AURORA MEDIANT

Black Halo Requiem

Book I: Hope Immortal

First published by Reliqui Mortus 2025

Library of Congress Control Number: 2025912414

First edition

ISBN (paperback): 979-8-9992012-0-1
ISBN (hardcover): 979-8-9992012-7-0

Cover art by Breno Girafa
Editing by Crystal Durnan

This book was professionally typeset on Reedsy.
Find out more at reedsy.com

Dedicated to all those who are lost.

BLACK HALO REQUIEM

BOOK I
HOPE IMMORTAL

"Is that the tree of life?"

"... and death.. everyone always forgets the death part."

I

Part One

Chapter 1

The soulless howl of wind echoes through the old-growth forest, causing Gabriel to shiver. Taking a moment to breathe, he rests curled against the trunk of a tree, leisurely sketching. The temperature plunges as the once sunny midday sky darkens considerably from fast-moving gray nimbostratus clouds.

Thunder cracks. *No, not thunder*, he thinks, *it's something breaking*. A scream follows from the same direction, jarring Gabriel as the harsh wind stings his skin. After moving his wavy, medium-length light brown hair out of the way, he looks past the bridge that crosses a stream and the rustic trail leading home. He shakes his head, refusing to ignore whatever it is, and drops his art supplies, sheltering in his light-blue blazer as he fights against the wind heading toward the well-worn wooden bridge.

A sound, like that of an ancient ship groaning against the sea, causes him to shudder. His heart freezes as he sees the impossible: a large shadow gliding across the ground like a giant snake. The massive shadow darkens the treetops of the old-growth Pennsylvanian forest and, for a moment, Gabriel sees a large, misshapen, obsidian-colored creature in the sky. At least, he thinks he did. It's gone in a flash, diving down into the forest, heading in the direction from which the scream had come.

Without hesitation, Gabriel breaks away from the path of safety, digging his feet into the ground as he heads toward what turns out to be a fallen tree branch. His heart seizes as he realizes there is a rope tied around the end of the branch and someone is pinned beneath it.

"HEY—" he begins to yell, but the wind takes his breath away.

He moves the large branch off a young woman who is wearing a frayed black shirt and faded gray jeans. All at once, the cold wind ceases then travels in the direction of the young woman, who has gold medium-tan skin and long, wavy, cardinal-red hair. The young woman coughs so hard it sounds like she's choking. Struggling to stand, she wavers. Gabriel is afraid she is about to pass out when her mahogany-colored eyes flicker in his direction. The young woman puts her hand to her throat, touching the rope that binds her to the tree branch. She pulls at the knot of the hangman's noose. Gabriel steps forward. The woman draws back, shaking her head.

"Let me help you," Gabriel pleads, cautiously staying near the large tree branch.

"No." The young woman's voice wavers as she holds her hand up. Tears stream down her cheeks.

"At least let me help untie you. Are you hurt?" Gabriel tries to see if she is injured. *She seems to be okay... at least physically.* He doesn't know her reasons for attempting suicide, but he understands. The plague of depression is a constant companion, a shadow he can never quite escape. He looks up to evaluate how far she has fallen. The branch is high, but the rope is long. She must have climbed the smaller, easier-to-reach branches before it broke.

Gabriel lifts the heavy branch, tilting it upright, rough bark scraping against his skin. He leans it against the trunk of the tree itself. The end of the thick beige rope is attached to a black boot she must have used as an anchor as she is still wearing the other boot.

First, he unties her shoe and then finishes untying the rope from around the branch but not around her neck. Cautiously, Gabriel places the boot next to her before taking a step back. When he comes near, she suddenly looks frail and turns away from him, shivering.

"I know what it's like," Gabriel starts to say.

"Don't—" she says, suddenly looking straight at him. "Don't pretend like you know what it's like."

Gabriel falls silent and respectfully nods. "If you want to talk, I will listen. Come to my house and have a cup of coffee with me and tell me why you…" His words trail off as he looks at the wreckage of the branch and the rope leading to her neck. "My name is Gabriel," he says, putting his hand out without thinking. After a moment he lets it drop to his side. "Please? At least for a few minutes?"

"Dawn," she says, still staring into the distance. Finally, she removes the noose before putting on her other boot and picking up a navy-blue backpack that was tilted over next to the base of the tree.

He motions for her to follow. Eventually, they come upon a well-worn and expansive house that resembles a cross between a cathedral and a long-forgotten fortress featuring weathered gray bricks marked by imperfections. It always looked out of place, yet it was home. Gabriel never knew who built it, nestled away in a forest, or why it was designed the way that it was. He always daydreamed that it was transported brick by brick from across the sea, from some ancient land whose soil was steeped in mystery—a place green as far as you could see, and knights roamed the countryside.

Leaves and sticks crunch beneath their shoes as they trudge along the rustic trail. Gabriel finds himself unsure of what to say, so he looks up at the treetops and the veins of branches highlighted by sunlight.

"You should look up some time," Gabriel says.

"Why?"

"Because, there's so much in this world to see." Gabriel jogs ahead of her to open the door. The right half of the wooden double doors creaks open. Curving black metal vines cross the tops and bottoms of the doors, the wood weathered with age, solid despite cracks along the base. The dark-red paint on the doors is vibrant but peeling.

They walk inside, and it looks modern if not somewhat cavernous, with high ceilings like the insides of a church.

"Don't mind the mess. My father is an archaeologist. He brings his work home more often than you would think." Gabriel makes his way past a table and television to a dark wooden dining hutch with drawers at the bottom, a table space in the middle, and glass doors at the top. "Please, sit anywhere you like."

Dawn finds a chair without any odd artifacts on it.

"Don't worry about messing anything up. I would have cleaned but I wasn't expecting company. The important stuff is probably in the museum-grade display boxes anyway." Gabriel shrugs.

"What is that?" Dawn asks, looking at the machine sitting on the hutch in front of him. It is composed of glass and metal, making it look more like a science project with a cylindrical glass container sitting above a bulb-like glass that hovers above a tealight candle.

Gabriel reaches into the shelves for a mug and sets it down next to another one. He answers her question as he fills the top glass of the machine with water from a pitcher. "It's a siphon coffee maker. Basically, it's an old way that brews an optimal cup of coffee." Gabriel strikes a match and lights the tealight candle.

"It's nice," Dawn says.

"Sometimes, tradition still works. Things that might otherwise be lost to time, sacrificed in the name of convenience. Build on what we have only when we can improve upon what is there." He looks over at her and adds, "Something my father would always tell me. I don't know if it's something I fully agree with."

"You must not have company often."

Gabriel is momentarily dumbstruck by her observation and stops what he is doing and nods.

"You only had one coffee cup ready to be used," she explains.

"Yes, you are correct. How do you take your coffee?"

"Very sweet."

Gabriel goes back to tending to the siphon coffee maker. He removes the round glass pot and pours the freshly brewed coffee. Leaving a small amount in the glass container, he puts out the flame and spoons in generous amounts of sugar before setting it on the small end table near her.

Dawn picks up the cup and breathes in the distinct aroma before taking a sip of the surprisingly strong, complex, sweet, bitter drink.

"That's good coffee," she says, her eyes downcast, words devoid of happiness they might normally convey.

"Do you want to talk about it?" Gabriel asks, momentarily haunted by his own darkness, his ever-present anxieties that constantly threaten to seep into his conscious mind. He takes a seat near hers, trying his best to be a sympathetic listener.

"Well, there are a lot of reasons I want to die. It's not easy to talk about." Dawn clasps the cup, taking another sip before setting it down on the wooden end table.

"I understand what you're going through," Gabriel says, trying to reach her. "I feel the same way sometimes. I talk to a therapist. It can help."

"I can't afford help," Dawn says, staring too intently at the coffee in the mug.

"There are places that will treat you for free if you qualify. It's called a sliding-scale fee." There is no response from Dawn, so Gabriel continues. "You observed that I rarely have visitors. I want to make an observation of my own. My guess is that you're homeless."

Dawn's looks at him, eyes welling with tears. He feels as if it's the first time that she's really looked at him.

"It's your backpack. Either you're in college or you're homeless and you carry around everything that you need." He hesitates before carefully asking, "Is that why you want to die?"

"Part of it? I guess? I—I don't know. I've been homeless for years. I ran away from an abusive foster family years ago. Something happened… something I don't want to talk about."

"It's all right. I'm just trying to understand."

"It—it happens the same—" She looks down at the burgundy carpet, falling silent.

"It's okay if you don't want to talk about it," Gabriel says, his concern for her growing.

"I do. It's just—I don't—it just keeps happening. They take a special interest in me. As time went on, their behavior increased to stalking. And then…" Dawn's words fade, her eyes close as tears stream down her face. "Then they try to—they—they try to—hurt me."

Gabriel sets his mug down, listening to what she has to say.

"Then… they die."

✦

The flow of conversation is interrupted. The room dead silent. There is an unsettling disconnect between her words and the reality of what she just said. Logically, there is no sane reason why anyone would say that. Her words, "Then… they die," was it a confession? A lie to get a rise from him? After taking a moment, Gabriel inhales deeply, focusing on steadying his hands from shaking. "What do you mean?"

"I can't explain it. They just die. Last time it happened I didn't even tell anyone. What's the point? Who would believe me?"

"How did they die?" Gabriel calms himself, refusing to allow anxiety to dictate his actions, striving to offer compassion and not snap judgment.

"Natural causes, I think? Heart attacks, strokes, aneurysms? At least… the ones I know about. They claimed they love me!" She spits her words, her face contorts as if she had eaten something incredibly sour. "They didn't love me! How could they?" Dawn shakes her head, eyes glistening with tears. "No. No, that's impossible. They lost their minds and became something else. You don't believe me? Do you?"

"No, I believe you. I—I have no reason not to believe you."

"It just keeps happening. I want to die because I don't want to be here anymore. I live in hell. I should go." Dawn stands and wipes away tears.

Without thinking, Gabriel sets down his coffee and stands as well.

"How can I be sure that you'll be all right?" Gabriel asks.

"Gabriel." She offers him an empty smile, one that only highlights the pain etched into her features. "I won't be. You have been… It's nice to meet you."

"Wait." Gabriel walks past her, stopping in front of a row of dust-covered museum-grade acrylic boxes sitting on a sturdy rose-wood shelf. He rummages through the junk drawer, sifting through small items, trying to find what he is looking for. He turns around too quickly, unaware that she is directly behind him. Gabriel holds out a gold pocket watch and flips it open. "It will remind you that you still have time."

"I couldn't possibly. Wait, I recognize this." Some of Dawn's hair hangs down as she leans forward to study the intricate geometric design of the watch face. It features a central symbol with two rings wrapped around it, a ring of Roman numerals, followed by a ring of planetary symbols. The sign in the center consists of two overlaid triangles, a solid one facing up and the broken lines of a triangle pointed down. The ends of the watch hands symbolize orbital patterns of the sun and a moon. The sun, astrologically represented as a circle with a dot in the center, shines with a golden sheen. While the moon in crescent form is silver upon a dark navy-blue circle representing the night sky. Gabriel shows her that the outer lane of the planetary symbols is movable, clicking it clockwise.

"I modified it myself." Gabriel hands her the cold, heavy watch.

"This is the same design as the clock at Café Noctem, downtown," Dawn says. "Except that one doesn't have an extra planetary symbol on it. Why is there an extra one?"

"An extra what?"

"An extra planetary symbol. There's the sun, the moon, nine planets, but that only equals eleven. What's the extra one between Mars and Jupiter?"

"I'm really not sure."

"How are you not sure? I thought you said you made this?"

Gabriel smiles, shifting his weight before explaining. "I did it in my sleep."

"You... made a watch... in your sleep?"

"I modified a watch in my sleep, yes."

She is silent for a long moment before she actually smiles. "All right, Gabriel, don't tell me."

"I'm serious. It's like sleepwalking."

"I can't accept this," Dawn says, holding the watch back out to him.

He shakes his head. "The watch will stop one day." He gently closes her hand around the watch. "It will remind you that there is still time. Where will you go?"

Dawn shrugs. "There's only one shelter in town. It's not far from Café Noctem."

"The café is open all night as well," Gabriel suggests. "Just tell them that the owner says you can stay as long as you like."

"What do you mean?"

"I'm the majority owner." Gabriel reaches into his pocket and pulls out a business card, handing it to her. "If you ever need anything."

Dawn walks over to her backpack and places the pocket watch and card in the front pouch.

"I've never seen you there before," Dawn says.

"I've been having trouble leaving my property, sometimes."

"Sorry to hear that." Dawn slings her bag across a shoulder and nods to him. She stops at the door and looks back. "Thanks, Gabriel, for trying to help."

"Anytime. Remember, as long as that watch ticks, you still have time, even if the ticking stops. Please, do something for me, would you? Promise me to hold on to hope, especially when nothing else remains."

Dawn gives Gabriel a sorrowful smile before heading out the red wooden door. He watches as she leaves until the door, with a crack at its base, shuts behind her.

Chapter 2

In the midnight hour, Gabriel sits hunched over his desk, scrawling upon cream-colored paper. The only sound in his mostly empty room is the scratching of his fountain pen as he writes, which increases with the ferocity of his thoughts. Ink flows from his modern cigar-shaped black fountain pen with gold accents. A lone desk lamp, the only light in the room, points to the letter he is writing.

Raphael,

I hope you are well. I wish I could tell you that things have been calm, but they haven't. I still have trouble leaving the house and haven't visited work in a long time. I've been struggling a lot. I don't feel like I am good enough.

I met someone. I was sketching outside when the weather turned. Thank god it did though, because I'm sure it helped break the tree branch she was trying to hang herself from. I don't think she fell very far, even though the branch landed on top of her, because she didn't seem hurt, at least physically.

When I invited her in for coffee, she started talking about some really strange things. About how people would die around her when she was in trouble. I don't know what that's about. She said that people would become obsessed with her and it escalated to stalking.

I really wish you were here. I'd have someone to talk to. I can't stop thinking about what happened. I mean, what almost happened or the fact that she is homeless.

I know you say to always take the opportunity to help someone if you can and I tried. I just don't feel like I have done enough.

Gabriel

◆

Dawn races through the ice-cold rain, trying to get to the homeless shelter in time. She hadn't been late the entire week since attempting to hang herself. All she wanted right now was shelter and warmth.

One of the few passing cars speeds up and swerves, intentionally spraying her with water. She hurries, telling herself, *ignore the cold. Ignore the water. I'm already wet.* She looks down the road to the homeless shelter nestled between other buildings about a block away. She is wearing the same frayed black shirt and faded gray jeans she had on when she tried to hang herself. It was one of two sets of clothing that she owned. Like the rest of her clothing, her thin, well-worn black jacket clings to her skin. As she swings the door open, papers taped on the inside of it flutter.

"You're late." The administrator makes no effort to hide her annoyance, tapping her fingers loudly on the counter in front of her. The portly middle-aged woman with curly brown hair rolls her eyes, clearly exasperated at the sight of Dawn arriving late.

"I'm sorry." Dawn glances at the flier-covered door, listening to the storm outside.

"You know the rules. If you're not here by 8:30, you can't stay the night. I was just about to lock up." The administrator stands.

"Please, it's raining outside," Dawn pleads. "I have nowhere else to go."

The older woman lets out a sigh, likely for Dawn's benefit. "I'm sorry, Dawn, but rules are rules. Work harder on being on time tomorrow if you want a place to sleep."

Dawn lets out a deep sigh and turns to the door, heading back out into the frigid rain. If she were crying, no one would be able to tell. She pulls the drenched hood of her jacket over her head and walks in the direction of a nearby park. The sound of the falling rain makes it impossible to think of anything until she takes shelter under the bridge near a river that crosses the park. There is a span of concrete from the water to the edge of the bridge at an angle with a small patch of earth between the concrete and river.

Sitting on the frigid concrete, Dawn sets her backpack beside her. It contains all that she has in the world, which isn't much. Reaching into it, she takes out the heavy pocket watch that Gabriel had given her. She stares at her reflection in the face's glass covering before clicking the outer ring several times. Out of exhaustion, she drops her head down and curls up, forearm resting on her knees as she grips the watch tightly and snaps it shut.

"I'm trying," she says, talking to the watch. Lost in the moment, she feels the heartbeat tick calm her. She places the watch back into her backpack and pulls out a small black silk bag with a red inner lining. Inside is a pocket-sized Rider-Waite tarot deck she's had for years. The tarot cards are wrapped in a black piece of fabric. The card-back design is a deep blue that resembles the night sky laced with light gold geometric symbols throughout, and an occult star symbol in the center.

She lays the piece of fabric on the ground and begins shuffling, letting intuition tell her when to draw a card and how many cards for each position.

A simple past, present, and future three-card spread. For the past, she draws the Hermit. She thinks it may be about Gabriel. The next card, representing the present, she draws the Nine of Swords and the Tower. *Accurate,* she thinks, as they stand for painful loss, change, and misery.

She pulls three cards for the future: Temperance, Judgment, and the Lovers card. Staring at the three future cards, she internally denies what she sees but takes out her notebook and writes it down anyway.

After shuffling, she pulls her cards into no particular spread. First, she draws the Queen of Cups, a card that represents her. Then she draws the Knight of Cups, a card she feels represents Gabriel. While idly shuffling, the Two of Cups falls out—the enduring lovers' card. She stares at it, not knowing what to do. She jots down the spread into her notebook and puts her tarot cards away.

Thunder cracks, and Dawn looks up at the underside of the bridge, listening to the sound of the rain as the storm increases. Despite it all, the sound of falling rain comforts her, and she is grateful to have at least some shelter from its unforgiving onslaught. Making the most of it, she reaches into her backpack and pulls out a well-read copy of *Edgar Allan Poe's Complete Tales and Poems* and a small book light. She curls up, lying down on the cold concrete. After she sets the book flat upon the ground, she flips through the well-loved pages until she reaches a makeshift bookmark made of a scrap of torn paper. She smiles and rests her hand on the familiar page as she begins to read the same story she has read countless times, escaping reality, at least for a short while in her mind.

◆

The next night, Dawn intentionally avoids the shelter. She feels unwanted and afraid that no matter what time she shows up, they wouldn't allow her to stay. Instead, she spends her time in the basement computer room at Café Noctem. The clicks of the mechanical gaming keyboards in use around her fade into the background of what she is consciously aware of as she stares at the computer monitor.

"Come on, stop roping me." She huffs, throwing her head back in frustration. The rope timer ticks down on the screen, every moment trying her patience. She is playing an online conquest card game. Her opponent is running out the timer, hoping she will forfeit. Dawn throws herself against the back of her chair a bit roughly before turning on her phone, which is charging. She swipes through an assortment of apps, many of which most wouldn't recognize unless they were privacy-conscious.

"You know, we don't allow hackers in here," Gabriel says from behind her. Turning to the familiar voice, she looks into his light brown eyes and realizes he is joking. Briefly, she looks at his clothing; he is wearing a dark-gray casual business suit with a white dress shirt.

She smiles, finding herself lost for a moment, as he is strikingly handsome. Internally, she pushes aside her growing attraction. Telling herself it is superficial, that she doesn't even know him and he only cares about her because she is in a vulnerable position. Every time someone had come close to her, it had only resulted in death.

Dawn snaps out of it and turns her attention back to the computer screen. Her eyes widen. "Oh, it's my turn." Dawn leans in, looking at her cards.

Gabriel points to a card that her mouse is hovering over. "If you wait to play that, you'll have more resources for the late game."

"You know how to play Stratagem Terra?" Dawn has a small smile on her face.

"Yeah, it's actually one of my favorite games."

"Interesting." Dawn does a poor job of paying attention to her game and panics once the rope timer starts ticking down on her end. Her opponent concedes, likely thinking that she is roping them in return.

"Want to play a local match?" Gabriel takes the seat next to hers.

"Sure." She shrugs.

Gabriel types in his information and pulls up the game. "Ready."

Dawn hits the button to search for local matches. As the game begins, they each roll an electronic D20 to see who goes first. Dawn rolls a zero. Gabriel rolls a ten, so he gets to decide who goes first. He concedes the first move to her.

"Why didn't you choose to go first?" Dawn briefly side-eyes him before looking at her cards and then begins placing units of troops in territories across the global 3D map.

"Well, first, I was being nice. And there is a strategy going second." Gabriel places his units on resource points. His troops show up as green and hers blue. Finally, the AI populates the empty spaces with bots.

"What do you say we take out the AI before attacking each other?" Gabriel suggests.

"Oh, so you can get a feel for my strategies before engagement?" Dawn smiles at him.

Several hours pass as they are playing total victory mode. The game has gone back and forth with Dawn currently in the lead due to her uncanny knack for rolling high on the random number generator, especially during key battles.

"Give up?" Dawn asks.

He rolls his eyes and smiles. "I still have a few troops left."

"Come on, Gabriel, the game's over."

Gabriel shrugs. "Not till we're all dead."

Dawn shakes her head and waits for him to look at the few cards he has left. He plays one that draws more cards, but at this point, only a miracle would win him the game.

"Fine." Dawn clicks her mouse as she amasses her troops around Gabriel's few.

In response, Gabriel plays a portal card that teleports him to one of the best resource points in the game, far from Dawn's troops. Gabriel can't help but laugh as a trap set at the resource point instantly kills the last of his troops. His screen dims with the words Game Over. "You're pretty good at this game."

"Thanks. You, too. I thought you had trouble leaving your property?"

"I do but I thought about what I said to you the other day, about looking up sometimes. Figured I should probably take my own advice. Besides, you might be here. I wanted to see if you were all right."

"I'm fine, Gabriel." Her tone is annoyed as she suppresses her anger.

"Are you really?" Gabriel's eyes lock with hers. "You don't have to fight, you know. I mean—"

"Gabriel, you couldn't possibly understand what I go through."

"No, you're right. I don't. But I want to."

Dawn glares ahead at the computer screen before checking to see how much battery her phone has left. "You'll end up like them if you're not careful."

"Is that a threat?" Gabriel asks.

"No. Why would I threaten you?" Dawn grabs her things and gets up to leave.

Gabriel stands as well. "I'll go. You stay here, all right? As long as you want. I've already talked to the staff."

"I need you to do things for me now?"

"I'm just trying to help," Gabriel pleads.

"You've helped enough. I don't need your charity." Dawn turns away from him.

"You can't keep running your entire life."

"Watch me." Dawn's stance changes, her feet planted firmly on the ground.

"It's okay to let your guard down sometimes."

"No, it's not." Dawn's voice wavers as pain swells inside. Her eyes narrow with anger. The rush of blood drowns out most other sounds. "You wouldn't understand."

"Let me help you," Gabriel says, frustration rising in his voice.

Dawn shakes her head. Her breathing becomes rapid, and she runs up the stairs, Gabriel trailing behind. Halfway through the café's main seating area, she stops and turns around, glaring at him. Gabriel freezes, standing next to the door to the stairs that lead to the computer room. Dawn takes this opportunity to run, throwing open the front door, causing the bell on the door to ring as she races into the night.

✦

The rhythmic tempo of Dawn's boots pounding against the concrete sidewalk slows to a halt as she stops to look back in the direction from which she came. Accompanied only by the stillness of the night, its peaceful nothingness works to calm her. The shimmering glow of scarce lights are dotted here and there along the rows of empty shops. The nights are growing longer and colder. It's so cold that she can see her breath.

She pushes away the thought that she is, once again, locked outside for the night. It is too late to go to the shelter. The familiar pain in her chest demands attention, yet she refuses to acknowledge it. Instead, she forces herself to walk to the library and sits down on a bench near its front door. It's closed, of course, but the Wi-Fi still connects. As soon as it does, her phone chimes, indicating she has an email, one of the few ways anyone can contact her. She hesitates, hand poised over the screen, ready to delete it. At a cursory glance, it looks like spam. Her heart seizes as she reads the subject line. Written in caps is not only her name but the name of the town that she escaped, Trastel, Minnesota. The email is time-stamped only minutes ago, relayed through an anonymous service, as evidenced by the masked address.

Dawn, I pray this reaches you in time. I've been invited to a group dedicated to stalking you in private messages. They know where you are. You are not safe. Godspeed.

Attached to the email are a series of screenshots of the group chats, including an image of a tarot card spread she did just days ago inside Café Noctem. Dawn is dizzy. The world blurs. The connection between her mind and her body is severed as she stares far too long at the image of the tarot spread. It is a spread with no standard structure: the Fool, the Knight of Wands, and the Lovers card under the Ace of Cups; the Seven of Cups beneath the Ten of Wands; and finally the Death card. The beginning shows a journey, a spark of fire carried by a knight, the lovers highlighted by emotion. The middle, a range of possibilities, an unseen future, overlaid by the Ten of Wands symbolizing this present ordeal, a heavy burden. Finally, the Death card. Dawn knows that most people get understandably frightened when the Death card shows up in a reading. She knows that the Death card doesn't necessarily signify a literal death but a death of a situation or the end of something rather than anything to fear. But sometimes... sometimes, the Death card really does mean death.

She had posted it online under a pseudonym that no one in real life knew. She didn't bother to wipe the metadata off an image posted to an anonymous blog she kept only for herself. Highlighted in the metadata is an IP tracing her location.

There is a series of images, screenshots, from the group's private chat sent by user Kate Lynn Anders. "I'm going to make sure that black widow can't hurt anyone ever again." Followed by a photo of a matte-black semi-automatic pistol with the word *karma* crudely carved into its side, just above the trigger. "I can't wait till that bitch meets karma ;)."

Panic grips her. *Don't let it take over*, she pleads internally but knows that this is a battle she cannot win. Her heart beats faster as she stares in the direction of an avenue that leads to the main road, one she can take out of town. The avenue runs west, past Café Noctem.

Several blocks from the library as she is heading to the main road, Dawn forces herself to move faster, deliberately looking away from the brightly lit block to her left. Ignoring the very existence of Café Noctem. Focusing instead on the blurry stoplights in the distance that mark the main road that leads out of town. *No*, she says to herself. *You can't ask for help. Don't ask for help. You cannot ask for help.*

Remembering Gabriel's words, when he tried to reason with her, 'it's okay to let your guard down sometimes,' grows louder in her mind.

"It's not okay. It will never be okay," she says, arguing out loud.

"Dawn?" Gabriel's voice calls from behind her. "Dawn, are you all right?"

"No. I'm not." Her eyes reluctantly meet his before looking to the direction of the main road.

"Come inside," Gabriel insists, holding the door open for her.

She hesitates, taking in a deep breath before walking into the café. Gabriel motions to an open table near the door, not far from the series of oversized windows that face the street. Feeling exposed, her hypervigilance kicks into overdrive, processing every potential threat.

"Dawn. Dawn, look at me. What's wrong?" Gabriel leans in, clearly trying to comprehend what happened in the short time since she had left the café. "Please, talk to me."

Dawn hangs her head down. She pulls out her phone and opens the email. Speechless, Gabriel's eyes widen as he scrolls through the messages.

"I'm calling the police," Gabriel says, his voice monotone and his phone already against his ear. "Yes, this is Gabriel Morgaine. I'm at Café Noctem, downtown. A... friend... of mine is actively being threatened." Gabriel glances at Dawn, who glares at him. She reaches for her backpack but then decides against it. "Yes, I do believe it is a credible threat. If you could send someone here, it would be appreciated. Thank you." Gabriel hangs up.

"Why did you do that?" Dawn moves back, away from him, feeling betrayed. "I—I have to go."

"No. Dawn, you have to stay here."

"I have to go. I have to."

"Go where, Dawn? Where are you going to go?"

"I don't know!" Dawn's emotions grow cold, lost in hopelessness, like the blotting of the midday sun by a storm, a storm she's sure she can not weather.

"They have to see this. These people are threatening you."

The door slams open, crashing into the wall with a bang. A disheveled middle-aged blonde woman enters the café, her hazel eyes narrowed at Dawn. "I finally found you, you little bitch." She lifts her arm, aiming the gun inscribed with the word *karma* directly at Dawn.

All Dawn can do is stand, frozen in shock, staring at her former foster mother. Everything inside urges her to run, but her feet will not move. She hadn't seen Kate since the last time someone had died in front of her. The man who died was Kate's husband. Dawn's fists tighten. She pushes aside the traumatic experiences inflicted by her former foster father, Jake. The unwanted advances, the crazed obsession ending in death. She can't rid herself of the memory of his body writhing in pain on the floor before it stopped moving entirely.

Dawn isn't paying attention as Gabriel pulls her behind him, planting himself between her and the assailant. She stumbles before quickly regaining her balance and booting the table forward, taking cover behind it.

"Get out of my way, boy!" the woman screams, pointing the gun at Gabriel.

"Kate, he didn't do anything! Don't shoot him! Do you want innocent blood on your hands?" Dawn pleads from behind the overturned table.

"Then stop hiding!" Kate screams, gripping her gun, charging in Dawn's direction. Her gait is like a bear standing on two legs. She sways, as it is cumbersome for her to move quickly.

Dawn catches a glimpse of another person, Kate's son Connor, who is recording and possibly live streaming the entire thing on his phone, while laughing and providing commentary.

The world blurs around her. Anxiety chokes her, causing her throat to close. Adrenaline forces her heart to pump so hard that she can hear it. Her mind flashes to the most recent deadly attack, when she was cornered, helpless, and alone.

Dawn didn't remember what excuse he had used to call her in. All she can remember is that she had been growing more and more scared of being alone with her foster father, Jake.

Jake had turned from his workbench and glared at her as if she was the source of all evil in this world, yet in his features was a crazed hunger, befitting a wild beast on the hunt. Dawn turned to leave, gripping the cold metal door handle and screaming at herself internally to get the damn door open.

"Don't you go leaving now!" Jake hollered. He knocked over tools on the workbench, staring at her with a feral hunger. Dawn cowered, deciding to defend herself the best she could, and hid behind her forearms, curled up.

She pulled herself into a tighter ball as if that would help somehow. There was a sound of something large smacking against the garage floor. The sight of another dead body before Dawn, too, fainted.

When Dawn opened her eyes, Jake was lay dying on the ground. Her mind skipped through memories: running, the cold, the loneliness.

The blurry reality of the back of the overturned table in the café comes into focus. She peers out and sees Gabriel's back as he stands between them. "Stop! Please!" She puts her hands up and stands from behind the table.

The out-of-focus barrel of Kate's pistol, aimed directly at her, comes into focus. Connor cheers and laughs, followed by a ringing series of bangs with evenly spaced pauses between the *pop pop pop*s. Small, disconnected waves of reddish-orange glow, like that of an overly bright firefly, light the air. The world fades as she collapses.

✦

Gabriel wraps his arms around Dawn, protectively tackling her to the ground. He stares at her unconscious body as the male accomplice's laughter turns into a scream. The young man drops his phone and runs to Kate. A halo of blood splatter stains the white tiled floor around Kate's head.

Looking up in awe, Gabriel sees something he couldn't possibly be seeing: a sickly black dragon missing patches of scales. The dragon twists through the air, encircling the main floor of the café. Time slows as Gabriel's heart beats hard against chest. It is a moment of silence, a pause from the chaos around him. He looks back at Dawn, feeling like a failure. The black dragon enters through her chest and vanishes. Gabriel searches her body for wounds and signs of life. Dawn's mahogany-colored eyes flicker open and look up at him weakly. A wave of relief mixed with stress rushes through him.

Jack, a manager with short bright blue hair, jogs over to them. "Are you two all right? Everyone else seems to be fine… besides the shooter. The idiot she was with ran off, but he dropped his phone."

"Thanks, Jack," Gabriel says as he helps Dawn stand.

Jack points to the windows. "Looks like they got him."

Gabriel sees the male accomplice handcuffed against a police car.

"You *have* to watch the footage." Jack insists, scrolling to a time on the video before handing him the phone. "Of course, we'll check our own security cams as well."

Gabriel nods and looks at the phone before pressing play. Several bullets narrowly missed Dawn. One ricocheted off a granite wall fountain behind her, sending it straight back through Kate's head, causing a small stream of blood to spray, before lodging itself into the wall near the front door. He doesn't see any sign of a black dragon and assumes it was merely an anxiety-induced hallucination… one he has seen before.

"Why did you collapse?" Gabriel asks. He looks at Dawn for her reaction to the video. But she isn't even watching it. Instead, she is staring at the corpse of her former foster mother.

"Stress? Maybe? I don't know. It happens every time." Dawn shrugs.

"You lose consciousness every time something like this happens? I want you to stay with me, at least for tonight. You shouldn't be alone right now." Gabriel's eyes lock with hers.

Dawn winces but doesn't look away. Silently, she nods.

"Wait for me. I'll talk to the police," Gabriel says, gently squeezing her arm before getting up.

Chapter 3

J ust past midnight, Dawn rests on a rustic rope swing at the edge of the woods, near Gabriel's house. It has a sturdy wooden plank suspended by thick ropes strung from a tree branch. As she swings slightly, head facing down, the prickly texture of the rope scrapes against her skin. She looks at the thick ropes, the color of which is faded by weather and barely visible in the dim light. The faint, unsettling creak of the swing heightens her stress. She looks up at where the ropes meet the tree branch above her, reminded of the unusually cold day she met Gabriel. The day she stumbled through the forest, feeling lost and holding back tears as she silently said goodbye to her life. That day, she felt nothing but emptiness—an emptiness that she continues to carry with her to this day.

Dried leaves crunch under Gabriel's shoes as he trudges across the small clearing, calling her attention. He stops a few feet away, the soft glow of moonlight offering some sanctuary from the darkness. The only other light is a dim orange glow from the windows near the front door of the old, large gray-brick structure Gabriel calls home.

"Are you all right?" he asks.

Dawn shakes her head, closing her eyes.

"I'm sorry, Dawn."

"I never asked for any of this." Dawn pauses, silently looking past Gabriel. "I've always felt alien to this world and how it works, like I'm not supposed to be here."

"I know how you feel. I'm not sure anyone fits in, not really."

"Every time things seem to be okay, something happens. My dreams are only nightmares anymore. I don't know what to do about it. This must be what it feels like to be cursed."

"You're not cursed, Dawn."

"No?" Dawn takes a deep breath. The crisp night air stings her lungs. "It sure feels like I am."

"Curses aren't real. Sometimes, when you think that you're stuck in the same situation forever, it turns out you were wrong. Listen, Dawn, I want you to stay here for as long as you need to. There's more than enough room."

Dawn turns away, gripping the ropes of the swing tighter.

Gabriel takes a step closer. "Please, Dawn. I know I wouldn't stop worrying if you were somewhere else."

"Okay," Dawn says, her voice soft and resigned.

"I'll be inside if you need me."

"You don't have to go." Dawn shrugs.

"What do you want to do?" Gabriel asks.

"Can we start a campfire?"

"Sure, I'll get the matches."

Dawn looks up at the tree branch, worried it may break as Gabriel heads inside. She hops off the rustic swing and begins to survey the ground for sticks and dried leaves.

She spends a few minutes gathering materials for the fire. The creak of the old wooden doors breaks the stillness of the night, accompanied by the rustling of fauna and chirps of insects as Gabriel returns. They pick a spot in the narrow clearing between the house and the forest. Dawn places the sticks and leaves she's collected on the ground. Gabriel places the matches next to the pile.

Sitting down on her knees, Dawn digs into the soft earth.

"What are you doing?" Gabriel asks before sitting on the grass.

"I'm digging a fire pit. The ground is soft enough."

Gabriel clears the area around the small fire pit. Dawn gathers the sticks and shoves them into the soft earth, creating a triangle shape in the hole she has dug. Then, she stuffs dried leaves in the center and strikes a match. After taking a moment to watch the orange-red flame, she places it into an open pocket beneath the arranged leaves. Finally, she sits back, relaxed, as the fire begins to crackle. The scent of smoke and sulfur fills the air. Dawn picks up a sturdy stick and tends the fire.

"Do you think there is anything out there, beyond what's here… anything beyond death?" Gabriel warms his hands near the campfire and glances at the blanket of stars resting above.

"Of course," Dawn replies.

"You say that with such certainty."

"There are some things you just know." Dawn brushes some of her long hair behind her shoulder.

"Did you ever know your family?" Gabriel asks.

Dawn shakes her head no as she tends the fire. "You said your dad was always gone. Gabriel, where is your mom?"

"She died in a car accident when I was eight. Drunk driver going down the wrong side of the street. I was in the car."

"Oh. I'm sorry, I didn't know."

"It's okay. I was young, and my memory is really fuzzy. It's one reason I really don't like being in cars. Growing up without a mother, it never hurt me as much as you think that it would. Mother's Day commercials, seeing other people with mothers. It was such a long time ago."

"I mourn for something I've never had, yet you don't mourn for something you did have. Was she not a good mother to you?"

"She was kind and caring. I see life going in a certain direction. If things hadn't happened the way that they did, I might not be here talking to you now." Gabriel looks at the fire, then over at Dawn, who has fallen silent. "Do you still want to commit suicide?" Gabriel asks.

She ignores him, concentrating on the warmth emanating from the flames before turning back to him. Silently, she studies him. His question seems genuine, and he looks as vulnerable as she feels.

Dawn looks down and nods. "I just… think that it would be better that way. To have an escape."

"Dawn, there are better ways of solving problems."

"Maybe if you're you."

"What is that supposed to mean?"

"Nothing. It's just that sometimes it's okay—"

"No, it's not, Dawn. Whatever is at the end of that sentence isn't good."

"Why? I have nothing to live for."

"I would be lost if you died."

"Gabriel, you hardly know me."

"I thought you died earlier. I can't help the way I feel—the way I've felt since I met you."

Dawn looks at him and is met with sincerity. She leans closer to get more kindling and his eyes shift from brown to blue.

"What?" Dawn stammers.

Cautiously, she moves back and forward again. The colors shift with consistency. "What color are your eyes?"

"They're brown. Why?"

"Nothing, it's just—up close they look blue," she says

Gabriel smiles. "They're definitely light brown. Maybe you have synesthesia?"

"What is that?"

"I'm really not sure. Something about seeing colors where there aren't any."

"Maybe?" Dawn sits back and his eye color shifts back to normal.

✦

Dawn is asleep in the guest room of Gabriel's home. Nightmares have plagued her for as long as she can remember. Tonight is no exception. In the nightmare, she is barefoot and wearing a simple black dress that hangs off her like rags. Large, cold black metal cuffs encircle her wrists with no chain linking them together.

Ominously hovering in the back of the dark, cramped, and unfamiliar room is a diseased-looking black dragon missing patches of skin. Various scales jut out sharply, forcing an unnatural silhouette. The dragon's body forms a winding river that resembles an Eastern dragon, although its face looks Western.

The dragon is not looking directly at her. It stares at something just beyond her... she looks but sees nothing. *Something isn't right*, she thinks, staring at the gray wall and wondering what the dragon is looking at. *It isn't looking past me... it's looking at me.* Only then does Dawn notice that the cuffs are... moving. Dawn is forced to the ground as if her wrists were magnets and the floor metal. She struggles to get up but finds the effort to be in vain.

The dim light in the room is only enough to highlight the pebble-like pattern of scales. Her heart wrenches as she stares blankly and realizes that they are not handcuffs but twin obsidian-colored snakes. Dawn screams. A third snake rises from the ground and wraps itself around her throat, silencing her. Each offending scale slices her skin like shards of glass.

"Listen to me and nothing will go wrong," an authoritative voice commands.

Are the snakes talking to her? Is it the dragon? she wonders. *No... it's something else.* The voice sounds as if it is coming from inside her head.

"Listen to me..." the voice says, "...and only to me." The snakes slow momentarily.

Dawn shakes her head and is reprimanded as the snakes tighten their grip around her.

"No!" she manages to choke out as hot tears fall down the sides of her face.

"Yes," the voice replies.

The serpent coiled around her neck painfully constricts, as if to say *it is not your choice.* "Listen to me... and only to me."

The voice fades. The snakes vanish, leaving only the dragon in the dark.

✦

Dawn sits up in bed suddenly, drawing in a sharp breath, dazed and lightheaded. Her heart rate begins to slow as she recognizes she is awake and not in the nightmare.

The feeling of a comfortable bed is foreign to her. After slowly looking around the sparsely furnished room, she realizes that she is at Gabriel's place. There is a desk in the corner and a dresser directly across from her.

Forcing the nightmare from her thoughts, Dawn gets up and takes a shower in the bathroom attached to the room. While savoring the hot water, she thinks about how those who have don't understand what it is like to go without. Not wanting to leave the shower, she lingers in this rare moment of luxury, steam filling the small bathroom.

After getting out, she gets dressed, changing into the same clothes she had on the previous day as they are cleaner than her spare.

There is a squeaking sound as she uses a hand towel to wipe away condensation from the fogged mirror. Singing softly to herself, Dawn opens her small cosmetic pouch. Slowly, the song's volume rises before dropping to a hum as she starts applying compact powder. The melody stops mid-hum. Her eyes widen and her breath slows as she sets her compact on the counter, eyes transfixed on her reflection. She tilts her head to the side to get a clearer view of the bruising on her neck—splotches of black resembling a Rorschach test, highlighted by the deep red of broken blood vessels. On closer inspection, the marks look like what could have been left by something pressed tightly against her throat.

Her breathing slows, and her heart feels frozen. Placing her fingers on her neck, she briefly presses the discolored spots. She winces, finding it tender. "No. No. No." She applies a layer of powder over the black-red splotches. The makeup only dulls the discoloration.

For a split second, her vision narrows and blurs. In the mirror, instead of her own reflection, a man with long black hair, an angular face, and a pale complexion stares at her with bright copper eyes. Then, as quickly as it came, it was gone.

There has to be a reasonable explanation for this. There has to be a reasonable explanation for this. Doesn't there?

Habitually, she takes her backpack and walks down the hall. She stops and knocks on Gabriel's door. There is no answer. She can smell something cooking. *It must be pancakes or waffles,* she thinks. At the end of another hall, down past the living room, she finds Gabriel in the kitchen, cooking pancakes.

"Oh, you're awake," Gabriel says. "Are you hungry? Coffee? Pancakes?"

"Um, sure?" Dawn sets her backpack on the ground next to the long counter and sits at the end of a row of mismatched chairs. Her arms rest on a black marble countertop with white swirls that remind her of Jupiter.

"What happened to your neck?" Gabriel asks, placing a plate of pancakes in front of her.

"I don't know," she says softly, staring too intently at the butter slowly melting into the pancakes. "I had a nightmare. When I woke up, the bruises were here." For a brief moment in time, she wonders if it is safe to tell Gabriel anything. Shoulders relaxing, she feels at ease when she looks into his eyes and sees that he is genuine—and relatively confused.

"Weird. Do you want to talk about it?"

"No, not really. I have nightmares all the time. I just try my best to forget about them."

"I'll listen to you if you ever feel like talking," Gabriel says, absentmindedly stirring a cup of coffee. "I made it the way you took it the other day." He sets the coffee near her plate.

Dawn clasps her hands around the cup. The heat of the mug draws her mind to the comfort of last night's campfire. In a disturbing flash, her memory shifts to the nightmare.

"Black snakes wrapped around me… choking me… pinning me against the ground. A black dragon watching." Her fingertips feel numb, like when the serpents restricted her circulation. "They were wrapped around my wrists, my neck. There was a voice ordering me to listen… to him."

She opens her eyes and her pupils dilate, adjusting to the light.

"To who?" Gabriel asks, leaning on the counter.

"I don't know."

Gabriel sits on a stool across from her. "I don't know a lot about dream

30

interpretation, but I can tell you I've had the same night terror for as long as I can remember."

Dawn nods, cutting her pancakes while listening to him. "The same night terror?"

"Yeah. It always seems to happen when I am caught in that space between being awake and asleep. When the paralytic prevents you from moving, but you're still awake. Fully awake. A man comes into my room and stabs me with a dagger, straight into my chest. I can feel it cut into me every time."

"I'm sorry to hear that," Dawn says, concerned but not knowing what else to say.

"I've never told anyone that before," Gabriel says in a slightly disconnected matter-of-fact tone, indicating it was a thought that had only now occurred to him.

"Why did you tell me, then?"

He smiles and shrugs. "I don't know. You told me about your nightmare. I felt the need to tell you about mine. Besides, I don't know why, but I trust you."

"You have no reason to," Dawn says, deliberately looking away from him.

"I know," Gabriel says, "but I do."

✦

In his room late that night, Gabriel sits at his desk with a black fountain pen accented with gold in hand, writing a letter.

Raphael,

Things have been weird. You may have heard about what happened at the cafe. I've included a newspaper clipping if you haven't. Despite that, things have been all right. I think I am in love. I know what you would say. That I've fallen in love too quickly. I say that there isn't anything to be afraid of. If there is anything worth fighting for in this world, it's love.

I think about her all the time. Even when I am asleep, I dream about her. She has been here for a few weeks and I can't believe how much we have in common. We like the same type of music, TV shows, and movies. She hasn't come with me to the café since it happened and I don't blame her. I cleared out a spare room for her to use. She makes me a better person just by being around. I have been going to the café more often.

I don't know how to tell her how I feel. I'm afraid she might leave if I do. With everything she has been through, I just want to be there for her. She's beautiful and intelligent and we get along as if we have known each other our entire lives. It feels like I've found a piece of myself that has been missing for a very long time.

Gabriel

Chapter 4

Gabriel absentmindedly scrolls through a news article he isn't even reading on his laptop. Sitting on the living room couch, he takes the time to listen to the deep voice of the host of a nature documentary coming from the television. As he watches the penguins on the screen, he thinks about how having something on in the background always made him feel less alone. He pushes back the memory of countless hours trying to find something, anything to escape the emptiness inside.

Then he glances at Dawn, who is reading a book at the far end of the couch. He wants to tell her the difference she has made in his life. Instead, he asks, "Do you want to go online?"

She shakes her head. "You really can't game on that thing."

"Too bad none of the decommissioned gaming rigs work. I have a bunch of them sitting in that closet." Gabriel points to a door at the far end of the room. "I use them for spare parts."

Dawn sets down her book on the arm of the couch, walks over to the closet, and opens the door. "Why were these decommissioned?"

Setting his laptop beside him, Gabriel shrugs. "Various reasons, hardware failure mostly."

"I could look at them for you." Dawn kneels and wipes dust off a computer tower. "I need a screwdriver."

Gabriel gets up and retrieves a screwdriver kit from the dark wooden hutch that houses the siphon coffee maker. "You know, if you can fix computers, you could always work at the café." He hands her a black rectangular zip case of screwdrivers.

"If I don't fix things, I tend to break them beyond repair," Dawn says, examining the tip of a Phillips screwdriver. She hauls out a tower, lugging it to the dark walnut coffee table in front of the television. Gabriel picks up a box of junk cords and carries it over.

"How come you know so much about computers?" Gabriel asks, heading back to the closet and picking up another computer tower.

Dawn sighs, connecting the HDMI from the television to the computer. "When I had a home, for a while, my room was known as the computer graveyard. It allowed me to do something alone, but I could interact with people from a safe distance if I wanted to. I accumulated junk computers that no one else wanted, so I fixed them."

She presses the power button on the computer but instead of booting up, it just beeps at her.

"See, it won't start," Gabriel says, setting the tower he is carrying next to the other one.

"Motherboard beep codes tell you what piece of hardware is failing." Dawn removes the side panel of the tower. "Can I use your laptop?"

He opens his laptop and hands it to her. "The passcode is 5747."

Sitting down, Dawn sets the laptop next to the open computer tower and searches for the motherboard manual.

"I built these myself. Most of the parts are the same, so they should be interchangeable if you can get any of them to work." Gabriel shrugs, sitting down next to her.

"I'm having trouble finding the beep codes for this motherboard. Let's start by resetting the hardware: the RAM, CMOS, and video card. We can also reset the CPU if you have thermal paste."

"I do." Gabriel walks back over to the dark wooden dining hutch and roots around a junk drawer for the thermal paste. He finds it and walks back to her. As he is handing her the thermal paste, their hands briefly touch. She jolts back, knocking the thermal paste to the floor.

Cautiously, he watches her expression as he picks up the thermal paste and holds it out for her. Frozen, she doesn't move. Strands of cardinal-red hair are frayed out of place. She continues to look away from him. Gabriel tells himself not to give in to his reactive anxiety that says he has done something wrong, knowing it is the echoes of trauma. Still, it doesn't make it hurt any less. Carefully, he sets the thermal paste on the coffee table and looks at her, feeling helpless.

"If there was anything I could do to make things different in your past, I would."

"Gabriel, there is nothing you can do."

"No, but there is something I can do now. I can be there for you, no matter what. Dawn, I love you, and I think you might feel the same. My father always told me, 'Love is a promise that, in the absence of reason, I will be there for you.'" When he looks into her eyes, he sees fear. "Dawn, I—"

Gabriel's words are cut short as her lips press against his, leaving no doubt in his mind that this is where he belongs. Where he has always belonged. Falling into the moment, he wraps his arms around her. After several heartbeats she draws back, breaking from the kiss. Her eyes connect with his before she nestles her head comfortably against his chest.

✦

Dawn is lost in another nightmare. The walls are composed of black stone, same as the ceiling and floor. She shivers, a stinging cold prickles her skin and heightens her anxiety.

"I'm afraid this is none of my concern," a familiar baritone voice says. It is a low commanding voice that sounds like the one from her serpent nightmare. She cannot help but feel as if she were pinned to the concrete floor, again, unable to breathe. Gasping for air instinctively, she forces herself to focus on this nightmare's reality.

She takes a closer look at the man, and it is the same man as the visage she saw in the mirror. There is an air of rigid nobility that surrounds him. He sits semi-casually, yet properly, against a large intricately carved black wooden throne-like chair. His chair is slightly larger than the rows of chairs on either side of the long black metal table with golden accents. The pale, tall man has long black hair and is dressed in tailored Victorian Gothic-esque attire.

He waves his hand dismissively, deep in conversation with a figure sitting directly across from him. The figure is hauntingly emaciated, but somehow beautiful with glowing deep midnight-blue wings folded behind his back, partially covered by strips of a blue-black tattered cloak. Otherwise, he wears black linen rags. He has striking ice-white hair, a pale and somewhat blue complexion. The body language of the lanky figure cannot hide the fact that he is highly introverted in nature.

"You must be concerned about this," the figure in rags pleads, his voice wavering. He rests his hands protectively on three large books sitting in front of him on the table.

Dawn feels hollow when she looks at him. She does her best not to move but isn't sure they can see her.

"There is no mention of him in the books," the pale figure in rags says.

"No mention at all?"

"Neither of them. Nothing in the Book of Life, the Book of Death, nor the Book of Fate. Have you seen anything that might give us an indication as to what is going on?" The ragged figure's eyes search his expression for answers.

The man with unnaturally bright copper-colored eyes and bone-white skin looks bemused before his expression drops to an unamused baseline. "No. Even if I did, it is none of your concern."

"It is my concern. Everything is my concern." The figure in rags collects his large books, hands shaking. He lets out a deep sigh. "I have to find out what is wrong."

"You worry too much."

"Are you not concerned?"

"Oh, I am."

The man from her nightmares looks directly at her. As their eyes lock, she stumbles backward, and the black stone floor shatters on impact.

Dawn falls through a tunnel. The nightmare shifts into the distant past, where Dawn is a child, cowering against the back wall of a closet. Angry shouting grows louder as one of her former foster mothers slams the door open, grabs her wrist, and forcefully drags her out.

Time shifts in her nightmare. Dawn is older and has locked herself inside a bathroom, the only safe room in the house. Just wanting to be left alone, she sits on the ground waiting for the screaming and pounding on the door to stop.

"You can't stay in there all day!" shouts the semi-hoarse voice of her last foster mother, Kate, before she stomps away. Dawn feels as if she has a few minutes to breathe. But then the nightmare transforms into the latest attack as her vision refocuses to the barrel of a gun pointed at her, followed by bursts of light leading to darkness. Opening her eyes, she sees soft light fall upon Kate's dead body on the floor of an otherwise pitch-black room.

More corpses appear, populating the room. She backs away, tripping over a dead body. Dawn lands hard, inches away from someone's face. Lifeless, pale milky bluish-white eyes stare back at her. Even his hair has lost nearly all its color, leaving only dead husks of white-blond strands. Her heart seizes. "Gabriel..." She reaches out to him, placing a hand gently on the side of his face. It's ice-cold.

Suddenly, she opens her eyes and is met with the comfortable bed she had fallen asleep in.

Her heart strains as her mind races, saying, *It was just a dream. It was just a dream. It was just a dream.* And she desperately wants to believe that.

◆

Throwing her comforter to the side, Dawn gets out of bed. Dread rooted deep within unsettles her, as if she is still trapped in the nightmare. She chokes back a scream, blood pressure rising. *Gabriel is still sleeping,* she thinks, looking at the door to her room.

The quiet room feels foreign, yet also a little too comfortable. Her mind races. *Safety, stability lead to instability. Love only leads to heartbreak. You can't get hurt from the fall if there is no room to fall. Gabriel is not your family. No, you can't depend on anyone.*

"I can't stay," she says to the empty room.

She rushes to the dresser, fumbling with the drawer, hands shaking. Grabbing her spare set of clothing, she shoves it into her backpack before zipping it shut, then slings her backpack across her shoulder and turns to the door, leaving behind the clothing that Gabriel had bought her.

Carefully, she opens the door, wincing as a creak echoes down the hall. Leaving the door ajar, she tastes the stale, cold air from the drafty house and makes her way down the dark hallway.

The blood pumping in her ears is the only thing she can hear. There is a dim light at the end of the maroon-carpeted hallway. *He must have left the TV on*, she thinks, listening to the murmurs and benign audience laughter emitting from the television as she turns the corner into the living room.

Dawn stops, freezing as she makes eye contact with Gabriel, who puts down his pencil and sketchbook. He mutes the television and stands.

"Are you leaving?" he asks. The light of the television casts a semi-transparent dark-blue color across his features. "Can we talk about this?"

Dawn shakes her head, taking a step back and curling inwards, head down, eyes averted. Her right hand tightens, gripping the strap of her backpack.

"I know you're scared, and I don't know why. Let me help. Please, talk to me." Gabriel cautiously stays where he is. "I'm not going to stop you. You can leave if you want—you always could. But, Dawn, I don't want to see you on the streets. Come, sit down for a few minutes, please?"

Dawn walks over, avoiding the computer towers and artifacts, and sits on the far end of the couch.

"Talk to me." Gabriel turns on a light and sits next to her.

"I'm scared. I don't know what to do." She looks at him. His compassionate vulnerability disarms her. "Every time someone claims to love me, they die. They don't love me. They've never loved me. Love isn't real."

"Dawn, I am willing to die for you. I promise you that my love is real. I would do anything to protect you, okay?"

"Why?"

"Because the only thing I am sure of in this world is the way that I feel for you."

She looks into his eyes and sees genuine emotion, not the empty, obsessive loss of self that she is familiar with from when others have proclaimed undying love.

"Please don't leave, not without a place to go." Gabriel quiets for a moment, before he says, "I need you, too, you know."

Dawn shakes her head, afraid to trust his words.

Gabriel places his hand on hers. "Please, don't leave me." He squeezes her hand gently. She makes no response. He stands up to give her space, as he does, she reaches out to him and holds on to his hand.

"I'm scared of losing you, too," Dawn says, her eyes closed. A single tear escapes.

"Then please, don't go. Dawn, I love you." Gabriel sits back down and wraps his arms around her. She relaxes, resting comfortably against him.

Gabriel holds her for a few heartbeats and then squeezes her softly but firmly, as if to express a silent prayer that she will not decide to walk out that door. He smiles at her, a concerned smile with a touch of relief, before he gets up to grab the remote. As he sits beside her, he rests his arm across her shoulders and hands her the remote with his other hand.

She flips through the channels before landing on a Sci-Fi classic.

"I'm going to get you a new phone tomorrow, so if you do leave, you'll at least be able to call."

Dawn doesn't protest as she normally would, choosing instead to rest her head against the comfort of his shoulder. She's filled with a rush of hope that everything is going to be all right.

That feeling is cut short. Hope dies in an instant, its malformed remains twist into a knot painfully constricting her heart as soon as she sees what it is Gabriel was sketching. It is an unmistakable drawing of the man. The man from the mirror. The man from her nightmares.

"Why? Why did you draw that?" Dawn says, unable to keep her voice from shaking.

"That? Oh, that's the guy from my night terrors."

"Wh—What?" Dawn stammers momentarily. "No."

Gabriel looks at her. "Are you all right?"

Dawn freezes, her body stiffens as she flashes back to the nightmare she had just awoken from. The one with Gabriel's corpse on the ground. When she looks up at him, Gabriel's face decays in seconds, vividly mirroring the morbid image; his eyes cloud with milky-white swirls over a lifeless fully light-blue eyes, except this time they blink at her. His paler-than-normal face is framed by the dead white-blond hair. She shivers involuntarily.

"Dawn?" Gabriel says. His voice echoes in her head as if heard from a distance. She turns away. When she looks back, his appearance shifts to normal. "Dawn, you all right?"

"No. That drawing—that man. I've seen him before, in my nightmares." She holds back telling him about seeing the man in the mirror, because who would believe her?

"That's impossible."

Dawn gets up and walks over to pick up the sketchpad, studying the loose, well-rendered pencil drawing closely. Her eyes widen at the Victorian-esque outfit, the angular nature of his face. Then she looks at the drawing's sharp eyes. Eyes that seem to stare back at her. "No." She loses her grip on the sketchpad. It falls onto the couch.

"Are you all right?" Gabriel asks.

"No, I'm not, Gabriel." Dawn shakes her head.

"Maybe it just… kind of looks like the guy from your nightmares?" Gabriel suggests.

"No, no. That's him. I'd know it—I'd know it anywhere."

"Dawn," Gabriel says, pulling her into his arms and back onto the couch. "Listen to me. Nightmares, night terrors, those things… they can get to you. But only if you let them. Recenter your focus on something else, like the fact that you are here with me."

"Do you want to meditate? It might help me calm down," Dawn asks.

"Sure, I'd like that."

Dawn closes her eyes and crosses her legs. He does the same.

"Breathe in," Dawn begins in a soft, peaceful tone. "Breathe out. The goal of meditation is to reach your subconsciousness and connect with everything. Relax and breathe in. Concentrate on your breath. Breathing is a subconscious act. You are connecting to your subconscious when you meditate. Relax and let go. Concentrate on peace, on nothing. Breathe in. You may have a thought, allow it to leave. Sit beside your thoughts, observe them, and allow them to leave. Know that these thoughts are not you. Open your hands, palms facing up. Breathe in and let go."

Chapter 5

Gabriel can't remember a time he has been happier. He hasn't formally asked Dawn to be his girlfriend, but they have an unspoken understanding. Although the bond between them is growing, deep down, Gabriel is afraid Dawn will leave him if he asks her to make things official. He squeezes her hand gently but firmly as they walk along a trail in the forest, making their way to the stream by the bridge, near where they had first met.

All around them, fallen leaves in shades of brown, auburn, and yellow litter the trail beneath their feet. He admires her as she stops to pluck a crimson apple from a tree. Weighing it in her hand, she tosses it softly into the air. After catching the apple, she notices he is staring.

They continue down the trail until they reach a trickling stream and sit beside it. The sound of the water is calming. Even though he has been near nature his entire life, the awe-inspiring serenity of the woods is never lost on him. Dawn rests her head on his shoulder, and he places his arm securely around her. There is a crunch as Dawn bites into the apple.

"It's nice out here." Dawn shrugs, casually picking up a rock and tossing it into the stream.

"You shouldn't do that," Gabriel says.

"Why not?"

He smiles at her, then his expression changes as he looks at the water. "You never know what repercussions your actions will have. Would you like to hear a story?"

"Sure."

"A long time ago, when I was younger, my dad was away on an archaeological something or other. This wasn't long after my mother died, maybe a couple of years. I had a caretaker, but for the most part, I could do whatever I wanted. I would spend most of my time in the forest. I was walking around, it was my birthday... no one showed up. Which wasn't surprising because I was home-schooled. I heard a voice inside my head, he said, 'I can be that friend.'

"He said his name was Semoel. I told him I didn't care who he was or why he was there, that he had to leave. Then I decided that since he was the only one to actually show up for my birthday, he might as well stay. We often walked together in the woods. One day, he told me he wanted to show me that which is nature. 'See the trees, how they form, how they grow.' He told me to pick an acorn and choose the best place to plant it. Showing me the simple choices we have in the world is our path as humans. We can greatly affect that which is around us, for good or ill.

"I was throwing rocks into the stream, watching the water ripple. 'The causality, like a spider's web. We are all tied together,' Semoel said. I picked up another smooth river stone. Semoel warned me that every action has a consequence, even if we don't intend them to. To be careful about the impact we make on this world. To live with forethought and caution. 'What if,' he said, 'a fish was swimming by and got hit by the rock?' I threw the rock in anyway. Not long after, a fish came up to the shores of the river, dying, clearly bludgeoned in the head.

"Every action has a consequence..." Gabriel says, his thoughtful tone is disconnected as he stares at the spot on the shore as if the fish were gasping for air on the riverbank. "I didn't mean to. I didn't understand. It was a hard lesson, watching that fish die. It looked like it needed air, but that's not how fish work. I kept a river stone I was going to throw next as a reminder. I carried it everywhere. Well, until my dad threw it in the North River about a year ago. He said I had an unhealthy attachment to it."

Dawn nods. "That is quite a story, Gabriel, but I believe you."

"You have no reason to believe me. I don't even believe me."

"You believe me when I tell you things. Why shouldn't I believe you?"

"I haven't talked to Semoel in a long time." Gabriel falls silent, then takes out his phone. "Picture?" he asks. She leans in close, getting into frame. He grins and kisses her on the cheek, then takes a picture of her reaction.

After enlarging the photo on his phone, he looks at it with a sense of comfort because, in it, she is smiling, something Gabriel never thought he would see.

She holds the apple out to him. He takes it after kissing her again. Gabriel bites into the ripe apple, tasting the sweet yet tangy fruit. Overhead, a flock of blackbirds scatters from the treetops.

"Did you know," Dawn says, gesturing toward the water, "humans are fascinated by shiny things because of the glimmer of water? It's in our instinct. Our ancestors were drawn to it, to stay close to water sources to survive."

"I didn't know that," he says, holding her and kissing her on the cheek. She rests her hands on his forearms.

They talk until day turns to night, about everything, about nothing.

After night falls, they move their conversation to Gabriel's room. His bedroom is almost identical to hers, except there are more items on the dresser and tabletops.

Gabriel lies in bed with Dawn in his arms, laying across his chest. She looks up at him and smiles. *She is so beautiful*, he thinks before kissing her and holding her tight. Night turns to day and they continue to talk until Dawn is too tired to stay awake any longer. She gets up to go back to her room. He holds onto her arm for a heartbeat.

"You can sleep here you know," Gabriel says, before letting her arm go.

"I'm not your girlfriend, Gabriel." Dawn has a half-smile.

"No? Could have fooled me." He smiles at her.

Dawn rolls her eyes and rests her head against his shoulder. He puts his arm around her, finally feeling grounded. Gabriel kisses her hair and breathes in her scent. She often burns incense, sage, and palo santo. Today, hints of palo santo linger on her hair and clothing.

"If you hold me and tell me you will be there for me, never let me go." Dawn adjusts her body against his, her head resting against his chest, listening to his heartbeat.

"I promise." Gabriel squeezes her soft, warm body against his.

He commits to memory this exact moment. The moment in which he feels whole.

✦

The chill of winter fills Gabriel's lungs. A cloud of water vapor is visible, even through the dust mask he is wearing as he exhales. The wood paneling of the shed is a weak shield from the frosty winter night. First, he adjusts his safety glasses and then the arm of the magnifying lamp attached to the table in front of him. Through the magnifying lens, Gabriel looks at the gold pocket watch he gave Dawn the day they met.

Occasionally, he glances at a printed paper on a clipboard propped against the shed's wood panel walls, sitting atop his large workbench. The paper is a reference sheet of a calligraphy-style cursive font often used in weddings. He is sketching on the pocket watch, which is cushioned by a hand towel and held in place by a clamp. Eventually, he draws out a pattern on the outer gold ring of the watch face, their names, Gabriel and Dawn, just beyond the circle of planetary symbols.

A buzzing noise like that of a tattoo gun fills the small workshop as Gabriel powers on his electronic graver. Putting the graver to metal, small strips of gold begin to peel away from the pocket watch.

Gabriel enters a flow state and loses track of time. Finally, he shuts off the graver and sets it aside. Using a cloth to polish the engraving, he does his best to ignore the strong stench of chemicals.

Leaning back against his chair, he admires the gleam of the metal before picking up an open, crinkled brown paper envelope. Turning it upside down, a small item wrapped in plastic slides onto his workbench. Unwrapping the coin-shaped object reveals a custom-sized metal print of him and Dawn near the river, which shines against the work lamp. He places the small metal disk inside the lid of the watch. It fits perfectly—almost too perfectly, as he has trouble removing it. After consideration, he resorts to prying it off carefully with a flathead screwdriver.

It pops off, landing on his workbench. Turning to the side, he adjusts the pocket watch sitting in a clamp and cleans the inside of the lid and the back of the metal picture. He applies a thin layer of flux and small amounts of solder in carefully chosen spots.

After putting on bulky but comfortable heat-resistant welding gloves and replacing his safety glasses with green-tinted safety goggles, the world around him darkens with a muted green tone. Grabbing his hand torch, he looks at his project and ignites the bright flame, which has an odd green-tinted blue through his goggles. He heats the solder and turns off the hand torch, working quickly to place the metal picture into the watch lid.

Breathing out slowly, he holds the picture to the inside of the watch lid, waiting for the metals to bond. Finally, he removes his safety equipment and checks his phone to see if Dawn has messaged. She hasn't; he figures she is still asleep. He heads back inside to watch TV until the watch is sufficiently cooled.

Several hours pass. It is late into the night. Gabriel goes to retrieve the watch and notices that one hand points to the strange planetary symbol he had never seen before. He hadn't even realized that he didn't recognize the symbol until Dawn said something. No matter how much he searched online, he couldn't find a matching symbol.

Gabriel reaches into his pocket and takes out a small, dark-blue jewelry box. He opens the small ring box, revealing an engagement ring he designed and ordered from a jeweler near the café. He takes it out, feeling the solidness of the platinum band, and holds it under the work lamp. In the center of the ring is a Celtic love knot made of the same platinum as the band, the bottom of which is wrapped around a light-blue semi-translucent Prince Rupert's drop. The teardrop's glass glitters with specks of silver and gold harvested from non-working computer parts as well as sand from the shore near the riverbank where the picture was taken. To the sides of the centerpiece of the ring, on the simple platinum band, are two round diamonds representing Dawn and himself. After he places the ring in a small scrap of dark-purple fabric, he snaps the watch shut. The cold metal burns mildly against his skin as he feels the heartbeat-like tick of the watch.

She will say yes. She will say yes. She has to say yes, Gabriel thinks, trying to convince himself that there isn't any way she will say no. He slides the watch into his pocket before trudging back to the house, following the path of his footprints in the snow.

Carefully opening his bedroom door, he finds Dawn fast asleep in their bed. Quietly, he changes into his night clothing, a long-sleeved white shirt and gray sweatpants. Gabriel smiles before climbing into bed and getting under the covers, pulling Dawn close and holding her in his arms.

✦

Dawn sleeps peacefully, curled up, lying on her left side. Her head rests against Gabriel's arm, his other arm is secured around her waist. Her breathing becomes ragged and shallow as if the air around her is running low.

Get up, she tells herself, but any attempt to do so is in vain as her body refuses to listen. Only through great effort do her eyes flicker open for a moment, and she sees him. The man from her nightmares, the man from Gabriel's drawing, the man from the mirror.

"Shh. It's all right," he whispers softly, stroking her hair. His icy hand rests on her forehead.

Get up, she begs herself as she falls deeper into near-comatose state. All at once, memories of her life, all the suffering she has endured, overwhelm her. Although she is asleep, tears begin to fall. His hand moves to the center of her chest and her back arches up, body stiff with the pain coalescing in her heart.

Falling further away, Dawn is lost in a dreamless sleep.

✦

Gabriel shivers as a frigid draft blows across his face. He adjusts his arms tightly around Dawn to protect her from the cold and tells himself to remember to do something about the insulation in this large old house. Drifting off to sleep, layers of subconscious thoughts rise to the surface. Unable to rid himself of the nagging anxiety of his upcoming proposal, he thinks about the engagement ring sitting wrapped in fabric inside the watch in his pocket. He has no idea what she is going to say. *She might say no. She might leave. I can't think like that.* Gabriel tells himself. *She'll say yes. I know she will... I hope she will.*

The bedroom door creaks open. Gabriel looks toward the door, half dazed. Boots clank against the wooden floor of his bedroom. Panicking, Gabriel tries to move but finds himself paralyzed. He can only open his eyes as a tall, otherworldly figure comes in to view above him. *It's a night terror*, Gabriel assures himself. *It was bound to happen eventually.*

The figure looks like a man displaced from time. He wears a well-tailored suit and a long Victorian-style overcoat lined with embossed gold buttons that shine in the dark, providing a low luminosity around him. The gold glows against his angular face with its sharp features and bone-white skin. He has long black hair that reaches down his back, and his unnaturally bright copper-colored eyes are fixated on Dawn. He whispers to her while softly stroking her hair. The man places his hand on her forehead, and her breathing is slow and shallow. Her body wrenches in pain, arching upward as a bright white light emits between the man's palm and her chest.

Uselessly, Gabriel fights against the sleep paralytic.

Dawn's expression of agony vanishes. She slumps over, crashing onto the bed, limp as a rag doll.

Screaming internally and fighting to move, Gabriel is unable to do anything but move his eyes. Thunder cracks with the loudest boom he has ever heard. The room lights up in a bright flash of white light as lightning strikes the window, shattering the glass.

Gabriel strains to keep sight of Dawn. Pale golden light from the man's overcoat casts a soft glow across the features of her face. Even though tears stream down her face, wetting his arm, he isn't sure she is even breathing.

The ground rumbles, tremors causing office supplies to chatter against his desk, threatening to fall. Pieces of the ceiling break apart and crash onto the floor. Cold winter winds howl into the room through the broken window. None of this is typical of his recurring night terror. Part of him wonders if he is actually awake.

The man reaches into his overcoat. The sound of something solid scrapes against metal as he unsheathes a weapon. The man grips a red crystal dagger with gem-cut serrated edges in his right hand. It would be beautiful if it wasn't so goddamn terrifying. The man drives the dagger into Gabriel's chest swiftly and without mercy. The red crystal blade of the dagger dissipates, melting into his bloodstream. The man withdraws the hilt of the now-bladeless weapon. Gabriel chokes, gasping for air. It feels as if his blood is on fire and warm poison is rising up his throat.

The dark figure turns his bright copper-colored eyes back to Dawn. The trespasser lifts her and drapes her body across his right shoulder. Gabriel continues fighting the paralysis. Somehow, he manages to lift his arm. His hand grips the man's forearm.

The man strikes Gabriel across the face with a powerful backhand. His face goes numb as the impact hurls him against the bed. Behind the man is a strange midnight-blue portal that emits white noise. The man takes a long, thoughtful look at Gabriel before turning and walking toward the portal.

There is a thud as Gabriel falls to the floor, reaching out for Dawn, who is still draped across the man's shoulder. The man turns and walks to Gabriel. Momentarily, he wears an amused smile, but it fades into mild annoyance as he leans down and picks up Gabriel by his throat. Lifting him into the air with one hand, he tightens his grip and hurls him into a wall near his now-overturned desk.

There is a succession of crashes as something structural collapses close to Gabriel's room. He doesn't have the strength to get up as he watches the figure casually walk away and disappear into the vortex.

What in the hell is going on? Gabriel thinks as he tries to move, but still finds his body rendered useless.

Broken, defeated, and just having lost the only thing he cares about in this world, Gabriel allows himself to drop against the hard wooden floor, surrendering to the paralytic. Left for dead, his mind is trapped, replaying the nightmare scenario as the ceiling continues to collapse, striking him and burying him in rubble.

II

Part Two

Chapter 6

T he old, weathered gray bricks of the cathedral-esque fortress buckle and collapse. Gabriel lay paralyzed, buried under rubble, dazed but somehow conscious. Warm poison runs through his veins. His eyes are fixated on the spot where Dawn had vanished.

Cutting through the sounds of the storm and the harsh wind is static louder than before, like when a radio is tuned between stations. The noise becomes so loud it drowns out the destruction around him. A twisting vortex of black clouds against a sea of dark blue appears.

A pale figure emerges from the vortex; tufts of billowy white hair stick out from under his hood. The ends of his stringy hair point in different directions. The cloaked figure turns and looks directly at Gabriel, his expression mute, his pale, emaciated features invoking an air of hollowness not helped by the fact that his irises are gray and nearly colorless.

The mysterious figure is draped in torn black rags under the remains of a cloak. The tattered ends of the blue-black cloak flow like feathers as he walks. Gabriel's blurred vision sharpens but only for a moment, focusing upon the tips of large semiopaque dark-blue feathers that drag across the wooden floor as the figure approaches. The temperature plunges as if an aura of bitter cold emanates from the figure itself.

This is it. This is how I die, Gabriel thinks, feeling strangely at peace. As numbness spreads throughout his body, the figure picks him up. Moments later, a dangerously large chunk of the stone from the ceiling strikes the ground where Gabriel was. The figure gracefully turns away from the pile of rubble.

As Gabriel is carried to the vortex, sorrow grips him. His final thought before leaving this world is, *I'm sorry, Dawn.*

Disoriented by the deafeningly loud radio-like static, Gabriel feels entirely disconnected as the air around him crystallizes into a deep midnight blue.

The figure lays Gabriel on the ground, which is colder than the light-blue-gray mists filling his lungs. A hypnotic melody fills the air. The hauntingly beautiful hymn does not allow Gabriel to ignore the fresh, deeply cut wounds of grief. The song, like a soft banshee's wail that echoes the forgotten halls of a bygone cathedral is an unrelenting funeral requiem.

"What... song is that?" Gabriel asks, closing his eyes, unable to ignore melody.

"There is no song." The figure's eyes look skyward. "What you are hearing is not music but atmospheric resonance discharged from the ether as it merges in and out of the bordering planes."

Gabriel isn't sure what he said, so he looks up, his vision finally focusing. He is rendered speechless by the haunting majesty of the sky above. Obscured partially by the mists, the cloudless, starless sky flows at an unnaturally fast pace as if it were a storm fully contained above and not below. The swirling sky is composed of gradients of deep, dark blues, like a tempest sea, coalescing in splotches so concentrated that they appear pitch black. Gabriel finds that he can finally move his body and turns to his rescuer.

Through the grayish mist, the figure is illuminated by the strange light that the world seems to be composed of so he can see just how decayed the angel's clothing really is. The tattered blue-black cloak, mostly comprised of strips of torn fabric, is adorned with a patchwork of large, clumsy yarn-like stitches.

The angel rests a cold, pale, slightly blue hand on Gabriel's forehead. All at once, voices flood his head, a myriad of foreign words, many in languages he is certain he has never heard before. Gabriel shivers, confused, expecting to see his breath in the mist-filled air, but does not. Taking a few moments to collect himself, Gabriel stays on the cold, uneven ground before standing. His body is sore; every muscle movement is painful. He wonders how much of it has to do with being stabbed with that strange red crystal dagger.

Placing his hand near his fresh chest wound, Gabriel asks, "Am I... dead?"

The strange figure does not reply. Instead he stares intensely at something Gabriel cannot see. After several long moments, the angel closes his eyes and tilts his head down for a heartbeat.

Finally, the angel lifts his head back up and responds. "No, Gabriel, you are not dead." When the angel speaks, his voice is monotone and carries a supernatural echo. But when Gabriel listens, really listens, the sorrow in his voice is unmistakable, yet it also conveys gentle kindness.

Looking down at his wound through the hole in his white long-sleeved nightshirt, Gabriel presses against it and winces, finding it to be tender. The wound is seared shut by a black crust of poison mixed with traces of blood. There are branches of black veins inching out from the point of impact.

"Who are you?"

"I am Azrael, the Archangel of Death. I have unlocked the power of Bable within you. Anything written or spoken in another language will be translated, with a few exceptions such as High Enochian."

Gabriel locks eyes with Azrael and then quickly averts eye contact. Etched in Azrael's face is a haunting melancholy, so much so that Gabriel focuses on the freezing cold and the pain in his chest to keep the morose feelings of hopelessness at bay.

"What happened? Who was that? Where is Dawn? Where... am I?"

"The man you saw is Lucifer. Dawn is out of reach. You are in the Ethereal Realm. You are Gabriel."

"Yes... I am Gabriel. Is that a question or...?"

"But you are not Gabriel." An enormous old beige colored book materializes, hovering just above the palm of Azrael's left hand, as well as two nearly identical books hovering to each side of Azrael. Finally, a worn black staff materializes in his right hand. The honey sand-colored pages of the book flip on their own, and Azrael leans to one side, resting on his staff. The top of it looks jagged, as if something had been torn off but never bothered to be replaced. "You are not in the Book of Fate, the Book of Life, nor the Book of Death."

Gabriel glances at the pages of the book and sees nothing but diagrams of mathematical equations with signs he has never seen before.

"I'm sorry. I don't know what any of this means," Gabriel says.

Azrael blinks, then the large book closes on its own. "Neither do I."

"Where is Dawn?" Gabriel asks.

"She is… home."

"Home? What does that mean?" Gabriel, eyes wide with frustration, gestures emotionally as he talks. "Why was there an earthquake? Am I dreaming?"

"Home… where she belongs," Azrael says, his voice devoid of emotion. "The earthquake is a mystery. And no, you are not dreaming."

"What do you mean? Where she belongs? She lives with me."

"Lived." Azrael blinks.

"What do you mean 'lived?'" Gabriel's jaw clenches, eyes narrow, and he looks directly at Azrael.

"She is home," Azrael insists.

"What happened to me, Azrael?" Gabriel's voice wavers as he pleads for answers.

Azrael pauses, making no reaction. His stature is lanky, and he leans forward slightly, as if his spine is curved.

After several long moments, Azrael says, "I am not the one to answer your questions."

"Why not?"

Azrael sighs. "It is not my place. I found long ago that it is better to stay out of the affairs of others. To allow things to grow organically, to die naturally. When you upset the balance… no, that is when things get out of hand."

"What does that even mean, Azrael? I need help. I need answers. Where is Dawn?"

"She is home."

"You keep saying that. What does that mean?"

"You, too, must go home." Azrael nods in a particular direction in the vast, seemingly unending, void of midnight blue.

"What?" Gabriel shivers, trying his best to ignore the eerie, unrelenting hymn. Through the mists in the distance sits an enormous, dark-blue, semiopaque, twisting tree whose branches split into veins connecting to the sky.

"You, too, must go home if you are to stop the spread of soul poison. The Crown Realms is where you belong, with your father Gabriel."

"My father's name is Raphael."

"I'm afraid it is not. You are a double of Archangel Gabriel, down to the molecular level. You both are and are not Archangel Gabriel."

"What?" Gabriel throws his arms up in confusion. "Then who is Raphael? And my mother Emily?"

"I have said too much."

The soul poison pulses in Gabriel's body, veins on fire. He doubles over in pain, pressing his right arm against his chest.

"As an archangel, the rate of your cellular regeneration should keep you from dying. However, you will suffer constant pain. It is in your system, it will progress. There may come a time when you are beyond a healer's abilities. Heed my warning. Take care of it now before the infection spreads."

A scream pierces his mind.

"Dawn." Gabriel, although unnervingly calm, balls his hands into fists as he searches the direction from which he heard her, but sees nothing.

"You must seek aid for your injury. I cannot help."

Azrael's words fall upon deaf ears as Gabriel continues to search for any sign of Dawn. "I don't care. I need to get to her."

"You need help," Azrael says more insistently.

Another scream, louder than before, echoes in his mind before it descends into words of a broken prayer, a plea for... for him before the sound goes silent.

"Tell me how to get to her!" Gabriel shouts, his heart pumping harder, amplifying the pain from the soul poison in his chest. His shoulder blades strain as his giant wings spread behind him.

Gabriel looks back at his wings, speechless. They are a concentrated midnight blue, as dark as the tree in the distance. Moving throughout his large, midnight-blue wings are speckles of light-blue dots and clouds of smoke. The elegant fluid movement is reminiscent of satellite images of clouds, as if a scoop of the midnight sky was captured in a blue-tinted glass bottle, the stars flowing with the clouds.

He looks at his wings and then back at Azrael. "What?"

"What part of Archangel Gabriel do you not understand?"

Dropping to his knees, Gabriel cries out in anguish. His wings fold behind him, he lowers his head as tears fall.

"I don't know what I'm doing. I don't know where I am. I don't know where to go. I'm lost." Gabriel raises his eyes to the strange sky above, anxiety coursing through his body. "Please! I beg you, have mercy on me." Gabriel lowers his head. "I would do… anything… to have her safe in my arms again."

Standing up, his head is bowed until he looks up and locks eyes with Azrael, whose conveys no emotion. "Are you talking to me?"

"No, Azrael. I'm imploring the universe for help."

"The cosmos cannot aid you," Azrael says solemnly.

"I know. Okay? I know." Gabriel's glossy eyes search the vast midnight-blue landscape, finding no sign of an answer. Deeply sighing, he drops his shoulders. "You don't understand… Dawn is everything to me. I need her more than she will ever know. I didn't even get the chance…"

Gabriel's words fade as he removes the engraved pocket watch that holds her engagement ring. His knuckles turn white as he grips the watch tightly, feeling the tick… tick… tick… thinking about what his life could have been… what it was promised to be.

"I've lost everything… she is the only thing that matters to me. I need her, Azrael. Without her, there is no me. Without her, I have no purpose—nothing."

Azrael blinks in confusion. "You are Gabriel. With your power—"

"I don't care about power, Azrael. Why would I care about power? I only care about her."

"Is this love or obsession?"

"Love is obsession tempered by compassion."

"Don't allow love to blind you to reason," Azrael says evenly. "Seek balance."

"Balance? There is no balance! Reason and love are not compatible. Love, love will never know reason. How could it? And reason, reason asks you to forsake everything you know in your heart to be true in favor of cold, rational calculations. I will not deny what I know to be true, and there is only one truth of which I am certain. I love her. I would do anything for her because the truth is… I am nothing without her."

Azrael takes off his tattered cloak and drapes it across Gabriel's shoulders. The broken ends flutter in different directions as it falls over his wings.

Gabriel looks up at Azrael. Without his cloak, Azrael looks smaller in his dark linen robes. Spots of pale skin with a soft touch of light blue can be seen through the many holes in his clothing.

"Why are you giving me this?" Gabriel picks himself up.

"You'll need it where you are going. Where I cannot stop you from going."

"Why?"

Azrael mumbles words of an incantation Gabriel can't understand before looking at him and saying, "When you're in another realm, your wings will be hidden here in the Ethereal. Wings are made of the same essence as this realm. The Ethereal permeates the bordering realms."

"Is there any other help you can offer me?" Gabriel asks, slipping the pocket watch back into his pants.

One of Azrael's large beige books glides through the air and stops, hovering in front of the Archangel of Death. Its pages flip faster than Gabriel can read until the final page is open. Azrael tears out a large honey-sand-toned page.

"Take this." Azrael holds out the paper as the book closes on its own and returns to the archangel's side.

Taking the paper, Gabriel stares at it but is unable to see anything but a blank page. Full of questions, his eyes flicker to Azrael. The ragged figure, however, stands silent with his eyes closed. The page darkens, ink spreads like watercolor until the entire paper is midnight blue as if the realm itself were bleeding onto the page.

Darker, more concentrated spots emerge, forming several circles that look like planetary orbits. The ink continues to spread, varying in shades, marking the planets, but the rendering is so impressionistic that Gabriel can read none of whatever the shading is meant to indicate.

"A star system?" Gabriel asks.

Azrael opens his eyes and looks back at him. "It was. You will find Dawn here." Azrael gestures to the darkest, smallest, innermost planet on the map. A sense of foreboding chills him as he stares at the small black dot.

"What do you mean *was?*"

"The star is dead."

"Ah."

"This is a living map of the Sine System. It will alter, based on your location, as well as the current positions of the other realms in the system. You may not notice a change unless you put it away for a while," Azrael explains.

The other side of the map has nearly translucent lettering. Its elegant, elongated symbols are a language Gabriel cannot read. Through the power of Babel, the symbols morph, reforming into groups of phonetic clusters that Gabriel can pronounce. He silently mouths the strange writing to himself.

"This incantation is not meant to be spoken lightly. A careless misstep can mean the end of everything," Azrael warns him. "Forcing a wormhole bridge between the realms tears a hole in space-time. If the realms are misaligned when that incantation is evoked, it can potentially create a magna black hole."

The blue-black lettering on the back of the map fades before being replaced by another set of phonetic clusters.

Azrael explains. "The incantation alternates frequently as a safety mechanism. In the front pocket of your cloak is a cosmoversal crystal. Hold it in your hand and repeat the incantation written on your map when it glows its brightest. The crystal will show a path if one is open. If the alignment is correct, it will beam you back here."

"Beam?" Gabriel asks, fishing the crystal out from an inner pocket of the cloak. It looks like ordinary quartz.

"Yes, you travel on an electromagnetic wave focused by that crystal to a fixed point in space when space-time aligns between the planes of existence." Depression is evident in Azrael's eyes, although there wasn't a moment when he did not look somber. "I have interfered enough as it is."

Gabriel inclines his head. "Thank you, Azrael."

"Don't thank me. Walk with me."

They walk for a while through the seemingly endless void of midnight blue, traveling away from the tree he saw in the distance and directly toward… the same tree in the opposite direction.

As if to explain, Azrael looks at the tree in the distance and mumbles, "That's Hurbur."

"Is that the Tree of Life?" Gabriel asks.

"… and Death… Everyone always forgets the death part," Azrael says quietly.

As they walk through the seemingly endless void, Azrael's books float in the air, orbiting him. His black wooden staff is utilized as a walking stick. Gabriel can't help but wonder about the jagged top of the staff. What, if anything, was there before? The soul-chilling hymn continues its ever-present funeral requiem, broken only by a disjointed buzz that increases in volume the closer they approach a pitch-black vortex portal under the tree.

"Are you certain this is the path you wish to go?" Azrael looks at him.
"Yes."

"Then go, Gabriel, but know that they will not welcome you, and your wound will only grow with time. This portal is one way," Azrael warns him.

"Understood. Does it take me to the innermost planet?"

"No."

Gabriel nods, steadying himself for what is to come. Anxiety spikes inside, provoked by the loud static white noise emitting from the vortex.

"Remember." Azrael proceeds to say something that does not translate and then explains. "It means thoughts become words, words lead to actions, and actions set the course of destiny. Break the links between them to alter your course."

"Why are you telling me this?"

"Because, Gabriel, all things share the same fate. Now go, if you are to go."

Gabriel nods respectfully, hoping to convey his appreciation before taking a deep breath of mist-filled air and forcing himself to walk through the portal into the unknown.

✦

Something is wrong. Dawn finds herself blindfolded. A series of straps restricts her movement. They are secured around her head, neck, wrists, and upper midsection. Her head is forced to the right, pressed against a wooden board, her body forced into a sharp S shape; her knees rest on an incline, ankles cuffed at a thirty-five-degree angle behind her.

Her wrists are secured to a pole, the chains of which jangle as she struggles. She tells herself no matter how real it feels, *this is a nightmare*.

Breathing in slowly in an effort to calm herself, she expands her chest as she inhales, painfully constricted by the tight restraints. A burning cold slices into the skin on her back, which increases to a searing pain as if she were being branded for an excruciatingly long amount of time. Dawn cries out. What starts as a whimper gives way to a scream. Shaking her head, her body stiffens as she thrashes uselessly against her bonds. Striking pain, a burning cold cauterizes her skin, is the singular sensation dominating her mind.

She starts babbling incoherently. "Gabriel! Gabriel! God, Gabriel. Please, God, help me."

Dawn's wailing escalates to a piercing banshee scream.

A comforting hand rests on the side of her face, while another is pressed firmly against her throat. The scream is silenced.

✦

A light, blustery wind carries a flurry of snow past Raphael as he surveys the wreckage of what once was his home. Large soft flakes of snow accumulate on the ground, obscuring the debris. He adjusts his black knit cap securely over his long, medium brown hair that is tied back into a ponytail. Creating distance from the sense of loss, he treats it like an archaeological dig. As he sorts through the familiar items, he examines damage on a small copper artifact before wrapping it in fabric and placing it in the side pouch of a coffee-brown tactical gear bag slung over his shoulder.

His mind races as he pieces together a probable chain of events. Snow crunches underfoot as he walks south, past where the aged wooden red front door once stood. Chunks of it litter the ground, much farther south than most of the debris.

Raphael stops to pick up a larger piece, the soft snow covering it sliding off as he does. Staring at the chipped red paint on the jagged chunk of wood Raphael mumbles a quiet prayer. "Blood, life, sanctuary."

After placing the chunk of wood into a pocket of his muted earth-toned cargo pants, he heads back. Careful not to disturb the crime scene more than necessary, he observes pieces of computers, artifacts, and many everyday household items.

He heads east and sifts through the remains of Gabriel's room. There is a makeup brush next to tarot cards strewn about. Reaching down, Raphael picks up a tarot card, the Page of Swords. The card is water-damaged; its ink bleeds together, especially in the warped bends. After placing it into a ziplock, he puts it in the main pouch of his gear bag.

A silver picture frame glints in the sun near the remains of a dark wooden desk. Carefully, he picks it up, allowing broken glass to slide off the photograph. Swallowing hard, he looks at the black-and-white weather-damaged photo of him and Gabriel. The picture was taken with an antique 1940s-style press camera. Gabriel had wanted to see if it still worked. He remembers it as if it were yesterday: the bright flash of light still seared into his mind, how excited Gabriel was to learn how it worked. So much so that he dismantled it—with permission. The pieces of the camera never did quite make it back together.

"Did I do the right thing?" Raphael looks to the sky, his light brown eyes begging for an answer.

"I'm sure you did everything you could," a stern voice says from behind him. "Everything, except telling me."

Raphael turns around. Steadying himself as he sees Mikhail and two of her soldiers, as well as the leader of the Order of Agies, James. The typical form Mikhail has chosen for the past several millennia is Nubian.

"Mikhail," Raphael says.

Mikhail inclines her head. Her features are angular and exceptionally beautiful. Her long black hair is pulled back and intricately styled in large, neat braids. Several are adorned with a matte golden ribbon that crosses the braids in an X pattern. The front half of her large braids are pulled back to just below her ears before hanging freely down.

"Do you want to tell me what is going on here?" Mikhail strides toward him wearing a business casual black wool jacket, much like Raphael's. The rest of her outfit matches the coat in a sleek yet understated manner. She stops a short distance from him, with James beside her and the two soldiers flanking them. They are all dressed similarly. James has on a plain black jacket and dark-gray military fatigues.

Raphael holds up the photograph.

"He's not allowed here," Mikhail says, as if it the statement were obvious.

"That's not who you think it is," Raphael says in a nearly whispered tone, his shoulders down, resigned.

"Clarify." Mikhail's expression doesn't change as she stands rooted in a firm stance.

Raphael begins to absentmindedly pace, debris crunching beneath his work boots.

"I really don't know the whole story. I've been watching over him. I thought nothing would happen because it was safe here. There were precautions. Anxieties, so he wouldn't stray far from this leyline, illusion in appearance, false memories." Raphael stops pacing, tears forming in his eyes. "I only did what I had to do to help him. Once he wrote me about her, I had to confirm that she is who she looks like she is."

Raphael takes out a picture from his bag and shows it to Mikhail. "He sent me this in his last letter."

The image is of Dawn and Gabriel sitting in the woods near the stream. James leans in, studying the photograph. His face is unreadable as he looks at Raphael, holding his gaze for a moment.

Breaking the silence, Mikhail says, "You should have come to me."

"I was sworn to secrecy. It doesn't matter. Now, there is no way to protect him. I made a mistake. I was only trying to do what was right. They refused to let me help them otherwise."

Turning away, Raphael hunches his shoulders and tilts his head down. When he turns back, Mikhail and her lieutenants are gone, leaving only James standing beside him.

"We should have told her," James says in a serious, somewhat angry tone.

"We were right to stand by our word to Gabriel and Uriel."

"I was never comfortable hiding his existence from her," James says, looking far off into the distance. His body language is resolute but weary.

Feeling broken, much like his home, Raphael allows himself to sigh and says nothing.

Chapter 7

The blue light of the Ethereal Realm fades behind him, and tear-splitting, disjointed static vibrations drop in octave while increasing in volume. Everything is pitch black. Gabriel's skin cracks, frosted from the drop in temperature. Then, slightly less cold but still freezing air blasts him as he finds himself falling, solid ground quickly approaching.

Gabriel scrambles to remember anything he knows about surviving a fall. *The key to increasing the chance of surviving a fall is to relax and control where and how you land.* Spreading his arms out, he uses air resistance to angle himself from landing on his head. Below is an expanse of gray dust in every direction. *I should have removed the cape,* Gabriel thinks, with only seconds left to impact. *Not that I know how to fly.* Closing his eyes, breathing out slowly, he relaxes his muscles, moments before he slams into the ground.

Utterly disoriented, body numb, Gabriel lies in the small crater, inhaling dust kicked up on impact. He is certain the fall damaged something in his brain because everything looks as if it were viewed through the lens of a broken black-and-white television with a malfunction of purple hues. The dirt cloud settles, caking him with dust. After the numbness fades, he wonders how he isn't severely injured. The only pain he has emanates from his chest.

He gets up and starts trudging through the endless gray expanse. Gabriel stops to take out Dawn's watch, flipping it open and looking at it through the strange violet vision. Sorrow grips him as he stares at the metal picture of them together on the inside of the watch lid. He tells himself to hold on to the feeling of having her safely wrapped in his arms. When she is with him, all the problems in the world fade away. Breathing out deeply, Gabriel relaxes. Blinking, his vision returns to normal, and Dawn's hair in the picture returns to its signature cardinal red.

Inside the watch and wrapped in a piece of dark-purple fabric is Dawn's engagement ring. Gabriel tries to dull the stinging pain in his chest that has nothing to do with the physical wound as he picks up the ring and unwraps it. What hope left inside is dying, but it's not dead yet. Despite the dim light, the pieces of gold, silver, and sand inside the translucent light-blue teardrop-shaped glass centerpiece glimmers. While wrapping the ring back up, he silently promises Dawn that he will hold on to that spark of hope, even if only an ember remains.

After winding the watch, he feels the heartbeat tick in his palm before snapping it shut. Pieces of the ragged feather-like cloak move as he slides the golden watch into his pants pocket. Even though the fabric of Azrael's cloak looks rough, in actuality it is incredibly soft.

Gabriel decides to remove the cloak, and the immediate area illuminates with light from his large, ethereal wings. Then he remembers the vague warnings Azrael had given him. So, he puts the cloak back on, and the light dims as his wings disappear.

Looking up to the sky, he can see a pale spot, as if it were a faint memory of a star. Deciding to follow the star, he heads in that direction. After some time, suffering from neither hunger nor fatigue, Gabriel wonders if he really isn't dead after all. Finally, he sees a red glow of fire in the distance. He makes his way toward it and travels down a steep decline into a crater.

Gabriel pauses to take in the view. He is surrounded by towering white marble ruins of statues, tablets, and pieces of what was likely a building, lying broken and forgotten. *Why does it feel like I'm standing in the middle of a graveyard?* he wonders. Reaching into his cloak's pocket, he takes out the impressionistic watercolor-like map and notices the center has moved to a darker spot on the map. Wishing he could read it more clearly, he folds the map and puts it away.

He heads to the fire and the gray stone columns that are half his height, the top of which are indented, forming a basin, and filled with opal-like white stones. Gabriel marvels as the stones appear to fuel the fire, but unlike charcoal, these stones are not consumed by flame. Although the fire is a standard color, it moves like water.

Turning to the side and walking further into the ruins, Gabriel observes the statues of angels: ones with missing noses, arms, some lying sideways, half-buried in the gray dust that composes the ground. Near what Gabriel figures is the center of the crater is a row of upright statues—in pristine condition aside from the fact that all but one have been decapitated.

Walking up to the fully intact statue, he inhales sharply.

"It can't be," he says, looking up at the oversized statue. "It's him..." Color drains from his already pale face, and he places a hand on his chest where he had been stabbed. "It can't be..." Gabriel swallows hard, staring at a statue of the man from his night terrors, the man who abducted Dawn. His heart pounds harder inside his chest, exacerbating the pain of the soul poison. *Keep it together, Gabriel.* The feeling of pins prickles his skin as he is overcome with a foreboding realization that this is real.

Willing himself to move, even though it feels like his feet are rooted to the spot, Gabriel walks past the row of mostly headless statues to a giant mural carved into white marble, the symbol-like carvings are missing pieces, making it impossible to translate. Gabriel's mind reels with questions as he looks at the elaborate carvings of angelic battles and weaponry.

"Why didn't I pay more attention to this stuff before?"

He knows the basics—something about an apple and a snake. There doesn't seem to be any of that here. Just below the mural of angelic battles are depictions of humans working in fields.

"What is this?" Gabriel says, talking to himself. He moves his hands across the cold marble; his fingers pick up dirt as he feels the indentations and smooth texture. An unfamiliar sound spikes his anxiety, causing him to turn around defensively. "Hello?" Gabriel calls out into the ruins.

It is the rumbling of rocks and gray dirt kicked up by the boots of a figure gliding down a nearby decline, weapon in hand. The black-clad figure wears a silver helmet, fashioned into the visage of a mythical sea monster. The metal mask covers his entire head and features jagged fins flaring out from the sides and top. The face of the mask has unsettling, sharp, smiling teeth.

The figure sharply turns his feet sideways, halting his momentum. A menacing black halberd accented with gold points directly at Gabriel.

"The Ruins of Daath are off limits," a commanding voice echoes from beneath the metal helmet.

Gabriel urges himself to do more than just stare wide-eyed at the sharp end of the halberd. The figure has on a long-sleeved black shirt that wraps around his right shoulder, joined by a horizontal row of silver buckles. A matching set of buckles pin the shirt together down the left side. The long shirt flairs out at the ends, slits on each side, reminding Gabriel of medieval tabards. The man's black-gloved hands tighten around the shaft of his weapon.

Gabriel shakes his head, his hands up. "I'm lost."

"Lost? Aren't we all?" In a fluid but aggressive motion, the end of the halberd strikes the ground, the dark figure rests against it. He looks around and says, "By the way... you're surrounded."

"I'm what?" Gabriel's heart races as he scans the area. To his left, just past some ruins, he spots the glimmer of a large golden weapon.

"Come on, Marce, we're going to be late," says another from the right side of Gabriel, just beyond an enormous chunk of what was once a wall. He is dressed the same as the others. This one has a sword drawn with a rounded pommel that features a red cross inside of a shield surrounded by silver.

Several more appear, forming a semicircle around Gabriel—a pair from each side, plus the one in front of him. Gabriel stares at the golden staff, which looks more like a very large axe. It features a set of crescent blades facing skyward on one side and pointed toward the ground on the other. The blades facing down look like plague doctors' masks, while the blades facing up look like angel wings. Carved around the length of the weapon are twin snakes.

"Over here, pretty boy." Marce demands his attention.

"I said we're going to be late," repeats the one holding the medieval-looking sword. He takes off his helmet, revealing medium-length curly black hair, dark skin, and emerald-green eyes. Sliding his sword back into its sheath, he says, "He's clearly not a demon."

"Clearly," echoes another one, with a bandolier of knives and strange-looking circle weapons hanging from the end of his sash. "You look vaguely familiar. Name, rank, unit?"

"Gabriel, um... what?"

One of the two hanging back, this one with a large broadsword, steps forward. "Gabriel?"

"Yes?"

Everyone else takes their helmets off. The one with the halberd has curly black hair and pale skin. He looks at him with bright green eyes. "What do you mean Gabriel?"

"I mean my name is Gabriel?"

"It can't be," whispers the one with the broadsword, short brown hair, and round face, in awe.

"It very well may be," says the one with wavy blond hair holding the golden staff evenly.

"Guys, we're going to be late. Do you want to lose?" insists the one with the medieval-looking sword.

"We're going to lose anyway, Saphrael," Marce says, resting against his halberd in his left hand. "Now, Gabriel, what are you doing here?"

"I'm looking for my girlfriend."

There is a chorus of laughter. "Good one, Gabriel," says the one with the knives and long white hair.

"We are going to be late. I'm Saphrael. This is Marceriel, otherwise known as Marce," he says, gesturing to the one with the halberd before pointing to the one with the broadsword. "Spud, real name Paderael. The one with the knives is Loth, and finally Cadence."

"Nice to meet you, Gabriel." Cadence puts his black-gloved hand out to him.

Gabriel shakes his hand. Having absolutely no idea how he is supposed to react in this situation, he falls back to keeping quiet.

"Why don't you join us in our match? We don't have a full roster and could use any help we could get." Cadence looks around at the others. "If it's okay with everyone."

"Why not? Couldn't hurt our chances of losing," Marce says, glancing over at Loth, who has his arms folded in front of him.

"No one in their right mind would join us," Loth argues.

"Luckily for us, he's clearly out of his mind." Marce smirks.

"Put it to a vote," Saphrael says. Everyone except Loth raises their hands. Saphrael looks at Gabriel. "You in?"

"I guess? If you can help me."

"What is it you need?" Saphrael asks.

"Information?"

Loth disappears, walking off alone.

"We're still going to be late. We have to go and we have to go now. It'll take time to make it through Thale Forest."

Saphrael starts walking. The rest follow, except Cadence, who hangs back with Gabriel.

"Late for what?" Gabriel asks, making his way up the incline of the crater that houses the ruins.

"It's tournament season. Surely, you know about the tournaments?"

"No? I have so many questions."

"So do we, Gabriel." Cadence puts his helmet back on. "So do we."

Cadence catches up with the others, Gabriel trailing behind. A sense of unease fills him. Anxiety pulses in his veins. He has no idea if he can trust them, but he has nowhere else to turn. Gabriel catches up with the others, afraid that any answers he finds will only lead to more questions.

◆

The black-uniformed unit travels at an inhuman speed, each moving so fast they blur into streaks of black with traces of silver as they travel through the dreary Thale Forest. The sheer magnitude of the oversized trees dwarfs everything around them. Gabriel has no time to stare in awe at the humbling majesty of the giant, decrepit, dead-looking trees, their twisting serpentine trunks reaching out into a curving array of branches devoid of foliage.

Gabriel struggles, barely keeping the others in sight. Mist and light rain obscure his view. On occasion, Cadence, identified by his golden staff, slows to guide his path. The group starts walking at a normal pace once they reach a trail just outside the forest.

The border of the forest is lined with rows of identical black metal structures. They remind Gabriel of square-shaped shipping containers. Each building has a large rectangular banner flag posted to the left. Every banner flag has different colors and symbols along the bottom.

On the buildings, dominating both sides of every door are two giant black flags that feature a silver Celtic cross-like symbol. The same symbol, forged out of black metal, adorns the tops of the doors.

As they walk, Gabriel studies the variety of colors and variations of symbols on the flags beside the buildings. The symbols at the bottom shifts from nonsense into numbers and letters. The designs in the center of the flags remind Gabriel of family crests, each topped with the same black symbol that marks the buildings.

Trying to find the right questions, Gabriel prepares to ask what the predominant symbol stands for when they start talking.

"Where'd Loth go?" Spud asks, looking back the way they came.

"He's not here—that's all that matters. At least we have Gabriel." Saphrael keeps his eyes forward, looking ahead at a large, gray oval building with arches along its base. Gabriel wonders how it is made of stone without being made of brick. Each entrance is marked by the same giant rectangular black flags with the silver symbol posted on every building they passed.

They walk under an arch and into a wide stone hall. It is not long before they stop in front of a door. This door, unlike the others, is shoddy and barely holding itself together. Saphrael takes out a large, rusted brass-colored key and unlocks it. It creaks open, revealing a cramped, poorly lit locker room lined with wooden benches. There are flags on the walls. Strewn about are additional weaponry, wooden boxes, and bags.

Dominating the room, encompassing the entire back wall, is the symbol made of black metal—the same symbol that is everywhere. It has two outward-facing crescent moons over a Celtic cross with a wide base. The outward-facing ends of the symbol bow in the middle, tips flaring out.

Saphrael tosses Gabriel a helmet. He catches it. It is heavier than he thought it would be. The cold metal warms against his skin. He studies the design of the helmet: the smooth bumps of the eyes, the sharp ends of the fins that jut out, and finally a malicious smile. The silver helmet is solid; there are no eye holes, nor openings in which to breathe.

"Is this some kind of sea monster?" Gabriel locks eyes with the helmet, eerily haunted by the feeling that it is looking back at him.

"It's a Tiamat," Marce says while buckling plates of armor.

Gabriel shrugs, having no idea what that is.

"It's a female leviathan." Marce rolls his eyes, clearly annoyed.

"Oh, I think I've heard of that before." Gabriel sits on the end of a wooden bench, helmet in hand.

Saphrael drops a large black duffle bag in front of him. "It's Loth's stuff. If he gets mad, he can deal with it because he's not here. Get dressed."

Setting the helmet on the wooden bench, he unzips the long duffle bag and starts taking out equipment. He finds plate armor with straps and buckles: an arm guard, a shoulder plate, and a leg plate.

"There isn't a full set here," Gabriel says, quieting as he looks around and notices everyone is missing pieces. The gear they do have is barely usable, scuffed, and on the verge of being junked.

"Yeah, we get what we can. I'm sorry," Saphrael says, sitting on the bench beside him, equipping a left-leg plate over his pants and proceeding to wrap frayed leather strips around the silver metal several times before securing it with a buckle.

Gabriel unties the front of his tattered cloak exposing the wound and hole in his shirt. Idle chatter fades into silence as they stare at him.

Cadence walks over, looking directly at the wound. "Where did you get that? It looks like a soul poison."

Gabriel closes his eyes. "I was assaulted one night, while I was in bed. The love of my life was taken from me that night."

Everyone is silent. Their responses are a mix of confusion and disbelief. Marce rolls his eyes, as if it was the dumbest thing he has ever heard.

Cadence looks sympathetic, briefly resting his hand on Gabriel's shoulder. "Well, it's nothing I can treat. Nothing any healer I know can treat. It will get worse before it gets better. You're an angel. You should be fine."

Gabriel senses a genuine but patronizing concern for the state of his mental well-being.

"He says he's Gabriel," Spud says, as he finishes securing a shoulder plate.

"He's not Gabriel." Marce leans against the doorframe, arms crossed.

"Guys, we're late," Saphrael repeats, picking up a small, weathered brass-like horn with copper-esque fittings. It curves like a bull's horn and is etched with symbols Gabriel doesn't recognize. Saphrael places the copper-colored chain attached to the horn across his right shoulder, the horn resting on his left side. "We can discuss who's an archangel and who's disoriented from discere later. Come on."

Saphrael hands Spud one of two rectangular flags on black metal poles. They are the same black and silver flags that adorn the locker room's walls. The ones that remind him of family crests if they represented military units. The door shuts after everyone else has left the locker room. Gabriel rushes causing him to fumble with a strap as he is awkwardly trying to secure a spaulder.

"Hey, archangel, we don't have all day," Marce says, coming back into the locker room. He roughly pulls the strip of leather and locks it into place. It compresses tight against his shoulder. His wound pulses with pain. "Don't forget the helmet," Marce says, leaving the locker room.

Gabriel grabs the helmet, hurrying to catch up, jogging down the wide stone hall.

Once he catches up to everyone, Saphrael explains, "Name of the game is Capture the Grail in case you forgot. It's pretty easy. Get the grail, bring it back to our side past the goal line marked by the flags and we win. Just try not to die and you'll be okay."

"You're joking," Everyone is focused, ignoring Gabriel. "He's joking, right?"

✦

The thunderous beat of rhythmic drums echo down the gray stone hall. The rest of the team has their silver Tiamat helmets on. Gabriel places his over his head and sees absolutely nothing. He takes it back off, trying to figure out how it works.

The drums stop. The ends of metal from weaponry and the flag poles drop sharply to the floor then bang twice in unison before they stand rigidly in formation at an entrance to the arena floor. Saphrael and Spud are in the lead holding flags, followed by Marce and Cadence. They all carry a weapon—everyone except Gabriel.

While working up the courage to say something, Gabriel gets interrupted by a trumpet blast and drums as the music starts again. The team marches forward. As soon as they step foot onto the floor, they are met with jeers. Some even hurl items. A small fragment dings, bouncing off Saphrael's helmet, followed by a piece of metal he deflects with his arm guard. Gabriel lines up beside the rest of his team on the far end of the arena. The majority of the sparse crowd is wearing the same base uniform as his companions: plain black with different colors of faded trim. His attention is drawn to someone being dragged down one of the many rows of stairs, being taken by what look like military officers.

The music pauses before intensifying as a team enters from the other end of the field. The crowd erupts, cheering as the opposing team enters and starts their introductory lap. The imposing team jogs past, flag bearers in the lead. Their flag is black and silver with a symbol of a bat mid-flight in the center. Light from the pillars topped with fire just outside of the arena floor glint off their well-maintained armor. The most striking feature of their armor are wings that arch sharply out of their backs. No one on the opposing side is missing any armor.

Gabriel counts ten members on the other team, starkly aware there are only five on his side. Once both sets of flags are planted at the goal lines, the music stops and the musicians march out. In the center of the field is a gray stone platform with stairs on all four sides that lead up to an embossed golden grail with silver accents sitting on a pillar. The large cup is lined with shimmering gems, each a different color. It shines with the quiet brilliance of a bygone era.

Four lines mark the ground. Gabriel recognizes the goal lines but isn't sure what the two near the middle are for. Across the field, the opponents are removing the metal wings from their armor, twisting them sideways, unlocking them from their place. Some hold on to the wings and use them as a shield.

"Get a weapon." Saphrael's voice echoes from inside of his helmet as he points to the weapons racks mounted on the sides of the arena's inner walls.

Gabriel walks over and surveys the arsenal of melee armaments. He is drawn to a rapier with a golden circular swirl hilt and a curved cross guard. Picking it up, he weighs it in his hand allowing muscle memory to guide his movements. For a moment in his mind, he is in his backyard, the green grass of Earth beneath his feet. The sound of swords clang in his memory as he remembers training with James, a friend of his father's. More jeers from the crowd, something directed at him, snaps him back into the grim reality he has found himself in.

Nervously, Gabriel rejoins his team along the middle line. Saphrael blows his horn. The opposite team responds with their horn. Gabriel puts on his metal helmet and is met with nothing but darkness. Before he can say anything, another horn blares across the field. The thunderous noise, a cross between a trumpet and a train whistle, reverberates in his helmet.

Seconds later, Gabriel is knocked back, slamming on to the ground, his head crashes against the inside of the metal mask. His sight shifts to the strange, disjointed purple vision he had seen before. In shock, he draws in a sharp breath, staring at the beating heart of his attacker. Gabriel can see the expression on his opponent's face, even through the mask his adversary is wearing. The opponent swings his mace back but stops mid-swing. Gabriel's eyes widen as the attacker's head is severed from his body and falls to the ground, a fountain of blood spouting up before the body drops beside him. Gabriel rolls out of the way and picks himself up. The killing blow came from the sharp blades of Cadence's golden staff.

Gabriel stares at the blood in the dirt and the strange fuchsia aura it has in this vision, thrown off by the hues of the blood that range from deep magenta to bright pink, clumped into gradient variations that remind him of smooth pixelated radar images. Cadence half turns in a swing, engaging with an opponent who has a pike, powerfully hammering the blade of his staff into the pike wielder's shoulder, but it gets stuck. The pause leaves an opening in his defense. Saphrael steps in, blocking an opponent from getting an open shot.

Gabriel sees a member of the Bat team running up the stairs. He races to stop him. Briefly, amid the chaos, Gabriel can see Marce get bashed in the helmet with one of the large metal wings-shields.

In a split-second decision, Gabriel readies to attack an opponent, who has a sword-staff. The competitor thrusts the sharp end of it at him. Gabriel blocks with the rapier at an unfortunate angle. The sword-staff glides through the opening in the rapier's swirl guard, slicing straight through his hand. The combatant pulls at his sword-staff still stuck in Gabriel's hand. His screams echo inside the silver metal mask. Closing his eyes, Gabriel grabs the sword-staff stuck through his hand.

Getting into a painful tug of war with his opponent, but only briefly, as Gabriel plants himself, tightening his grip on his opponent's sword-staff and swings launching his opponent into the air in an elegant powerful move. The opponent is catapulted. The sword-staff glides out of Gabriel's hand, blood spraying from the wound. His rapier, now free, tumbles down the stairs. The opponent lands halfway across the arena.

Several opponents sprint up the stairs, all charging to the grail. Gabriel takes a deep breath in and throws himself at it. Wrapping his arms around the grail, bracing himself as he crashes down the gray stone stairs. Once he hits the ground, he gets up and starts running.

The few defenders watch as he slides, coming to a halt past the goal line his body curling inward. He screams in pain at the same time the crowd erupts, drowning him out. Gabriel looks at his own strangely colored circulatory system as the blood from his hand pours into the grail.

His eyes travel down the trail of blood that leads past the goal line, where he sees Saphrael yelling at a judge, but they are too far away for him to hear. Gabriel's blurry vision sharply focuses on a flag near him. He takes off his helmet and drops it to the ground as the image on the flag of a bat mid-flight comes into focus. He goes numb as he realizes he just won the match for the bats.

Chapter 8

Dawn wakes from a deep sleep, her body sinks comfortably into a soft mattress. She turns, reaching out for Gabriel, but her hand falls on nothing but blankets.

"Gabriel?" she says. He rarely ever gets up first. She looks around, dazed from sleep. The first thing she sees is the frame of a black wooden four-poster bed, elaborately carved with roses, vines, and thorns.

Dawn places her hand on the soft, polished headboard. In the center is a hauntingly beautiful rose, the petals of which are wilted and torn. The air is bitterly cold. The walls and floors are made of black stone and engraved with symbols.

In the center of the walls, dotted in perfectly aligned spaces, are glass wall lights. They are sleek and futuristic yet possess an old-world charm. Cool, blue-tinted light emanates from within diamond-patterned glass. Strips of rounded rectangular glass fan out in a squarish, circular form around the light source. She gets out of bed, and a chill bites the soles of her feet.

"Gabriel?" She looks down at a long silk purple nightgown she has never seen before. "Gabriel?" she repeats in a heightened, strained tone.

She runs to the only window in the room, a small flower-shaped window with bars running across it. Looking through the bars, she sees an unfamiliar landscape. Its muted tones are dark and make her feel uneasy. The dull skies remind her of layers and layers of dark-gray wool. It is as if time itself stopped and the realm froze, sealing the land into a perpetual gray twilight. In the distance are a set of four oblong black buildings, two on each side. Her view is slightly off center and far above the tops of the buildings.

This is a nightmare. It has to be. Her nightmares have felt real before, but this is different. Deep down, she knows that this—this is real.

Dawn runs over to the large wooden double doors and pulls on a handle, but it doesn't budge. Desperately, she slams her fist against the solid mahogany-colored door before grabbing hold of the metal ring and pulling with all her strength. Tears form in her eyes as she lets go of the handle. It clangs against its mount as metal hits metal.

"Gabriel!" Dawn screams.

There is no answer.

Taking a step back, she fully views the arching double doors. The beautifully evocative mural carved into the dark wood tells a story, one she doesn't fully understand. On the left half of the door is a woman with long flowing hair who almost looks like her. The woman is falling, reaching out to a man on the right half of the door. He reaches back in futile desperation but the man is bound by chains, which are carved all the way to the boundaries of the arch. A symbol she has never seen before, composed of two crescent moons, a circle, and a cross, adorns the top center of the doors. The bottom is embossed with an intricate floral design that matches her bed frame. The door itself is encased with gray stone bricks with symbols carved into it, none of which she can identify.

Removing the handle on this side would do nothing. Due to the size and thickness of the doors, any attempt at brute force would not be successful. So, she turns back to the room.

At the far end is a large closet. She opens it and finds dresses, few of which are to her taste. Desperate for answers, she turns back to the room searching for anything that might help her. There is a beige paper sitting on an ornate silver table. Picking it up, she reads the handwritten note, the script of which is elongated, narrow, and elegant.

Dawn,

Welcome. This is your room. Everything in it belongs to you. There is a closet full of dresses and boots. You will find accessories and makeup in the drawers of the vanity. There is a bath in the room next to the closet. Things will become clear in time.

The note is unsigned. Setting it down, her eyes flicker to the silver candelabrum that's embossed with floral designs sitting upon the table. It has four branches in two tiers holding black candlesticks. An obsidian snake-like design wraps around the silver base. Four of the candles are topped with orange flames, the holders of which are shaped like closed purple roses. The center candle holder, however, is forged into a blooming purple rose. Its candle is topped with a violet flame.

The chair in front of the candelabrum is carved from black wood, the back of which curves in the shape of a heart and has a burgundy-colored cushion. She sits and stares at the flame, entranced by the varying shades of purple laced with deep blacks; the colors sway like the cosmic dance of a nebula. She gazes into the flame for an unknown amount of time.

A sharp knock jolts her from her haze and she stands defensively. The double doors are opened by a pair of guards in silver-white featureless masks and black fabric uniforms. Each has a pair of hook-swords hanging from the sides of their cloth belts. The hook weapons come to a point at the end and feature a sharp crescent guard.

A man in the center of the two guards wears an elaborate black uniform with rich dark-red accents. He has an officer's hat with the same symbol that adorns the doors. There is a bright gold insignia on his jacket, indicating high rank.

The officer has an olive skin tone and brown eyes. He clears his throat and in a strange accent she cannot place, he says, "Your father has requested that I retrieve you."

"My father?" Dawn repeats. Her eyebrows raise as she lowers her arms, dropping her guard.

"Yes, it is best not to keep him waiting," the officer insists.

"What do you mean, my father? I am an orphan."

"Just because you were an orphan doesn't mean that you do not *have* a father, does it? Come along."

The man turns, exiting the room. As she walks past the guards, they give no response. They don't even move until they suddenly form behind her, keeping pace.

The footfalls of boots echo down the dark, high-ceilinged yet narrow hallway lined with the same lights as her room. Taking a closer look at the lights, through the distorted diamond-patterned glass, she sees a blue glowing crystal cluster as she passes by. Dawn stays quiet, slowing her pace behind the officer. She can see black hair under his hat. They walk down a set of spiral stairs into another long hallway.

Dawn's eyes dart from side to side without turning her head before she makes her move. *It's now or never,* she thinks to herself, before she shoulder checks the officer into the wall and bolts. Swiftly, she processes her path as she speeds past rows of doors, barely slowing as she comes to another set of winding stairs.

Her heart pounds. She races down the stairs too quickly and loses her balance. She inhales sharply and braces for the fall. Suddenly, her fall is halted, caught by the officer's grip on the back collar of her nightgown. The officer forcefully redirects her momentum, ripping the delicate fabric of her nightgown as her body strikes the cold stone wall. Even though she is numb, Dawn responds with a punch aimed at his face. The officer firmly catches her fist and sharply twists her arm. The masked guards position themselves on both sides, hook-swords drawn.

"If it isn't too much trouble, you should be aware that this is an inhospitable place. You wouldn't want to end up making a careless mistake, losing everything, and gaining nothing but pain." He finally releases her arm. She curls forward and does not look up at him. "You are expected." The officer gestures down the stairs. Dawn sighs.

As she continues down the set of winding stone stairs, there is a sound, quiet at first, that grows louder as they descend. It is the mournful cry of a violin. The world around her fades as she gets lost in the enchanting sound.

Unconsciously, she begins to walk in step with the music, nearly forgetting the threatening presence of the officer and faceless masked guards. They stop at a set of large black double doors, carved with symbols. Dawn wonders if they are a ward, a warning, or sigils to draw power. Perhaps it is merely decorative, but she doubts that.

The masked guards take their places on either side of the entrance as the officer opens the door.

Without thinking, Dawn walks in, freezing as soon as she sees him... the man from her nightmares, the man from the mirror. The music increases in volume. Dawn forgets her fear, and for a short time, the violin's melody is the singular thing occupying her mind.

In the center of the room is a man with long black hair and bone-white skin. He is well-dressed in a tailored eighteenth-century suit, sans its accompanying jacket. His eyes are closed as he plays, lost in the music. Dawn holds her breath as his bow reaches its final note. The man smiles and sets the dark beige violin into its case along with its bow. Dawn cautiously stays near the door.

"Come in." The man gestures to a seat. The room is full of artifacts in and out of cases, much like in Raphael's collection. Although this room is far more organized, sleek, and spacious. Dawn slows her pace as she notices a row of what appear to be deteriorating statue heads lined up on a mahogany-colored shelf. *The one at the end... almost looks like Gabriel. But that's impossible* she reasons, so she puts the thought out of her mind.

There are several long couches and chairs centered around a table. The room is cavernous. Shivering from cold and the pain in her right shoulder, she approaches a chair identical to the one in her room. Her brow furrows as she searches for the right words to tell him that she has seen him before. Something inside warns her that it would be dangerous to allude to such things.

"I know you have many questions," the man says as he sits down in the middle of a long baroque-style black couch with an intricately carved frame. "You do look so much like an apparition. Tell me, why didn't you pick a dress from the ones I left for you?"

"I didn't care for them," she says, keeping her eyes down, feeling vulnerable and exposed in her nightgown.

"We will have to do something about that. The dresses were collected for your mother. I have been holding onto false hope that one day she would return to me. I know you must feel lost and afraid. Trust me, you are exactly where you belong. As for any questions you may have, I will do my best to fill in your lack of knowledge."

Dawn doesn't look up.

"My apologies. Where are my manners? My name is Lucius. I am your father. It is a pleasure to finally meet you." The man rises from the couch and places his hand in front of her, which she ignores.

"My father...?"

"Yes."

Lucius sits and picks up an elegant glass carafe with a frosted diamond-shaped base accented with metal and polished black stones. The carafe is filled with blood-red liquid. Dawn's heart races as she stares at the sharp end of the carafe, which looks more like an artfully designed weapon.

Lucius pours burgundy liquid into two silver chalices accented with dark-gray metal vines. He offers her a glass.

She accepts it and quietly studies the drink. It shimmers like the red swirling clouds of a sunset. "May I ask what it is?"

"Xerotes is a liquor processed from a rare berry that is produced from a tree that exists only within this realm."

Dawn sniffs the liquor. It has a pungent but sweet aroma. As she takes a drink of the bittersweet liquid, a rush of warmth flows through her veins.

"Where is Gabriel?" she asks, holding the chalice in her hand. "My boyfriend. Do you know where he is?"

"Gabriel is not with us," Lucius says, rather harshly adding, "Do not speak of him again."

"What do you mean, 'Do not speak of him again?' He's my boyfriend. I love him. He saved me."

"*I* saved you from the pitiful existence your mother doomed you to on Earth."

"You know my mother?" As soon as Dawn says it, she sighs, knowing it is a truly dumb question.

Lucius smiles. "Of course. She was extraordinary." He spends a few moments deep in thought before gesturing to a book on the table in front of them. "This is a historical account of Eden. It is my personal account transcribed by our historians."

Dawn looks at the large, dark-brown book with aged paper sticking out the side. She leans forward and opens the book. It is written in a strange but elegant language composed entirely of symbols. The ink of the foreign script is raised, sitting atop the paper rather than being absorbed into it completely. She traces her fingers along the ink, finding it to be bumpy. The beige pages are textured but soft. "I can't read this."

Lucius places a cold hand on her forehead. A variety of voices in foreign languages rush by. "Now you have access to the power of Babel."

She looks back at the book. The symbols bend and reshape into a language she can understand.

"What? How?"

He smiles. "There is much to learn. Now, go. Adam will escort you back to your room, where you can read."

"Adam?" Dawn asks.

"Yes, *the* Adam of Eden, or rather correctly pronounced Eridu."

"What about Gabriel?"

"Study," is all he says.

Lucius knocks sharply twice on the table.

The door opens and the officer, Adam, enters the study and waits next to the door.

"I will answer questions you have about our history once you read the account." Lucius picks up his bow and violin and begins casting his spellbinding music once more.

Dawn walks slowly, lightheaded from the Xerotes, her footsteps in rhythm with the melody. Adam holds the door open for her. She clutches the heavy book close to her chest as she walks through the doors.

✦

In another nightmare, Dawn walks ceaselessly. Her body is broken and tired, but there is no place to rest. So, she does all she can do and continues walking. Thunder grumbles in the sky above. She pulls up her frayed black jacket. Inside, she knows this is a nightmare, but she is so conscious that her mind doesn't accept otherwise. It begins to rain, softly at first, but quickly becomes a downpour.

Although her stomach cramps with hunger pains, she forces herself to continue along the never-ending sidewalk. She stops to peer over the side of a bridge. Instead of crystal blue waters, the rapids are coal-black, except for the white foam forming around a large threatening vortex.

She tries to walk but can't move her body and is shoved off the bridge by an unknown force. Instead of falling into the water, she lands on anti-homeless spikes that jut up beneath the bridge. The impact punches her chest, radiating pain. Dawn lies contorted across the spikes as if they were a medieval torture device; the sharp points drawing blood. Bruises blossom on her skin, blue-black with hints of red.

Suddenly, she is on the bridge again, looking down at the shell of what she used to be. As she turns away from the sight of her malnourished and abused form, she hears a voice whisper, *Never return.*

She begins to walk again, the never-ending walk. There is no destination. There is no Gabriel. The ominous, sickly black dragon hovers in the sky following her.

In the distance, the sound of a violin reminds her of where she is.

✦

Dawn wakes up exhausted, as if she hadn't slept at all. She moves her thick black blanket embroidered with golden vines to the side and sits up, setting the heavy book she slept beside onto her lap. The book's rough texture is soft and worn with age. Opening the book, she reads a section titled Promethean Angels.

Long ago, in a place far from Earth, the angels led a peaceful existence. Lucius was their leader and Gabriel his second in command. Michael ran the military. Eight flames, properly known as numinous, burn within each archangel, whose power far exceeds that of standard angels. The flames grant heightened abilities that are unique to the color of the flame. Lucius is the bearer of the divine psychic numinous.

Dawn's eyes flicker to the purple-flamed candle in the center of the candelabrum and the wax that never seems to melt. When she reached out to it before, she found it to be cold.

Turning back to her book, she reads about how the angels cultivated the development of Earth. They watched over as humankind evolved and helped guide them without making themselves known. At one point, fishermen, shepherds, and the first organized farmers came together near the Tigris and Euphrates rivers. It is there that the entire council of archangels came down to aid humanity. This place was called Eridu. In stories, the name would be passed along as Eden.

The rest of the historian's transcription has been torn out. *Why would Lucius give me a book with most of the pages missing?*

Dawn walks to her closet, sighs, and digs through the dresses, finally settling on one that resembles amethyst-colored rose petals. She changes out of her silky purple nightgown. The amethyst-colored rose-petal dress is soft and comforting.

She smooths out her dress before heading to her makeup table. The drawers are filled with an assortment of vintage-looking makeup in solid metal containers embossed with designs.

There is a knock on the door. Adam strides in, holding a proper military posture.

"Your father has requested that you spend time with him today." Adam nods to her. "I've been instructed to retrieve you."

"I've assumed as much," Dawn says, working on her makeup. "If I am to wear dresses, I should actually do my hair and makeup. If you don't mind."

"Find anything interesting in the book your father has given you?" Adam asks, taking a step closer.

"No." Dawn stops for a moment, then continues putting on powder. "In fact, most of it seems to be torn out."

"I'm sorry to hear that. I've never had a chance to read it myself."

"You are from Eden, as it were, maybe you could just tell me what happened."

Adam hesitates. "…It was a very long time ago. The mind has a way of forgetting."

"So, you don't remember?"

"Not entirely. If you don't mind, Princess, your father is waiting."

Dawn puts down the powder puff slowly. "Princess?"

"Yes, Princess," Adam says.

Dawn pushes away from her makeup table, not knowing how to respond. Part of her wants to ask him if he's being sarcastic, but she knows he isn't. Dawn finishes her makeup and follows Adam down the halls, the masked guards walking behind them. She assumes that they are posted outside of her room at all times, but she isn't sure since she has never actually heard them talk. Adam opens one side of the large black double doors as the two accompanying guards fall into place on either side of the entrance. Adam and the guards stay in the hall.

"So glad you could join me." Lucius stands, gesturing for her to sit in her chair.

"Do I have a choice?" Dawn asks, annoyed, arms crossed in front of her.

Lucius inclines his head. "You do, of course. If you are referring to being kept in a locked room, that is for your own protection. The intent was never to keep you as a prisoner."

"Protection? From what?"

"From everything, Dawn. You are valuable, not just to me, but to everyone. They will want your help, or they will want to destroy you."

Dawn looks away. He rests a colder-than-expected hand on her cheek and turns her face to his.

He locks his gaze with hers as he says, "You must face hardships, defeat them, and be stronger for it."

She shivers and turns away, not used to his unnaturally bright copper-colored eyes. "You have no idea what I've been through."

"Oh, but I do, Dawn. It doesn't take a strategist to analyze what has transpired on Earth with you. Your mother cultivated an aura of obsession, of seduction, a pull greater than a month to a flame. I can only speculate on the horrors you must have endured. Tell me, what happened on Earth?"

Dawn turns away again, only to find his firm but gentle hand guiding her back to him.

"Tell me, what happened on Earth." He enunciates his words, this time less of a question.

She curls inward, closing her eyes. "The longer I was around someone, the more obsessed they would become. Taking locks of hair, pictures without consent. Endless phone calls, letters, propositions. Sometimes they would corner me. When things got more than harmless... they would die. Every time they claimed to love me, that they couldn't live without me. That even the thought of being without me brought them physical pain."

Lucius is quiet for a long moment before saying, "Vivus mortuus sanitas. It means living dead sanity. I am impressed. The ability to drive lesser beings past the brink of sanity must have been quite useful."

"What? No—lesser beings?"

"Yes, Dawn. What would you have me refer to them as?"

"Humans?"

"Ah, humanity. The very name is synonymous with compassion," he says with a smirk. "That failed to be your experience with them... has it not?"

"Gabriel..." Dawn starts to say.

"Gabriel is not human," Lucius cuts her off.

She looks at him, lips parted in surprise. "What do you mean... Gabriel is not human?" Dawn searches him for answers.

All he responds with is, "As I have said before, we are not to discuss him." Lucius studies her for a long moment before clearing his throat. "Tell me, Dawn. These humans that became obsessed with you. How did they die?"

"Heart attacks, aneurysms, strokes, a ricocheted bullet... the ones I know of, anyway."

"Have you ever been raped, Dawn?"

She shakes her head. "Not that I know of. Every time someone came close to hurting me, they would die."

"Your mother had a seduction aura but not one that protected her as well. Not as far as I know. She always used it to her advantage."

"I don't see how this could ever be an advantage."

"Anything can be a tool. Have you ever enticed someone to bring them to death?"

"What?" Her eyes widen and meet his. She is confused but realizes that he is serious. "No. Of course not. It was always an accident. I had nothing to do with it besides existing. I would never—"

"Even if your combined powers would allow you to proactively protect yourself?"

"No."

Lucius is quiet again. She feels as if he is evaluating her. "I promise you that if I were around, none of this would have happened."

"How can you be so sure?"

"Dawn, this is the reason you are kept safe here in the citadel. I'm not sure how much the seduction aura's pull would have on those around here. The guards are specifically cultivated for their status, loyalty, and rank. As you may be aware, they are, under no circumstance, allowed to talk to you."

"What about Adam?"

"Adam is no royal guard. His rank is hierophant, which is basically the leader of generals."

"Do you trust a human around me?"

"Adam has ascended beyond the level of a standard human." His words trail off and he looks directly at her. "I trust him... enough."

"So, I am safe with him?"

"Yes, I believe you are. If he steps out of line, I will swiftly show him his place."

"Why did you give me a book on history if most of the pages are torn out?"

"I wanted to familiarize you with the subject before diving into it."

"Why are there pages missing?"

Lucius doesn't answer. Changing the subject, he says, "I will have a tailor sent to speak with you shortly. Walk with Adam back to your room."

Lucius knocks sharply upon the table twice. The door opens to Adam waiting to escort her.

✦

Having no way to track time, Dawn is uncertain how many days have passed. No one has visited since she last met with Lucius. Whenever she peers through the bars of her flower-shaped window, she is met with the same dark-gray landscape. It is as if time is frozen in perpetual twilight. Sometimes she wonders if there is simply no nearby star at all.

Lately, she has been opting to spend most of her time soaking in the hot waters of an indoor thermal spring. Her head is laid back, eyes closed, body resting comfortably against the black stone. Humid, steam-filled air fills her lungs. A sharp knock on the door causes Dawn to open her eyes.

"I'll be out in a moment."

Letting out a deep sigh, Dawn forces herself to leave the relaxing waters. She lifts herself, placing her hands on the seemingly naturally formed ledge behind her. Her feet warm against the heated rock while water drips onto the ground.

Drying off, she uses a towel not made from any fabric that she is familiar with. It looks like linen but is much softer and far more absorbent. After she puts on her undergarments, she slides on her amethyst-colored rose-petal dress. Hurrying, she squeezes water out of her hair. When she opens the door, the air pressure change blows a cold breeze against her skin.

"Sorry to keep you waiting," she says, expecting to see Adam, but instead sees a man resting his hand on an oversized light-blue bag slung across his shoulder. The uniform he is wearing, if you could call it that, is rather informal. The pale eggshell-blue outfit is made of mismatched patchwork aesthetically arranged in an oddly pleasant composition. There are three others accompanying him, dressed more formally than he is, with long-sleeve black outfits featuring silver buttons lining the left center of their shirts. He looks at her with rich brown eyes that speak of kindness and has short sandy-blond hair. He bows to her in greeting.

She nods courteously to him, before her eyes are drawn to a large, angled mirror they have placed in the corner of her room near her four-poster bed. The large three-fold mirror has a black stone frame, and a purple crystal rose adorns the center of the frame.

"Princess, I am your tailor, Ketis." The tailor bows respectfully and looks at the mirror as well. "The mirror—yes, your father commissioned this design. The lights are activated by blood."

"The wh—what?" Dawn stammers.

"I'm sorry, Princess, I do not fully understand your question." Ketis lowers his head respectfully.

"...The lights are activated by blood?" Dawn can't believe that she has to clarify the statement.

"Yes, Princess, it is standard. Angelic blood interacts with the crystal frame."

Ketis gestures to a dagger sitting upright on her silver metal table near the candelabrum. The handle of the thin silver blade flairs out on each side and features a purple heart-shaped crystal. The pommel is crafted in such a way that allows the blade to point upright. The dagger is silver-colored, except unlike typical silver, the shadows are deeper and far darker than she has seen before. Dawn glances at Ketis before gingerly picking up the blade.

"A touch of blood anywhere on the frame will activate the light. Mind you, it does fade gradually with time," Ketis explains. "If you have any issue with—"

"No." Dawn shakes her head. "I'll be fine."

Slowly, she approaches the mirror and stands before its trifold design, staring at her reflection. Dawn pricks the index finger of her left hand. A spot of blood emerges, and she touches the black crystal frame of the center mirror. As soon as her blood touches the cold stone, it glows with a bright gray ethereal light that spreads. Her lips part in awe as she watches the veins of light travel until they encompass the entire frame. Finally, it reaches the purple rose centerpiece, the light traveling much more slowly through the purple crystal, which, when fully lit, glows the brightest of all.

"If you don't mind, Princess, I do require proper measurements." Ketis roots around in his oversized bag and pulls out a simple piece of string and gestures for her to walk to the other side of the mirror. Dawn realizes that it doubles as a privacy screen.

"Of course," Dawn hurries to put the dagger back on the table. Nervously, she slips behind the mirror and is silent once again, marveling at the crystal of the back of the mirror. It reminds her of obsidian glass, black and dimly reflective.

Ketis clears his throat to get her attention. "Forgive me, Princess, you must remove your dress for me to get accurate measurements."

"Oh! Of course, I'm sorry. I've just—I've never seen anything like this mirror before." Dawn pulls her dress off and allows it to fall into a pile on the floor.

Ketis gets to work taking measurements. When he is done, he picks up her amethyst-colored rose-petal dress and holds it out for her.

Dawn inclines her head and says, "Thank you, Ketis," before putting her dress back on.

The tailor folds a side of the mirror and allows her to go before him. When Dawn walks past the barrier of the mirror, her smile fades and she suppresses a shiver, silently staring at the royal guards who are now inside her room. Ketis notices her discomfort and gestures instead to his attendants, who stand with a poised rigidity that reminds her of Adam.

"These are some of your assistants, with specializations in artistry for makeup, hair, and tradition," Ketis says.

A few of his assistants nod as they are introduced—all except one. Dawn nods to each in turn, even the one who didn't acknowledge her. Trying and failing to hold back confusion, her mind reels as she stares at the tall, humorless angel in his formal uniform. "Tradition?" is all she manages to say.

"Yes, your tradition specialist works in integration of codes and formalities. He also works to heighten your status socially."

"What does that mean?"

"I believe another word for it is publicist, as well as a liaison to… things that publicists need to be a liaison for, I suppose. It is an honor to be your tailor, Princess."

"I'll just be happy to have something that fits." She smiles shyly.

"We can do more than that." Ketis takes a sketchpad out of his oversized bag and asks, "What do you have in mind?"

"No one's ever asked me that before."

"Well, take your time."

Deciding the best way to describe what she wants is to show him what she does not like, Dawn goes to her closet and opens the sliding doors. "Inelegant. Not the right color scheme. Too revealing."

Ketis takes notes as she examines the dresses.

"There is just something not right about almost all of them."

"I think I know what you are going for, Princess." Ketis puts his sketchpad away and takes out fabric swatches, clasped together by a silver metal loop, and shows her a midnight-blue swatch shimmering with silver dots like stars in the night sky. Dawn nods.

The assistant who specializes in tradition steps forward and whispers to Ketis.

"Yes, yes," Ketis says to the tall man with brown hair. Then he turns back to Dawn and flips through the swatches, stopping at a deep royal purple. "Your father has requested this become your signature color."

"It's my favorite color," Dawn says before glancing at the attendants and wondering if they are not allowed to talk to her directly.

The tailor then asks a series of seemingly inconsequential questions, such as, "Do you prefer birds or flowers, trees or starlight?" Most of her answers are ethereal in nature.

"…And you will want a military flair," Ketis mentions offhandedly. "To match everyone else, of course. And to signify rank."

"To what?" Dawn's hands unconsciously tighten.

"Rank, Princess. In the military hierarchy."

"I have no rank."

"I'm afraid you—" He looks at the tradition specialist and then at the guards. "I'm afraid I don't know what I'm talking about. I assumed in a military monarchy, Princess is a rank. I meant nothing by it."

"A military monarchy?" Dawn says in disbelief. Everything she has been trying to ignore floods her mind at once. From seeing flashes of Lucius in the mirror to the snakes coiled around her wrists and neck, she feels as if she can no longer breathe. Shaking her head, she steps back in fear, unable, at least for a moment, to ignore everything she has been sheltering herself from acknowledging. "No! No, no, no!"

The royal guards step between Dawn and the visitors. One points a hook-sword in the direction of the doors. Silently, Dawn observes everyone's movements while ever so slightly adjusting her stance, leaning weight onto her left foot, and bending her right knee slightly. Before the tailor and his attendants leave, she bolts, running barefoot. A guard charges at her, shoulder first. Dawn dodges him, nearly running into the second guard, who is blocking the exit.

From behind her, the tall attendant, who specializes in tradition, grabs her and violently pulls her to him. He glares at her with a cold unreadable expression, saying nothing. Dawn cries, struggling to break free as his grip tightens painfully around her arm. The tradition specialist is raising his hand to reprimand her when a royal guard shoves the end of his hook-sword through his back piercing his chest. Wordlessly, he drops to the ground as the royal guard who attacked him continues to assault him.

Dawn screams, a reverberating banshee's wail. The loud, high-pitched shriek disorients everyone in the room, shattering her window. Various mirrors form veins of cracks, fracturing but not fully breaking the glass. The guards grab hold of Dawn and drag her out of her room. As they do, the boots of the royal guards crush the fingers of the body on the floor. The tailor and others have already gone.

The guards force her down the long hallways and winding stairs. They open a door and shove her into a room with a long, gilded black metal table surrounded by dark-brown throne-like chairs, and charts litter the walls. Dawn lands on her knees. Lucius, Adam, and an unknown individual are mid-conversation when they get interrupted.

Lucius stands. "What is the meaning of this? Why were you screaming?"

Her eyes flicker to Lucius, and she picks herself off the ground, angrily staring down the guards as if she is about to take a swing at one of them.

Adam finds this amusing. The unfamiliar figure with snow-white hair and matching white irises is silent. Dawn's eyes connect with his for a moment.

"Dawn," Lucius says with a forceful but gentle tone, "tell me what is going on."

"They—they killed one of the tailor's assistants," Dawn stammers.

Lucius has a flat and somewhat bored expression, elaborating, "Why did they kill an assistant, Dawn?"

"Ketis—the tailor—he said—I am a part of the military hierarchy. I tried to run, and one of his assistants grabbed me."

Lucius waves his hand, dismissing the guards.

"That seems natural. Tell me, is that something you have a problem with?" Lucius asks evenly, although it sounds more like a statement than a question.

"No, of course not. They killed someone."

"Focus on my question. Is being a part of a military monarchy something you take issue with?"

"Military monarchies are the worst, most corrupt form of government." Tears well in her eyes, and she doesn't understand why he is talking about this instead of the murder.

"Are they? Or are they just the worst form of government that you have seen? The principle on Earth is that the strong lead and will have strong offspring that can also lead. Did you assume you are titled princess as a term of endearment? Or rather, practical purposes? Accept your role and apologize to your tailor and your guards, for they are correct."

Her mouth hangs open before she shuts it and glares at him.

Lucius continues. "I understand that there will be a period of adjustment. Yet, I expect you to settle into your rightful position with time. Adam, escort the princess back to her room, or would you rather stay here in the war room and learn why things work the way that they do?"

"Someone is dead. You're acting like nothing happened. Maybe someday you can explain to me why things are the way that they are, your highness," Dawn says sarcastically.

Lucius nods to Adam, who walks to the door and holds it open.

As she walks out of the room, Lucius says from behind, "Do learn to control yourself in the future. And Dawn, never forget that peace is only afforded through the cost of war."

Chapter 9

G abriel slouches in front of the shoddy locker room door. *I shouldn't even bother*, he thinks. *Are you going to let anxiety run your entire life?* he asks himself. *No? Then open the door.*

He takes a deep breath, placing an unsteady hand on the door handle. The door creaks open, and Gabriel stands there unable to enter the locker room. Everyone else is busy removing their gear and packing it into equipment bags. The mood is downcast, but no one seems angry. Well, no one besides Marce, who glares at him with his arms crossed. He shakes his head before shoving a silver arm guard into his bag harder than necessary.

Saphrael walks over, places a hand on Gabriel's shoulder, and ushers him into the room.

"It's all right. We would have lost anyway," Saphrael says, his last sentence spoken while looking directly at Marce.

"Think about it like we reached our end goal a little faster." Spud shrugs, holding his arm outstretched as he is being tended to by Cadence.

"You don't... care that I lost you the game?"

"Why would we?" Cadence shrugs. "Losing is what we do best."

Marce growls in frustration, then he turns to face Gabriel. Throwing his arm back, he hurls his helmet at Gabriel. The metal helmet narrowly misses him, nailing the stone wall with a bang before dropping to the floor and coming to a rest on its side. "We were doing okay for once!"

"We were outnumbered," Saphrael says as he sits and allows his head to hang down.

"We're always outnumbered. We had a chance this time." Marce huffs and stomps over to pick up his helmet.

"No, we didn't." Saphrael lets out a sigh and mumbles, "Grace in forgiveness. Understanding in death."

"All I know is that we lost because of this genius's lack of ability to read a basic sign."

Saphrael ignores Marce and glances around the room. "Is everyone okay?"

Shrugs and nods answer him.

Gabriel holds up his hand, and warm blood streams down his wrist, soaking into the cuffs of Loth's borrowed uniform. Carefully, he sets the silver-colored helmet onto the bench. Droplets of blood race down the Tiamat helmet.

"Look, I'll just go," Gabriel says, his hands raised in a sign of resignation. "I'm sorry."

Before he walks out the door, Cadence says, "It's all right, really. Let me see your wound," Cadence gestures to the bench beside him.

Why is he still wearing his helmet? Maybe he can see better with it on? Gabriel wonders as Cadence begins to clean his wound.

"You'll be okay in no time... barring that soul poison," Cadence says, deftly threading a needle into the skin of his hand, sewing the wound shut with shiny golden thread.

"What happened, Gabriel?" Saphrael asks.

"I caught a sword-staff at an odd angle, and the blade sliced through my hand."

"No. Not that." Saphrael points at his chest. "The soul poison."

"Oh... the soul poison. Yeah, it's kind of a long story."

"We don't have anywhere to be," Saphrael says.

"...Where am I?" Gabriel holds his hand up, examining the golden stitches.

"What do you mean? Where are you?" Marce asks.

Gabriel puts the bloody helmet back on. Switching his vision, he sees the heartbeats, muscular, and circulatory systems highlighted in strange colors in those around him. He removes the helmet and sees the same colors, except they are darker and blurrier. Closing his eyes, he wills his vision to return to normal.

"I mean... where am I? You said if I helped, you would give me answers."

"As much as we can, Gabriel," Saphrael says.

Marce points at Gabriel. "He didn't help."

Before he can argue further, Saphrael gets up and walks over to Marce.

"He very well may have saved us some injuries or worse by losing the match so quickly. We're only being docked five points each."

"Whatever, Saph." Marce throws a hand up in a dismissive gesture and sulks on a bench.

Saphrael sighs and shakes his head before saying, "Let's finish removing our gear so we can head back and figure out what's going on."

◆

The team travels a gray dirt path, carrying their weapons and equipment bags. Their boots kick up pebbles and gray dust as they walk. The decrepit, oversized forest looms to the left. They walk past a city's worth of matte-black metal buildings.

Gabriel stays silent, guilt-ridden about losing the match, knowing he has let them down.

"I heard Merodach lost last night. Big surprise." Marce rolls his eyes and smirks at Cadence, who is beside him.

"It was five against one," Cadence says, briefly glancing at Marce before looking to the path ahead.

Both Cadence and Marce use their weapons as walking sticks, Cadence with his golden staff and Marce with his halberd.

"Tournament season just started. I'm sure he will claw his way back to Hod somehow," Saphrael says with a hint of anger. Gabriel isn't sure why, but he doesn't feel that it is all right to ask.

"You'll make it back there someday, Saphrael." Cadence gives him a reassuring look.

"From what I heard, Merodach hates it here," Spud says, resting his hand on the hilt of the broadsword at his side.

"Why wouldn't he?" Marce half-shrugs.

Gabriel has no idea what they are talking about, so he stays quiet. Eventually, they reach a lonely structure close to the forest's edge, marked by a large, dilapidated flag that matches the flags in their locker room.

"We're home." Spud smiles and spreads his arms as if he is going to give the strange metal building a hug.

"Why are you speaking English, anyway?" Gabriel asks.

Everyone stops dead in their tracks and looks at Gabriel—a mix of stunned and puzzled faces. Shoving him out of the way, Marce shakes his head and grumbles something Gabriel doesn't understand, but knows it was an insult.

"I'll talk to him," Saphrael says to everyone. Then he takes Loth's equipment bag from Gabriel and hands it to Spud. "Give this to Loth, would you?"

Grabbing the bag, Spud hurries inside, leaving Gabriel and Saphrael alone.

"I don't know what is going on. I don't know what's wrong with you. We're speaking Enochian. You may be speaking English, but we're not," Saphrael says, his arms crossed.

"Oh," Gabriel says, remembering Azrael mentioning something about the power of Babel being able to translate.

"What is going on, Gabriel?" There is kindness in Saphrael's eyes that he has already come to expect.

"What do you mean?" Gabriel asks.

"I mean everything. How bad was it that you are this delusional? You think we are speaking an Earth language? You think you're Archangel Gabriel? None of this makes any sense. It is necessary to take time to recover your memories after a psychotic break."

"There is nothing wrong with my memory. My name is Gabriel. I don't think I'm an archangel..." Gabriel briefly thinks about his conversation with Azrael. "I honestly have no idea what is going on. I need help."

"I promised you I'll help as much as I can." Saphrael opens the door and walks in, Gabriel trailing behind. The interior is cramped and lined with cots along walls as well as dressers to the side of each cot and various bags on the floor. Adorning the center of each wall is the unit flag surrounded by weaponry.

"Welcome to the Wonder Brigade." Saphrael shrugs.

"The what?" Gabriel asks.

"The Wonder Brigade," Saphrael repeats.

"As in, I wonder why they bothered to show up?" Spud says.

"I wonder who they'll lose to next?" Loth says, not looking up from whatever he is writing. There are a variety of knives mounted on the wall behind him.

"We were never going to make it past the qualifying rounds anyway." Spud sighs, looking at the floor's reddish-brown wood.

"You never know," Saphrael says. "We've got Gabriel now. If we help him recover, we'll have another member of the team."

"Recover from what?" Gabriel asks, still standing near the door.

"From discere, Gabriel," Marce says, with his usual tone of annoyance.

"Discere?"

"He doesn't even remember the centers," Marce says to Saphrael. "That level of denial is dangerous."

Saphrael ignores Marce and clears off one of the few disused cots piled with junk. "You can use this one."

Gabriel nods and says, "Thank you," before walking over.

Spud is reading something while Cadence pretends not to be in the conversation as he organizes his medicinal sling.

"If you would just tell me what is going on, I can try to explain how I got here. What is discere?" Gabriel asks, sitting down on his cot.

"The discere centers on Chesed," Marce says. "You know, the place you go when they need to reform you."

"What? I'm from Earth."

"It's okay to talk about, Gabriel. You can't be so delusional that you really think you're from Earth," Saphrael says.

"Pretend I know nothing about anything. What's with the masks?"

"The Chokma masks?" Marce asks.

"Tell him nothing," Loth warns them in a flat, monotoned voice, taking his notebook with as he leaves once again.

"You get used to it," Spud says after the door closes behind Loth.

"It's a Chokma mask. Each unit has a mask representing their team. The blacksmiths don't really care for us, so they're not the best quality," Cadence explains.

"We're only supposed to wear them in sacred places, such as in battle, in the Axion, or during training," Spud adds. "To do so otherwise is considered bad luck."

"Some do anyway." Cadence sighs. "Mostly when they attack us. Masks of the losers get taken after a significant loss and are hung in shame on the outer walls of the Axion for another tournament season before being melted down so the Chokma metal can be reused. Obviously, we get new ones each season. While the winners keep their masks for quite some time. Except for the tournament's ultimate champion, their masks reside in Emperor Lucius's citadel. Having an old mask is a sign of continued victory."

"Why do yours look so old then?" Gabriel asks.

"Like I said, the blacksmiths don't care for us, and the Chokma metal purity isn't the best. It's not like we can just go get more pure Chokma metal because there isn't access to the Chokma anymore," Cadence says.

"Sorry, I get a little lost. Why isn't there any access to Chokma?" Gabriel asks.

They are silent for a moment, exchanging glances with one another.

"Gabriel, what do you know about the war?" Cadence asks.

Gabriel shrugs. "Which war?"

"Any of our wars?" Cadence says.

"Nothing."

"Let's put it this way, the universe was once whole. Then, during the first great war, it shattered into pieces. Most of us just happen to live in the areas that were lost," Cadence explains.

"Wait, so you guys are angels?" Gabriel asks.

"We were, once. Now? I'm not sure." Cadence says.

With a flourish, Gabriel removes Azrael's cloak, exposing his ethereal midnight-blue wings with smoke and starlight speckles flowing throughout. His wings illuminate the small housing unit, casting a blue light on everything in the barracks.

Cadence rises from a sitting position, mouth agape. "You are Archangel Gabriel."

"No, I'm just Gabriel. I mean—I don't know."

"Those are archangel wings. You don't just look like him. You are him," Spud says in awe.

"I'd keep that cloak on if I were you," Saphrael advises him as he throws the feather-like soft fabric cloak over Gabriel's shoulders, causing the light in the room to dim dramatically.

"All the time?" Gabriel asks.

"Yes, all of the time," Saphrael says.

"Is it even legal for him to compete? I hope you know what you're doing," Marce says, glaring at Saphrael.

Saphrael sighs and shakes his head, taking out a rag from his equipment bag. He removes his sword from its sheath to clean it before sitting on his cot.

"Nice sword," Gabriel says.

Saphrael hands Gabriel the sword. He admires it and weighs it in his hand. The blade has a rounded pommel that features a red cross inside of a shield accented by silver markings. It features a dark-brown hilt with a silver hand guard. There is writing on the fuller, the indented groove in the middle of the blade: the words are written in Latin, *Sanctus Praesidium*, with letters following it. The letters don't translate, but the words arrange themselves to say *holy protector*.

"Thanks. I call him Solomon," Saphrael says as Gabriel hands him back his weapon.

As Cadence changes his shirt from one long-sleeve shirt-jacket to another, Gabriel notices two large, distinct scars on his back over his shoulder blades.

Saphrael tosses Gabriel clothing before carrying over a pair of worn boots. It is the same uniform everyone else wears, except it is gray instead of black, worn with time. He puts the shirt on through the hole of the cloak. Then he changes out of his gray sweatpants, holding Dawn's watch as he changes into the uniform's faded gray pants.

"What's this?" Marce snatches the watch from his hand.

"Hey!" Gabriel says.

Turning his back to Gabriel, Marce opens the watch and looks at the picture. Slowly, he turns to look at Gabriel. The purple fabric holding the engagement ring falls onto the ground. Gabriel rushes to pick it up.

"You have to see this!" Marce shows everyone the picture inside the watch.

"Is that—" Cadence begins to say.

"It's Lilith!" Spud says.

"No... it's not," Cadence says, from the other side of Saphrael. "Look at her face. Gabriel, who is this?"

"That's my girlfriend, Dawn."

Saphrael takes the pocket watch back from Marce, who glares at Gabriel.

"That... is your girlfriend?" Marce asks, his usual angry tone undercut by something. What, Gabriel isn't sure, until he looks into his eyes and realizes that it's fear.

"Yeah... why?"

Marce points at Saphrael and says, "Either he leaves or I do."

The others move out of his way, except Saphrael, who stands with his arms crossed near the door.

"Why?" Gabriel repeats.

"Why? Why? Why!" Marce takes a moment to collect himself, controlling his breathing. "... I don't know what's going on, but I don't like it." He looks Gabriel up and down before saying. "Nothing good ever happens... not to us." Marce gives Saphrael a look of you're an idiot and says, "Captain," before heading out and slamming the door behind him.

Everything is so quiet that Gabriel hears his heart beating in his chest.

The sting of rejection and its accompanying loneliness may be something he is used to, but it doesn't make it hurt any less, nor does it allow him to understand why they are reacting this way.

"Let's go for a walk." Saphrael nods toward the door.

✦

After the door shuts behind them, Saphrael hands Gabriel his pocket watch. He flips open the heavy lid and looks at the picture of him and Dawn, his grip tightening around the watch. Moments pass as the tick of the watch beats against his palm. Sighing, Gabriel concentrates on his memories, begging them not to fade. In Gabriel's other hand is Dawn's engagement ring, the ring she never got a chance to see. Saphrael watches quietly as he unwraps the fabric, revealing the ring. It shimmers in the low light. Gabriel's hand shakes involuntarily. He closes his eyes, pushing away thoughts of what might have been.

Saphrael stands solemnly near the door, giving him a sympathetic look. Gabriel wraps the ring in the protective dark-purple fabric and places it back inside the watch, snapping it shut before he places it in one of the inside pockets of his tattered cloak. Saphrael walks in the direction of the forest with its oversized, decrepit trees. Gabriel follows, silently looking at the twisted, misshapen branches that inspire a hauntingly hollow feeling within him. He doesn't know where they are going, or why.

After they are deeper into the forest, a fair distance from anyone else, Saphrael says, "Keep your watch hidden."

"Why?"

"I don't think you understand what you are dealing with. You're lying to us or suffering from some form of amnesia. Either way, you bring with you great danger."

"I'm telling you the truth." Gabriel stops walking, and his shoulders slump.

Saphrael stops as well before turning to face Gabriel, their eyes meet.

"The truth as far as you believe." Saphrael looks apologetic, holding eye contact. "You can't stay with us. I'll help you find your way around, for as long as I can, but you can't be here."

"Why? Saphrael, I need help."

"Gabriel, I don't think you fully comprehend what is going on."

"Then tell me."

Saphrael gestures to the watch inside Gabriel's pocket. "As far as I can tell, your girlfriend is the child of Emperor Lucius and Lilith. Your girlfriend, Dawn, is the child of Lucifer."

"So?" Gabriel shrugs.

"So? Is that all you have to say? Even if you are Archangel Gabriel, you must see reason."

"What reason, Saphrael? What is it I'm supposed to be seeing?"

"That this is a lost cause. You can't fight him. You may be strong, Gabriel, but this is no mere tournament fight you're preparing for. Doesn't it bother you? That you didn't even know? And now that you know, you don't even care?"

"I love her. Nothing is going to change that."

"It's probably just part of her nature," Saphrael says while looking up at one of the nearby trees.

"What are you talking about?"

Saphrael sighs and sits down, resting against the trunk of a massive tree.

"Legend has it that Lilith had an aura that drew people to her. If that is her child or some other descendant, and it looks like it is, she probably has the same aura. It isn't your choice to fall in love with someone like that. That's just how it works."

"I have no idea what to say to that. I love her, Saphrael. Haven't you ever been in love?"

Saphrael closes his eyes, collecting himself. "Do you have the slightest idea where you are?"

"Yes," Gabriel says.

"Then you must realize that no such thing as love exists here."

"I refuse to believe that."

Saphrael sighs.

"Where am I, Saphrael?"

"You're in the Sine System. Imagine Earth's universe is a circle with a hole in the middle."

"Like a doughnut?" Gabriel asks.

"What's a doughnut?" Saphrael looks confused. "Sure, I guess, maybe? Anyway, there's a bubble on top of Earth's universe, which is the Crown Realms. The space between is the neutral realm. Then, opposite the Crown Realms is the lower realms, which is where we are. To be specific, you're on Basalt, fourth realm from our central star, Sine." Saphrael gestures to a pale dot in the sky. "Any other points of light you see in the sky are other realms in this system." Saphrael pauses, then says, "If you get lost, the city to the north is Arali. Maybe you'll find something there. I have to get back to my team."

"You're abandoning me?"

"No, I'll check back in a few cycles. I promise to help the best I can, but you have to be careful. You have no idea what you're dealing with."

"Cycles?" Gabriel asks.

"The passage of time relative to whether Tiphareth is facing Sine."

"...What is Tiphareth?"

"Another realm."

"I thought you said we were on Basalt?"

"We are."

"Then... why—"

"It's a system-wide regulation. A set standard."

Gabriel shrugs and figures it's just something he is going to have to get used to.

"I need help, Saphrael. I can't do this on my own."

Saphrael offers him a merciful smile before getting up and walking away. Feelings of abandonment and loneliness flood his mind.

Whenever I open myself up, something happens, he thinks to himself.

I'm still here, a voice replies.

"Semoel?" Gabriel says out loud.

Shh, yes, it's me, but talk to me inside your head.

They don't want me around.

Do you blame them? They are right. You carry a large target on your back.

I just... wish that I had someone to help me.

I'm here, Gabriel, and I'm not going anywhere.

Gabriel heads further into the heart of the woods, feeling a pull in a certain direction. Eventually, he comes upon a large body of water, an expansive lake filled entirely with inky black water.

He reaches out to touch the surface of the strange waters.

I wouldn't do that if I were you, Semoel warns.

Gabriel notices his reflection on the surface of the black waters. He is not used to his altered appearance. His hair is white-blond and his eyes are light blue.

Why am I drawn here?

Why is anyone? Semoel says.

A pale, rotting hand, like that of a corpse missing chunks of flesh, emerges from the black waters, swiping the air inches from Gabriel's leg. Panicking, Gabriel stumbles backward, hitting the ground hard. The arm sinks back into the coal-black water, causing ripples to form on the surface. The ripples turn still at an unnaturally swift pace. Gabriel's heart beats hard in his chest as he looks at the eerily calm waters.

"What was that?" Panic rises inside, but he finds himself completely alone.

✦

Dawn follows Lucius up a set of winding stairs. She feels out of place wearing a ceremonial dress that once belonged to her mother. The garment is one continuous piece of cloth wrapped around her, the end draped over her right shoulder. The deep crimson fabric is well preserved for as old as it must be. As for what occasion it was reserved for historically, she was never told, only that she was to wear traditional garments for something special her father had in mind.

She adjusts her elaborate bronze headpiece that sits heavy on her head.

The adornment reminds her of a crude representation of the morning sun if it were just beginning to rise across the land, the rays of light represented by a row of blocky, polished lapis lazuli stones.

Lucius stops at the top of the stairs, holding his hand out for her. Cordially, she takes it and he leads her down a short hall to an exceptionally large set of doors with a tree embossed on it. They are the largest doors by far that she has seen in the citadel. "Are you listening to me, Dawn?" Lucius asks as she marvels at the intricate detailing on the doors.

She shakes her head, and instead of beginning again with whatever he was lecturing her about, he says, "I have a feeling this may become one of your favorite floors of the citadel."

He opens both large doors. Dawn's heart freezes as light streams out, illuminating the dark hall. After taking a few steps inside, she stops stuck speechless. It is as if she were on Earth, surrounded by lush greenery and flowing streams. She curiously touches a fern that is far larger than any she has ever seen. The plants are somehow familiar but incredibly foreign at the same time, all nestled in a myriad of gray stone pathways, stairs, and statues.

They walk along a path through the lush arboretum. Next to Dawn is a level divider made of natural dark-gray rock that has a faint sparkle of silver where the light hits. She looks up at the bright ceiling far above, the entirety glows an orange-yellow. The light feels like sunlight on her face... but there is no sun. Throughout the floor, veins of trickling streams branch out, flowing into ponds here and there. Her pace slows as she notices an out-of-place, lone twisted gray tree that she thought was long dead until she notices blood-red berries at the end of its branches.

"Come here, Dawn." Lucius kneels beside a small pond.

She walks over and watches as he gently examines the buds of a small aquatic plant system, causing the flora to sway in the water. The closed light gray plant buds float throughout the surface of the pond, accented by a series of leafy dark green dots. Dawn muses that the small green plants look as if someone had tossed in hundreds of bunched-together clover petals.

110

"They aren't ready yet," Lucius says softly.

He takes out a clunky yet beautiful dagger from a pocket of his elaborate black overcoat. It has a dark-blue lapis lazuli handle inlaid with half-rounded chunks of gold. Lucius removes the weapon from its simple black leather sheath, the blade is also gold, yet a darker shade than the handle.

"Ritual sacrifice was commonplace in your mother's time. This was her ceremonial dagger. Gold was never quite the proper choice for a weapon, at least one that is to be employed. In order to protect your mother, I had the blade reforged with syr, an exceedingly rare metal, even to us."

Dawn notices splotches of discoloration on the blade and wonders if it is stained with blood. She receives her answer as Lucius slices the palm of his right hand and holds it out, dripping blood into the water. Most of the flowers die, decaying rapidly after the buds open, blossoming for only a moment. The shriveled gradient petals turn gray, rapidly decaying as the tips fade to black and fall upon the surface of the water. It looks as if a bird was torn to shreds, leaving only feathers. The dark green clover-like flora is somehow not affected. Lucius puts the dagger away. Then he picks a half-opened bud and gently pries the flower apart. She watches as he reaches into it, removing a small, blood-colored circular mass.

"This is the heart of the blood flower. It has properties that allow one to unlock blood memories. Take it and you will experience visions, memories from your past or your ancestors. While you fall asleep, I want you to concentrate upon mother."

Lucius hands her the heart of the blood flower, but Dawn doesn't take it. Instead, she is staring silently at the aftermath of the blood flower harvest.

"Dawn, pay attention. Now, eat this, and we will wait for the results," Lucius says.

Dawn huffs and takes the squishy, dark-red heart of the blood flower. It is cold, slimy, and unpleasant. She lifts her head and looks at her father. "You—you said if I take this, I can see my mother?"

"Yes, Dawn, as long as you concentrate on her as you fall asleep, you will see her."

Dawn closes her eyes, pops the heart of the blood flower into her mouth, and swallows as fast as she can. Even so, a bitter taste remains.

"What was she like?"

"Oh, she was unequaled. She had long red hair and golden-tan skin like you. Her eyes were enchanting." Lucius seems to be lost in memory for a moment. "Tragic, what happened."

"What happened?"

"It is a long story, Dawn. I think you should start at the beginning."

Dawn feels a deep pull of sleep, quickly finding it difficult to keep her eyes open.

"Soon you will enter a dream-like state where you will experience the past. Hopefully, we will find some answers."

Her vision blurs the greenery around her. The world spins, as if she were inebriated. The feeling speeds faster until she loses the ability to hold herself upright. The last thing she feels is Lucius catching her as the force of her limp body hits his arms, causing her body to arch downward and her headpiece to fall.

She opens her eyes to an ancient time. The walls of the strange room are painted white, and the texture is like that of clay or dried mud. Yet when she attempts to move, she finds that she has no control over her body. It is like watching television: she can't affect things, yet at the same time, she is fully present with every sense intact. A hand rests on her shoulder. A rush of endorphins floods her senses. *No, not her shoulder, Lilith's shoulder*, she realizes. Lilith is wearing the same dress that Dawn has on.

She lightly caresses the back of the man's warm hand before bringing it up to her cheek and nuzzling against it. When Lilith looks at him, Dawn is surprised to see Adam. His hair is a touch longer, and his eyes are darkened with eyeliner. He is wearing a knee-length light-blue tunic robe and brown sandals. Adam bends down, kissing her. Inside, Dawn is sufficiently on edge. He looks the same yet so different, and not just in age or clothing. Beneath it all, Dawn doesn't believe it could be the same person. The man standing before her has a spirit in his eyes that speaks of a gentle kindness, of love.

Adam kisses her, tenderly embracing her. He whispers, "I love you," into her ear. Lilith blushes and answers him with a passionate kiss, pulling his body flush against hers.

Tenderly, Adam breaks from the embrace and looks into her eyes. "I'll see you at the harvest festival?"

"Of course." Lilith traces her fingers across his forearm. This is the first time Dawn has ever heard her mother's voice.

Adam squeezes her hand before he leaves. Lilith gets up and tends to an assortment of primitive, difficult-to-see-through glassware on a woven wicker wood table topped with a sheet of bronze. The only light in the room burns from a mollusk shell oil lamp engraved with deteriorated symbols too faded to translate, inlaid with lapis lazuli. Reed baskets line the walls, and a storage chest made of wood sits beside the table.

Dawn can hear Lilith's thoughts, but they are calculations of the stars and measurements of what is to her, foreign methods and ingredients.

The door to the room opens. Dawn expects to see Adam, but it is her father, Lucius. Tall and imposing as ever, he is dressed in long, dark-gray robes, and an animal fur is slung across his shoulders. He, too, is wearing eyeliner, his skin is golden tan, and his eyes look normal.

He strides over to Lilith, observing the glass vials. "I see you have been busy."

"Not busy enough," Lilith rolls her eyes and places her hand lightly on the center of his chest.

"I passed Adam in the hall," Lucius says, not bothering to mask the bitterness behind his remark.

"He isn't one to give up easily. Are you going to help me or not?" Lilith asks, leaning in, inspecting the glass vials.

"You understand I disapprove."

"I'm well aware," Lilith says flatly. Instead, her concentration is focused entirely on the liquids in the vials.

Dawn's blood runs cold as Lucius doesn't have an immediate response. Instead, an unamused thousand-yard stare chills the marrow in her bones before he says, "No matter."

The world goes dark as Dawn's vision blacks out. In an instant, the room reappears, and Dawn's heart seizes as she sees a woman with long, dark-brown hair, eyeliner, and a light-blue dress with the ceremonial knife buried in her chest. She isn't dead... at least not yet, as evidenced by the sharp rising of her chest, accompanied by a horrible gurgling sound as she struggles to take what are sure to be her final breaths.

The image fades, and Dawn is surrounded by darkness once more. When she comes to, Lilith is tied to a chair, surrounded by a few figures Dawn can't fully see.

A male voice says, "Azrael, please, it's time."

If Dawn didn't know any better, she would have sworn it was Gabriel. A pale bony hand reaches out and touches her forehead. Lilith's memories begin to fade, along with emotions tied to them. As visions of her memories speed past in her mind, ones of her forbidden love affair with Lucius surface. Then Azrael notices something... he notices her. Not Dawn as she is now, he realizes that Lilith is pregnant.

Azrael hesitates, and in that moment of weakness, Lilith seizes the opportunity and grabs hold of Azrael's essence through the connection, drawing it into herself like a psychic vampyre enhancing her power and seduction aura.

The vision skips through a quick succession of horrors: Lilith luring victims, blood dripping onto an altar from the ceremonial dagger, a symphony of shrill screams and cries of agony. A pile of corpses unceremoniously stacked in a dark room illuminated only by torches from the hall. Zombies shamble through the streets of an ancient city. *It must be Eridu*, she thinks in wonder before the vision alters, this time to a cabin deep in the wilds. Lucius has a small smile on his face as he grips the ceremonial dagger. Lifting the dagger to his face with one hand and cupping Lilith's cheek with the other, he makes a haphazard cut vertically across his lips. He grabs Lilith's waist, pulling her close. Dawn's heart races in fear or perhaps Lilith's in excitement. *No, no, no,* Dawn begs as she tries to pull away, but there is nothing she can do. As his lips meet Lilith's, a coppery, metallic, burning acidic taste seeps into her mouth. Dawn feels the physical toll taken as Lilith is poisoned with angelic blood. It feels as if every cell of her body is on fire. Time skips once more, and Lilith is outside patting dirt over a freshly tilled grave. She places a flower on the soil near the twisted juniper tree next to the cabin for yet another child lost. The tree is nearly identical to the dead-looking one in the arboretum. Left buried under the juniper are the decaying remains of Dawn's lost siblings, reduced to soulless husks of bones and unripened flesh. They lost so many trying to conceive.

Then darkness. The only thing that remains is a disturbing, inharmonious chorus of agonizing screams. The screams cease, and Dawn opens her eyes to the bright lights of the arboretum, surrounded by lush green and the calming sound of rushing water. Lucius is beside her, his hand resting on her forehead just below the bronze headpiece. She gets up too quickly. A deep feeling of sickness washes over her, and Lucius pulls her into an embrace.

"I think your nightmares started to seep in at the end, my dear," Lucius says, holding her close.

Chapter 10

Adam walks briskly to the far end of Lucius's study to an imposing desk carved from a single tree harvested from the giant forests of Basalt. It extends from one end of the cavernous room to the other, carved to resemble a black dragon. Adam waits, listening silently near the evocative head of the dragon, whose mouth is open, fangs bared. The heavy clank of Lucius's boots echoes as he descends the stairs inside the desk and walks out of the dragon's mouth.

"Adam, I am going to need you to do something I have never asked you to do before." Lucius looks directly at him.

No matter how long he has been around him, Adam has never gotten used to the feeling inspired inside of him when Lucius's unnaturally bright copper-colored eyes set upon him.

"Yes, my lord?" Adam's posture is stiff. His expression gives away nothing of his personal feelings.

"I want you to remember the past." Lucius strolls, crossing the room while Adam falls into step behind him.

"Human memory, even enhanced, can only retain so much. Besides, those memories were blocked long ago. If I could recall them easily, they would be at your disposal."

"They were purposely blocked. However, I want to remove those blocks."

Adam keeps pace a step behind Emperor Lucius. "Wouldn't that potentially prompt an unpredictable effect? We blocked my memories for a reason."

"Now I need you to remember."

"Why? May I ask?" Adam knows it has something to do with Princess Dawn. But what? He has no idea.

"It will become clear in time. For now, we will remove the blocks and prompt your memories to resurface."

"Yes, my lord. How do we proceed?"

"I want you to spend time with Dawn. I need you to watch over her while I attend an important meeting."

"Yes, my lord. And what of the lesser Gabriel?"

"We have tracked him to the desolate world of Basalt. I want you to welcome him."

Lucius stops in front of a case of ornate weapons mounted on the wall. He opens the glass door before reaching in and taking hold of a serrated red crystal dagger. This one is a darker shade than the ruby-colored one Lucius depleted earlier.

"Since he survived the less concentrated version," Lucius says, weighing the dagger in his hand before holding it out to Adam.

"There are so few of these left. Are you certain?"

Lucius nods, and then Adam grips the cold intricately embossed silver-colored handle. Quietly, he admires the haunting elegance of the skillfully crafted blade.

"What is our aim, sir?"

"My aim is none of your concern. You are a weapon, Adam. Do as you are instructed."

"Of course, my lord." Adam gives him an apologetic bow.

✦

Gabriel sits at the edge of the lake for what he assumes are days. It's impossible for him to tell. He doesn't understand why he is drawn to the strange black waters. Finding himself unable to leave, he is weighed down by the suffocating weight of hopelessness. The waters are eerie and still.

He isn't sure that the waters are moving, even where the lake breaks off into deep fjords in the distance.

He lies on the ground and looks up at the deformed, knotted, serpentine branches that curve out haphazardly, feeling as twisted inside as the trees look on the outside. It is unnervingly silent. He has not seen a hint of wildlife and wonders if wildlife even exists here.

Thinking about his former life, he holds onto the thought of having Dawn wrapped safely in his arms. The feeling grounds him, providing him strength, yet at the same time intensifying the emptiness that accompanies loss. His train of thought is broken by a noise coming from the woods.

He picks himself up, hoping it's Saphrael coming to tell him he has changed his mind. Instead, he is greeted by an officer in a pitch-black uniform with red accents. The officer projects a threatening aura as he walks toward him. Gabriel takes a defensive stance. His heart beats faster, anxiety rising. The officer's medium brown eyes meet Gabriel's evenly. As he gets closer, Gabriel can read the name on his uniform: Adam.

"What do you want?" Gabriel forms a fist.

"I see you've joined the ranks of the Wonder Brigade." Adam smirks. "Fitting."

Gabriel glances at the water, pushing away the darkness calling to him. "I don't know what you want, but maybe we can work together. I need help."

Adam stops directly in front of him and responds to his question by punching the side of Gabriel's face. A stinging numbness spreads across his cheek.

"I am not here to bargain," Adam says, unsheathing a dark-red crystal dagger.

Gabriel's eyes widen, and he lowers his arms without thinking. Adam does not hesitate to utilize this break in defense. He tosses the dagger from his left hand to his right, leaving a red streak in the air. Then, with inhuman speed, Adam maneuvers under Gabriel's right arm. Before Gabriel knows what hit him, his left shoulder is being pulled back; at the same time, Adam knocks his heel into the back of his right calf, sweeping it upward. Gabriel slams into the ground, landing dangerously close to the coal-black waters.

Adam falls to one knee, using momentum to plunge the dark-red crystal dagger into Gabriel's lower right abdomen. The dark-red crystal blade melts into his bloodstream. Gabriel chokes, gasping for air. A burning pain runs throughout his body, somehow worse than before.

The officer is expressionless as he uses his boot to turn Gabriel to his side and kick him, driving his boot into the mid-center of his back, causing Gabriel's body to arch before turning him to the side and booting him into the lake.

The world turns dark as he plunges into the black water. Pale, decaying corpse-like hands reach out of the darkness. He panics as the nightmare comes to life around him. Inside, depression grips him, easing his anxiety. *What's the point?* he thinks to himself.

You're worthless, a voice tells him.

You are nothing, a different voice says.

Gabriel lets go, continuing to sink, the creatures dragging him deeper into the lake. The feathered ends of Azrael's cloak cling to him, as if it were trying to shield him.

He instinctively breathes in the cursed water, causing negative emotions and the feeling of sickness to amplify.

Give up, a voice says to him.

Inside, he knows that the voices are from the rotten creatures. It no longer matters to him where these negative voices come from. Allowing himself to let go, he lay on jagged cliffs that line the bottom of the deep lake.

✦

Laughter and screams echo from a carnival held in the middle of the forest at night. A blood-red moon hangs low in the sky, far larger than Dawn has ever seen, casting a red light over the carnival. She shivers, finding herself in a gown that has been shredded and torn, reduced to ragged, shiny strips of black fabric. There is a silhouette of the black dragon upon the blood-red moon. Dawn wonders if she is dreaming.

She stumbles into the crowd, surrounded by extravagant costumes and stunning masks worn by those with traditionally angelic features. The beautifully eccentric masks are made of various materials: some porcelain, some metal, and others wood. Feathers adorn the sides of many of the masks. A young woman walks by in a mask shaped to resemble butterfly wings, which are translucent and protrude far above the form-fitting mask.

Dawn searches the crowd.

"Gabriel!" she cries. "Gabriel!"

But no one responds. It is as if she has said nothing at all.

Deciding to follow the bright lights, she walks a central path, following garish signs pointing to the midway. Her eyes widen as, instead of rides, the midway is full of medieval torture devices.

Dawn's blood turns cold as an adult plucks the eye out of the face of a victim who is screaming and tied down, being stretched by a rope and pulley system. The adult has a mask with a snow-white hat attached to it, which is framed by a sparkling silver rope. The entire mask is heavily jeweled, reminding her of what a gaudy aristocratic sycophant might wear if they were masquerading as a religious leader at a party. The adult hands the baby the eye with the nerves still attached to it. The baby shakes the eye, making it look as if the eye is searching the crowd. The air is filled with sick laughter punctuated by cries and screams. The baby grows tired of its toy and drops it on the ground. The mother and child stroll away.

Dawn stares in horror at the eye. It is a deep, rich medium brown that reminds her of her own eyes. Two women pass her, talking about how they can't wait to get to the food court. They step on the eye, crushing it without even noticing.

Inside, her stomach twists into knots. *I have to get out of here, now*, she thinks, searching for an exit. Picking up her pace, she hurries, quickly finding herself in the food court. Human limbs hang from meat hooks visible through the windows of dilapidated black brick buildings. The disturbing scent of searing flesh, far more potent than any barbecue that Dawn has ever had the misfortune to smell, makes her nauseous. *Keep it together, Dawn. You can't let them know you're not one of them.*

She fights to stop tears flowing, but still, they fall, and suddenly a hand grabs her upper right arm, its grip like a vice. She looks up and is met only with a blank porcelain mask with no adornments. The large, gruff individual crushing her arm says, "Can't have you wandering 'round like that."

Dawn desperately plants her feet into the cold, wet grass.

"No! Where are you taking me?!" Dawn tries to pull away but can't.

The man in the porcelain mask says nothing as he drags her back to the midway.

He locks her into a cylindrical glass case with a wooden floor. The small round target hanging like a sign off to the side indicates she is in a dunk tank. The wooden floor has gaps around the edges.

Dawn slams her fists against the thick, unforgiving glass. "Gabriel!" she screams in desperation. "Gabriel!" She tries to kick down the door, but it doesn't budge.

A group of silver-masked men dressed in black approach her cage. Dawn desperately pulls at the door. It is securely bolted shut.

"Gabriel!" she cries in vain. "God, please, Gabriel. I need you."

"Why do you think anyone is coming to save *you*?" says one of the masked men, who seems to be the leader.

He picks up a black wooden crossbow and aims it directly at her, finger on the trigger. Dawn cowers as he breaks into laughter—laughter echoed by his friends. The leader walks closer and removes his silver mask, which is fashioned into the visage of a monster.

"Gabriel." Dawn's breath becomes shallow as she doesn't believe what she is looking at. His face is illuminated by the red moon.

"She knows my name..." he says softly, almost gently, before his expression hardens. "Guess they finally learned how to talk." His entourage responds with more laughter. "What good are they anyway?" The look in Gabriel's ice-blue eyes speaks of neither love nor kindness, but hatred. Gabriel slams his fist on the barrier between them, startling Dawn. "What good are you anyway?" His lip twists. "Pathetic."

Gabriel fires an arrow into the ground directly in front of the cage. He smirks as she cowers, her eyes closed, as if she could escape the situation.

He strolls over to the lever and watches her as he punches it. But the floor does not open. Instead, pitch-black waters from below bubble through the wooden floor. It rises quickly, filling her prison-tank.

"Gabriel!" she begs, hoping beyond hope that he will turn around. "Gabriel!"

But all she hears is laughter from the group, as their backs are turned and they walk away, blending in with the grotesque crowd.

"Gabriel!" Dawn cries, as the coal-black water rises past her throat.

The water is cold. She closes her eyes and tilts her head back, trying to keep her head above water. The cold black water fills the entire tank.

As she holds her breath, she remembers what Gabriel said to her so long ago. *Promise me, to hold on to hope, especially when nothing else remains.*

Dawn inhales sharply. When she does, she opens her eyes and is met with her own quiet room. Frantically, she looks around, heart beating wildly. She sighs and puts her head down, telling herself, *it was only a nightmare.*

She gets up and runs to her door and pulls on the solid metal circle. It doesn't move. Dawn kicks the door out of frustration and lets out a loud cry of distress. Then, she curls up and slides down against the wall next to her door, hot tears running down her face.

◆

Gabriel lies on the jagged lake bed of the cursed obsidian waters for an unknown amount of time. With every breath, he ingests cursed water. The creatures inhabiting the lake no longer attack him.

Will I ever see her again? Does she still care about me? Will I forget her smile? Her touch? The softness in her voice when she said my name?

You will forget. We all forget, the voices of the lake creatures whisper to him. Their chant increases in volume until it is the singular thought dominating his mind.

Finally, a break from the torment as a familiar voice says, *If you forgot, perhaps you would be happier without this burden on your shoulders?*

Semoel? Gabriel's eyes open wide, but he sees nothing but a cold black void. In the back of his mind, Gabriel hears Dawn sobbing.

Think very carefully. Would you give everything for this one girl?

If I could extend her life by mere moments, I would sacrifice everything without question.

"Gabriel!" Dawn's voice rings clear in his mind, giving him the strength he needs to fight. He pushes up from the jagged floor of the lake.

"Gabri—" Dawn's voice is cut off.

The incessant whispers of the lake creatures are silent, but the thoughts holding him down are not. His mind flashes to the night he failed to protect Dawn. The night everything changed. Using sheer force of will, he swims upward, determined to make it no matter how long it takes.

I'm coming, Dawn, he thinks, ready to fight the waterlogged creatures, but none come at him.

Finally, he starts to see through the surface of the pitch-black waters, he imagines Dawn reaching to him from the shore. He breaks through the surface of the lake, breathing in hard instinctively.

Saphrael sits on the lake shore.

"Little help?" Gabriel swims toward him.

"This is something you have to do on your own," Saphrael says looking sullen.

Gabriel wonders if the suffocating depression is amplified in Saphrael as well from being near the black waters as he pulls himself onto land. Saphrael grips his hand and helps steady him onto his feet.

"Those who are lost, are lost of their own accord," Saphrael says. "If you couldn't get back on your own, you deserve to be lost."

Gabriel breathes in hard, trying to reorient himself. "Well, that's pretty dark, Saphrael." He looks back at the waters. "What was that?"

"That?" Saphrael gestures to the lake. "That's Black Lake. The creatures who inhabit it are known as the Lost. I thought you might end up here. Most everyone does."

"I didn't jump in because I wanted to." Gabriel points at his wound and hole in his worn gray shirt-jacket. "I was thrown in. Someone named Adam."

Saphrael raises an eyebrow and says, "Come on. I thought about it, and I can't just leave you on your own."

"You've thought about it. What about the rest of them?"

"I'll talk to them."

"Maybe… it is best if I didn't return. Adam seems to know who you guys are."

"No, you need our help. Just—don't tell the others about Adam."

"Why?"

"It'll just scare them."

"Why… did you come back for me?"

"I need to be true to my word. I said I would help you, so here I am. Understanding and forgiveness are disciplines I actively practice. So much so it is in the Wonder Brigade's motto."

"You said something like that after the match. Forgiveness in death?"

Saphrael laughs and shakes his head. "No, Gabriel, the motto is 'Grace in forgiveness. Understanding in death.'" Saphrael looks out across the coal-black waters and is silent in contemplation for a long while. "Eliminate every weakness… it's something we live by. Something we are forced to live by." Suddenly, Saphrael looks tired. "Allow the random violent nature of the cosmos to shape you or take control. Forgiveness allows us the opportunity of choice. Existence is a never-ending battle. Forgiveness is a strength, it's a choice, a vow. It's not about being right. Only through forgiveness may we find peace. And only in peace can we hope to understand without the shadow of ego clouding our judgment."

Gabriel is silent as he looks across the waters as well. He is sure that he knows far less that Saphrael does and when it is wise to listen.

"It's not easy…" Saphrael hangs his head down before he looks up past the waters in contemplation. "Revenge… revenge is easy. Retaliation without forethought is driven by lack of control." He looks at Gabriel with compassion. "I don't know what you've been through in discere, but try to forgive yourself. If you don't, every action will be motivated by pain."

Gabriel nods, listening to the wind rush through the forest. "I want to understand."

"I think you do," Saphrael says. "Let's get back."

✦

Dawn sits curled against the stone wall in what, she is fairly sure by now, is her prison. Hugging her legs, she rests her head against her knees, unable to stop the flow of tears for what seems like hours since waking from her nightmare. Someone clears their throat. Startled, and with hot tears falling down her face, she looks up to find Lucius holding his hand out for her. She hadn't even heard him open the door.

Silently, she looks at his hand while he stands, giving her time. She takes his hand, and he helps her up and pulls her into an embrace. She rests against his chest, unable to stop the flow of tears.

Weakly holding onto him, she says, "I miss Gabriel..."

Lucius tightens his hold before letting go. He looks at her, his expression unreadable as he says, "I understand. However, I told you before, I don't want you mentioning him."

"Why?"

"Dawn, some things are done for your own good. You may not understand now, but think of the sorrow this brings you. If there is anything I can do to alleviate your distress, allow me to do so."

"What could you possibly do?"

"I could spend more time with you to ease your loneliness, or commission things to be made, anything you like. All you have to do is ask."

She looks down, thinking the only thing she wants is Gabriel. Instead of answering, she straightens her nightgown. Lucius places his hand below her chin and lifts her head, forcing her to look up at him.

"Anything you need, all you must do is let me know." He holds eye contact.

"I want to leave the citadel sometime."

Lucius pauses before inclining his head. "I will see what I can do. For now, would you like to spend time together? Come, we can talk in my study." He holds the door for her. Dawn grabs her boots, puts them on and laces them up before walking into the hall and falling into step beside Lucius. The guards stationed at her doors follow a few paces behind.

"It's so cold here." She holds her arms, shivering. "Why is it so cold, all the time?"

"An unfortunate side effect of this system having a dead central star. Be sure to ask your tailor as to what can be done about it."

Their footfalls echo on the black stone floor. Dawn quiets as she looks down the hall, the hall she ran down, trying to escape, when Adam had escorted her. She remembers making it halfway down the winding stairs before Adam slammed her against the hard stone wall, twisted her arm, forcing her to obey.

"Why do you keep Adam around anyway?"

"I know you didn't have the best introduction to my chief adviser, but rest assured, he is to be trusted."

Lucius opens the door to his study, and they walk inside. He sits on his black Victorian-style couch and she in her chair. He picks up the carafe of Xerotes. The red liquid sways inside the frosted diamond-shaped carafe.

"Xerotes?" Lucius offers.

Dawn hesitates before nodding. He closes his eyes, inclines his head, and pours her a drink into an ornate silver metal chalice. She drinks it quickly, averting eye contact as he stares at her from his usual spot in the middle of the long black Victorian-style couch, studying her.

"Tell me, Dawn, what is it you were crying about? If anything, beyond Gabriel?" he asks, pouring her another glass.

Dawn drinks, her body relaxing.

"I had a nightmare," she says, barely audible.

"Tell me about it," Lucius asks, refilling her glass.

"There was a dark carnival held in the middle of a forest at night, a large crimson moon hung low in the sky, casting red over everything and everyone... It was grotesque but the patrons wore the most beautiful masks. In the center of the fair, the midway, was not filled with rides but torture devices and death for the amusement of careless, heartless people.

126

I was locked in a dunk tank until water filled the tank completely with pitch-black water."

"Be sure to log a full account in your dream journal. Are your dreams often like this?"

Dawn nods. "Most of the time, though, there is something I can't quite figure out."

"What would that be?"

After drinking more Xerotes, she smiles. "It makes no sense. It just doesn't."

"What makes no sense, Dawn?"

"The dragon."

"What dragon?"

"Sickly-looking, skinny dragon-snake, missing scales and—I don't know. I don't even know why I'm talking about it."

"It's all right, Dawn. You can tell me anything."

"It's always just there, in my dreams. I don't know why—hovering ominously like he's waiting for me to die."

"What did his face look like?"

"The dragon's face? Like a dragon? How am I supposed to know? Like a Western dragon, I guess, but its body looked Eastern."

"Has the dragon ever talked to you?"

"What? Um, no? Not that I can remember. He's always just there. Well, most of the time, not always."

"Dawn, you're rambling."

"I'm just trying to answer your questions."

He smiles. It is a half-smile but a genuine smile. Then his demeanor changes. "The next time you see the dragon, I want you to kill it."

"You want me to what?" Dawn finishes yet another glass of Xerotes. "You want me to kill the dragon?"

"Yes, Dawn. If it is indeed the source of your nightmares, you might be better off with it dead."

Not knowing what to say, she sets her chalice down on the table. Lucius continues to pour her more.

"How am I supposed to kill a dragon?" Dawn asks.

"In any way you can."

Chapter 11

Gabriel follows Saphrael through the door of the Wonder Brigade's barracks. His posture is slumped as he looks around at the Wonder Brigade, all milling about in the cramped space.

"I thought we told you to leave," Loth says, glaring at Gabriel before turning to address Saphrael. "What kind of captain are you anyway? You have the nerve to bring him back without asking."

"He's right," Marceriel says, looking over at Loth from his cot.

"I need help." Gabriel stands next to Saphrael, near the door to the barracks.

"And we need to be clear of whatever wrath comes your way. How is it possible that you are even walking around freely?" Marce stands up. "If he doesn't leave, I will."

"Maybe we should give him a chance," Cadence says, doing his best to be diplomatic.

"Yeah!" Spud sits up in his cot. "What do we have to lose?"

"Everything, Paderael," Loth says.

Saphrael waits to see if Loth is done talking before addressing everyone. "You are concerned I didn't ask you beforehand. I apologize for that. It was my mistake. But we have the opportunity to discuss it now and vote on whether or not Gabriel stays. Those of us who want to keep Gabriel on our team and risk whatever comes our way, raise your hand. We will fail without him this tournament season, but this isn't about us. This is an opportunity to help someone."

"A traitor," Loth says.

"He has a point." Marce shifts his stance uneasily. "This is beyond reason. You have abandoned sanity, Captain."

"Anyone who wants to help Gabriel and allow him join our team, raise your hand." Saphrael surveys the room.

Cadence, Spud, and Saphrael raise their hands, leaving Marce and Loth as the outside votes.

"You have no idea what you are asking," Marce says through gritted teeth.

"We have some idea, Marce. We voted as a team." Saphrael looks at Marce who shakes his head, allowing his anger to get the better of him.

Marce storms past Saphrael and stops in front of Gabriel, half his lip curling in disdain before leaving the barracks. The door slams shut behind him.

◆

Deep in the heart of Arali, Marce waits inside a small decorative office, hands resting on a table. The office belongs to the head loyalty officer of the Wonder Brigade's district, Darius. Marce has a decent rapport with him and occasionally visits as a responsible soldier. Darius, as all loyalty officers tend to be, is known for his ruthlessness and cruelty. Marce personally never had a problem with him.

Darius has an angled face with a sharply defined jaw and protruding chin; thick black eyebrows sit close to his blue eyes. His medium-length black hair sticks out from under his officer's cap. He seemed to always favor Marceriel while hating the rest of the Wonder Brigade, though Marce isn't quite sure why. Even so, Marce was astonished that Darius agreed to the impossible.

The loyalty officer sits at his desk, looking through paperwork as Marce distracts himself from his nerves by tapping on the table in a rhythmic beat. He stops as the door opens and in walks Hierophant Adam.

"This better be worth my time," Adam says as he strides in, glaring at

Marceriel and then nodding to Darius.

Marce is temporarily struck silent by the air of gravitas Hierophant Adam's presence commands. It makes him feel insignificant. "It is, Hierophant," Marce scrambles to say, his posture is stiff as he holds his chin respectfully tilted upward.

The hierophant stops behind an open chair across from Marceriel. Opting to stand, Adam rests his hands on the back of it before gesturing impatiently. "Well, get on with it."

"Adam, sir, Gabriel—a Gabriel or someone who looks like, and may be, Archangel Gabriel is here."

"Indeed? And you offer this information freely?"

"Yes, Hierophant, it's the right thing to do."

"Do you have any other information?" Adam asks, his formal, stern attitude unchanging as he waits for Marceriel to answer.

"No. Only that he is looking for his girlfriend. Her name is Dawn."

Moving his head from one side to another, Adam mulls the information. "Is that all?"

"Yes, Hierophant," Marceriel says, putting his head down in a sign of respect.

"Return to your unit, Marceriel. This will not be forgotten."

"Yes, Hierophant."

"Return if you discover any new information."

"Of course," Marceriel says, before hesitating. "Is—is Dawn here?"

"Princess Dawn," Adam corrects him.

"Of course, Princess Dawn. So… she is here."

"Do not tell Gabriel a word of what you think you may know."

"Of course, Hierophant."

"You were right to call for me." Adam nods to Marce, showing him a small sign of respect.

With that praise, Marceriel allows his shoulders to drop, relaxing. Marce reaches into a pouch. There is a heavy thud as he drops Gabriel's pocket watch on the table. Adam picks up the gold watch and opens it, quietly studying the image.

"She looks happy," Adam says, with a thoughtful tone before snapping it shut. "You have done well, Marceriel."

Closing his eyes, Marce struggles internally, steadying his trembling hand as he reaches into his demon leather pouch once more. Marce lets out a sigh and drops the ring wrapped in fabric on the table.

Hierophant Adam picks up the ring and studies it silently.

The hierophant places a hand on Marceriel's shoulder. "I will be sure to inform Emperor Lucius that these items of value came from directly from you. Perhaps someday you could find your way out of the Wonder Brigade, and on to somewhere your skills and loyalty are more appreciated."

Marce keeps his head down. "Thank you, Hierophant."

"Tell the rest of your unit nothing. Leave things the way they are."

"Are you not going to arrest him?"

"No, it is not my call."

"But—"

"Follow my orders." Adam sneers momentarily and pockets the items.

"Of course, Hierophant," Marce says.

Hierophant Adam pauses, taking a long look at Marceriel before leaving. Calling attention to himself, Darius clears his throat after the door closes. He walks over to Marceriel and drops a small black bag that clanks as it hits the table. From the sound it makes, it is clear what is inside: payment.

"For your time," Darius says evenly.

"I don't want this." Marce looks away from the small pouch.

"Do spend it wisely." Darius pauses. "I hope you got whatever it is you needed from this."

Marce stands up, nods at the loyalty officer, and then reluctantly pockets the reward.

"Keep an eye on him and report back to me if necessary. Any new information, regardless of how inane it may seem. I would like to hear it."

"Yes, Officer," Marce says.

◆

A startling noise blares outside of the Wonder Brigade's barracks, a mix between an air-raid horn and a tornado siren. There is a tinge of brassiness about the sound that makes Gabriel think it may be some sort of horn.

"Time to go," Cadence says as everyone gets up.

Marce shoulder checks Gabriel on his way out of the door, and Saphrael balances him by putting his hand behind his shoulder.

"Just stand with us and you'll be all right," Saphrael says.

From the nearby barracks, other teams are filing out and standing in lines.

The Wonder Brigade lines up, standing beside their giant, tattered flag.

Saphrael nudges Gabriel. "Just do what we do, and you'll be okay. Don't draw attention to yourself for any reason."

An officer in uniform similar to what Adam wore approaches. Next to his insignia is a name tag that says Darius.

"Loyalty officer," Saphrael says quietly from beside Gabriel, Marce on his other side.

Darius's black boots kick up gray dust as he stops abruptly before the Wonder Brigade, glaring at them.

"Who is this?" Darius asks, striding up to Gabriel.

"The newest addition to the Wonder Brigade," Saphrael says, holding his posture straight and perfectly still as he stares ahead.

Darius examines Gabriel for some time before saying, "How come I've never seen you before?" A loaded question, and one Gabriel doesn't know how to answer.

"I'm new here," Gabriel says with a smile.

The loyalty officer pulls out a small dagger. In one sharp flick, the otherworldly chromatic shine from the blade creates a colorful visual effect before slicing the side of his face.

"I will not suffer insubordination." Darius sneers.

Gabriel stiffens and looks at the others, who are all staring straight forward.

Saphrael speaks up. "Sir, he spent time in the Black Lake."

"Someone crawled out of the gutter to join your team? That's enough of you pathetic lot." Darius scoffs and then turns on his heel before stopping. "Oh, I highly recommend that you do not consider skipping your qualifying free-for-all this season. We will not only be re-educating the losing champion, but the entire team, if you are among the first to lose. Which, according to tradition, you will be." Darius turns back to Gabriel. "Are you certain you want to even join this unit? There are other, stronger, better units in the legions."

Gabriel nods. "Yes, loyalty officer. I'm sure."

"How you've managed to lure someone to your ranks is beyond me, wonder team," Darius says, surveying each of them carefully before walking away.

In the distance, there is a disturbance as an officer beats someone curled into a fetal position on the ground, offering no defense. Everyone looks over at the commotion and then quickly turns away. One of the twin flags that flank the door has been ripped in three places as if clawed by an animal.

Loth sneers. "Serves them right."

Gabriel searches but cannot see what everyone else seems to be seeing.

"Don't let them catch you," Saphrael turns him away from staring in that direction.

"Why?"

Marce scoffs, "Idiot. What do you mean, why? If you interfere, you will be treated as an accomplice. If you're lucky, you'll only be treated as a disturbance."

"I can't look at them?"

"It's not safe to... no." Cadence gives Gabriel a look of appraisal. "You'll be fine soon." He turns Gabriel's face to the side and applies a medicinal paste.

"Thanks, but it really doesn't bother me." Gabriel's blood mixes with the paste, forming a seal.

"All right, everyone, time to run formations," Saphrael says, standing in front of the group.

He shouts commands. Gabriel looks to the side and follows along a step behind everyone else. They practice different forms of combat maneuvers.

When they are done with tactical formations, Saphrael hands Gabriel a black leather-bound book. He flips through the pages. It is full of fighting forms, reminding him of martial arts katas.

"Study," Saphrael advises.

"I know some martial arts. This shouldn't be too difficult," Gabriel says. They head back into the barracks, and Gabriel sets the book down onto the dresser next to his cot. "So, what was going on with the flag?"

"Do not say a word," Loth warns from his cot.

Cadence laughs, his back turned as he messes with medical items in a drawer. "Why? You think he's going to lead the charge against Emperor Lucius?"

"What?" Gabriel asks, looking back and forth.

"Three slashes across the emperor's crest is a sign of the resistance. What? He's going to hear about it sometime, it might as well be from us," Marce says.

"There's a resistance?" Gabriel asks, sitting down on his cot.

"It's a myth," Loth states.

"I heard—" Spud begins to say.

"Nobody cares what rumors you've heard, Spud." Loth snaps.

Saphrael is keeping a wary eye on the situation in case it needs to be diffused.

Gabriel decides to do so himself by asking another question. "I've been meaning to ask: if you're angels, where are your wings?"

Saphrael softly says, "That's a very human question."

"I'm sorry?"

"It's okay. It's ignorant, but understandable," Saphrael says, pausing to find the right words. "It's... cultural."

"Cultural?" Gabriel asks, looking around the room. No one seems happy. "That's not really an answer."

"Don't you have strange customs on Earth?" Saphrael asks.

"Well, of course, but—"

"It's just how things are," Saphrael says.

"Did you ever have wings?" Gabriel asks.

"Yes, we did, before the war. Before the sundering of the realms. Before… all of this," Saphrael says.

Loth glares at him from across the room. "It's none of his business if he doesn't know."

"How are you so sure?" Saphrael says.

"They get cut off," Spud says from his cot as he lies back and stares at the ceiling. "It hurts, and they don't regenerate. Not even when you change form."

"Change form?" Gabriel asks.

"This guy is deaf and stupid," Loth says.

Marce laughs.

"Don't listen to them. It's tradition when you lose, and everyone has suffered a loss at some point," Cadence says.

Gabriel still looks confused.

"Like I said, it's cultural," Saphrael says. "Get some rest while you can."

◆

In the dead of night, everything is quiet, save for the gentle rustling of those asleep. Gabriel, however, is wide awake. His mind will not stop racing through scenarios of impending disasters. He doesn't know if his body needs rest, but he knows that his mind does. Briefly, he glances at Marce's empty cot and wonders where he goes on his frequent late-night walks.

Unable to rest, he watches the faint dark-blue glow of a time crystal sitting across the small room on Cadence's dresser. The blue dot in the opaque white crystal ranges from a deep midnight blue to that of a pale sky. It is starting to turn a brighter, lighter color, indicating the beginning of a new cycle. During the zenith of a cycle, the entirety of the crystal glows a bright pale blue. Time crystals are aligned to royal time set to Tiphareth's cycle. In reality, the atmosphere outside is perpetually dusk.

The metal door of the barracks screeches open. Marce looks over at Gabriel and throws something at him. Gabriel catches the shiny silver object with both hands as if it were a basketball. He looks down at a pristine Wonder Brigade Chokma mask.

"I remember what you said to Darius... when he asked if you were sure you wanted to join," Marce says, looking off in another direction. "If you're going to be a part of the team, you're going to need this."

"Thanks," Gabriel says quietly, trying not to wake the others, most of whom are already getting up. "I don't know what to say."

"I do," Saphrael says, getting out of his cot and walking up to Marceriel. "Where did you get the money for that, Marce?"

"I called in a favor. It didn't cost me anything," Marce says, averting eye contact.

"Marce," Saphrael repeats in a harsher tone.

"I said I called in a favor. I don't want to talk about it." Marce comes face-to-face with Saphrael, directly meeting his challenge.

Cadence, on his cot, says nothing but exchanges a look with Saphrael. Spud snores and turns in his cot.

Gabriel gets up and walks over to Marce. "Thank you, Marceriel."

Marce nods, saying nothing for a long moment. "Anytime, Gabriel," Marce says softly.

Gabriel wants to ask him what's wrong but considers how defensive he got with Saphrael. As Marce looks at him, Gabriel sees something in his eyes. A look of pain? He isn't sure, but he doesn't know Marceriel well enough to pry.

"Really, thanks, Marce," Gabriel repeats.

"Sure," Marce mumbles.

"Would you all shut up?" Loth complains, turning his back to them.

✦

Gabriel sits on the wooden bench inside the shoddy locker room assigned to the Wonder Brigade. Everyone is there, except for Loth, who said he had better things to do than help train a traitor. Gabriel can't help but think about the last time he was here, how dejected he felt after he single-handedly cost them the match against the bats.

He picks up his Chokma mask and stares at his distorted reflection, thinking about how everything the Wonder Brigade did, even the games they played, were devised to sharpen the blade of war.

"How come everything you guys do seems like you're preparing for a war? A war that may never come?" Gabriel asks.

Marceriel looks over at him while tying on a leg plate. "The threat of war is constant. Defenders, aggressors—it makes little difference who wears the self-righteous crown when there is a blade in your back, in the backs of your friends. Peace is fiction, just war taking a breath."

Gabriel looks around the room. "Loth's equipment bag is gone. What am I supposed to wear?"

Saphrael unties an arm guard and holds it out to him.

Gabriel looks at the already sparse armor that Saphrael is wearing. "I couldn't."

"I insist." Saphrael sets the piece of armor on the bench beside him and looks around the room. Cadence tosses a leg plate from across the cramped locker room. Marce sighs, walking forward with a shoulder guard, and drops it in the pile. Spud hands him an arm guard directly.

"Thanks. I don't know what to say," Gabriel says, looking at the equipment.

After gearing up, they head out onto the arena floor, carrying their weapons and Chokma masks.

Cadence and Spud sit a long wooden bench on the sidelines of the floor level, talking to one another as Saphrael, Marce, and Gabriel find an open spot to practice on the arena floor.

"Hey, Wonder Brigade, give up already!" shouts someone from a distance. Gabriel looks back to where the shout came from, scanning the lower-level seating of the amphitheater, but all he sees are other teams resting or preparing to practice.

"Just ignore them," Marce says. "Saphrael is the best fighter we have."

"Go. Find your soulmate," Saphrael says, nodding in the direction of something Gabriel doesn't quite understand.

The only word Gabriel manages to say is "What?"

"Your weapon," Saphrael says, pointing to the weapon racks mounted on the walls.

"Why—why would you say it like that?" Gabriel asks.

Both Marce and Saphrael look at him, trying to figure out what he is on about.

"Like what?" Saphrael asks before exchanging a look with Marce.

"Soulmate, why would you use that word for a weapon?"

"Because that's what soulmates are," Marce says, his words laced with not just anger but confusion.

"No, I mean... on Earth—that's not what it means," Gabriel explains.

Saphrael and Marce look at each other again before Marce rolls his eyes, and Saphrael answers. "I don't know what it means on Earth, Gabriel. But here, your weapon is an extension of yourself, another arm, a part of your soul. You guard your weapon, and it guards you. That's what makes it a soulmate."

Breathing in deeply, Gabriel says, "Okay," before he walks to the weapons racks, Saphrael following.

"There are a lot of things I could tell you about fighting, but no amount of preparation will get you ready for an actual fight. So, it's better to just get to it. Spend some time getting to know the weapon, as well as the other weapons on the racks. Get to know their feel, their weight. Maybe practice with some targets." Saphrael points to the targets, most of which are in use. "Use everything to your advantage. In a real fight, every choice you make or do not make will have severe consequences."

Gabriel scans the weapons, thoughtfully considering the importance of what Saphrael had just said. His fingers trace the handle of a spear at the bottom of the rack, before appraising a large claymore at the top. It has a crossguard that angles down on each side, and its thick blade is etched with runes. While moving to the claymore, a glint off a golden rapier's swirl hilt captures his attention. It is still stained with blood... probably his blood, he thinks, the roar of the crowd after he lost the match with the bats crossing his mind. Drawn to the blade, he picks it up and swings it around, testing its form.

As he does, he gets hit on the leg by an arrow, scraping his skin. Before he can register what happened, several more are fired at him. The incoming arrows tear his clothing and graze his skin, without piercing him. The adversarial group walks up to Gabriel while Marce and Saphrael form up behind him.

"Nice clothes. Freak," says a larger member of the group, this one, unlike the majority of them, does not have a bow in his hands. They form a semicircle around Gabriel, there are roughly ten angels surrounding them. Their Chokma masks are fashioned into the shape of a tiger's head. Gabriel grips the rapier's handle, holding it up defensively.

The team laughs at him.

"Nice choice," one of them says sarcastically. "*Gabriel,* is it?"

"He does kind of look like Gabriel," another one replies, his arms crossed.

"Archangel Gabriel makes a glorious appearance, dressed in rags and a worn-out gambeson, all to join the Wonder Brigade? Yeah, I don't think so," says the leader.

Spud and Cadence join Marce and Saphrael around him.

"Heard you spent some time in the Black Lake?" a shorter one says.

"Must have been so hard," the one to his right says, mockingly. The larger member shoves Gabriel, who stumbles, thrown off psychologically.

"Wonder—how you ever got out." The one who pushed him goes to take a cheap shot. Saphrael glides in front of the punch and blocks the hit.

"Not here. Not now. You want us all to get sent to the cage?" Saphrael grits his teeth.

"Watch yourself, *Gabriel,*" the leader says. The harassing team walks off, laughing.

"Who were they?" Gabriel asks.

"That's the Tigris team. They think they're the best, but they don't ever do well. That's why they live here," Saphrael says.

"That's why they live here?" Gabriel repeats.

"Ranking, winning, determines everything—who gets the most resources, who gets to live in the best places," Saphrael explains.

"What's the cage?"

"Detention barracks... you know, jail." Saphrael says.

"Why didn't the arrows do more damage?" Gabriel looks down at the scrapes from the arrows.

Saphrael shrugs. "As far as I know, archangels are only vulnerable to specific types of metals and to varying degrees at that. My guess is that the metal of the arrows was only strong enough to graze your skin."

"Won't they figure it out?" Gabriel wonders aloud.

"No, there are other ways angels can increase their constitution. Besides, the willfully ignorant only see what they want to see and nothing more."

Cadence and Spud walk back to the bench. Marceriel stands at a distance with his halberd.

"Ready?" Saphrael asks, putting his Chokma mask on.

Gabriel stands on the arena field, his Chokma mask hanging upside down in his right hand.

"Are you okay?" Saphrael asks, taking his helmet off.

"I can't, always, ever really see well with this on," Gabriel admits.

"It's all right. You need to be retrained on how to use magnus sight."

"You still think I'm some lost angel?" Gabriel mumbles quietly.

"Yes, I think we all are." Saphrael motions for Cadence to come over.

"Everything all right?" Cadence asks, trying to figure out if anyone is injured.

"Yes." Saphrael glances at Gabriel. "He doesn't remember how to use his magnus sight. Can you explain it to him?"

"Not a problem," Cadence says, then points to his own pupil. "Magnus sight is the ability to see the range of the ethereal spectrum. The Chokma metal has absorbed enough ethereal radiation because of its close proximity to the point of impact when the cosmoverse shattered."

"Cadence—" Saphrael interrupts. Cadence looks over at him. "He doesn't need to know the academics, just tell him how to use it."

"I thought that's what you were asking me. In any case, let go of your controlled vision. Unfocus it so you can refocus on the other levels of sight."

"What?" Gabriel asks, confused.

Marce rolls his eyes and yells from a distance, "You just want me to hit him really hard?"

Cadence ignores Marce and says, "Just try to make your vision blur with the helmet on, and you should be able to switch over."

Saphrael puts his Chokma mask back on.

Gabriel tightens his grip around the hilt of the rapier and puts on his mask with his other hand.

It's dark inside the cold metal helmet, even the sounds sound different, more industrial. Then, all at once, as if someone had flipped a switch, the world around him lit up with strange bright colors. The arena glows, dimly fluorescing here and there where blood had recently spilled.

Saphrael, standing nearby, is as identifiable as he would have been without his helmet; the bright outline of his features has a semi-transparent purplish-blue glow, brightly lit magenta blood runs through his veins, and he watches as his heart beat inside of his chest.

"Gabriel, Hey! Gabriel! Pay attention." Metal crashes against metal, and Gabriel's head rings. Saphrael knocked him in the side of the mask with the hilt of his sword. After stumbling back, Gabriel finds his footing and blocks the next swing.

Saphrael maneuvers to the side and then advances, utilizing speed and skill to his advantage. Although awkward, Gabriel manages to block with his rapier again and again. A growl emanates from Saphrael's mask as he shoves Gabriel backward anticipating his block.

"You have to do more than just block, Gabriel. This is a fight, so fight." Saphrael stands in a ready position.

Disoriented, he responds by swinging wildly at Saphrael, who backs away from his errant swings. Marceriel puts his Chokma mask on and gets into a fighting stance, his halberd tilted in his hands. He advances, taking a swipe at Gabriel who stumbles back, nearly losing his balance.

"I thought it was one-on-one?" Gabriel says, keeping his distance from them both.

"Yeah…" Marce says, "in real a fight there are no rules. Nothing is fair. Get used to it."

Gabriel dodges another swing from Marce's halberd. Backing up, he focuses on tracking their movements. Saphrael and Marceriel work in tandem as if they were one. They split, advancing on both sides.

Making an odd strategic move, Gabriel drops his rapier onto the ground and takes a fighting stance, waiting for them to come at him. When they attack simultaneously, Gabriel runs bolting forward, out of the way of them both. Saphrael and Marceriel narrowly avoid a collision. Saphrael twists his feet to the side, quickly halting his momentum. Marce's reflexes are not as well trained, and he stumbles forward. Marceriel regains his balance and swings the sharpened blade of his halberd at Gabriel.

After dodging, Gabriel runs at Marce, watching his heartbeat through the Chokma mask's enhanced vision. Marceriel's heartbeat appears to slow as Gabriel moves faster. Lowering his stance, Gabriel spears him with his shoulder. As Marce slams into the ground, he drops his halberd. Gabriel lifts him up in a chokehold. Marce manages to choke out, "Okay! Okay!"

As soon as Gabriel lets him go, Marce punches him in the midsection, impacting his most recent wound.

"Hey!" Gabriel shouts in pain before racing to grab Marce's halberd, taking hold of it defensively.

"There are no rules in a real fight," Marce says, enunciating every word.

"You know there is such a thing as hon—" Halfway through saying the word "honor," Gabriel feels a cold pain slice through his midsection on his left side.

"Honor gets you killed," Saphrael says, letting go of the blade.

In disbelief, he drops the halberd and turns to Saphrael before looking down at the sword impaling him. Blood trickles from the corner of his lips, his hand rests near the sword, body curled inward.

"Come on, Gabriel, fight. Get up," Saphrael says, taking a sparring stance.

His only response is to scream, a scream that reverberates throughout the arena.

"You think that hurts? You think that hurts? You are facing threats far worse than anything we can throw at you. You expect to defeat Emperor Lucius? You can't even take a hit, pathetic." Marce spits on the ground before he retrieves his halberd, gripping it tightly as he turns back to face him.

"Marce… We're here to train him how to take a hit," Saphrael warns.

"I'll train him. Train him not to cry over every little thing. You think that he stands a chance of survival here? I don't." Marce shifts his weight to his right side and sidekicks the hilt of the blade, lodging the sword within him fully.

The kick knocks Gabriel off his feet and onto the ground, where the sword is painfully forced at an angle, warm blood soaks into a puddle around him, obscuring the bottom half of his vision. Saphrael and Marce are arguing. Their words begin to fade as Gabriel loses consciousness. The last thing he sees is the unit's healer, Cadence, running up to him.

Chapter 12

As the days pass, Dawn has been spending more and more time alone, at least that's how it feels. Stacks of books sit on shelves and tables, with even more piled on the floor. Much of her time on Earth was spent avoiding people, and now she just wants someone to talk to.

As she sits at her small ornate silver table, she briefly looks at the purple-flamed candle on the candelabrum. Then she turns to the stack of books on her table and picks up a small black journal from the top. She opens a bottle of black ink and picks up a wooden-handled dip pen with a silver nib. She isn't used to writing with it but has been practicing.

Lucius orders guards to escort me to his study frequently. I have no way to keep track of time here. In one of our last meetings, Lucius explained that cycles, as days are called here, are gauged on Tiphareth's relative position to Sine. Yet the star is dormant and doesn't provide adequate light or heat. Most days I can't see through the fog to even try to see the faint dot in the sky. When I can see it, it only reminds me of home. I guess this is my home now, isn't it? Nothing feels right without Gabriel. I'm not allowed to talk about him, yet, for some reason I'm allowed to write about him. Lucius is gone for some important meeting, though he will be back soon. Meanwhile, Adam is in charge. I have been told to expect a visit, but I'm not sure I want him to be around, especially with Lucius being gone.

A knock on her door breaks her concentration.

"Yes?" She leaves the journal open on the table.

She gets up and walks to the door. As she walks, the tail of her long dress glides on the floor—one of her new dresses that Ketis, her tailor, dreamed up. It has an exposed back, is primarily deep purple with accents of black. Its material is like satin, form-fitting and comfortable.

After she opens the door, Adam walks in, dressed how he always is, in an officer's uniform. To the sides of the door are the ever-present but silent masked royal guards.

"Hi, Adam." Dawn smiles softly, happy to at least have someone to talk to.

He inclines his head and nods in the direction of the door. Together they walk down the corridor, guards trailing behind.

"Where are we going? I thought Lucius was going to be away?" Dawn asks, catching up with him.

"That's true. I have been tasked with taking care of you, along with everything else."

He didn't sound annoyed about it. Perhaps he was good at hiding it, or maybe he really didn't mind.

"Where are we going?" Dawn asks as she falls into step beside him.

"Not far, it's one of my favorite places."

They make their way down sets of stairs to the main floor of the citadel. As they walk down the hall, a wingless angel with white irises looks at them. Adam walks by, not bothering to even glance in the man's direction. "Come along, Dawn."

Dawn stares at the stranger's white irises, snow-white hair, and matching uniform before forcing herself to follow.

After a short distance, she asks, "Who was that?"

"His name is Zunael. He's another one of your father's advisers."

"Oh, what does he advise?"

"Many things, Dawn, none of which are your concern."

"You don't like him, do you?"

Adam stops, looks at her, and half-shrugs. "It is not my place to question your father's choice of advisers."

They reach a set of dark reddish-brown wooden double doors. Even though the paint is peeling off due to its age, it holds a quiet elegance. The guards take their place along the sides of the entrance.

"I imagine you might require some peace." Adam opens the door to a spacious room with incredibly high ceilings and statues lining the walls. There are rows and rows of ornate dark-brown wooden pews.

"What is this place?" Dawn asks as she leans in, taking a closer look at one of the statues. She is fairly sure it is a statue of an angel, but it has no wings. It looks to be in good condition for as old as it must be.

"Is this a church?" Dawn asks.

"It's more of a museum, a monument to a bygone era. Although I guess the more appropriate word for it would be chapel." Adam strolls down the aisle between the pews. He stops in the middle, takes a sharp right, and sits at the end of the long wooden bench before tilting his head to the side in a gesture for her to join him.

In the center of the room, on a rise, is a large dark-cherry-red box that is ornately carved with floral designs.

"What is that?" Dawn asks, looking at the box.

"It's an altar."

"I've never been inside a church before."

"I can tell." Adam pauses. As he holds her gaze, his expression softens. "You look so much like your mother, a relic from a lost time."

"And you're not?"

"Touché," Adam says with a smile forming on the corner of his lips.

"Why do you talk like that, anyway?"

"Talk like what, my dear?"

"Like Lucius?"

"Tell me, what is it you expect me to sound like?"

"Well… not like Lucius. I guess, not like anything. I don't know."

"Lucius, I suppose, is someone I have been around for several thousands of years. It is not unlikely that I would form speech patterns that are similar to his in that regard."

"I guess that makes sense. Have you started thinking like him, too?"

"I suppose I have."

"Aren't you worried about that? Shouldn't you be yourself instead of someone like him?"

"Dawn, Adam died long ago. Now, I exist with purpose. My reason for being, as it were, is to be whatever Lucius needs."

"Why?"

"You wouldn't understand." He leaves it at that. Perhaps ignoring the conversation, Adam kneels, resting his hands on the back of the pew in front of him.

Dawn watches him. After a few moments, she asks, "What are you doing?"

"I'm praying." Adam straightens his uniform as he rises, returning to the pew.

"I thought this wasn't a church."

"My dear, one doesn't need to be in a church in order to pray. I come here often to do so. It seems like the most appropriate place."

"What did you wish for?"

"Dawn, praying is not wishing. But if you put it that way, I wished for a decent life. I also prayed for you."

"I'm fine. I don't need prayer," Dawn says a little too defensively, thinking of when people would tell her they would pray for her when she was homeless.

"Sometimes, hope is enough to get you through another day. Prayer is hope, hope that things will get better. But we must forge that path ourselves, don't we?" he says, turning to look directly at her, then adds, "Do have a chat. With someone besides Lucius sometime. Come now, I have something to show you."

✦

"Wait." Dawn steps back from an exceptionally tall set of intricately carved black wooden doors. There is a symbol forged at the top. No one has told her, but she knows it is Lucius's sign. "Are we leaving the citadel?"

Adam waits patiently by the doors.

"Yes, but not the forbidden realm. It will be all right, Dawn."

"Lucius told me never to leave the citadel." Dawn shakes her head and takes another step back. Even though she asked Lucius if she could leave sometime, she can't shake the feeling that something is wrong.

Adam sighs. "Your father is correct. However, you are under my supervision. We are only going to my quarters. It is not far."

"Lucius said—" Dawn pleads.

"I know what Lucius said." Adam takes a moment to collect himself before adding, "Dawn, I vow to you I will protect you, if necessary."

Adam opens one of the large ornate doors. As she steps outside, she is hit with a blast of cold air. It is even colder than inside the citadel. The chill wind blows back Dawn's hair and stings her skin. She listens to the rhythmic beat of their footsteps as they make their way down stairs that never seem to end, although far into the distance she can see the courtyard and a myriad of stone path ways.

She stops to look at the pale stone statues that adorn the sides of the stairs. One in particular captures her attention. It is a human on their knees. It reminds her of the woman in the mural on her door. She assumes that it's Lilith. The statue of Lilith is wearing flowing robes that look just like what Dawn wore in the arboretum. Her mind flashes to the horrors she saw near the end of the blood flower memories.

In front of it are statues of three angels. The center angel has a sword drawn, pointed directly at Lilith. The statue of the sword-wielding angel, wings outstretched, her expression carved so realistically, inspires fear.

Stopping as soon as she did, Adam stands silently as she looks at the statues.

Dawn nods and looks over to him. "Maybe—maybe you could tell me about that sometime?"

"I cannot. My memories of that time are blocked or long forgotten. I only know the legends."

"You could tell me them, too."

"I'm afraid that I don't want to unintentionally cloud the truth. Best to talk to Lucius, perhaps gain entry to the vault."

"What's the vault?"

Adam starts walking again, toward the four buildings Dawn can see from her room and Dawn walks beside him.

"It is a collection of knowledge, in the form of books, scrolls, and things of that nature. Located in the deepest levels under the citadel. I'm unsure how many levels the vault actually occupies. Legend has it that when a book disappears from Earth, a copy of it finds its way into the vault."

Dawn is quiet as they continue walking. Once they reach the four oblong buildings, they turn to the first one on the right. Adam opens the door, and they walk inside. There is barely any sign that someone lives here.

"I don't spend much time here," Adam says, as he picks up some clothes from an end table. It is a plain set of clothing, with buckle straps down the right-hand side of the long-sleeved shirt. He holds out the plain black uniform.

"Why do I need that?" Dawn asks, looking at the clothing.

"It is a standard-issue gambeson uniform. Put it on. I have a test for you." Adam holds out the long-sleeved shirt-jacket and matching pants.

"Okay? What kind of test?"

Adam turns away, but doesn't leave the room, nor does he answer her question. Dawn sighs as she takes off her boots and slips the pants on under her dress. Then she turns away from him as she takes off her dress and puts on the rest of the uniform. Her uniform is plain black with no insignia or name tag. The buckles on the shirt-jacket are made of black metal. She places her dress on the side table, then sits on the floor to put her boots back on.

"I'm done," Dawn says, standing up.

Adam turns to face her. "Shall we proceed?"

Dawn follows Adam into a dark and increasingly narrow hallway. Normally, she isn't claustrophobic, but she can't stop her heart rate from spiking as they descend a set of winding stairs made of untreated planks of wood, haphazardly put together, which creak under their footsteps. Blue crystal lights behind a simple orb of glass dot the black stone walls, providing dim light.

At the bottom of the stairs is an empty room. In the distance sits an old dark-red wooden door. It reminds Dawn of the door to Gabriel's house, but the sense of safety that Gabriel's door projected is absent. This door gives her an unpleasant feeling that nudges at her subconscious.

"Don't be afraid," Adam says as he unlatches a lock on the outside of the door.

Dawn flinches as the old wooden door creaks open. Adam holds it for her, waiting for her to enter. Echoing from inside the room is the strangest cry, a half-whine, half-growl. Dawn steps into the dimly lit room. At the far end is a small, rusted metal cage. He observes her silently. Dawn walks in slowly and stops, gasping, her eyes wide as she shakes her head and turns around. But Adam closes the door and shoves a plank of wood that locks the door from the inside.

"What is going on?" Dawn asks in desperation.

Adam points to the cage at the far end of the room. She squints, straining to see. Suddenly, something hurls itself against the bars. It's some sort of creature. It looks up at Dawn and suddenly stops its mournful cry. Then it looks at Adam and snarls, thick saliva and green blood drip down its sharp teeth. A similar green substance is oozing out of the porous holes in its discolored skin.

"What—what is it?" Dawn asks, walking closer, straining to get a better look at the creature through the bars of its cage.

"This is one of your mother's creations. It is a demon—more specifically, a rage demon. Demons tend to conform to an emotion, be it lust, rage, greed, cardinal sins, and so forth. This one is considered a weaker demon—a child, if you will." Adam hands Dawn a ceremonial-looking axe. It reminds Dawn of a rune-engraved Viking axe, except instead of runes, it is adorned with angelic sigils. They must be wards, she assumes, that do not translate. The demon's eyes fixate on her. The axe weighs heavy in her hands.

"Demons rarely react this way to anyone, yet your mother being the mother of demons…"

"Does—does that make me a demon?"

"No, Dawn, you are clearly something else."

Dawn looks at Adam, swallows hard, and slowly approaches the cage. The creature has oddly formed growths under its discolored, dull gray skin. Its eyes are entirely black, and its arms are longer than its legs. There are claws on its hands and feet. It is hunched over by a crooked spine and is naked.

"What is it you want me to do?" Dawn asks, looking at Adam before turning her attention to the demon.

The demon stares back at her. In its large pitch-black eyes, she can see her reflection holding the axe. Suddenly, it hurls itself against the bars. Metal screams as the door swings open. The creature charges at her. She trips backward. Adam catches her as she falls. The axe clangs onto the ground.

Still with Dawn in his arms, Adam boots the demon in the face, knocking it back. Then Adam shoves Dawn toward the demon. It lunges at her but stops inches from her face, calmly sniffing her. It looks up curiously and blinks with its strange, fully black eyes.

"Interesting," Adam says thoughtfully.

Hand shaking, Dawn holds onto the demon's hand, and leads it back to its cage.

"The axe, Dawn."

"No." Dawn glares at Adam before turning back to the demon and begins singing.

She has the hypnotizing voice of a siren. The demon lies down and falls asleep listening to her. Adam says nothing. Dawn looks at him afterward, and he seems dazed.

"Adam?"

He shakes his head out of the trance he is in and nods at her. Adam walks forward and secures the lock on the cage.

For a moment, he rests his hand on her shoulder. "Come, you should get home."

As they walk, Adam doesn't talk. Dawn isn't entirely sure why. He carries her dress, as she is still in the standard black uniform. Guards meet them at the citadel's entrance and follow them inside. When they reach her room, the guards hold the doors open.

Adam hands Dawn her dress, which she sets on her bed.

"How long are you going to keep it in that cage?" Dawn asks.

"As long as necessary. Make no mistake, they are vile creatures." Adam pauses before he says, "Get some rest."

"I always have nightmares," Dawn complains, looking to the side, staring at the wall. "I don't like sleeping."

"Well, Dawn, I know you are accustomed to sleeping. I don't know if you necessarily have to sleep. Something to think about. Goodnight," he says, looking her in the eyes before shutting the door. He still has a strange, far-off look.

She glances at her mirror. Admiring the way the uniform looks on her before sitting down on her black heart-shaped chair with the comfortable burgundy cushion. Resting her elbows on her table, she glances at the bar covered flower-shaped window, thinking about the demon alone in the cold, dark basement.

✦

Lucius gazes across a vast sea of cloudy light-blue luminescent water whose edges and creases project a soft pastel multi-hued glow that shines brightly where the light hits, like a pearl. He removes a small corked hexagonal glass vial from an inner jacket pocket, opens it, and fills it with the luminescent water. After pocketing the vial, he takes out a finely crafted black journal from a pocket in his overcoat and starts writing in it with a black fountain pen with a gold nib.

Dawn, I wish you could see the beautiful waters that cover this realm of Zera. It is far too dangerous for you to accompany me to this meeting. I understand you are rightfully upset that the book on the Promethean Angels was incomplete. Allow me to rectify the situation by writing to you in this journal. I shall do my best to present you with knowledge.

My daughter, you have reminded me of the power and mysteries of life. I miss your mother greatly, although—truth be told, I'm not sure she was ever truly mine to begin with. Odd, I do not sense such outright defiance in you.

The light-blue and white waters that cover this planet are calming to say the least. Long ago, Raphael the Archangel of Healing, cleansed these waters. Careless of him to expend that much raw energy to transform this once acidic ocean world. Now these waters possess healing properties.

There is a black ring far above the atmosphere that protects this realm as it was unnaturally requisitioned from Earth's universe, from a system close to the Alpha Orionis system; you may know it for its star, Betelgeuse.

A black hole was tearing the system apart. We decided to save what we could of the system and its star, Crea. Only one planet and the star survived the journey. They were hauled by a former lover of mine, Uriel. She used a powerful device known as the Nox Obitus. Forged by a brilliant engineer named Kyael. Long ago, it was used to quell the dinosaur populations on Earth. Uriel, in her anger, attempted to turn the Nox Obitus against humanity. She acted in haste and miscalculated the planetary orbits. In doing so she obliterated a planet known as Pallas, it was the fifth planet from your sun. The remains of Pallas have long since been reduced to an asteroid belt that exists between the inner and outer planets of your Sol System.

The Nox Obitus now resides in the pinnacle of the highest and central peak of the Crown Spire, a building that houses offices for the Divine Council. The Crown Spire is a circular building with eight entrances, one for each archangel. A stone sigil above the door marks whose passage it is. The building is stone as well, glossy pitch black laced with shimmering silver in an erratic pattern like that of broken glass. When viewed from afar the building resembles the shape of a crown, each of the arching spire an entrance.

The central spire always faces Crea because the Nox Obitus holds the realm firmly in place. The very top of the Crown Spire pierces the black ring around the atmosphere.

I cannot write much longer as the meeting is set to start soon. I wish you could see the architecture here. Most buildings are white granite veined with metals as are the circular platforms that make up the ground above this water world.

The buildings are generally uniform, made primarily of the same white stone, besides the Crown Spire, of course. There are golden statues placed like guardians at entrances and windows of most buildings. The structures generally have a circular arching top, much like the buildings your senate employs. There is a similar type of ultimately useless system here as well, called the tribunals. They are composed of an equal number of members from each side of the higher realms. I have just finished reviewing papers from the tribunals: proposals, amendments, anything I need to review.

I do hope Adam is taking care of you in my absence.

Your father,

Lucius

Lucius gazes at the waters once more before turning back and walking past groups of guards with no acknowledgment to them. Although the tribunals are split evenly between the Sine and Crown Realms, the guards on this realm are a branch of Mikhail's army known as the Finitimus. The Finitimus uniform is silver with white trim. It is as ceremonial as it is functional. It features long sleeves wide enough for concealed weapons and a large skirt. Their fighting technique is uniquely designed to hide stance, weapons, everything—to obscure what an enemy knows and can anticipate.

A set of assigned Finitimus guards stand on each side of his door to the Crown Spire. The door is marked with his sigil. A statue of Lucius is on a ledge above, depicting him when he had wings; they are outstretched and dominate where the eye is drawn to, even above the glowing purple orb in the outstretched palm of the statue. Dark emotions threaten to surface. Lucius tilts his head back and centers himself.

Light glints off the silver metal mask of the guard standing to Lucius's right. Every member of Finitimus has the same mask regardless of rank. It is a neutral face, unidentifiable in gender, yet slim, angelic features lean toward the feminine.

He strides into his office on his way to the Divine Council's Inner Sanctum. Like most of his living spaces, this one is filled with artifacts and mementos of times long past. The rooms are divided, half into an office and the other half into a living space. Doors leading to the sanctum are only accessible from a council member's designated space. Quarters for the dead archangels, built in honor of their memory, have gone on unused.

Lucius stands before a large gray stone door at the end of the room. The door is inscribed with warnings and symbols written in the most basic Enochian script, followed by a poem.

Immortalis Immurement awaits any who trespass against this sacred ground.

In darkness, you repent.
Pain, your sole companion
Your scream is silence.

The stone itself has been processed by alchemists into tinisium. The material is formulated to burn away, but only while an archangel's flame touches it. Rapid self-healing properties allow it to reform nearly immediately after the flame is no longer active. Lucius holds up his palm, and purple flame melts the barrier.

He steps into a faintly glowing midnight blue tunnel that leads to the Divine Council's Inner Sanctum, known as the Heart Chamber. It is located in the very center of the cosmoverse. Traditionally, when one traverses these tunnels, they undergo a form of meditation known as the Walk of Contemplation to temper emotions and allow one time to gather their thoughts. The funeral hymn-like sound, hauntingly loud in the Ethereal Realm, is muffled as if the spirits singing were far, far away. This "music" lowers in volume the further one descends.

As he nears the final door, which is made of dark wood and not tinisium stone, he steadies himself, taking a deep breath and steeling his mind for the confrontation ahead. Lucius straightens his Victorian-esque black overcoat and walks through the door into an expansive oval-shaped room with high ceilings that is Inner Sanctum. The walls match the large oval table made of ornate white stone veined with smatterings of gold and silver. It has an iridescent shine, like white fire opal. Around the table are eight large elegantly carved dark-brown wooden thrones, each aligned to a door. The most striking feature is the rounded ceiling above that burns with a warm bright blue light. It looks like clouds composed of fire raging violently. Taking the time to view the chaotic fire storm of what is the heart of Hurbur. It is no less majestic now than seeing it for the first time.

Beside the doors are sets of paintings each archangel has chosen. The pillars between the paintings contain candles. Each of Lucius's chosen paintings are flanked by purple-flamed white candles. The barrier has fail-safes—if someone unauthorized touches the barrier or the candle, they would lose all of their senses until broken by an incantation spoken by an archangel. The candles reserved for the yellow flames and green flames remain unlit.

Through the blue mists, at the other end of the table is Chancellor Gabriel with an impatient expression. He is a near-perfect replica of the other Gabriel. Although no one would mistake one for the other. Chancellor Gabriel commands an air of confidence, his eyes are a brighter, lighter shade of blue, and his hair is more yellow-blond in tone. He wears standard regalia for one from the Crown Realms, light silver robes with a pale-blue stole accented with white, crossed in the center, his sigil embroidered on the ends. Large archangel wings sit folded behind him. Through magnus vision, Lucius views the bright, colorful aura encompassing Chancellor Gabriel. He can easily read physical and spiritual health as well as emotional disposition, among other things. Reading his aura, Lucius observes that Gabriel seems well prepared for their meeting.

"Thank you for coming." His voice reserved, Gabriel briefly nods.

Lucius inclines his head, then acknowledges Mikhail, who is standing near her door. Mikhail's uniform is white with red accents, and the symbol of the crown's army, Unus, sits near her upper right chest. Unlike her subordinates, she wears a simple golden armlet cuff lined with bloodstone beads. Her midnight-blue archangel wings add to the glow in the blue mists around her. Her physical aura is strong and full of vitality, yet her mental disposition as indicated by a faint yellow glow, that can appear as orange and even red, is weak indicating she is weary.

"Gabriel, I have important things to do. I simply do not have time to entertain whatever it is you want to talk about. Yet, in the spirit of diplomacy I am here. This meeting was arranged outside the set schedule. I do not appreciate the discourtesy you have displayed," Lucius says, sitting down directly opposite of Gabriel across the long rounded-oval table.

Chancellor Gabriel's stone-cold ice-blue eyes level with Lucius's. His hardened expression makes no apology. "I know you must be busy with an entire system to subjugate."

"Refrain from your pleasantries, Gabriel." Lucius waves a dismissive hand in his direction.

"Very well. I wish to discuss changes," Chancellor Gabriel says, leaning back in his chair. "I wish to amend the *Treaty of Ordo* with the name of my successor."

"As do I. You do realize once you seal your successor, that individual is bound by the same constraints as you are, correct?" Lucius eyes narrow, closely watching his response.

"And yours as well."

"I hardly think that is fair. Do you? Besides, successors must be aware that they are chosen and willing to fill the role. Tell me, Gabriel, is your successor aware and willing?"

"No," Gabriel says, barely audible. "No," he says louder. "My successor has not yet been informed."

"Then why are we here?" Lucius's voice is low as he forcefully enunciates every word.

Mikhail's hand rests on the hilt of her sword. She is the only archangel allowed to carry a physical weapon into the chambers.

"So, we are in agreement that successors need not be bound to the same restrictions as we are?" Gabriel asks.

Lucius offers him a smile and says, "No, by all means they should adhere to the law."

Chancellor Gabriel studies him in silence, before saying, "You're fine condemning your daughter, binding her fate with yours to that accursed place you call home. See reason, old friend. Allow them passage to the

Crown Realms where they can live under my protection."

"Protection from what, Gabriel?"

"Protection from you. They would be much happier in the crown. You know that."

Lucius fails to hide his anger. The silence in the room is deafening.

After a few moments, Chancellor Gabriel sighs and says, "Give me my successor and I will stay out of your affairs regarding your daughter. I will also compel my son to follow suit. He would be bound to the Crown Realms, after all."

"Is that an offer or a threat?"

"Can't it be both? I needn't remind you that you recently set foot upon Earth, which is a clear punitive violation if found guilty, which we both know you are. Regardless, I could find a way to forgive this transgression and encourage the tribunals to do the same. The Tribunal of War is already assembling."

"I agree to nothing."

"You risk all-out war?"

"And you do? Or have you forgotten that nine out of every ten citizens of the higher realms are under my jurisdiction? No, I'm afraid you hold no leverage. Gather the council against me, it makes no difference." Lucius stands up to leave but lingers for a moment. "Tell me, Gabriel, have you informed your people about the existence of the other Gabriel?"

"No," Chancellor Gabriel says, looking off to the side.

"Nonetheless, your secret was found out." Lucius turns to Mikhail. "And you, you're fine with him breaking the rules over the existence of his son?" Then Lucius turns back to Gabriel. "Tell me, why try to hide something so big? Did you err on purpose? Or was it all just a mistake? You clearly had improper follow-through."

Without a word. Gabriel gets up, ignoring Lucius's existence, and heads to his door.

"Do send my regards to Uriel," Lucius calls after him.

Gabriel answers by slamming his door.

Lucius turns to Mikhail. "Did you know?"

"No," Mikhail says, her expression gives away nothing.

"Pleasure as always to see you, Michael."

"Lucifer." Mikhail nods in acknowledgment.

"When the time comes, I do hope that you will fight for what is right, even if I happen to be on that side."

"Good day, Lucius."

Mikhail exits the Inner Chambers through her own door marked by a red candle.

✦

The gray stone floor of the dark basement is cold and discolored, with splotches of dried bodily fluids. Adam picks up the sigil-engraved axe. Adrenaline pumps through him as he tightens his grip around the handle. A sadistic half-smirk forms on the corner of his lips. The axe's blade is sharp but does not shine in the dull light.

With a flat expression, he stares in the direction of the rusted cage before slowly walking over and unlatching the metal door. The demon growls at him before he stomp-kicks the side of the cage, booting it straight into the back wall. The cage lands on its side with a bang, door hanging open. The deformed creature cowers against the back of its small, rusted cage. Impatiently, Adam thrusts his arm in and chokes the demon, dragging it out by its throat.

He lifts it into the air and throws it. The creatures already open wounds smear green blood as it hits the wall. It crashes onto the ground with a thud. Adam waits, unmoving like a predator stalking its prey. The demon gets up and charges, running on all fours, screaming in wild desperation. Its scream is high-pitched and more of a gurgle. Adam grins, axe held at the ready. He aims for its body and waits for the perfect timing to swing. Gliding forward, he hacks into the demon's left shoulder. It howls in pain before dropping to the ground, its arm still attached by a small strip of flesh. The demon desperately crawls, trying to get back to the safety of its cage.

Adam stomps on its back, then swings the axe, bashing its throat with the wooden end of the axe handle. The strip of flesh holding its right arm tears completely, leaving a deformed arm lying on the ground next to the demon, who is struggling to breathe. Green blood sputters from its mouth and pours from its armless left shoulder.

Dropping down, Adam drives his knee into the side of the demon's face. Shifting his weight, he presses down, pinning it in place before he takes a deep breath and attempts to ignore the rotten acidic stench of demonic blood. The demon swipes at him but only manages to nick the cuff of his black uniform undershirt.

Adam gets up, swings around, and drives the axe blade into its neck, severing its head from its body. Rivers of dark green blood pour out onto the floor.

Slinging his jacket over his shoulder, Adam carries the axe in his other hand. The pungent smell of demonic blood hangs heavy in the air as he leaves, making his way up the narrow stairwell and setting the axe against the wall of his bedroom. After undressing, he picks up a beige linen towel and dips it into a rustic leaf-shaped metal basin sitting on his dresser. The unique metal keeps the water warm. It is one of the few luxury items he owns. He wrings it out before wiping himself down, and sets the towel back in the basin. The green blood gets pulled into the water and then vanishes, returning to the pristine warm waters it was moments ago. He picks up the cloth and wrings the water out. If he left it in the basin, it, too, would eventually break down into nothing.

Turning to his closet full of standard-issue uniforms, he pulls out a new set. Being one of the highest ranks in the legion, if he wanted to wear different clothing, he could—with approval for the design, of course. However, he enjoys the stability and reassurance this life provides.

His heart starts to calm down from the intensity of the excursion. He hoped that the exercise would be cathartic, but has not found that to be the case. Adam briefly thinks about being the only human in the Sine System. *No, I'm not the only human here, not anymore. Dawn's part human, isn't she?*

He considers this as he changes. *Why is she here?* Which raises the question of how she is even in existence. Angels are not able to procreate. It is the balance of their immortality.

What a stepping stone in power it would be to marry her. No, I was once in love with her mother. Would that be morally gray or acceptable? Neither, he thinks, *there are different rules for those who have lived for so long. Isn't there?*

His mind continues to wander until it lands upon Lilith. He hasn't been able to stop thinking about the idea of her since Dawn arrived. His first love, or so he has been told. He glances at the axe dripping with dark green blood, and part of him wonders just what he has become.

Glancing at his mirror beside his closet, an image flashes in his mind. It's Adam, but Adam from long ago. His reflection shows the same black hair, but his demeanor is different, untouched by what he has gone through. He is innocent. He is caring. *He is dead,* he tells himself.

Forcing the image from his mind, his vision refocuses on his present-day appearance in his crisp uniform. Smoothing out his hair before putting on his officer's cap, Adam lifts his head, watching the mirror as he straightens his uniform, ensuring absolutely everything is in order.

Chapter 13

T he celestial timepiece sits on her silver table, near her candelabrum, the center of which glows brightly, indicating the time of day. The golden branches of the timepiece hang off a black cylindrical trunk, each holding an orb representing a realm of the system. The base of the celestial timepiece is a semi-translucent black octagon-shaped crystal. In the center of the crystal is an orbital map. The entire timepiece sits in the center of a circular navigational chart of the system made of some strange black leather.

She looks at the faint glow of the central crystal representing Sine before scanning the symbols written in High Enochian, she has been trying to learn. Her eyes rest on the third realm from the center, one labeled Geburah. That's where she and Adam were heading today, to go to an amphitheater known as the Axion. She has been ready for hours and is excited to go, even though last time she left the citadel, she had what she likes to think of as a nightmare, the demon encounter.

Her surprisingly comfortable dress is a rich, deep violet with a metallic sheen of blues that frame her figure beautifully with highlighted tones as varied as the sea. The signature of her dress is a large crystalline, semi-transparent purple rose that covers the entire right half of her bodice. The rose doesn't appear to be made of any material she has ever seen before—not quite glass, not quite stone. The texture and thickness of the extraordinarily large crystalline rose is like that of well-made, soft parchment. The long-sleeved dress features strips of purple fabric tied around her upper arms, just above the elbow, and hanging from a soft purple cloth belt is a pennant-shaped violet fabric that accents the giant rose.

The bulk of her hair rests down her back, while the top is composed of a series of braids woven into a larger crown wrapped around her head, the braids are adorned with metal rings and diamond-cut amethyst gems. On the back of the crown of braids sits a heavy, metal emperor's crest.

Ketis and his assistants had brought in her outfit as soon as the light started shining blue in the time crystal. Hours had passed as they prepared her hair and makeup. She tried to tell them that she could do it herself, but Ketis explained that today was going to be the first day many would get a chance to see her, and because of that, everything had to be perfect.

Alone and bored, Dawn starts to sing and dance. The ribbons of her dress float gracefully, like ribbons of a midsummer's maypole. The petals of the rose ruffle before settling. She stops dancing and turns to her mirror, sighing. The right side of her double doors opens, and Adam strides in, before stopping next to the door.

"Hi, Adam." Dawn walks up, and they leave her room; the masked royal guards follow close behind. Adam doesn't seem to be in the mood to talk, so she silently walks beside him as they journey down the winding stone stairs, passing the spot where he had thrown her into the wall when she tried to run when they first met. Her heart races, and she tries to tell herself, again, that it was a nightmare, though she knows that it wasn't.

Another set of royal guards joins them as they leave the citadel's main entrance, following down the grand stairs lined with rows of statues.

Dawn stops and shivers from the frigid temperature, but Adam keeps walking. Something seems off about him. She has no idea what. *Maybe he is just normally like this, and our conversation the other day was the exception,* she thinks.

As they reach the end of the grand stairs, they turn to the right of the citadel, heading to a sigil burned into the ground. It is a circle marked with various symbols written in High Enochian that do not translate. It reminds

Dawn of a helicopter pad, but much larger.

"This is your first time traveling between the realms," Adam says, finally talking to her. "You will see a flash of light and it will be over before you know it." Adam hands her a crystal.

The markings on the inside of the crystal represent the realms of the Sine System. The design matches the orbital pattern of the timepiece in her room.

Two of four royal guards with their silver-white faceless masks vanish before her eyes. The other two wait for Adam and Dawn to follow.

"Step into the sigil and concentrate on Geburah, the third realm from the center on the map in the crystal."

Dawn nods and steps into the sigil. She instinctively squeezes the warm crystal tightly and imagines the celestial timepiece pattern, concentrating on Geburah. Suddenly, she feels detached from her physical self, shot like a bullet, rapidly launching forward through deep blue energy. She stares at her hands in wonder. They are dark magenta and semi-transparent, as if she were nothing but a spirit. The crystal, affixed to the palm of her right hand, glows a brilliant white.

In a flash, she opens her eyes and finds herself somewhere else. She looks at the crystal. It seems ordinary, besides the map etched in the center.

The air is filled with the chatter of a lively, densely packed crowd. The two royal guards who went ahead are positioned around the sigil, warding off anyone from coming near. Dawn feels exposed and out of place. Most of the crowd is wearing uniforms similar to the one she had on the other day when she faced the demon. The angular-faced men of those not wearing silver masks seem astounded as they stop out of shock before forcing themselves to ignore her. Their jovial voices drop to a hushed tone as they walk past.

She waits for Adam but doesn't see him anywhere. That is, until a solidified shadow, like a specter whose features are highlighted by a brilliant white, fades into existence beside her, solidifying into Adam in the blink of an eye. The two guards appear beside him moments later. Part of her didn't think that it would work, but here they are. There is an aura of blue highlighting everything in the area, which gets brighter around the edges of the land. She has been told that the realm of Geburah is unique, as the surface is entirely covered in an ocean of blue fire. *Well, at least it's warm here*, she thinks.

Adam steps onto the gray cobblestone path that leads to the giant oval-shaped amphitheater. There are stalls outside of the Axion selling banners, cloaks, and knick-knacks, each roughly large enough for the merchant and their wares. Dawn stares at the fabric hanging down the top of the merchant stalls, staying close to Adam.

As they approach the dominating structure, Dawn inhales sharply, stopping dead in her tracks, when she notices prisoners in metal masks chained, their arms spread to each side, pinning them into place on their knees. These unfortunate souls line the outer walls. No one bothers to look at them, except those inflicting physical abuse. Dawn winces and turns away as a prisoner near an entrance gets chest-stomped backward, but only as far as the taunt chains allow before they hold him in position. His silver metal mask faces downward before he lifts his head back into an upright position. No matter how he tries to hold his posture, he is clearly exhausted.

"What is going on here?" Dawn looks at Adam, who is a few feet ahead of her.

"What exactly are you referring to, my dear?" Adam says, sounding impatient.

"Those prisoners are being abused. What did they do to deserve this?"

"They are being corrected. Trust that there is a reason for everything." Adam stands waiting for her.

"But—there can't possibly be a reasonable explanation for this."

"You will find life much easier if you do not question what cannot be changed."

Dawn falls silent as they walk under an archway that leads to the emperor's box. Adam gestures to a seat near the emperor's large, ornate throne. He takes a seat next to Dawn, leaving the emperor's chair open.

"You really must begin to understand the way things work around here.

The fittest thrive, as nature has always intended," Adam says.

"I am a pacifist."

"You won't be for long," Adam states as if it were fact.

Dawn looks out onto the Axion floor, crossing her arms. As she scans the packed stands, she feels something is off. Then she realizes there are only men as far as she can see.

"Why are there only men here?"

"You're here," Adam says, not even turning to look at her.

"That is not what I asked."

"This is not Earth, and they are not strictly male. Angels are trans-binary; they can appear any way that they choose."

"Oh, but—"

"There are things you do not understand, culturally speaking."

Dawn glares at him before looking at no particular spot on the divider in front of them.

"You could explain," Dawn says, annoyed.

"It's cultural."

"If they are angels, where are their wings?"

"Again, cultural."

Dawn slams back into her chair. She looks at the reddened dirt of the Axion floor—no doubt darkened by blood.

"Why did you insist on bringing me here? This place looks barbaric."

"Barbarity is one being closer to nature, is it not? So-called civilized societies from your world play courtroom games of words and paper, followed by mass executions called war. I hardly think that system of killing is any less barbaric."

Dawn's attention is drawn to the Axion floor. The crowd erupts into cheers as a flood of dinosaurs runs out onto the large open space. They are small for dinosaurs, but still twice her size, and extremely agile. *Must be some type of raptor*, she thinks. Her eyes widen, and she winces as arrows skewer the dinosaurs. One falls hard onto the Axion floor, skidding into the divider in front of them.

A rain of arrows follows, darkening the skies. The sheer number of arrows offers the dinosaurs little chance, as none escape being hit and most fall to the ground. The crowd is deafeningly loud.

"What is the point of this?" Dawn looks at Adam.

"It is based on legend, a metaphor for when the archangels brought destruction to the unforgiving land of predators to pave way for the eventual rise of humanity. There is a saying that humans and angels share a common ancestor, though I am not sure if I believe that."

"Why?"

"The differences are too immense."

Dawn turns away, trying to block out the shrill dying screeches of the dinosaurs as the archers jump down, armed with oversized knives featuring brass knuckle hilts.

"This is no different from bullfighting in your world," Adam says.

"How do you know about bullfighting? Also, I'm against bullfighting."

"Just because our realms tend not to care about the human one, does not mean that we are ignorant of it."

"Why don't they care what happens in the human realm?"

"Why should they?"

"You're from there, too."

"I was," Adam says.

Dawn looks back into the arena and regrets doing so, as she sees mangled dinosaur corpses being dragged out of the amphitheater. The ground is littered with scattered feathers and trails of dark-red blood.

"I want to go back to my room," Dawn complains.

"In due time. The matches haven't even begun."

Dawn huffs, gripping her armrests in anger. Adam grabs her forearm, constricting it painfully.

"Perhaps, my dear, it is time you learned what survival of the fittest truly means."

He nods to the royal guards, who respond as if they have already been instructed on what to do. The guards force chains on her wrists and drag her out of the emperor's box.

◆

The day had long passed since Gabriel had felt the cold and unforgiving bite of Saphrael's blade. Although he understood what they were trying to teach him, he couldn't help but feel like something was wrong.

Real archangels don't pass out from a hit like that, Spud had said, albeit he did sound disappointed. It was nice to have someone who believed in him, if only for a moment.

Maybe it's a mental barrier since he's been on Earth for so long, thinking he's human? Cadence replied.

Human is the right word, Marce scoffed.

He's obviously not human, Saphrael replied. *He's already healed. Would probably even heal faster without the soul poison, I'm sure.*

Gabriel doesn't understand why Saphrael always seemed to be there for him. Having friends wasn't anything he was ever particularly skilled at.

"Keep your cloak on. Don't draw attention to yourself," Saphrael whispers to Gabriel, breaking his train of thought and drawing him into the present.

The Wonder Brigade is just outside the Axion, among the crowd near the lively merchant stalls. Saphrael walks alongside Gabriel, and the rest trail behind, talking to one another. They're all wearing their Chokma masks. Gabriel's rapier rests at his side. Everyone has their weapons, even if they are not fighting today. Recently, he had been practicing how to focus his vision so he can see through the Chokma metal normally, but it takes effort and eventually gives him a headache.

Saphrael seems distracted and turns away from those chained outside the Axion. Gabriel looks at the line of chained prisoners, arms pinned to their sides, wondering what they had done to deserve such humiliation. He is about to ask Saphrael when someone in the group ahead of them starts hurling insults. The unprovoked aggressor laughs and then strikes the bound prisoner, causing him to waver and the metal chains to crash against their bindings. Their Chokma masks are fashioned to resemble vipers, and they wear blue accented gambeson uniforms.

"Your name means nothing to anyone."

"Except loser," replies another from the group.

"Right, except loser."

Saphrael stops walking. Gabriel looks at him, trying to figure out what is going on.

The entire team turns to face them.

"You got something to say?" The abuser steps up to Saphrael who silently stands his ground.

"No," Saphrael says, doing his best to be diplomatic while subtly shifting his hand closer to his weapon.

"I thought so." The team stops harassing them and moves along their way.

The Wonder Brigade pushes through the overcrowded arena, eventually finding an open spot in the upper levels big enough for them all. Gabriel looks out across the Axion, allowing his vision to shift into magnus sight. The view is incredible, the angel's ethereal colors range from a light blue to bluish-purple, with the majority glowing dark blue.

"We missed the culling," Spud says sadly.

Gabriel looks at the arena floor and sees dinosaurs being dragged out. He is amazed to see dinosaurs at all, much less through his Chokma mask. Their spirits glow from dark red to black, from dead and dying.

Marce reaches over Spud to punch Gabriel's shoulder. "Your girlfriend's here." Marce points down to the floor level, and Gabriel sees Dawn sitting next to Adam. He instinctively puts his hand over where Adam had stabbed him and stands.

Saphrael looks at him, quietly saying, "Not here, not now."

Marce says loudly, "Let him go. It would be entertaining."

Cadence, at the far end past Loth, shakes his head. Loth says nothing, ignoring them all.

"What's going on?" Spud asks, looking in Dawn's direction. "She's being taken away."

Gabriel looks to where Spud is pointing, and through the long rectangular window on the floor level, Gabriel sees Dawn being forced from the royalty seating area.

Saphrael grabs hold of Gabriel's wrist, stopping him. Gabriel instinctively pulls away, still facing where she was.

"It isn't safe now," Saphrael says quietly.

"Yeah, Gabriel!" Loth says loudly. "Shut it."

"Gabriel! Wait!" Saphrael calls but Gabriel is too busy pushing his way through the crowd.

Marce rolls his eyes and mutters, "Stupid," under his breath.

Gabriel shoves those walking down the hall aside as he races by. *I have to reach her. All I have to do is reach her and everything will be okay*, he tells himself.

"Dawn!" Gabriel screams as he turns a corner in time to see her being shoved down the hall. His voice echoes inside his mask.

She looks directly at him but doesn't recognize him because of the Chokma mask. Using his magnus sight, he looks at Dawn. Her ethereal form is different from any other he has seen so far. It is dark violet, like his own, but with a reddish hue.

"It's no use, Gabriel. They're bringing her into the arena," Saphrael says from behind him.

Gabriel doesn't stop staring at where she was just moments ago.

"Come on, let's go see what this is about," Saphrael says, nodding in the direction they came. Gabriel shakes his head and starts down the hall after her.

"This is a forbidden hall. Gabriel, trust me," Saphrael pleads.

"What are they going to do?" Gabriel says his hand on his rapier.

"You want to be tortured? You want to be thrown into the void or worse?"

"What?"

"That's what will happen if you set foot down that hall. You'll never reach her that way. Gabriel, please,"

Gabriel pulls away from Saphrael and charges ahead.

✦

Dawn struggles against the iron grip of the royal guards as they shove her onto the Axion's floor. She falls, kicking up red dust as she hits the ground. They pull her to her feet, hands cuffed, and she coughs from the dust-contaminated air. A dinosaur's feather sticks to her bodice near the large crystalline purple rose before falling as the guards roughly turn and uncuff her. The first thing Dawn does is throw a swing at the closest masked guard, who swiftly blocks with his forearm.

She knows that she is outmatched as she has no formal training. Tightening her defensive stance, she holds her ground as the four guards surrounding her draw their hook-swords. Adam yells something from the emperor's box that she doesn't understand but the guards do. They turn and immediately leave. Everything feels so large and small at the same time, she can't help but feel isolated compared to the massive size arena. The metal gates screech shut. Dawn's heart strains inside her chest. A loud horn blares and the crowd cheers.

Gabriel, she begs inside.

There is no Gabriel to save you now, something in her mind tells her.

Then comes a thunderous sound like that of a stampede. Her heart stalls, and her eyes widen as large demons flood the opposite end of the arena. There is weaponry on the walls, but it is too far away. Dawn shelters behind her forearm right before a charging demon runs into her, knocking her to the ground. The back of her head roughly hits the floor, causing her metal hairpiece to dig into the back of her skull. She curls up and lets out an ear-piercing banshee scream. All at once, the entire demon horde stops, turns, and faces Dawn.

◆

Dawn's scream echoes through the inner halls of the lower level of the Axion. As Gabriel wills himself to run faster, the world blurs. *Don't think about the guards chasing you. Don't think about the guards chasing you,* he tells himself. Stopping at a medieval-style iron gate, shoving it, but like the others, he finds it locked. A guard shouts from behind him, an arrow narrowly misses him, and Gabriel takes off again.

✦

The princess lies dazed, sprawled upon the ground, caked in bloodied dirt. Her large, crystalline rose is crumpled and torn. Somehow, Dawn manages to get to her feet. Finding it difficult to stay upright, she stumbles, nearly falling. The Axion's interior, seen through strands of hair clumped together by blood, blurs. Through her vision, each demon doubles, then triples. Each mirage moves in tandem. The ground rumbles a terrifying noise like that of a stone avalanche, the thunderous drumming of a demon stampede.

All is lost, Dawn thinks, her vision darkening as her body begins to move on its own. She holds her arms to each side, palms facing the sky as black smoke begins to swirl directly above her. A harsh wind howls throughout the arena's halls with a hollow scream. Her billowing hair flows with an eerie grace in all directions as she stands, eyes closed.

✦

The wind blasts Gabriel as he is pursued by more and more guards, until he comes to a large metal gate at the end of the hall. Stopping, he kicks it open. Everyone chasing him stops before they shut him in, locking the gate. *This is either a very good thing or a very bad thing*, he thinks. There is a crackle of thunder. Gabriel looks up but sees nothing but the stone ceiling of the large, open room.

A lone angel peers through the gates to the Axion floor. Gabriel runs at him and rams his shoulder into his chest, slamming him against the wall beside the door. When he looks out through the metal bars, he realizes he is at the opposite end from where he started.

The angel lying on the ground wears a torn gambeson that is enhanced with extra-thick padding. Gabriel spots the keys at his side and says, "Sorry!" before punching him in the face, knocking him out cold. Briefly, he takes note of scratch marks on the angel's gambeson and realizes he must be some sort of beastmaster.

✦

On the Axion floor, there is a deafening roar from above. A myriad of lightning bolts strike simultaneously, frying the demons at once in a circle around Dawn. The demons drop dead as the air fills with the burnt odor of acidic flesh. Large, cold droplets of water rain down, quickly becoming a deluge, washing the dirt and blood off Dawn.

She looks over and sees Adam fighting the wind to reach her. She does not feel at all like herself.

"I'm sorry, Dawn!" Adam yells, looking briefly at the sky. A crack of thunder answers him.

The wind increases in pressure, making it nearly impossible for him to breathe. A fire tornado forms on the edge of the Axion's platform. The western edge of the arena starts to crumble. Stones crack and fall. The crowd starts to panic, crushing one another as they scramble to the exits.

✦

A familiar sound, that of an ancient ship groaning against the sea dominates even the thunder. Briefly, Gabriel looks back at open dark tunnels behind him before grabbing the keys only to find the door unlocked and tosses the keys aside, heading onto the arena floor. At the far end he sees Dawn in a trance. Gabriel's heart wrenches and he stares in awe at a blue-flamed fire tornado. A dark mist fills the Axion.

Dawn... Gabriel thinks as he races toward her but stops as the horrific sound becomes even louder. Black smoke forms in the shape of the dragon. Its body twists and turns, forming out of the black smoke, circling Dawn as she collapses. The wind grows more terrifying. Gabriel fights the intense wind, trying to get to her. The black dragon's winding serpent-like form picks up Dawn's body with its mouth. She hangs limp as a rag doll as it soars into the air above the Axion, curling itself around the now stationary blue fire tornado.

✦

Everything is silent and still. A coldness envelopes Dawn as the aura of warmth surrounding the Axion is gone. Deeply unsettled, she finds herself in the center of the ruins of the Axion. The stands are bare. The emperor's box, empty. She looks at the inner walls, or at least, what remains of the inner walls. The light gray stone is marred by blood, battle, and time; darker in areas where more blood had spilled. Hues of blacks, greens, and primarily reddish-browns stain the walls, varying in shades like watercolor splotches.

Trying to make sense of it all, she closes her eyes, meditating. A shiver runs down her spine as she braces, expecting to hear sounds of past, of weapons clashing coupled with barbaric screams or cries of terror and pain. Screams both recognizable and foreign, like the shrill shrieks of dinosaurs. Instead, she hears nothing. Until there comes a terrible sound, loud and nearby like that of a ship groaning against the sea.

Dawn looks up to where the sound is coming from, the ominous sky. Dark clouds coalesce, gathering above her. The black dragon roars, diving through the sky, heading straight for her. Pivoting her heel, Dawn races to the weapons racks mounted on the walls. She loses her footing, stumbling and nearly crashing into the weapon's rack before regaining her balance. Then, she quickly grabs hold of the nearest weapon: a brass basket-hilted sword. There are hearts pierced from the metal hilt, which is lined with dark-red velvet. A matching red tassel hangs off the pommel.

Turning back, sword held up in defense, she faces the black dragon. Her adrenaline spikes. Despite it all, she keeps her head up, swallowing her fear. Never before has she seen it so clearly. It is ragged and missing patches of skin. Its body is pocketed with unnatural bumps that force scales to jut out here and there.

Dawn has no idea if this is a dream. Her right hand grips the surprisingly soft handle of the sword as she backs up against the wall. The dragon's large, black, soulless eyes stare at her from a distance. *It isn't coming after me... it has every opportunity to do so, but it isn't coming after me*, Dawn thinks.

She forces her hand open and releases the sword. It clangs upon the ground.

"I will not harm you," she says, probably much louder than she had to, hoping it understands. Her words echo down the halls. She closes her eyes, turns her head to the side, and waits for death.

After a heartbeat, Dawn opens her eyes and is face-to-face with the black dragon. A strong wind forces Dawn to stabilize herself. She looks into its eyes and sees not a monster, but vulnerability and pain. Wind gusts pick up even more, and the dragon comes straight at her, entering through her chest. The world fades.

◆

The wind and the rain cease as the smoke-form of a dragon gently places Dawn's unconscious body in the middle of the Axion's floor. The weather cleared as soon as her body touched the ground.

"Dawn!" yells a masked figure from halfway across the Axion. Adam recognizes his ratty cloak and Wonder Brigade uniform. It could only be Gabriel. Turning away from Dawn, Adam grabs an axe from the weapon's rack and faces Gabriel, who is entirely focused on Dawn. Adam's fist tightens around the axe handle. He charges at Gabriel, moving so fast the world blurs.

"Dawn!" Gabriel reaches her, kneels down, and is about to take her into his arms when Adam rams his shoulder into Gabriel's chest. The force of the impact, coupled with the speed, throws Gabriel back several feet before he hits the ground.

Gabriel is dazed but quickly recovers; he grabs hold of his rapier, drawing his sword. Adam stands protecting Dawn, axe in hand.

He's unbalanced and distracted... good, Adam thinks right before launching a flurry of axe swings. Adam forces Gabriel not only away from Dawn but toward the rubble of what once were the western walls.

A figure descends from the sky, landing next to Adam.

"Emperor Lucius," Adam says. He is quickly punched in the stomach, followed by a decisive forearm strike, numbing his face. Dropping his axe, Adam keeps his head down.

Lucius walks toward Gabriel, his shiny black boots thunk with a low, dull, heavy sound as he stares at him. Gabriel looks back at Dawn's unconscious body before charging at Lucius. He swings his sword at the emperor. Lucius grabs hold of the blade, his purple flame burning with a darker color. The flame begins to harden in concentrated spots, and a solid crystal encases the rapier. Gabriel drops his weapon right before the crystallized flame reaches the hilt. In a split-second decision, Gabriel predictably turns to Dawn. Adam shakes his head. He had thought that, for a moment, maybe he wasn't quite as stupid as he appeared to be.

Unbelievably, Gabriel runs to Dawn, reaching for something in his ragged cloak. Panic causes Gabriel to lose his balance, and he falls hard on the ground next to her.

What could he possibly be thinking? Adam thinks to himself.

Gabriel reaches out to Dawn. Just before he touches her arm, Lucius grabs hold of his shirt collar and shoots into the air, flying without wings. Gabriel throws a desperate punch at Lucius's face. It connects but has little effect.

Lucius rips Azrael's cloak off Gabriel before dragging him, midair, over the edge of the Axion's platform, exposing Gabriel's midnight-blue wings. Adam walks over to pick up Gabriel's now crystallized and discarded weapon, and he stops to observe them, watching as Emperor Lucius reaches to Gabriel's back and cracks his left wing where it meets his shoulder blade.

Gabriel's howl of pain echoes throughout the Axion as Adam returns to Dawn. His eyes are drawn to the beautiful, torn violet rose; its semi-translucent petals are now stained with blood. After checking on the back of her head where the metal emperor's crest holds her crown of braids, he thinks, *She'll live,* and lifts her up.

Adam looks over in time to see Lucius drop Gabriel into the ocean of blue fire. Gabriel spirals as he falls, one wing outstretched, the other broken and half-folded before he falls from Adam's view.

Lucius takes a few moments to watch Gabriel fall before returning to

Adam on the Axion floor. Adam holds Dawn's limp body in his arms. The few observers who were brave or dumb enough to stay fled when Lucius arrived.

"Not a word," Lucius says.

Adam keeps his mouth shut and holds Dawn out.

"Bring her back to the citadel. There is much you must atone for."

Chapter 14

Dawn wakes, dazed, on the couch in Lucius's study. *What am I doing here?* she thinks as the room comes into focus. The nightmarish demon roars echo in her mind, and she thinks, maybe, it was another nightmare. Her hand drifts across the soft, parchment-like, crystalline material of the bloodstained oversized purple rose and torn dress, still wet from the rain. The heavy emperor's crest she wore in her hair is on the table beside her.

"Hello?" she calls out, searching the room.

Her heart rate starts to rise before she turns to the other side of the room and finds Lucius studying papers. He sets his pen down and rises from his chair, which matches its vintage ornately carved black wooden desk framed with silver metal.

Shaking her head, Dawn feels as if she is going to have a breakdown. Walking over, Lucius opens his arms, inviting her into an embrace. She looks up at him and cannot get the image out of her mind of the first time she saw him, when he appeared to be watching her through the bathroom mirror. Or the first time she is sure she heard his voice, in the nightmare where the snakes pinned her to the cold concrete. But the individual standing in front of her has, so far, proven to be none of those things. He has only shown her patience, compassion, and protection.

When she does not walk to him, he inclines his head and says, "Adam, although clearly mistaken, did what he thought was best for you in my absence. Revenge is not justice even if it masquerades as such. I assure you, justice, not revenge. He will atone his transgressions against you, my dear." Lucius approaches her and places a cold hand softly on her cheek as she closes her eyes, giving in to his comfort. "Dawn, do try and find forgiveness within your heart." He places a hand on her back and gestures to her chair. Lucius walks over to the center of the couch and sits where he typically does.

"You were quite impressive. You not only managed to hold back demons but incite a weather change. I don't believe I need to inform you that weather of that nature is not typical for Geburah. Your mother had similar powers, but not to this extent. It must be attributed to the power of Enkiael. Enkiael was an archangel, one of the Promethean Angels. When he died, your mother absorbed his essence. Once, he was the bearer of the green flame of creation. You are a truly unique combination, and I am sorry I didn't take better care of you while I was away. Adam mentioned he tested you against a lesser demon, and you coaxed it to sleep with a song. He was expecting you to do as much in the Axion. Yet, he acted without permission and has been demoted from his position as hierophant. He placed you in great danger; it is now his penance to keep you safe."

Lucius gets up and reaches into his long Victorian-style overcoat, pulling out a small black patch that's embroidered with golden thread and places it in her hands. The fabric is frayed around the edges, evidence that it had been torn out by force. She recognizes it from Adam's uniform.

"What do you mean?" Dawn asks as she looks at the embroidered badge, trying to make sense of the symbol combination. Because of studying, she recognizes the rune-like symbols as a combination of Sumerian cuneiform. Yet, she has found that not everything always translates.

"I am reassigning Adam to be your personal guard and adviser."

"What? I don't want to see him. I don't want anything to do with him."

"Dawn, this is the best course of action for everyone involved."

"How? How is it the best course of action for me?"

"Adam is more than a capable guard. He must atone for his actions."

Dawn falls silent.

Lucius continues, "Things work differently here. As Adam has pointed out, you were never in any real danger. Talk with him. Dawn, I promise you that I will never allow such a thing to happen again," Lucius places his hand below her chin and tilts her head up to look at him. "Adam will be along shortly." When she sighs, his voice softens, "You are so passive, so kind. I pray you do not lose your soft touch. However, you must learn to control your outbursts. With your innate power, unintentional misuse can lead to devastating consequences." Lucius's bright copper eyes meet hers.

"I saw the black dragon again… in the Axion," Dawn confesses.

"And did you kill that which has been plaguing you?"

"No," she says, turning away.

"Things tend to work out in the way they are meant to, Dawn."

Lucius looks at her for a long moment. There is a knock on the door.

✦

Adam takes a moment to collect himself before walking through the door. Without saying a word, he locks eyes with Lucius, who inclines his head before ignoring him, walking past and out of the room.

After the door closes, he takes a deep breath and forces himself to walk over to Dawn. His hair is uncharacteristically disheveled. And he no longer wears an officer's uniform but casual faded-black military fatigues with no rank insignia.

Guilt weighing him down, he slows his pace as he approaches Dawn. She is understandably angry and not even looking at him. Her reserved composure is betrayed by her strained breathing and the subtle shaking of her hands.

Adam bows his head as he stands solemnly before her. He drops to his knees, head facing the floor, holding his hands together, as if in prayer.

"Princess Dawn, I beg your forgiveness. I misjudged the danger. I'm sorry." Lifting his head, he looks at her, only to find her still looking away. "I knew you weren't in any real danger. It was against demons, after all. The way of battle is the only thing I have known for such a long time. Rumors of your presence have been reverberating. Citizens have been asking to see you. I wanted to show them."

"Show them?" Dawn glares at him.

"That their princess is truly worthy." Adam breathes in deep, steadying himself, bracing to be hit.

"I don't care what they think."

"I know you don't."

"What you did is unacceptable."

"Understandable. Though I suspect you are far too kind to hold on to anger and hatred for long. I do not deserve your forgiveness, but I beg it of you anyway," Adam says, bowing his head, still on his knees.

"Forgiveness is not a word I know the definition of," Dawn says, looking away again.

Adam studies her expression and body language. "So much like your father." His tone is soft, saying it more to himself.

"So, you're my personal guard and adviser now." Dawn crosses her arms.

"That is correct."

"Which means we'll be spending a lot of time together."

"Yes, Princess."

"What is to become of your old position?"

"I'm afraid that will be up to your father."

"So, you will stay in the general's quarters?"

"No, Princess, you are my sole priority; therefore, I will be present wherever you are. Your father asked me to give this to you. I was allowed only to do so to mend our relationship."

Adam reaches into his pocket and pulls out a cloth-bound item, holding it in front of her. Dawn takes it and unwraps the fabric. It is a set of oversized tarot cards. The cards are well crafted, each with a hauntingly eerie image painted upon it. They are encased in a clear yet durable material she cannot identify. The watercolor technique used displays the ethereal movement of smoke or gray storm clouds on many of the cards. Although the cards are primarily dark blood red in color. The card back is deep crimson with the emperor's crest inscribed in black with elegant silver accents.

Dawn closes her eyes as she fans the cards out and draws one, moving instinctually. *The Ten of Wands.*

Reluctantly, she shows Adam the card and sighs. Her shoulders slump. "It reminds me of the battle I was just in."

Pain evident in her eyes compels Adam to speak. "Dawn, I will do everything within my power to assure nothing like that happens to you again."

"Protect me from your own actions... you mean," Dawn says, her words laced with anger and sarcasm that, above all, mask pain.

"Dawn..." Adam's voice trails off. His heart wrenches.

Dawn glares at him and he finds himself silent with remorse. Finally, she asks, "Is this watercolor?"

"It is crafted from blood and other relics that the artisans powdered and turned into pigments, giving it distinct color and power," Adam explains.

"I can feel energy coming from them," Dawn says, shuffling the cards. They are comfortable in her hands, as if they were her own cards that she has had for years. Dawn pulls another card, laying it on the table. The King of Wands. Adam knows it represents Lucius but offers no interpretations.

"No one else is allowed to touch your cards beyond you and your father. There are safeguards if someone does. If anyone else lays hands on your cards without its protective cloth or attempts to use it for divination with gloves on, it will overwhelm them with telepathic voices that increase in number and volume until they cease."

Dawn studies the cards' art. Adam can tell she is uncomfortable with the origins of the cards—most would be.

"They're beautiful," Dawn says quietly. "You—you said it was painted with blood?"

"Yes, Princess."

"Whose blood?"

Adam clears his throat. "Various archangels, mostly. Your father has a collection of—let's call them—unique alchemy supplies."

"Okay..." Dawn pulls another card, the King of Pentacles, and lays it beside the King of Wands. She looks directly at Adam. Finally, she pulls a third card.

Closing her eyes, she winces, trying hard to hide her clearly evident pain. Adam looks at the card, the Knight of Cups, which unmistakably resembles Gabriel.

Chapter 15

Gabriel slams into the ground. Wind from his fall momentarily clears the ice-cold blue fire in a radius around him. The flame quickly reclaims its space, engulfing him. Pain branches from his left wing, veining throughout the entire upper left side of his body.

Strangely, the fire doesn't hurt—it energizes him. *She was so close*, Gabriel thinks before he screams in frustration. He rips off his Chokma mask and drops it next to him. It clunks against the ashen surface with a heavy thud. Engulfed by the blue flame, Gabriel breathes in deeply while visions of being so close to Dawn flash in his mind. "I had her. She was right there. I had her..." Gabriel closes his eyes and grabs his hair in frustration.

Gabriel, Semoel's voice says inside his head. *Gabriel... listen to me.*

Semoel? Gabriel opens his eyes and sees nothing but blue flames.

He sits up and hugs his knees, rocking back and forth, body racked with pain and a profound sense of loss. Reaching to his side, he grabs his Chokma mask with his black-gloved hands, making a mental note to ask Saphrael why their uniforms are fireproof. If he ever gets the chance.

Gabriel, listen to me. You belong here. This is your father's flame. Left after a great battle long ago. If you can harness it, it will give you strength. Enough power to defeat Lucius and rescue Dawn.

How do you know all of this?

Trust me, Gabriel. Have I ever led you astray?

No, you have always been trustworthy.

Gabriel closes his eyes and breathes out heavily, becoming increasingly aware of the pain of his fractured wing coupled with the poison running through his veins. He sighs, feeling broken and discarded.

I am lost. Gabriel grits his teeth and pushes back overwhelming depression. *I've lost her, haven't I?* Tears begin to form in his eyes. *I can't do this, Semoel.*

There is no reply.

Semoel! Please, tell me everything is going to be all right.

I can't tell you that. If I did it would be a lie. The truth is that nothing will ever be all right. Such is life. All you can do is focus on the path ahead of you and brave it the best that you can. So, listen to me and I will guide you through this. You must learn to wield the flame of the archangels. Now focus. Clear your mind, relax, and feel the cold fire run through you. Concentrate on directing the flame to a spot in your hand and release it.

Sighing, Gabriel sets his Chokma mask beside him, breathing in blue flame. He can feel it running like blood through his veins. Opening his hand, he concentrates on moving all the energy inside of him to his palm. The energy flows out of his hand like an electrical pulse searching for an exit. A whisper of a fire sparks inches above his gloved hand, concentrated flame darkens the ocean of fire.

Is this my destiny? Is this who I am? I don't understand. I need answers.

Gabriel, we are who we choose to be, not who we are born to be. Understand that, listen, Semoel instructs.

Why?

Just listen. I want you to concentrate, to meditate. Let go, relax, palms up. Connect to the world around you. The pain, the suffering, the charred ashes of the ground. See it and allow it to leave. Feel the flame inside you: each spark, every atom. Breathe in. Breathe in deeply. Breathe out the flame. Let go of yourself, the past aspect of who you thought you were, the future of what you think you could be. I want you to let go. I want you to forget where you are. I want you to forget who you are.

Engulfed in the blue flames, Gabriel thinks back to when Dawn taught him how to meditate. He focuses his thoughts and clears his mind. Nagging self-doubt threatens his well-being. He wants to let go but the profound sense of loss pulls him down. Thoughts whisper in the corner of his mind that he is not good enough, not strong enough, that everything is pointless. Visions of Dawn flash in his mind and he relaxes.

"I need to hold on, if for nothing else, I need to hold on for her," Gabriel says to himself before clearing his mind. He becomes drowsy as he views his stream of conscious thought and then lets it go. Breathing in deep, he concentrates on the air, connecting to the realm around him and the Axion above him. His mind ventures to the different realms of the Sine System.

Whispers, residue of his time spent in the Black Lake fill his mind. Then, he forgets and lets go. Centering himself, he becomes only conscious enough to know that he is in his subconscious. Breathing out slowly he connects to everything and nothing all at once.

Now take in the flame. It is yours to command.

He inhales sharply, calling flame to him. The fire starts to whirl around him and he pays it no mind. As he inhales the flame, it infuses into his every cell. His body is so cold that it feels like it is burning as it infuses. Gabriel's eyes are wide as he tries to hold on, but his body convulses in pain and consciousness fades as he can take no more.

✦

Gabriel opens his eyes to a world of barren ash pocketed with craters. The only light is the soft glow emanating from his large, ethereal midnight-blue wings. After picking himself up, he looks around but sees nothing. Part of him doesn't believe he could be in the same place that was once covered in blue fire, yet he can see the Axion's floating platform in the distance.

So, you are finally awake? Semoel asks. *I want you to stay here for as long as you need to in order to grow familiar with your powers. I will help you, if you let me.*

"I feel... different," Gabriel says aloud, as there is no one else around.

That is natural. It will take time to fully adjust. Remember what I've said and continue to practice. Direct the flame out of your hands, the soles of your feet, and practice creating projectiles.

Gabriel breathes in deeply, pushing back the thought of everything he stands to lose. However, no matter what he does, the thought of Dawn continues to stay ever present in his mind. To quell his emotions, he thinks about what it feels like when she is wrapped in his arms and the sound of her voice. It's hard not to be afraid that memories are fading. *Is she already gone?* He looks around at the charred gray surface, pocketed with craters, a shiver runs up his spine, and he thinks, *This is what it must be like if I were stranded alone on the dark side of the moon. Everything is so... quiet...*

Gabriel looks up at the Axion. "How am I going to get out of here?"

He takes a deep breath in and ignites a flame above his gloved hands. The fire erupts like a blowtorch. Not expecting such a large flame, he braces his stance to prevent being pushed back. Turning his palms to face behind him, he directs more energy to his hands and launches forward. Speeding recklessly, Gabriel loses his footing, stumbles, and nearly crashes. Instead of pulling back the fire, he accelerates. Gabriel angles his palms to face the ground, lifting himself off the surface.

Only when he finds himself a fair distance in the air does he realize he doesn't know how to decelerate. Gabriel pulls the flame in too quickly, causing him to free-fall. Although he is successful in relighting his flame, his trajectory is already heading down. The only thing he accomplishes is accelerating his descent. He falls like a shooting star, leaving an arcing blue streak behind him. Despite crashing into the ground, he picks himself up, feeling stronger than ever. He even feels his broken wing begin to reshape.

With caution, he lifts himself off the ground. This time with more control. He pulls the flame in, lowering himself to the ground.

I know where the broken pieces of your father's armor should be. Semoel guides him on which direction to go. Gabriel picks up his Chokma mask and starts trekking through the barren realm. After a while, he stops to rest, although it is rather unpleasant to breathe because of dust particles.

It's just a little farther, Semoel tells him.

"All right..." Gabriel hangs his head in exhaustion. The monotonous atmosphere is starting to get to him.

Don't give up. Dawn needs you.

Gabriel nods and pushes himself to continue. In the distance, a soft halo of light cuts through the darkness. After making his way to it, he sets down his Chokma mask and stares at something mostly buried in the ground. Grabbing hold of it, he pulls, nearly falling over as he expected it to be difficult to dislodge. Gabriel marvels in awe as the air fills with a light-blue glow from the triangular-shaped crystal in the center of the breastplate. Accenting the center gem are dark-blue triangles reminiscent of a compass star on a map. The chest piece is solid with circular designs and raised, thin pieces of metal artfully crafted into one of the most beautiful things he has ever seen.

Lifting it over his head, he puts it on and clasps the latches on the sides. The breastplate is split open in the back, so it doesn't fit as well as it should. In the ashen dirt, he sees something metal. Digging into the dirt, he uncovers a forearm guard. The arm guard is adorned with the same triangular compass-gem and circular designs of the breastplate.

This armor is forged from the rarest metals. It will protect you better than anything else you will find.

Semoel, how do you know all of this? Why didn't you tell me anything before?

I have been many places, Gabriel. I have seen many things for quite a long time.

You didn't answer my question.

Trust me, Gabriel, please.

He spends the next few hours practicing his newfound powers. When he feels comfortable enough to attempt to accelerate such a distance, he looks up at the broken Axion, takes a deep breath, and puts on his Chokma mask. *Here goes nothing*, he thinks as he launches into the air, leaving a streak of blue behind him.

✦

Saphrael sits atop a pile of rubble that was once part of the Axion's western wall. Hunched over, he is weighed down by inner conflicts and uncertain

189

he'll ever see Gabriel again, not after Emperor Lucius got hold of him. *Why did you to charge headfirst? Can't you take time to think? To plan?... I hope you're okay, Gabriel.*

He grips the tattered cloak he had managed to retrieve amid the chaos. The tear is sewn, rather clumsily, thanks to a field repair kit Saphrael carries in a pouch on his belt. *I should go. What is there to go back to? I've put everyone in danger. They're better off without me.* His mind drifts to the endless monotony broken only by painful treatments that await in the discere centers on Chesed.

Saphrael lets out a deep sigh. The stillness of the now broken Axion disturbs him. Cold wind stings his face. If anyone had told him that the ever-burning fire beneath the Axion was gone, he would have called them a liar.

A startling bang causes Saphrael to jump up as a flash of blue burns not far away. Past a pile of rubble, Saphrael finds someone in a Wonder Brigade uniform and Chokma mask picking himself off the ground. Saphrael stops, staring at the armor. It is highly reflective in the aura of soft blue light emanating from the gem in the center of his breastplate as well as his wings.

Saphrael takes off his Chokma mask and squints. It looks like he is wearing tetragram armor... but he couldn't be. "Gabriel?"

Gabriel removes his helmet as well, and his unnervingly bright ice-blue eyes stare back at him. Saphrael takes a step forward. "Gabriel, what is going on?" He holds his mask in one hand and Gabriel's tattered cloak in the other.

"I was hoping you might know." Gabriel may look different, but he still sounds the same. "By the way, why are the uniforms fireproof?"

"Why wouldn't they be? By the way, they're not fireproof, just highly resistant depending on the intensity of the flame." Even though there is no one else around, Saphrael hands him his cloak and says, "Keep this on."

"Saphrael, there is no one else here."

"You never know."

The blue light dims as Gabriel throws his cloak on. "I want to go to the Black Lake. I feel like it's calling to me."

✦

Gabriel stands next to Saphrael, both staring into the pitch-black waters. Inside, Gabriel has an odd sense of familiarity. When he looks at Saphrael, he notices his slumped posture.

The Black Lake must be affecting him as well, Gabriel thinks.

"We lost a lot of people here," Saphrael says, looking at the mists above the lake. "Some entered willingly. They never came up. They never wanted to. Do you remember seeing those disciplined outside of the arena?"

"Of course."

"I used to be one of the most successful champions Hod had ever seen. Hod is where you get to live if you win. That was... a long time ago." Saphrael quiets, lost in thought. "You know, I would have walked in long ago, if it wasn't for them."

"The Wonder Brigade?"

"Yeah."

Gabriel looks at his reflection on the surface of the black waters. "My eyes are lighter." His words are more question than statement.

Intrusively, a voice enters his mind. *You're not good enough,* it whispers. It is soon joined by a chorus of eerie, disjointed voices all speaking at once.

Gabriel faces downward sharply, breathing in harder. His fingers curl causing him to drop his Chokma mask.

"Are you okay?" Saphrael asks, surveying the area, alert for dangers.

"Yeah. No." Gabriel winces.

You will never succeed. There is no hope, repeat the voices.

Gabriel's flame ignites on its own, encompassing his body, protecting him.

The voices grow louder, as does his heart rate. *You will never see her again.*

"How do you know?" Gabriel screams. Dazed, he looks up at Saphrael. The world blurs, tilting beneath him.

A loud, isolated voice grates at his psyche. *She no longer cares for you.*

Gabriel falls to his knees.

"Gabriel!" Saphrael yells as the blue flame engulfing Gabriel grows.

Saphrael backs away. Gabriel fights to find his balance, he stands halfway, near the water's edge. Arms from the lake grab and pull him under.

She no longer cares for you.

She no longer cares for you.

She hates you.

I don't love you anymore, Dawn's voice whispers, an imagined fear.

Gabriel's eyes widen, and the flame encircling dies out. Inside, he knows it isn't really Dawn. Part of him doesn't care. Part of him thinks, *What if it is the truth?* Giving in, he allows himself to sink to the jagged cliffs that line the bottom of the lake.

Closing his eyes, he remembers what he said to her as if it were yesterday. "Dawn, listen to me. I promise you, I love you, and I would do anything to protect you. No matter what. Okay?"

He opens his eyes, and the blue flame ignites, burning any creatures nearby. The water looks clear for a moment after his flame burns the residue. Concentrating, he wills his flame to grow. The intense fire burns everything around it.

Inside his head, the voices of the Lost turn to screams of agony, followed by silence. The flame continues to grow until it encompasses the entire lake, spreading to the deep fjords that flow to and from the main body of water.

For a brief moment in time, the veins of water across Basalt were ablaze with blue flame. The water system evaporates in moments. Gabriel pulls back his flame. He finds himself hovering just above the bottom of a large crater strewn with bodies of the Lost. The spikes he lands upon are long, black, and crystalline in nature. The oversized jagged black crystals are lined with triangular bumps of smoky inclusions. Gabriel never imagined the bottom of such an awful place could look so beautiful.

"What just happened?" Saphrael walks up to him as he lands on shore.

"I don't know." Gabriel shrugs.

"You don't know?"

"No, I don't. I felt like I was—I could hear them—I was lost, drowning in hopelessness and... then, I remembered."

"Remembered what?"

"Dawn. She needs me."

"We need you, too, Gabriel. If you could just figure out some way to—"

"Some way to what, Saphrael? What is it you think I can do?"

"I don't know. It just seems like all you care about is Dawn."

"It is," Gabriel says, his hands open.

Saphrael shakes his head. "You're selfish, Gabriel."

Gabriel ignores Saphrael, looking into the deep, jagged crater.

"The Lost... do you think they are going to be okay?" Gabriel asks.

"They'll be fine."

"Are you sure?"

Saphrael shrugs. "Does it matter? They should regenerate with time, now that the curse is gone. Didn't know you could do that, by the way."

"Neither did I." Gabriel picks up his Chokma mask from the ground and tosses it to Saphrael. "I'm going for a walk."

Saphrael catches it. "But—"

"I'll be back, Saphrael... I just need some time alone." Gabriel turns away and heads into the dark forest.

Chapter 16

Dawn stares up at the ornately embossed black wooden ceiling of her four-poster bed, wondering if she will have another nightmare. Adam told her she doesn't necessarily need to sleep, but there is little else for her to do. So, she decides to sleep anyway. Adam watches over from his chair near the door, turns a page in the book he is reading, and says, "Rest well, Princess."

Ignoring Adam, Dawn adjusts her blankets, searching for a comfortable position. Taking a moment to relax, she feels herself sink into her soft bed.

As she is falling asleep, she hears her name. "Dawn... Dawn... are you asleep?" Drifting off, she loses her grip on consciousness. Dawn finds herself standing on the back of a black dragon in mid-flight. It looks like *the* black dragon, but it couldn't be. This black dragon is emaciated but no scales are missing. On closer inspection, she realizes that the scars from the lesions on its body are still there, just far less pronounced. Thunder grumbles as the clouds around her darken, threatening to envelop everything.

The same voice that called her name as she was falling asleep says, "There you are."

A figure in a featureless silver-white mask and plain black uniform stands up from sitting cross-legged at the other end of the dragon. He takes a step closer to her, yet keeps his distance. "We speak in code. Help us, so we can help you."

The stranger takes off his mask and reveals sandy-blond hair and blue eyes, then he rips off that face. He continually removes face after face, some of which she feels she has seen somewhere before.

"What do you want from me?" Dawn asks, her long hair flowing behind her.

"We need your help, and you need a warning. There are those of us who want to help you. There are those who want you dead."

A knife splits through the darkened clouds and speeds at her, narrowly missing her before flying off into the dark clouds behind her.

"No one is meant to be here, not even your father. This place… it poisons, it warps. It leaves nothing unaffected. Those with power," he nods at her, "have a greater ability to make change. Together, we can end this bloodshed. Help us, so we can help you."

"I'm fine." Dawn crosses her arms.

"Are you really? You're a prisoner. That much is clear."

"I'm safe," she says defensively before unconsciously taking a step back.

"Safe? Safe from what, exactly?"

"From danger? From everything? I am safer than I have ever been."

"I can tell you that, clearly, you are not."

A sharp steel blade of a guillotine howls, dropping inches in front of her. It is so close she can feel the wind on her face as it speeds past. The blade dissipates, turning into smoke when it hits the dragon they are riding.

"Dawn, Dawn, wake up," Adam says.

Dawn looks up, finding Adam standing next to her bed. "Yes?"

"You were talking in your sleep. I was afraid you were having another nightmare."

Dawn sits up, nodding. "Not exactly…"

"Oh?"

"Weird dream," is all she says.

"I see," Adam says, carefully judging her reactions. "Who is it you were talking to in your dream, just now?"

Dawn, still lost in the dream, closes her eyes and listens to the sound of the guillotine's blade. "…maybe it was a nightmare?"

"I'm sorry you keep having nightmares, Dawn."

Adam seems sincere, but anger over what happened at the Axion washes over her.

"Shall we transcribe your nightmare?" Adam asks.

She shakes her head before her mind sorts through the dream she just had and the stranger she just met. She feels she has seen him before, but where? Then she realizes his mask matches that of the silent royal guards commonly posted outside of her door. Refusing to detail her dream, she stays silent and turns away from him. Her heart races, uncertain of how severely Lucius and Adam would react if they knew. If she really was talking to a guard at all.

"Dawn, we should always transcribe your dreams. Why not this one?"

"I don't feel like it."

Adam is silent for a long moment, then nods curtly. "Very well, Princess." He goes back to his chair near the door and picks up his book.

◆

Later that cycle, Dawn sits at her ornate silver table, hunched over a book, struggling to concentrate. Her back faces Adam. He clears his throat. She pretends not to hear anything, turning a page in her book before closing it and deliberately turning away from her tarot cards that sit beside her candelabrum as well. The strange comments of the deck's creation never sat well with her. Yet, no matter how often she pushes the thought from her mind, the deck continues to call to her. Closing her eyes, she places her hand on the deck, fighting internally whether it is a good idea to use the cards at all. The sleeve of her dark violet dress, layered with black lace patterned with roses, rests upon the table. Her hand pulses from the immense energy radiating from the deck.

After removing the fabric, she shuffles the best she can, given the deck's awkwardly large size. *Speak to me*, she says internally. Using intuition to guide her on what cards to choose and in what order. She lays three cards on the table: the King of Swords, the Five of Swords, and the Queen of

Swords.

The footfalls of Adam's boots upon the black stone floor echo as he walks up behind her, breaking her concentration.

"What do you suppose it means?" Adam asks.

"I don't know," Dawn says, not looking over.

"You can't ignore me forever, Princess."

Dawn puts her deck back together, shuffling her cards.

"Do you really not know, or do you just not want to talk to me?" Adam says.

"I don't know—both? Just go back to reading."

"You are so much like your mother," Adam murmurs quietly.

"I thought you wouldn't know." Dawn sharply turns to face him.

"I know enough."

"Tell me about her then."

"She was… unique. At least from the stories I've heard."

"How come you don't know?" Dawn asks, setting her deck on the table.

"It was a very long time ago."

"I thought you loved her."

"I did."

"Then why don't you remember?"

Adam sighs. "Dawn, I don't remember anything from my life in Eridu. I'm not allowed to."

"Not allowed to?"

"No. Anyway, your mother, she was beautiful, powerful… dangerous. It wasn't always that way, at least from the stories I've heard. Her life was fine until…" He looks up at the ceiling and stops talking.

"Until what, Adam?"

Adam looks back at her and says, "Until she met your father."

He returns to his chair and opens his book, trying to escape the conversation he started. Dawn stomps over and opens her mouth, finger pointing at him, but before she can say a word, there is a knock on the door. Adam stands and straightens his casual faded-black fatigues.

He opens the right half of the oversized wooden double doors in a controlled manner before altering his stance and slamming it shut. The door doesn't fully close as the long end of a hook-sword is jammed inside. The assailants use the hook-sword to pry the door open, and two masked royal guards enter.

After stumbling back in shock, Dawn regains her footing, her heart racing. The pair focuses on Adam, who kicks his chair under one, while grabbing the wrist of a clumsy forward thrust from the other. Then Adam grabs hold of the assailant's hook-sword and pulls in, but the other guard bashes Adam over the head with the chair. Adam lets go of the weapon and falls to one knee before the other skewers Adam's shoulder with the hook end of his weapon. The guard pulls at the weapon lodged in Adam's shoulder, and he lurches forward before stopping, suspended in the air, held before being dropped. Dawn backs away as the other guard stomps Adam in the throat. He holds Adam down as the other one looks directly at Dawn with his eerie, faceless silver-white mask. She stares at him, frozen, willing her body to move but it does not obey.

Seconds tick by with each beat of her heart. She screams internally to move, but does not. The sounds of Adam being beaten, the guard approaching her... She closes her eyes and stress builds inside of her until the strained beating of her heart feels as if it may explode. Unable to think clearly, she closes her eyes and lets out a piercing banshee scream.

The spiderweb crack in her mirrors grows. With the assailants stunned, Dawn runs to her tarot cards and grabs a card off the top. The attacker recovers and grabs her from behind. She screams, and it echoes down the halls as she twists her body, throwing an elbow, aiming for his throat but she painfully hits the silver-white metal mask instead. He overpowers her, holding her still. The other royal guard starts walking over to them. She opens her mouth to scream, but the guard holding her headbutts her with his mask. Her head whiplashes back as the world blurs around her. A warm trickle of blood runs down her forehead. She manages to shove the tarot card down the back of his uniform. The guard drops to the ground and writhes on the floor, screaming. Dawn turns to the other guard and in that split second decides to run and bolts past, out the door.

Pale-blue dots, lights from the sconces, blur into lines as she races down the narrow black hall. She stops at the top of the stairs, hyperventilating. Fearfully, she looks at the spiraling black stone stairs, and her vision doubles. Without hearing anyone approach, she suddenly finds Lucius standing next to her. He wraps an arm protectively around her and holds her tightly, his other hand outstretched, palm facing the dimly lit hall. Closing her eyes, she curls her head against his chest. The already frigid temperature drops rapidly and bites her skin like the unforgiving winter wind. Dawn has flashbacks to when she was exposed to the elements, homeless, and alone. She opens her eyes to an intense purple encompassing the entirety of her vision. It takes her a moment to realize that Lucius is shooting a large jet flame down the hall. Lucius speeds away, gliding as if he were not even touching the ground.

Dawn shivers, folding her arms in front of her. Screams echo from down the hall, the sound of broken bones and flashes of purple light highlight her large wooden double doors. For a moment, it is beautiful, the purple glow of fire outlining the mural.

There is a noise behind her, someone is running up the stairs. Dawn turns. It is another guard. She has no idea if he is friend or foe. Her question is soon answered as he launches an attack, swinging his hook-swords. Dawn catches the hook end with her already injured arm, not caring if it cuts into her.

The masked royal guard shoves Dawn into the wall, but she manages to keep hold of the hook-sword but so does he. Planting her feet in a rooted stance, Dawn uses the wall to prevent the assailant from shoving her down the stairs. She holds on for dear life to the end of the weapon as he swings his other hook-sword at her. Lucius halts the weapon, grabbing hold of it midair. Seizing the opportunity, Dawn positions the other hook-sword, which is still cutting into her flesh, against the attacker's chest. Yelling as she shoves the hook-sword through the rogue royal guard.

He does not immediately fall to the ground. Her eyes widen as the sharp end of another hook-sword pierces through the attacker's neck, shoved through by Lucius. The assailant drops to the ground, taking Dawn with him, her hand pinned by the hook. Lucius pulls the hook-sword from the guard's chest and helps Dawn stand. She wavers, unbalanced, exhausted, and weary. Lucius's bright, pale copper-colored eyes shine in the dark, alert for any threat.

✦

Dawn rests against her chair in Lucius's study, wearing a deep purple gown that shimmers with small clear gems. It has a heart-shaped neckline and double straps wrap around her upper arms. Her long cardinal-red hair is down in large waves of curls. Earlier, her assistants had silently fussed over her, as if they were apologizing or doing what they could to make her feel better. With her hair and makeup done, no one would suspect that she was recently attacked, except for the shiny golden thread stitched in her right forearm. Although her dress, makeup, and adornments say otherwise, she is exhausted. She traces her hand against the bumps of stitches. The thin golden thread reminds her of tinsel. Adam had cleaned and cared for her wound.

Lucius places an ornate silver chalice of Xerotes in front of her. He wears a long black overcoat with gold buttons, a black vest, and matching attire.

"Adam is gathering information on what happened. I suspect it was a faction of zealots known as the resistance. They have been silent for quite some time, but it is not surprising that they decided to move now. I have dealt with the attackers. Although they are no longer a threat, that does not mean that they won't return or that others will not follow."

"Why would they attack me? I haven't done anything."

"Because you are my daughter. By existing, you are a threat to those who oppose me. You must understand that. You are beautiful, just like your mother. Dawn, you display both my abilities and your mother's—"

"Why do you both constantly talk to me about a woman that I've never met? A woman that I don't need to meet. A woman who abandoned me in that lonely, abusive place."

"Dawn, had your existence not been hidden from me, I assure you, I would never allow that to happen."

"You said I was safe here." Dawn throws her head back and drinks the entire glass of Xerotes at once.

Lucius takes a drink as well before carefully setting his chalice upon the table. "You are, Dawn. Safer than you would be anywhere else, I assure you of that. Truth be told, I may have provoked the zealous group in order to root them out."

"You... caused this?"

Lucius places the glass and wrought iron carafe pitcher with its diamond-shaped end and black stone accents in its metal frame in front of her, so she can pour drinks herself. The viscous red liquid inside is half full, it sloshes as Dawn picks it up and pours another drink.

"Yes. But I made certain they were fed false information that I would be absent when the suspected disloyal guards were on duty. Of course, I was there to ensure nothing happened."

Dawn rests her hand on her arm, feeling the thread of stitches once again.

"Rest assured, had I not provoked them, they would have moved regardless and in a much less predictable manner. This was a preventive measure. This is why I don't want you to feel comfortable leaving the citadel. You do not know who to trust. However, we need to present a united front against these terrorists."

"What do you mean?"

"I am arranging a celebration rally—I believe on Earth you call it a parade—in order to show those who attacked us that they will fail in their endeavors. I also want to properly introduce you to the citizens." Lucius pours more Xerotes into his chalice. "How have your cards been treating you?"

"Well enough." She steadies her nerves, wanting to ask how he got the blood used in the deck's creation, but decides it is better not to. "They are... accurate."

Lucius nods. "I want you to carry them with you at all times, so you will have some defensive abilities."

"I think I did okay."

"Always use what you have to your advantage. Keep your cards safe. What happened between you and the black dragon in the Axion?"

"I don't know. It's like I was somewhere else entirely. I was in the Axion but… it was in ruins, abandoned… empty. The black dragon came at me. I managed to get hold of a sword but I dropped it, refusing to harm him. Then, the dragon entered in through my chest."

"Have you been having nightmares since?"

"I haven't slept." She shifts uncomfortably, looking away to hide her lie.

"Try to sleep. Let me know what happens."

"Why didn't my window break this time? When I screamed, it only deepened the cracks in my mirrors."

"The windows have been reinforced after the first incident."

Dawn drinks more Xerotes. The urge to play with her tarot cards pulls at her, so she takes them out and unwraps them.

She lays the cloth on the table and pulls four cards. The Queen of Wands, the Ace of Swords, and the King of Wands, with the Hangman card behind it. Dawn knows the Queen of Wands represents her mother but doesn't say anything.

Lucius picks up the Hangman card, carefully studying it before placing it back down.

"I have been in a state of reflection, withdrawn from much of what goes on. Not wanting anything to do with it for quite some time. I allowed Adam to do his job, overseeing nearly everything in my stead. Now that he is guarding you, it has left more upon my shoulders."

Lucius touches the Queen of Wands card, fingers running across the textured surface. It's clear to Dawn how much he misses her mother.

Chapter 17

Excited chatter from the largest crowd Gabriel has ever seen fills the air. The Wonder Brigade is near the back of an expansive open-air venue known as the Laterem on the realm of Hod. The floor of the venue is composed of glossy black brick-shaped stones. Gabriel is relaxed, even in this large and unfamiliar place, because he is with his friends. He's never had friends before—not real ones, besides Dawn.

The crowd is a sea of soldiers clad in their standard black uniform. Various flags jut above the crowd, here and there. The rectangular flags come to a point at the bottom. Ceremonial in quality, the flags are lined with gold colored braided trim and held aloft by black poles topped with a golden emperor's crest. The Wonder Brigade did not have a formal flag for such occasions, so none of them carried one.

Gazing into the distance, Gabriel marvels at the soft light of an atmospheric crystal. Its luminescent glow could have been mistaken for the setting of a white sun, but instead of moving behind the skyline of the nearby metropolis, it sat nestled on the horizon before it. The end of the skyline stretched farther than Gabriel could see, composed of architecturally Gothic cathedrals. Their spires pierce the light gray skies. The excess wealth of this realm is undeniable and a stark departure from the resource-deprived Basalt, where it often feels like one eternal camping trip.

Gabriel rests against the short stone wall next to a wide, black stone path that runs down the center of the Laterem. He was told it is called the Path of Victory and warned that under no circumstance should he set foot upon it. It is reserved for tournament champions, royalty, and those of exceptionally high rank alone. The path is lined with finely crafted pillars crackling with violet flames.

Far above is a circular walkway that wraps around the entirety of the open-air stadium, supported by a series of large square-shaped watchtowers made of black stone. A sense of foreboding nags him as he looks at them. The medieval-looking black towers remind him that he is trapped in a dark and unforgiving hellscape. The towers are draped with massive black flags adorned with the emperor's crest, highlighted with gold embroidery. It makes him feel small and amplifies the fear he has been trying to ignore, that this has all been in vain. As time goes on, reuniting with Dawn feels more and more like an impossible dream.

"Are you okay?" Saphrael asks.

"Yeah." Gabriel puts his head down before looking back at his friend.

The silent expression on Saphrael's face says *I don't believe you*, but Gabriel is thankful that he doesn't press the issue.

"Has anyone found out what this is about yet?" Cadence asks, leaning on his golden staff.

"No, but I have a feeling we're about to find out." Marceriel points at the massive black stone structure behind them that serves as the entrance to the Path of Victory. It is marked by the largest of all the emperor's flags and flanked by watchtowers. The imposing black structure reminds Gabriel of the Arc de Triomphe. He grows cold, peering into the shadows that envelop the massive tunnel. A line of torches near ground level does little to light the darkness.

A succession of shadows dims the light of the dark violet flames as a line of high-ranking officers step onto the Path of Victory. They stride with an air of arrogance reserved only for those who occupy a superior station. The rumble of the crowd quiets into a hush as speculation grows. Some cheer, throwing fists into the air as commonly dressed armed competitors march out.

"Last season's champions," Saphrael whispers.

Commanding trumpets demand attention near the entrance. The musicians are lined on both sides of the Path of Victory but not upon it. The blaring sound carries unnaturally far. The melody calms Gabriel, transporting his mind to a peaceful time, a time he has never known but can somehow not forget. The trumpets cease, and drummers begin with a rhythmic beat that grows louder and more demanding.

The music stops. Everyone turns to face the arch. Then, out of the mouth of the giant black stone arch come flag bearers, carrying flags that are five times the size of typical ceremonial flags. They are followed by six figures in Chokma masks and standard uniforms, their bodies wrapped in chains. They lean forward yet stand proudly as they pull an elaborately ornate carriage. Shadows travel across the carriage as it enters the Path of Victory. The vehicle is a work of art, adorned with statues of headless angels reaching out to the sky positioned above each large golden wheel. The base of the carriage is black with gold vines crawling across it. Black curtains are pulled shut, obscuring his view.

Gabriel shifts his sight, hoping to see through the curtains. He can't, so he allows his sight to return to normal.

Everyone is not looking at the carriage but at what is behind it. Gabriel unconsciously takes a step back before bracing himself. His eyes widen and his breaths are shallow as his mind refuses to reconcile what he is seeing: soldiers in silver-white faceless masks carrying severed heads displayed on pikes, parading them in the air as if they were nothing but another flag. The grotesque spectacle is repulsive, and yet he can't look away. It is starting to sink in, the amount of danger he is in. What Saphrael, Marceriel… everyone has been trying to tell him—that he is in grave danger. Gabriel stares at the heads on pikes, his mouth slightly open, as seared into his brain is the blush-purple hue of their skin, the discolored black splotches of bruises marring their faces. The bruising on each head is unique, like an ink blot test. Their skin bares marks of ragged lacerations. Gabriel wants to believe the wounds had to be from an animal attack, but he has never seen any here. He stares at what he is sure now are knife wounds, the lacerations speak of the brutal and personal beatings they endured.

Those carrying the severed heads are dressed in clothing baggier than the standard gambeson outfit, these are reminiscent of martial arts uniforms. Each has a pair of hook-swords hanging from their cloth belts. Those in the center of the procession drag chains wrapped around the headless bodies. The dead wear the same uniform as those dragging their corpses. The clothing of the headless corpses are bloodied, burnt, and torn. The dead seem out of place, juxtaposed against the glossy sheen of the road. Closing off the procession is another set of emperor's crest flag bearers.

"What happened?" Gabriel asks, looking around.

"It's obvious what happened, Gabriel," Saphrael murmurs quietly.

Gabriel turns Saphrael to face him. "No, Saphrael, tell me what happened."

"The same thing that will happen to you if you're not careful." Loth says, his back to Gabriel as he watches the parade.

"I'm sure there's a reason for this," Cadence says.

"Yeah, this sort of thing just doesn't happen." Spud shrugs.

Loth turns around and glares at him. "This is a warning, Gabriel. If that is your real name. Heed reason, or next time it will be your head on the pike."

"All I'm trying to do is—"

"We know. You're trying to kidnap the princess," Loth says, turning his back to him once again to watch as the carriage pulls up to the large stage at the end of the long brick path. "Will you ever admit that you were in discere? You're dangerous, Gabriel, and frankly, I don't believe a word you say."

"I don't even know what you're talking about, Loth," Gabriel says.

"Why would you?" Loth sneers before turning his back to Gabriel.

"You guys believe me, don't you?" Gabriel looks around.

"I do." Spud offers him a smile.

"Marce, you're uncharacteristically quiet," Cadence remarks.

"I'm just trying to see what's going on," Marce says. He and his halberd rest against the wall.

Spud leans over Marce and looks down to the stage. "I can see Adam!"

Gabriel instinctively puts his hand over the wound Adam inflicted. Instantly, his mind flashes to when he was entombed in the Black Lake. The feeling of overwhelming hopelessness begins to suffocate him until he sees Dawn. She is being helped out of the carriage. His despair softens before transforming into anger as Adam's hand securely grips hers, stabilizing her as she is clearly not used to exiting the carriage. Gabriel can't hide his anger, but no one is looking at him.

Anger sinks into something darker as he sees what Dawn is wearing: a black and gold military-style dress. Three gold chains hang down her right shoulder, resting near her neck and looping around her back. The dress's gold buttons form a constellation-like pattern.

She doesn't seem fazed; in fact, she looks happy as she smiles at Adam, who walks directly behind her. They ascend a set of oversized stairs to the first platform, where the guards carrying the heads on pikes, champions, and high-ranking officers stand to the sides.

Dawn keeps her head down as they continue up a set of curved stairs, leading to an elevated stage. The bottom-most stairs are flanked by a sharp-angled decline that separates those in the first-level VIP area from the crowd. There are words carved on both sides, inlaid with gold. It says *Fortitudo, Vis, Virtus* on one side and *Quondam Victoria* on the other. Gabriel allows his vision to translate the words. The letters rearrange to *Strength, Power, Valor* on one side and *Certain Victory* on the other. Punctuated on both sides of each slogan is the emperor's crest in a circle, engraved into the stone highlighted with gold.

Adam follows directly behind Dawn with Emperor Lucius leading, walking onto the main area of the stage. The octagon-shaped stage flairs out to side stages and has sharp, slanted edges that make it resemble a massive black diamond.

The giant flags hanging on the towers are pulled to the side, revealing mirrors as large as the flags. On the stage, Lucius steps in front of two sets of mirrors, each composed of three panels; the two outward panels are tilted in at an angle. His enlarged image appears on every watchtower mirror. Gabriel's heart races as the towering images of his night terrors surround him.

As Lucius speaks, his voice booms across the venue with no visible amplification device. "We are here to honor our princess, my daughter, Dawn." He turns to face her. "You are stronger than you will ever know," he says softly before sharply raising his voice, once again addressing the crowd. His eyes briefly flicker in the direction of the severed heads, whose bodies were left discarded at the feet of the stairs. "Traitors, terrorists, thieves of things more precious than any material item: thieves of time, thieves of stability, thieves of peace. Those that wish to destroy all we have built, all that we stand for, infiltrated the ranks of my elite royal guards. These unworthy, honorless traitors assaulted our princess and threaten the stability of all."

"Dawn was attacked?" Gabriel looks around, trying to make sense of it all, but everyone is watching Lucius.

On stage, Lucius raises a black hook-sword encrusted with blood.

"Betrayed by the very ones entrusted to defend our princess. These three have chosen to throw away integrity, virtue, and chivalry. Make no mistake, these three did not act independently. They are but the claw of the beast, the body and head of which must be destroyed for the security of all. Our princess took out an assailant with her own hands. Come forth, Dawn."

Dawn walks up to Lucius, coming into the frame of the mirrors, projecting her image across the venue. Her posture is proper, and her eyes speak of intense shyness but also of something more, something hidden. Gabriel knows that look—it's fear.

Lucius thrusts the bloodied hook-sword into the air. "This weapon, meant to guard our princess, was instead forced by her hand through the chest of one of the traitors. The beast will be destroyed, just as these three have been." Lucius turns to Dawn, handing her the hook-sword. "My dear, you have been so understanding and valiant in the face of this near tragedy."

The words of Lucius's speech fade as Gabriel remembers the sensation of being close to Dawn. He feels disconnected as his sight sharply focuses on her current militaristic appearance and the bloodied weapon in her hand.

Lucius pins a dark-red octagon-shaped gem to the upper right corner of her dress. Gabriel struggles with a sinking feeling as he thinks, *She looks happy.* He closes his eyes for a moment, and when he opens them, he sees a small black flag held by the ruby-colored pin. He doesn't know what it means, but it looks like it has a name inscribed on it. *It must be the name of the guard she killed.*

"Dawn, you are a paragon if I have ever seen one," Lucius says with a soft touch to his voice, then his demeanor changes once again, hardening as he looks out, scanning the crowd. "If any of you hold these diseased ideals, let him come forth. If you hold enough conviction in your heart, I'm right here." Lucius has his hands open, raised slightly at his sides. "If you lack the courage to stand, remember this moment. It shows who you really are."

Gabriel starts to step over the wall next to the forbidden glossy brick path. Saphrael grabs his arm. "Gabriel, don't be stupid." Saphrael looks up at the circular walkway supported by towers. It is lined with archers, their sleek black crossbows aimed at the crowd, arrows ready to fire at a moment's notice.

The crowd gasps as one of the champions casually meanders up the stairs. Lucius looks at the archers and holds his hand up, motioning for them to stay. Adam steps forward. Lucius says something to him that Gabriel cannot hear, and Adam stops. The champion has his weapon in hand, a glaive with an imposing blade and short handle.

"I can't just watch this happen," Gabriel says, before jumping over the short wall. In midair, a hand grips the back of his shirt collar, and he is thrown backward to the ground. He lands beside Marce's dropped halberd.

"You're an idiot, you know that?" Marce says before his eyes narrow and he cocks his fist back.

Saphrael steps in between them.

"Mind your own business, Captain," Marce says, shoving Saphrael to the side. Then he looks back at Gabriel. "Don't make me put a boot to your neck."

Gabriel blanks out, forgetting everything. He screams and tackles Marce, his shoulder ramming into his midsection. They crash, knocking into those around them. Marce falls to the ground. Gabriel loses control, punching Marce repeatedly on the side of his face. Saphrael pulls Gabriel off him and places himself between them.

"This isn't going to get us anywhere," Saphrael says. "Except the cage or worse."

"Let them try." Gabriel balls his hands into fists.

A simultaneous gasp from the crowd causes him to look back at the stage in time to see history repeat itself as Dawn has her hand on the hook-sword lodged in the upper right chest of the champion. Dawn stumbles back, letting go of the hook-sword. Lucius puts a hand on her back, steadying her upright, as his other hand grabs hold of the weapon and forcibly thrusts the end fully through the angel. Lucius extracts the hook-sword, and swipes up, decapitating the assailant in one fluid motion. Blood sprays across Dawn's face and dress. The traitor's head lands face down on the first level of the platform before rolling onto its side.

A deafening roar fills the air as the crowd cheers. Lucius holds up Dawn's hand, along with the bloodied hook-sword. Fresh blood drips down the end of the weapon. Lucius hands her the hook-sword, then lifts the headless corpse, tossing it off the stage. The body lands near the right decline flanking the stairs, on the gold emblem next to the words *Quondam Victoria*. Then the corpse slides into the crowd. The crowd lurches forward, trying to get near it to do who knows what.

Gabriel squints, not believing what he is seeing: above Dawn's hands smolders a dark mist and her skin is covered in pitch-black scales. In the blink of an eye, everything shifts back to normal. His stomach sours as he sees Dawn embraced by Lucius.

"I've really lost her... haven't I?" Gabriel says quietly. Most of the Wonder Brigade looks over at him. Everyone except Loth.

"I'm sorry, Gabriel," Saphrael says.

"She's one of them now," Marce says, briefly putting his hand on his shoulder.

"It will be okay." Cadence has a compassionate look in his eyes.

"How? How is it going to be okay?" Gabriel strains to hold back tears.

"Dawn murdered them."

"It was self-defense, Gabriel, both times," Cadence says.

"They're not the only ones," Gabriel mutters. This gets Loth's attention; he turns around to face him.

"Whatever do you mean?" Loth asks, in his monotone voice.

"This isn't the first time something like this has happened." Gabriel works to calm the strained anxiety gripping him.

"Explain," Loth demands with a bite to his words.

"It's not important. It doesn't matter. Nothing matters." Gabriel turns away and pushes through the crowd.

"Gabriel! Wait," Saphrael's voice comes from behind him, but Gabriel doesn't stop until he reaches the teleportation sigils.

When he gets there, he sighs, lowering his head, feeling as if he can't go on any further.

Saphrael turns Gabriel to face him.

"Gabriel, what's going on? Are you all right?"

"No, Saphrael, I'm not all right. Why the fuck would I be all right?"

Gabriel pulls away and walks onto the teleportation sigil. Shoulders hunched, he is unable or unwilling to mask his depression. "I need to be alone."

◆

Time blurred since the attack. Dawn's mind insists it was just another nightmare, but she knows it wasn't. Playing on repeat in her mind is the moment she realized the saber-tooth masked champion was coming for her. The large venue seemed to shrink to the immediate space around her as her vision focused on the assailant, on the glint of the silver mask's elongated teeth and the sharp end of his large glaive. She saw her distorted reflection in the metal mask as he approached, like some twisted carnival mirror. She remembers wanting to shield herself, but being forced, once again, to use the hook-sword. Dawn shudders, remembering the sound of the weapon gliding through his body and the stifled groan that came from inside the metal mask. His body was pushed back from the point of impact, twisting counterclockwise, then lurched forward as Lucius extracted the sword. Then, in one swift, elegant motion, Lucius decapitated the assailant. Blood sprayed across her face, droplets resting on her lips. The abhorrent salty metallic taste seeped into her mouth. The altercation left a gleaming red mark on her right hand.

She is sitting in a large chair set against the wall of her room. Adam walks over with a few small glass vials. After he uncorks the vials, he cleans her wound with a cloth and water before applying a mixture of what looks like lilac and honey.

"What is this?" Dawn asks.

"It's an elixir comprised of tree sap and plants. It will help speed the healing process."

As Adam corks the bottles, Dawn thinks about how he doesn't show any sign of his own shoulder injury from the fight with the royal guards.

Deeply exhausted, she hangs her head down. She focuses on the soothing balm before she looks up at Adam, begging for an explanation. "Lucius challenged them. No arrows were fired. You didn't even try to stop it. Why did this happen again?"

Adam sighs as he places a small piece of cloth over her wound and seals it with tape. "Expelling infections has always been a painful process. Best that, if these attacks are to happen, they stay within a controlled environment."

"I've seen him before," Dawn says quietly, looking off in another direction.

"You've seen who before, Dawn?"

"Lucius, before I came here..." Her eyes glisten with tears.

Adam lets out a deep sigh and nods. "What took you so long to tell me?"

"None of it made sense. I was scared. It could just be nightmares..."

"I understand." Adams offers her a small smile but says nothing more on the subject.

"Adam, when humans die, do they come here?"

"No, since the *Treaty of Ordo*, neither side has wanted them. So now, orphaned souls are relegated to the Ethereal Realm until they move on."

"Doesn't any of this bother you?"

He is thoughtful for a long moment. Their eyes meet, but his expression is unreadable. "Emotions are a luxury I have only begun to afford."

"What do you mean?"

"To survive, one must adapt."

"And if we do not?"

"In that case, Dawn, you must force the world around you to be the one that changes. Do not forget that change is not always a bad thing, even though it may seem so at the time. Only in stagnation are we truly dead. I know things have been hard for you lately. I truly wish they were not."

Adam walks over to a chair close to hers and sits down. "Let me tell you a story. Once, there were twin boys, identical in appearance and moral inflexibility. One believed in self-sacrifice, honor, and duty. The other in selfishness, ruthlessness, and victory at any cost. They fought constantly. Some petty argument escalated to violence. Neither would back down... it only ended when one brother killed the other."

"Why are you telling me this story?"

"Because, Dawn, this fight rages within each of us."

"Isn't it better to just kill the evil twin, then?"

"No, Dawn, because then that is the twin you become."

Chapter 18

Gabriel wanders aimlessly through Thale Forest, his shoulders hunched.

"What is the point?" he says, certain that he has lost the only thing he cares about. Sorrowfully, he thinks, *Maybe I never really knew her to begin with.* After all, she fit in so well with her sleek military-style attire. For a brief moment, she even looked happy. Anger rises as his memories flash to the moment Marce threw him back midair, preventing him from getting to her.

She didn't need my help, though, did she? What were those strange scales on her skin? Does she even need me anymore? Does she still care about me... does she even still think about me?

Inside his chest, his heart strains, grieving the loss of his love, the loss of his former life. Sure, has friends now, but it isn't the same as having her wrapped safely inside his arms. Gabriel stops daydreaming and looks up before shooting into the air, momentarily leaving a blue streak of fire behind him. He decides to settle, nestling in the treetops, cradled by branches.

The scenic view is vast with an ambiance of muted gray-scale tones. Gabriel looks across the sea of treetops, the decrepit fingers of the twisted junipers devoid of foliage reach out in every direction.

There is a gap marking the divide of an empty fjord nearby. Letting out a deep sigh, he allows his body to relax, feeling the chill wind against his face.

Nothing is as it once was; his old life is fading from memory. Even so, he clearly remembers the argument with Raphael. His "father" rarely gave in to anger. Yet in those moments, few and far between, when his father allowed his anger to shine through, it could burn him in ways that never seemed to heal. That time, it was an argument over the river stone he carried with him everywhere.

You have an unhealthy attachment to that thing, Raphael had said. His "father" gave him no choice—he forcibly confiscated the stone from him and threw it into the river. Raphael didn't understand... but Gabriel never explained either.

I wish he was here, Gabriel thinks as he folds his arms, leaning back against the comfortable branches.

Sighing, he wishes the loneliness, the hollow pit inside, would leave. His mind drifts to the fact that Raphael was always gone. The familiar feeling of abandonment is preferable to the controlling whims of his so-called father. Gabriel knows he is being unfair. Raphael would help in any way that he could. Life never felt real until the last few years. Memories before that time are like watching a movie with no subtitles or sound, but the power of emotions rings clear.

Gabriel looks up, searching the sky for the central star. It provides a low light, but no heat. *Why is it dormant? Maybe the star is just old?* Switching his vision, he surveys the area. Everything looks surreal in the strange violet hue. Dark orange auras outline the giant, decrepit serpentine trees. Gazing up at the star, he strains, trying to see it more clearly. As he does, his vision alters again. His heart beats faster, and his eyes widen as flowing lines of radiant golden particles appear. The golden rainbows wrap around the planet, flowing north. Only a fraction of each arch is visible.

Speechless, he marvels at the golden rivers, which are arranged with mathematically perfect spaces between them. Looking down, he sees a large golden river moving south beneath the surface. The golden rainbows that originate from beneath the realm's surface flower out and curve with a sharper angle than the spectacular golden lines that jut out into space far above.

Semoel, are you there?

Yes?

What are these? Gabriel asks, staring at the display of small golden particles. They shimmer like millions of flecks of gold floating in a semi-viscous material traveling in the same direction.

What do you think they are? Semoel inquires.

Leylines?

No. What you are seeing are particles of cosmic radiation trapped within the magnetic field of Basalt.

Willfully turning away from the majestic natural wonder, Gabriel hangs his head down.

I think I've lost her, Semoel.

Don't think like that, Gabriel. You have a mission. You have a purpose.

She doesn't need me anymore.

It's not about need, Gabriel. Do you love her?

Of course I do, more than anything. Saphrael keeps telling me that I'm selfish.

You are not selfish, yet perhaps you are not selfless. Everyone is a mix of both.

Gabriel sighs. *I want to be selfless... but I think I am selfish. All I want is Dawn. She is everything to me.*

Why does that make you selfish?

Because... Saphrael thinks I can save everyone. I want to, but what am I supposed to do?

Maybe you can someday. Why don't you go back to the Wonder Brigade and see if they need help?

They don't need me either.

That is the lake talking, Gabriel. Go back, you have time.

Semoel, do you think Dawn still loves me?

I do. But I think your friends need you as well. And I know you need them.

Silently, Gabriel looks back up at the golden cosmic radiation particles traveling along the magnetic lines and centers himself.

✦

Despite knowing that idling with negative thoughts as his sole companion, his depression will only worsen, Gabriel stays isolated in the treetops ruminating over Dawn. *I've lost her*, is the incessant thought that plagues his mind. *I've lost her. I've lost her. I've lost her*, his mind continues to insist, louder and louder as if he had not heard it the first time. Clenching his fists, he closes his eyes, head bowed, straining not to scream.

There is a thunk as something hits one of the branches he sits upon. His heart races as he stares at the arrow lodged in the tree branch. Gabriel takes flight, his blue flame supporting him in the air. He surveys the muted grayscale tones of the bleak landscape surrounding him and sees... nothing. So, he returns to the arrow.

When he goes to remove it, he crumples paper affixed around the arrow shaft. Leaving the arrow lodged in the branch, he looks at the beige paper. It is held together by a black wax seal of the emperor's crest. *No, that isn't the emperor's crest.* On closer inspection, three strikes slice through the seal. Three distinct strikes through the emperor's crest, like the ones that defaced the flag on a neighboring barracks the day he met the loyalty officer. His hands shake as he removes the scroll from the arrow shaft and begins to read.

Gabriel,

Time runs short. We pass this along in hopes that one day you may in turn repay our kindness. Destroy this letter after you read it.

We have been watching you. We thought you might need this, a crystal with leylines mapped to the forbidden realm. Tell no one you have it, unless absolutely necessary. We speak in code but the language of suffering is louder than words.

"Crystal? What crystal?" He looks at the arrow lodged in the tree once again. In frustration, he grabs and dislodges it from the tree. On closer examination, he finds nothing, so he dismantles it, unscrewing the arrowhead. Inside the hollow shaft, a crystal glints, even in the dull light.

It glides easily out of its hiding place and into his hand. At first glance, the crystal looks ordinary, much like a common chunk of clear quartz, yet it has the faintest glow. The light accentuates the bumps, bends, and sharp angles of its form.

Gabriel concentrates and switches to magnus sight, pushing it further into the high-powered magnetic field vision he used to see the brilliant gold particles surrounding the realm. The light of the crystal grows brighter. A stream of energy flows to and from the crystal at the termination points. The crystal starts to grow so bright that it sears a bright white flash of discoloration in his vision when he looks away.

Blinking his sight back down just a bit, Gabriel can finally see the etchings of a map inside of the crystal. This one contains a more complete map of the Sine System than the one he previously used. It is hard to see clearly because his vision is still damaged with searing white-black marks. He opens his cloak and places the crystal in a front inside pocket, hidden with the other crystal that Azrael had given him.

Then he takes out the map and looks at the dark spot where Dawn is said to be. Tracing his finger near the dot that marks the forbidden realm on the impressionistic watercolor-like map, he reaches his other hand into his pocket to retrieve Dawn's ring.

He fumbles, almost dropping the map, before shoving it back into his cloak and hastily searching every pocket.

"Oh my god—Dawn's ring."

His mind reels, heart racing as he thinks of where he could have lost it. *The Axion? The lake? The barracks?*

He calms himself and secures the arrowhead back onto the shaft, then sets it to rest upon the branches. Lowering his head, he swallows, trying to shove aside the depression. Finding it to be in vain, lets out a scream that echoes across Thale Forest. For a moment, he wonders if it wouldn't be better to just give up.

Gabriel takes the letter back out of his pocket and ignites his blue flame, burning the crumpled paper and wax seal.

The wax drips into his hand and onto the branches below. After watching the paper turn to ash and float away, he feels a profound sense of loss over Dawn's engagement ring and pocket watch with their picture inside. *It's all I had left of her.* He closes his hand into a fist as if he were still able to hold the watch.

✦

Lucius opens the thick wooden doors leading to his war room. It is a long, narrow room featuring a black metal tablet accented with gold, surrounded by ornately carved deep chestnut-brown wooden chairs. Charts line the walls, most of which are hand-sketched with black ink set upon beige parchment whose edges faintly glow in his magnus vision. The charts resemble antiquated cartography, mathematical, and astronomical renderings from Earth in times long past.

Zunael, his architecta with a specialization in sociological concerns, is seated in a chair third from the center along the opposite side of the table. The architecta's striking snow-white eyes look at Lucius; he inclines his head to his superior with no change in expression. The action is stiff and reserved. Lucius does not reciprocate the greeting as is custom.

The angular-faced architecta, whose sunken cheeks and ghost-white hair give him the appearance that he is far more aged than the typical angel, scans his papers as Lucius takes a seat and then looks across the table to his adviser. As usual, Zunael wears a stark white custom-tailored uniform featuring sharply angled pockets. The rather sterile ensemble is flourished with a cape.

"Tell me, how does the press campaign fare?" Lucius inquires.

"As well as one can. I have been administering a less direct approach. By guiding the subconscious thoughts of subjects, grants them the facade of forming the ideas on their own volition. This technique has proven to be far more effective in the longevity and conviction of ideals, once solidly formed. We should continue to focus our resources on these psychological approaches: songs, mantras, target areas of celebration," Zunael clears his throat. "Such as the one that recently occurred. Your rally has transformed idle curiosity into reverence for our princess. They believe she is strong, which also makes her a greater target for those who wish her harm."

"Let them identify themselves and that will be the end of it," Lucius says, pouring himself Xerotes. Normally he doesn't drink during these meetings, but this is a celebratory glass for a successful mission. After setting the embossed silver decanter on the table, he drinks out of a matching metal chalice.

"Have you considered the possibility that there may be more differences between the Gabriels?" The angular-faced, white-haired angel leans in, waiting for a response.

Lucius nods in acknowledgment, allowing Zunael to continue.

"The lesser Gabriel's hair is a lighter shade than that of Chancellor Gabriel's. His cells do not regenerate at an optimal speed, especially for an archangel. This level of sustained cellular retardation has only ever been observed in subjects held in the deep," Zunael says.

"Ah, your experiment that studied the effects of prolonged exposure to void radiation. Furthermore, you are suggesting his deficiencies in cellular regeneration are evidence of void radiation damage." Lucius pauses thoughtfully before taking a long drink from his embossed metal chalice.

"Prolonged exposure, coupled with your soul poisons means that he is weak. Gabriel is primed to be harvested, my lord," Zunael says. "Yet, back to the subject at hand, comparing the lesser Gabriel with Chancellor Gabriel. Their abilities and interests clearly do not align fully with one another. Some can be attributed to nature and others to nurture. When you take two completely identical subjects, give them a different set of circumstances, they will form unique personalities. What I'm asking you to consider is the possibility that, at the source, we do not have two identical subjects."

"Tell me then, Zunael, what do you suppose these further differences may be?"

"Disregard nurture and look solely upon nature. Given certain traits, such as the modification of his pocket watch, it is possible that one Gabriel is inherently different from the other."

"What are you suggesting?"

"I'm observing. Long has it been since any archangel has displayed that sort of talent."

"Your point notwithstanding, it is entirely possible that this is purely nurture—Earth ingenuity."

"Yes, that is a possibility," Zunael concedes. "What about the extra planetary symbol on the watch?"

"The former planet that is now an asteroid field? How he knows about it... I don't know."

Zunael leans back and says, "That was honorable of Moraine to sacrifice himself for your cause."

"He thought so," Lucius says, setting the chalice carefully on the long metal table.

"Ah, so I was correct in assuming you arranged the former champion's involvement in your theatrics?"

"It was his idea."

"Really?"

"He asked if there was anything he could do." Lucius takes a drink from his chalice.

"I see. The princess seems to be adjusting well."

"Yes, her psyche has been kept safely in an acceptable range. Too far in one direction, and her self-destructive nature would take over. She hasn't tried to escape, as of late. Especially with Adam keeping watch. He provides her solace as well as aiding in our fine-tuning of her issues."

Zunael inclines his head. "How has she been progressing?"

"Better than expected. Not only is she naturally gifted, it seems that the black dragon has integrated with her, preventing her from dying."

"No one else knows of this?" Zunael asks.

"No, not even Adam. Only archangels can see the visage of the dragons."

"Did the dragon aid her in dealing with Moraine?"

"No, it tried, but apparently a Horseman of Death's splintered dragon cannot kill an angel."

"Which of Child of Eridu's half is it?"

"From what I've seen it must be Cain's."

"How is Cain?"

"The same as he has been."

"Why don't you wake him?"

"The Reliqui Mortus is far better off without his influence. Cain is reliable in reaction. Unfortunately, that reaction is often self-serving."

"Are you going to unite the fractured black dragon within Dawn? It would offer even greater power and protection. Perhaps, one day she may even use it offensively."

"Perhaps someday. For now, Able is under the 'divine protection' of Mikhail."

"At least the *Treaty of Ordo* keeps your lands clear of most interlopers."

"Here's to the law." Lucius toasts his chalice in the air.

"One might consider running tests on Dawn to fully explore the integration of Bedellus as well as identify and expel any lingering weaknesses due to the unique circumstances of her conception. For her protection, of course."

"And if she does not survive the process?" Lucius has a cold mask of indifference, but anger is more than apparent in his words.

"If she succumbs to her innate flaws, then nothing of value will be lost."

"No one is above the need for salvation protocol. Do you agree?" Lucius's piercing copper-colored eyes stare into Zunael's white irises.

Zunael's response is measured and controlled. "Of course, Emperor."

"Then, I suggest you take leave to be evaluated on Chesed." Lucius watches as the disciplined nature of Zunael's composure slips before he regains it.

"Of course, my lord." Zunael bows his head. "May my leave be suspended until after this orbium's tournament?"

Lucius looks at him, his chin tilted upward. "You care not for the games, Zunael."

"What I care about is the Circle Gala and what it represents. I wouldn't want to miss such an important occasion."

"Have been reading my files again?"

Zunael lowers his head in a sign of submission. "I merely put the pieces together, my lord, I swear." He looks to one of the many charts on the wall that looks like bent grids depicting connecting wormholes. "The alignment only happens when the orbium begins anew."

"Don't assume what you do not know, Zunael." Lucius glares at him. After a silent moment Lucius continues, "I grant you your request. Remember this kindness."

Zunael nods and gathers his papers. "Of course, my lord. You are more than gracious."

With much restraint in his composure, Zunael exits the war room. Lucius watches him, tilting the metal chalice to his lips once more.

Chapter 19

Dawn turns uncomfortably while drifting off to sleep and hopes that she will not have another nightmare. The world around her fades. A dark crimson apple floats in front of her midair, slowly spinning in a circle and bobbing slightly. It shoots off, flowing up and down, as if upon an ocean wave. The world around her is a deep midnight blue and has a bitter chill. The sky, at least what she can see through the light-blue mists, is a strange mix of blacks and blues. There is a mournful hypnotic hymn coming from nowhere.

The apple floats up and hovers inches above the open palm of a pale, white-haired angel with large dark-blue wings dressed in tattered black rags. A tinge of a smile pulls at the corner of his lips.

"Dawn?" The angel's voice echoes as he speaks.

"Yes?"

"I am Azrael, the Archangel of Death."

"I've seen you before. Am I dead?"

"No, Dawn, you are not dead. Your name is not written in the Book of Life, the Book of Death, nor the Book of Fate. I'm not certain you can die. Even if you could, I'm not sure that you would, especially with Bedellus protecting you."

"What?"

"Bedellus is my dragon—well, half of him anyway. Long ago, I gave him to the Horsemen of Death."

"Isn't it, Horseman of Death?"

Azrael doesn't answer. His head is turned to the side, intently staring at something she cannot see.

"Why am I here, Azrael?"

"There are things you need to know and nightmares that need to end."

"You can end my nightmares?"

"The least I can do is try. With any hope it will lessen. Come." Azrael walks, heading toward an ominous dark-blue tree that is like none Dawn has ever seen before; the branches of the overgrown tree are split two by two the ends of the veins connecting to the sky.

As Dawn stares at the twisted tree, Azrael says, "Tell me, what have you seen?"

"What do you mean?"

"Tell me of your life."

Dawn stops walking, her eyes well with tears, and she shakes her head.

"Is there nothing you want to remember?" Azrael asks, his light gray irises are worn yet kind.

"Gabriel," is the only thing she says.

"And the rest?"

"Of Earth? No... nothing."

Azrael nods silently before quietly saying, "I understand." They begin to walk again. "Tell me about your nightmares."

"My nightmares? Well, they're always different, but I always suffer. When I wake up, it feels like I was really there... wherever there was. The pain, the fear... it lingers and accompanies me throughout the day."

Azrael nods. "I understand," he says softly. "If I were to sleep, my dreams would be filled with nightmares as well. A natural consequence of my duty. Normally, my mind is scattered across a great distance, but I need to talk to you with a more complete mind. I don't understand you, Dawn. Which is complicated because I understand nearly everything."

Azrael reaches out to he and places an ice-cold palm gently on her forehead. He speaks a few words that do not translate, and she feels a sudden head rush as if she were connected to the strange blue space around her.

Suddenly, the hymn ceases. The world around her is gone, and she finds herself on Earth, walking in the forest near Gabriel's house. She looks up as she passes the tree—the tree where she tried to commit suicide. *Gabriel isn't far,* she thinks. But instead of heading there directly, she stops at a nearby wooden bridge. Something urges her to find Gabriel and to find him now.

"What happens when there is nowhere left to run?" she mumbles to herself, leaning against the tattered railings of the old wooden bridge.

An enormous black snake jumps from the water and grabs her, coiling itself around her waist. She wants to scream, but she cannot breathe. A cold rush envelops her as she is dragged under. The obsidian-colored serpent constricts painfully and sinks its venomous fangs into her shoulder. Warm venom is injected into her bloodstream. The already muddled water around her blurs, and she feels an overwhelming sense of peace. A sword materializes in her hand, but she refuses to use it against the snake.

"It will kill you if you don't," Azrael's voice echoes from nowhere.

Closing her eyes, she opens her hand and allows the sword to sink to the bottom of the river.

In an instant, she finds herself sitting beside Azrael on the edge of the bridge overlooking the water. When she peers into the waters, she can see a mirage of herself, relaxed and dying within the serpent's grip.

"Is there no way to make you see?" Azrael says, sadly gazing into the water.

"See what?" Dawn asks. Her purple nightgown is drenched, sticking to her skin.

"I thought you were safe. I thought you were where you belong. I am not certain of where you belong. Everything has a purpose. Everything has a place. Tell me, were you happier with Gabriel or where you are now?"

"I was happier with Gabriel. Of course, that might be the endorphins talking."

"Brain chemistry is only part of what love is, Dawn," Azrael waves his hand, and the image of Dawn wrapped in the coil of the snake vanishes. "I don't want to see you poisoned like your mother was."

"What are you talking about?"

"Your mother was a priestess. Then, she met your father. He whispered into her ear constantly. Told her how to act, that he loved her. Part of him was with her in spirit, always. I don't understand his need for control. Perhaps it stems from his own sense of fear?" Azrael falls silent.

"Maybe he did love her?" Dawn reasons.

"Maybe." Azrael has a small, sad smile on his face. "Be careful, Dawn. Life is a game of chess; move intentionally and with purpose. So I tell you this with purpose: Gabriel has been searching for you. He has sacrificed much of his own salvation in order to find you. You need to return. Tell no one that you saw me."

Azrael places a friendly but cold hand upon her upper arm. He offers her a smile as her vision blurs out of focus until she finds herself in her own comfortable room. The first thing she sees is Adam, seated in his chair, guarding the door.

He sets down the book he is reading and walks over. As much as she has grown used to his presence, it makes her miss Gabriel even more.

"Another nightmare?" Adam inquires.

"No... not really." Dawn shrugs, not knowing what else to say.

"Oh?" Adam waits for her to elaborate.

"It was... just a dream." Dawn leans away from him.

"Interesting, but are your dreams ever just dreams?" Adam says, his expression stoic but concerned.

"It's all right, Adam. Isn't it good that it wasn't a nightmare?"

He nods. "Yes, of course, Princess. It is just that—things are not always as they appear to be."

"Yes, you are right, of course. It was a dream, a dream that I wish to keep to myself, for once."

"I see... In that case, there is something I've been wanting to discuss with you." Adam breathes in, collecting himself before he says, "I am relieved to have been removed as hierophant and reassigned to guard you."

"Oh? Well, that's good, I guess. Didn't you have a lot of power as hierophant? Won't you miss that?"

"There is a burden of responsibility either way, Dawn. But to answer your question, no, I was suffocating under the weight of being hierophant. I had no way out."

"All right," Dawn says slowly, trying to fully process what he said. "It's nice that you are satisfied with your new role. To be honest, it's nice having you around."

"I am happy, Dawn. I do mean that."

Dawn gets out of bed. She grows silent before nodding to herself, lost in thought. "I forgive you for what happened in the Axion."

"I thought you did not forgive," Adam teases her, his eyes filled with appreciation, then his expression grows more serious. "It was a deeply regrettable transgression, one that I can never truly atone for. I placed you in danger. Now it is my solemn vow to sacrifice my time, and if needed, my life to ensure your protection."

Dawn is silent. She never thought about it that way.

"However, I stand by my stance that you were never in any real danger. The masses wanted to see their princess. With your abilities, demons pose no threat to you. If anything were to happen, I would have intervened myself."

"You threw me in the Axion with demons, Adam. Large demons."

"I know. Sometimes, if you want to see someone fly, you have to give them a push."

Dawn sighs and shrugs, then walks over to her closet while singing a low gentle tune. She quiets as she notices that Adam looks as if he is lost in a trance.

"Adam?"

Adam shakes his head, taking a moment to regain himself before saying, "Forgiveness, Princess, is all I ask."

"I already said I forgive you."

✦

Even though some time has passed, Adam struggles to concentrate on anything beyond the intoxicating trance induced by Dawn's song. The soothing, otherworldly melody placates his emotions. It repeats continuously in the back of his mind. She has no idea she is amplifying the effects of the seduction aura inherited from her mother. Adam is unable to voice concerns about her unintentionally misusing her abilities, as Lucius has ordered the handling of such matters to be left solely to his discretion.

From his seat near the door, Adam glances over at Dawn, who is at her vanity, scrunching her large, soft, spiraling curls with a light touch of oil. It is in this moment that he realizes that he can no longer deny just how attached to her he has become.

Feeling dazed, he grips the book he is holding before he composes himself. The song in his mind fades ever so slightly, and he looks down at the white pages of the leather-bound book open in his right hand. It isn't a book at all, not in the traditional sense. It is a Book of Literas, or rather, a book of letters.

Whenever Lucius sent a missive, which was often, he would write in a matching book, and the words appeared in Adam's copy as he wrote. In general, Adam finds the content, primarily composed of Lucius's philosophical views, to be malevolence masked by selective truth. He keeps a vigilant watch at the door, having already read over the last thing Lucius sent several times—words written in Lucius's elongated, elegant handwriting. Black ink sits raised upon the parchment made of stone and plant fiber, which reads, *I would like to see Dawn at her earliest convenience.* Which, of course, meant now.

Dawn has only ever asked about the book once. Not wanting to lie yet unable to tell the truth, he told her it was a "rather poetic philosophy book."

Adam stands and places the book into a large pocket near the chest of his faded-black fatigues before securing a button in place. He clears his throat, calling her attention. "Your father has sent word that he would like to spend time with you."

Dawn nods and stands. Her black lace dress is intricately designed, the skirt of which reaches the floor. Bowing his head respectfully, Adam offers her his arm. She looks at it with a bewildered expression.

"I can walk on my own, Adam." Dawn walks up to him, and he opens the right half of the large wooden double doors.

"Very well, Princess." Adam strides down the hall with the same demeanor that he had when he was hierophant. It was almost as if nothing had changed. But at the same time, everything is different now. Wishing he had someone to confide in, he buries his thoughts deep inside. She will never understand how grateful he is to be her guard. Fatigue lingers from his previous duties, but now he has time to rest, time to breathe.

Dots of pale-blue crystal lights line the narrow black stone halls. The royal guards follow silently.

Adam turns to Dawn and remarks, "There is a different air about you this cycle, Princess."

Dawn lets out a deep sigh and looks as tired as he feels.

Adam nods and tries to reach out to her. "I hope I am doing a decent job at alleviating your loneliness. I know I am not Gabriel—"

"I thought I wasn't allowed to talk about him." Dawn snaps.

Adam hesitates, wishing he could do more.

Before he has a chance to respond, Dawn continues, "I've heard some things—things that I don't even know if they are true." Dawn has a tremble of her bottom lip, but only for a moment. She is hiding something.

"As in… what, Princess?"

"Gabriel," Dawn says quietly, her voice broken as she says his name.

Adam stops and turns to her. The guards keeping pace stop as well. "Princess… tell me what is bothering you."

"They're just dreams, Adam. They don't mean anything."

"Forgive me, but dreams are often much more than what they seem. And yet, perhaps you are correct in assuming that sometimes dreams are just that. I know you miss Gabriel, but as a whole, you are far better off than where you were. If I were you, I would voice your concerns to your father."

Adam holds the door open. She looks at him as she passes, depression evident upon her face.

Dawn turns and nods to her father before picking up the chalice of

Xerotes waiting for her. She stares despondently at the silver metal chalice and the red semi-vicious liquid within it.

"Is there something wrong, my love?" Lucius inquires.

Drinking deep, Dawn downs nearly the entirety of the sweet, bitter red liquor at once. Adam takes his place, standing near the door. Dawn shakes her head and doesn't answer. Tears form in her eyes, but she fights to hold them back.

"I hear you've been escaping into dreams. Doing so gives permission to that which haunts us, the problem to be solved, to continue. Dreams are illusions and should be treated as such." Lucius rests against his elegant black couch, the wood around the top of it and arms flow out in curves. He tilts his head, studying her. "Tell me, has Adam been a suitable guard?" Lucius asks as he refills her chalice.

Shyly tilting her head down, Dawn is much quieter than normal. After taking a sip of Xerotes, she says, "Adam told me a story the other day."

"Did he now? Adam, you haven't been filling her head with false hope, have you?" Lucius turns back to Dawn. "Tales are designed to inspire, to alter the course of fate of those who hear them. What was the moral of the story he told you, Dawn?"

"It was about one brother murdering the other. One was dark and the other light. That if you kill, you become the dark twin."

"Disregard such information, Dawn. Fables only cloud proper decision-making."

"How can you say that?"

"There is no truth in tales. If there ever was, it has been falsified through embellishment. We must ask ourselves, what purpose does it serve? Stories are a synthetic comfort, shielding us from the cold reality where it doesn't matter how much you hope. A reality in which Goliath always wins, in which Daniel is food for lions. We must remove the weakness of false hope and instead utilize them as the tools that they are. Many are designed to keep armies marching into the jaws of death, if required. Tales of unending triumph in the face of death and insurmountable odds. Reality has a much darker tone. If you inspire fear, you risk the enemy becoming stronger by triggering natural defenses. If you hold ransom, they have purpose, inspiring them to fight harder. No. Remove hope and the enemy will defeat themselves."

Dawn is silent for a long moment, tears still welling in her eyes. Quietly, as if she is afraid to ask, she mumbles, "Is Gabriel the enemy?"

"Yes." Lucius has his trademark hollow expression.

"Why?" Dawn shakes her head.

"Dawn, you are a living remnant of your mother. Enduring proof of love that once was. Your mother had incredible prowess. I admired her strength, cunning, spirit, and intellect."

"I heard she was a priestess until you corrupted her," Dawn accuses him, looking directly at him, meekness evaporating into anger.

The unreadable expression on Lucius's face stays as such. He leans in, watching her closely. "Did Adam tell you that? Your mother was addicted to power. Once she tasted divine strength, she obsessively sought more, as all addicts do. Nothing would ever be enough." Lucius is lost in thought for a moment before he continues. "She may have loved me in her own way, but she loved power above all else. ... I loved your mother. Now, Gabriel wants to take the only piece of her I have left. That is why he is the enemy."

"Is Gabriel here? Is he coming for me?" Dawn looks up at him, her hand gripping the chalice trembles.

"Let me ask you a question, Dawn. How did you know of your mother's position in Eridu?"

"Someone told me."

"Adam?"

Dawn's bottom lip scrunches, pressing up against her upper lip as she refuses to answer.

"Now, Dawn, we must be truthful with one another." Lucius has his chin lifted into the air. Adam is never quite sure what Lucius is thinking. Then, he tries to read Dawn's reactions. His mind sorts through what he had said, and although they had talked about Lilith recently, he is certain he didn't tell her that she was a priestess in Eridu.

"I can't tell you how I know or how I know Gabriel is on his way."

232

"Azrael is the only one naïve enough to interfere. Have you been conversing with the Archangel of Death, Dawn?"

She shakes her head, but her eyes are wide and the truth is written clear upon her face.

"Adam, send word that Azrael is no longer welcome within our system." Lucius looks back to her. "Generally, he knows better than to interfere, but perhaps we need to send him a reminder. Further isolation may give him the time he needs to reconsider his actions."

"Sir, wouldn't further isolation potentially drive him to work against you?" Adam asks, walking over.

"Clearly, he's already working against me. Better a forgotten friend turned enemy than a spy who is actively working against you. Dawn, if I can tread back to the subject we were discussing earlier, how has Adam been treating you?"

"Well enough."

"Perhaps you are better off at my side than at his. I will leave things the way they are for now, but tell me everything, and I will do my best to make things right. Take a short break, and then we will continue training. I also wish for you to study fallacies and debate. If you are to rule, it is something you must know."

"Why place this burden on me when I have never once asked for it?"

"Because it is your birthright."

Chapter 20

I can't believe I lost Dawn's ring. Gabriel sighs deeply as he drags his fingers along the coarse fabric of his cloak. Igniting fire from his hands, he jets a short distance and lands at the edge of the crater that once housed the Black Lake. As he peers over the side, his memory flashes to when he was trapped deep underwater, locked away far from everything else. *Will I ever forget what it feels like in there?*

The overwhelming feeling that this has all been for naught plagues his mind. Gabriel hangs his head down, thinking, *Maybe it is better to just give up.* Then, his father's words echo in his memory: "A single spark of hope can light your path. You know what the good thing about the darkness is? It makes the light easier to see."

Taking in a steadying breath, he focuses his thoughts on Dawn. However, refusing to leave his psyche is the sight of her in that military dress, sharing the stage with Emperor Lucius and Hierophant Adam. *Emperor Lucius...* he thinks sadly. *Why has he allowed me to gain a foothold and allies?* He desperately wants to understand in order to fight against it.

Inside, he knows that ultimately the Wonder Brigade are soldiers of Lucius's army. Besides Saphrael, he isn't certain of anyone's loyalties. *Maybe he doesn't think I am a threat? If that were true, he wouldn't have bothered with me in the Axion. Why would he throw me into my father's fire? To see if I was strong enough? If I could survive? The simple answer is he wanted me there. This is an elaborate trap; a trap he knows I need to walk into. I have no choice. I have to save Dawn.*

Questions race through Gabriel's mind as he walks back to the barracks. *I can never go back to my life as it was... can I?* Deep down, he knows the answer that his life, as it was, is irrevocably broken.

Gabriel passes the large, tattered banner outside of the Wonder Brigade's barracks. He opens the door and finds everyone milling about inside.

"Has anyone seen my watch?" Gabriel asks, surveying the room. No one seems to even acknowledge his question.

"Saphrael told us what happened," Cadence says, standing up from his cot, his gaze meeting Gabriel's directly. "We can no longer deny it. You are Archangel Gabriel."

"What? No, guys, I'm not."

"You are Archangel Gabriel. There is no other possible explanation." Marce lets out a deep sigh, averting his gaze as he delivers the news. "I'm afraid that you're disqualified from participating in the tournament. You can't help us."

"He's not even from our realm." Loth glares at Gabriel with accusatory suspicion before he turns to the rest of them, not giving Gabriel the dignity of addressing him directly. "That alone is enough to disqualify him. Not just him either, the rest of us will be cast out alongside him if we continue down this path."

Saphrael sighs. "We won't abandon Gabriel. Even if it means a shared fate."

"Who made you the decider?" Loth glares at Saphrael, standing up, fists clenched.

"You all did," Saphrael says, meeting Loth's challenge. "I am still the leader of this team."

"Captain Nemos," Loth says sarcastically.

Gabriel looks confused.

"Nemos means no one. It's your only name in discere. Which is where we will all end up," Loth says.

Spud, who was trying to stay out of it by fiddling with a piece of armor, puts it down and leans in, asking, "Has anyone heard about Adam?"

Expectantly, he pauses, waiting for their reaction.

"What about him?" Marce shrugs.

"After the Axion, rumors are that he has been stripped of his rank. Now, he has to guard Dawn personally." Spud smirks as if he had been waiting to tell them the news.

"Who is taking over Adam's position then?" Saphrael asks.

"Jarael is taking over most of his responsibilities, at least for now. At least that's what I've heard," Spud answers.

"Adam... and Dawn?" Gabriel asks, looking more lost than ever.

Saphrael looks at him with compassion. Loth rolls his eyes and sits back down, successfully disarmed, at least for now. Cadence works to apply a mix of oil onto his staff and ignores the gossip.

"So, what now?" Gabriel asks. "I can't fight in the tournament for you. Is there anyone we can talk to about this?"

"No," Cadence says. "Where'd you get the breastplate from anyway? It almost looks like a cheap knock-off of Archangel Gabriel's lost tetragram."

"What is a tetragram?"

"That symbol in the middle but is also refers to the armor set. Powerful, sacred material, real tetragrams."

Gabriel becomes quiet. Would they believe him if he told them that he found it in the fire outside of the Axion? In the back of his mind, he remembers Semoel's warning to not to say anything.

"No, yeah..." Gabriel mumbles before forcing himself to snap out of it. "The armor's all right." He moves aside Azrael's cloak, showing him the broken part of the breastplate.

"Nothing a little tape won't fix," Cadence says, resting his large golden staff against the wall before grabbing what looks like a roll of duct tape off the top of his dresser and making his way to Gabriel. There is a *skreet* sound as he peels a strip of the highly reflective silver tape and wraps it around Gabriel's armor. Cadence works expertly as if he were bandaging an arm. "Good as new... sort of."

"Thanks." Gabriel nods to him and allows the feathered ends of the cloak to slide back over his shoulder.

"Too bad you're disqualified. We could sure use your help in the free-for-all." Spud shrugs.

"Has anyone officially come by and said that I'm disqualified?"

"Laws pertaining to the tournaments are clear," Loth says. "Archangels are not allowed to compete. Go to the library yourself and look it up if you don't believe me."

Cadence shrugs. "Saphrael will have to represent us in the free-for-all."

"Guys, it's time to go," Saphrael says, slinging a bag over his shoulder. Gabriel only now realizes they are fully geared. "Gabriel, get the rest of your gear on."

"Is it time for the free-for-all?" Gabriel asks.

"No." Saphrael takes a long, black, medieval-looking crossbow from the wall. He tilts it up vertically, the tip of the crossbow facing skyward, and puts on his Chokma mask with his other hand. "It's time to hunt."

◆

Although the Wonder Brigade traveled for some time at a brisk pace, no one is physically exhausted, but a mental toll has been taken from trudging through the visually endless, mute gray desert that encompasses much of central Basalt.

"So much gray," Gabriel complains, mostly to himself. His shoulders are slump, showing signs of fatigue. His worn demon leather gloves have flecks of paint from his run-down, secondhand medieval crossbow he carries. Although it is worn, the mid-sized crossbow is well-shaped and surprisingly light for as long as it is.

The others carry hiking bags with three vertical straps that wrap around. In it, they carry their crossbows in the center straps, and ritual knives hang off the right side. Saphrael is the only one who also carries a quiver, placed nestled against his crossbow. Their Chokma masks hang just below their ritual knives. Since Gabriel has no bag, Spud insisted on carrying his Chokma mask for him, so he trudges along with a mask hanging from each side of his pack.

"Think we're going to get anything?" Cadence asks, the sound of his large golden staff makes a *sht sht sht* sound in the dirt as he walks.

"Hopefully." Marce shrugs, adjusting his pack. "Saphrael could use lutum in his fight,"

"What is lutum?" Gabriel asks.

He almost regrets asking, as Marce sighs theatrically and even Cadence gives him an exasperated look.

The look softens as Cadence explains, "It's a boost made from demons mixed with enhancer plants."

"We do this before all the big matches. Believe it or not, we're usually pretty good at killing demons," Marce says.

"Someone explain the rules to Gabriel," Saphrael says, keeping his eyes forward as he walks.

"Sure, you get one arrow." Marce points. "The arrowhead holds a glass vial filled with your blood—angelic blood is toxic to demons. The vial of blood sits against an inward spike that breaks open a cap on impact."

"Okay, but why do you only get one shot?" Gabriel asks.

"You want to waste resources?" Loth rolls his eyes. "This is a game of accuracy and restraint—of intellect."

Marce rolls his shoulders, shifting the weight of his hiking bag to be more centered as his halberd is strapped to the side of his pack. His crossbow is slightly off center as a counterbalance.

Saphrael stops in a seemingly arbitrary place and drops his heavy bag. "This is as good a place as any. We can rest here before moving on."

Everyone follows suit as the sounds of unpacking fill the air.

"But we're in the middle of nowhere?" Gabriel squints, looking at the expanse of gray dust and wondering if there is something he is missing.

"Better here than being ambushed in the Lilthaen Forest," Saphrael explains as he digs through his backpack.

Spud takes out a blanket and sets it on the ground. It's the same blanket from his cot in the barracks since the Wonder Brigade isn't provided with luxury beyond basic necessities.

"Thanks, Spud," Gabriel says as Spud hands him his blanket, as well as a small bag of items he carried for him.

"Can you believe Moraine attacked Dawn? I thought better of our champions. I guess strength doesn't afford you loyalty or honor." Loth says the last part while looking directly at Gabriel.

Gabriel looks through the items, ignoring Loth, and takes out a sheathed ritual knife. He waves it around casually, thinking about how damaged and incomplete he feels without Dawn.

Saphrael stops him from waving the sheathed knife in the air by placing his hand on his arm. "These are not toys, Gabriel. They are ritual items, and they should be treated with respect," Saphrael says softly.

"Oh, I'm sorry, it's just—when I go camping it's not as serious."

Marce gives him a weird look, a look that says *What did he just say?* If everyone else was also confused, they didn't show it. Gabriel isn't sure why Marce gave him that look, until he realizes that there may be no good translation for the word camp. The concept of leisurely staying in the foreboding woods is entirely foreign to them.

"Remember, when we get there: stay in formation, follow my orders. Hopefully, we'll get a kill shot," Saphrael says.

"Do you guys need to rest, or do you just want to rest?" Gabriel asks.

"We don't need to stop, but it is wise to take your time when you can afford to. The mind needs time to prepare as well. Enjoy this moment of reprieve. We don't always get that luxury," Saphrael says.

"I always enjoy these moments of rest," Spud says, relaxing.

"I don't." Marce smiles a bit too sarcastically to show he is joking, but it is clear from his pained expression that he's not.

✦

Between hiking through the expanse of nothing and the lack of significant celestial light, Gabriel's mind grows ever weary. Spud has kept up most of the conversation by continuously telling everyone about things he has overheard. Everyone tended to humor him or outright ignore him.

"And then… Berosel threatened to throw the match just to spite Davael.

That shut him up real quick."

"Where do you get your gossip from anyway, Spud?" Gabriel asks.

Marce rolls his eyes, sick of the conversation, and answers for him, "Caelus. He gets his gossip from Caelus."

"Who is Caelus?"

"Not a who. It's a what. Caelus—you know, building of lakes." Marce makes a gesture with his arms that means nothing to Gabriel.

"Building of lakes?"

"They're called bathhouses on Earth," Saphrael mumbles.

"How do you know that?" Gabriel asks.

Saphrael shrugs and says, "I know some things about Earth," and leaves it at that.

"And then what, Spud? Did Berosel actually throw the match?" Cadence asks.

Spud half-shrugs. "They lost, if that's what you're asking. If he lost on purpose, I don't know. Davael sure seems to think so. They aren't talking anymore."

"Oh, would you shut up already?" Loth rolls his eyes. "It's bad enough we have to travel, do we have to listen to you the entire time as well?"

"Sorry," Spud says quietly, at least for a moment, before he points excitedly. "The Lilthaen Forest."

Gabriel squints, and sure enough, a forest is coming into view. The trees don't look as monstrous in size as those in the north, but it is hard to judge at this distance.

Saphrael stops and allows his heavy bag to fall to the ground. "All right, guys."

"Are we resting again?" Gabriel asks.

"No, we're preparing to hunt." Saphrael unbuckles the top of the quiver he carries and starts handing out black arrow shafts.

They all work quietly, in a well-practiced fashion. Meanwhile, Gabriel stands there wondering what it is he is supposed to do.

Spud takes what he needs from his bag and then tosses it to Gabriel, who catches with his free hand, holding the crossbow in the other. After observing silently, Gabriel follows suit, setting down the crossbow and locating a small black wooden box. The antique-looking box creaks open. Inside, he finds a handful of glass vials filled with plant material, a few objects he believes are tools, a couple of lids, and two arrowheads.

Silently, he struggles to keep up with what they are doing. He pauses in shock as Marce unsheathes a ritual knife, closes his eyes, and slices into his lower right forearm. He drops onto one knee and whispers something that Gabriel can't quite hear. Marce's blood runs down his fingers into the vial. The others drop down to one knee and do the same.

There is a *skrrrt* sound as Saphrael places a piece of shiny silver tape on his arm before pulling the long sleeve of his gambeson back down. He puts his gloves back on, makes eye contact with Gabriel, and walks over.

"Take the knife, hold it in your hands, and give thanks for the opportunity to be a hunter instead of the hunted. Roll up your sleeve and make an incision along your forearm. As the blood drips, allow it to curve down the tips of your fingers into the vial." Saphrael speaks quietly as the others are concentrating. "Try not to waste any. Concentrate on the beat of your heart."

"The beat of my heart?"

"It tells us everything. The beat of the drum calling us to war. Sacrificing a piece of yourself reminds us that we are not the only ones who suffer. When you do get a shot, make sure you stay centered," Saphrael says.

There is a series of clicks as the others load their weapons.

"Like in meditation?"

"No, I mean literally. If the string and arrow are off center, then your shot will be as well."

"Oh."

Gabriel grips the handle of the ritual knife and unsheathes it. Closing his eyes, he tries to ignore everyone watching him and makes a deep cut into his left forearm. Breathing out, he steadies his shaking hand as he positions the glass vial. The blood that fills it is a darker shade than the others. He isn't sure if it is because he is an archangel or because of the soul poison running through his veins. When the vial is almost full, he

241

carefully screws on the soft lid. It is slightly difficult to manage due to its hydrophobic coating.

After he places the arrow shaft together with the glass vial he asks, "How come no one uses crossbows normally? Aren't they more effective than melee weapons?"

"Yes, Gabriel, they tend to be. First of all, we try not to waste resources if we can help it. Metal that can pierce angelic skin is running scarce," Saphrael explains.

"We use it as a backup method, rather than the other way around," Spud adds.

Gabriel holds his hand up, stopping Cadence from coming over to help him then places the arrow shaft on the ground and patches himself up. The sticky tape is rough, and he is fairly sure that the silver tape they are using is the same one Cadence used to repair his armor. He's pretty sure the tape isn't designed to be used medically.

"Marce, you're left-handed," Gabriel says after noticing the strip of silver tape on his right arm, his sleeve still rolled up.

"What's it to you?" Marce says, half-ignoring Gabriel while he packs his bag.

"Nothing, I've just never noticed before."

"Observant." Marce rolls his eyes before fixing the sleeve of his gambeson, covering the silver strip of tape on his arm.

Gabriel picks up the nearly junk crossbow and the arrow. Marce had brought the crossbow several cycles before, and where he got it from, Gabriel doesn't know.

"Let me help you." Cadence walks over.

"Would you all quit babying the archangel? You think he needs our help? You think we need his? I think he's a spy or worse," Loth says, staring out into the distance of nothing to the north.

"What's worse?" Spud asks.

"Anything, Spud. Whatever you do, don't trust him." Loth adjusts his pack.

"Come on, guys, let's get going," Saphrael says, buckling the straps of his pack in an X across his chest. Everyone has a weapon in addition to their crossbows and ritual knives—everyone except Gabriel.

✦

The Wonder Brigade treads quietly through the forest. Even though the largest trees of the Lilthaen Forest are roughly half the size of the ones in the north, the monstrous trees surrounding them are still much larger and foreboding than Gabriel is used to. The twisting, thick vein-like branches reach out in all directions, making him deeply unsettled. The golden-brown bark of the trees is covered in a dark green moss. And, unlike the trees to the north, these ones produce richly dark green leaves that hang down from the branches in bunches of circles, reminding Gabriel of grapes.

They come to a thicket of what looks like densely packed, towering, withered oak trees. Saphrael communicates silently through hand signals. The unit splits, taking positions on both sides of a small rustic trail that cuts through the center of the thicket. Gabriel calms his shaking hands, worried he may accidentally set off his crossbow and look like a complete idiot. *Just remember what Saphrael said*, he tells himself, *'Don't shoot unless you have a kill shot, Anywhere the arrow pierces will be a kill shot due to the poison. Angelic blood is incompatible with demon blood.'*

He switches into magnus sight and the world flickers, becoming a bright, night-vision-like view with far more colors. As they wait, Gabriel can do nothing but think of Dawn. *How is she doing?* A small part of him hopes that she is miserable without him, but another part knows that is a dark thought. Finding it hard to forgive himself for having a passing negative thought, he reassures himself, *I am not my thoughts. It is my actions that determine my destiny.*

Gabriel's adrenaline spikes as he hears a crunch of branches—the footfalls of something running. Not well trained in magnus sight, he switches his vision back to normal and spots a large, mange-ridden black wolf with dark-red eyes that glow in the dimness of the forest, heading in their direction. Switching his sight back, the darkness obscures much, but highlighted

243

in bright red is the circulatory system, and the movements of muscle contractions as the beast runs.

Unlike the bluish-purple range he sees in his friends, the aura emanating around the demon is a necrotic black. Gabriel raises his crossbow. Saphrael holds his hand up in a fist, signaling for him to wait. The demon runs by, its large, clawed feet thunking against the ground as it races past. Saphrael points forward and, silently, they speed after their prey. Gabriel trails behind the group, not proficient at boosting his natural speed.

The group splits off in a formation that Gabriel had only practiced once, the crescent-guard formation. They form a semicircle around the demon, crossbows raised, driving it against a rock wall. The demon foams at the mouth, snarling at them, rapidly doubling in size. Its roar is so terrifyingly loud, it reverberates throughout Gabriel's skin. *Its fangs are the size of my forearm. Keep your crossbow steady.* His hands tremble as he tries not to think of how easily it could swallow any one of them whole.

In the semicircle around the demon is Marce, at the far-left end, next to him is Gabriel, farther back, out by a false opening are Cadence and Saphrael. Loth and Spud close the semicircle around the other side. Without a word, Saphrael's arm snaps forward, signaling to open fire.

Loth shoots first. As Gabriel watches the arrow fly, time slows. Visualizing the path of the arrow, Gabriel sees it will hit the rock wall. The demon turns to Marce and charges.

Inhaling deep, Gabriel pulls the trigger of his crossbow. His arrow speeds directly at the demon, causing it to panic and pivot back toward Loth's arrow. The glass vial of Gabriel's arrow shatters on the rock wall moments after Loth's arrow pierces the demon's leg. The creature lets out a wounded howl that echoes throughout the forest.

Loth rips off his Chokma mask.

"Hey, archangel! I didn't need your help!" Loth yells, aggressively coming at Gabriel, who also removes his helmet, ready to meet his challenge.

"Would you both shut up before we alert every single demon in this forest to our location?" Saphrael says in a low, firm tone.

"Your kill's getting away," Gabriel says to Loth.

Gabriel looks down at the trail of green blood that leads into the forest. Just out of view, the whisper of an untranslated prayer amplifies throughout the forest with disorienting echoes from different directions. There is a shriek soon cut short, followed by a sound of something falling.

Cadence emerges from the woods carrying a normal-sized human-looking head in his left hand. Green blood drips down the blades of his golden staff. He throws the head of the demon at Loth and Gabriel. It lands next to them.

"It's done," Cadence says.

No longer arguing, Gabriel is silent in shock because he always saw Cadence as the most stereotypically angelic of them all, in both appearance and demeanor. To watch him walk in, freshly killed demon head in hand, felt... wrong.

"Thanks, Gabriel." As Loth glares at him, Gabriel is deeply unsettled that he doesn't blink. His lip twitches as if he were going to at least pretend to smile but thought better of it.

"We did it!" Spud celebrates with a fist pump.

"We nearly didn't. Now, let's get out of here before we have to fight our way out. Loth, technically it's your kill," Saphrael says.

Loth sighs, picks up the severed demon's head, and trudges in the direction Cadence emerged. Loth hoists the demon's carcass across his shoulders. Rivers of green blood pour down the left side of his uniform. As he walks, he leaves a pungent trail of demonic blood behind.

The Wonder Brigade stops at the edge of the forest. Marce takes out black rope and throws it over a tree branch. Loth sets down the carcass and ties the end of the rope around its now-humanoid feet. Marce and Spud pull on the rope's other end, hauling the corpse into the air, feet first.

"What are we doing now?" Gabriel asks.

"Exsanguination," Saphrael explains as he looks up at the demon. The discolored, dark green blood drips onto the twig-covered ground below.

"Little late for that, isn't it?" Loth says, looking at the demon corpse before turning away, as if the smell was too much to bear.

"Get over it," Cadence says, who is also covered with pungent demonic blood.

Chapter 21

D eep in the vast gray desert, the wind whips dry dirt, pelting the Wonder Brigade as they trek back toward Thale Forest.

"Where do demons come from?" Gabriel asks.

Marce rolls his eyes but answers his question. "They are discarded pieces of human souls torn at the climax of a cardinal sin."

"Are we bringing this… thing into our barracks?" Gabriel gestures at Loth, who carries the demon carcass.

"No, we'll display its corpse on the pike for a few cycles before breaking it down into parts. Trade what we can and make lutum from the rest," Cadence explains.

"Oh, no wonder that second flagpole never has any flags on it," Gabriel mumbles.

"The second spike's a demon's pike," Spud says.

"Guys… can someone help me carry this?" Loth asks, the headless, exsanguinated demon weighing him down. He adjusts it, and his trademark array of knives hanging from his bandolier sways as he trudges forward.

"Hey, you know the rules," Marce says with a raised eyebrow.

"I'll help." Gabriel says.

"I don't want *your* help." Loth turns away from Gabriel.

"Well, that's fine because he's not allowed to help you carry it back anyway," Marce looks back at Loth, who lets out a deep sigh.

Spud looks at Loth, his body language saying *What can you do?*

Cadence and Saphrael are a bit ahead of everyone else and deep in conversation. As Gabriel catches up to them, he hears the word Quanta.

"Who is Quanta?" Gabriel asks.

"The Quanta is a what, not a who." Saphrael stretches his arms, tired from the arduous journey.

The Ruins of Daath come into view, meaning they are almost home.

"Though some do say that the Quanta is alive," Cadence speculates.

"The Quanta is everywhere!" Spud looks around wildly.

"What?" Gabriel asks, as he sees absolutely nothing.

Marce has fallen back and is talking to Loth.

"The Quanta is a system of caverns that exists beneath the surface of the realm. You know how yours is mostly water? Well, ours is mostly Quanta," Saphrael explains. "Where did you think we get all the crystals from?"

"I haven't really thought about it," Gabriel says.

"Blindingly glorious, the Quanta is dangerous." Spud hangs on the edge of Gabriel's shoulder, pulling down his right side for a moment.

"All right, Spud, you don't need to scare him," Saphrael says.

"No, I don't." He just smiles, looking at Gabriel, then continues forward singing, "Terrified! Buried alive! Surrounded by light, there is nothing but night."

"What's he going on about?" Gabriel points to Spud, who is a fair distance away now.

"Sometimes there are cave-ins." Cadence says with a shrug.

"Do we have to go to the Quanta?" Gabriel asks.

"We do if we want to make lutum," Saphrael says, his hands resting on the straps of his backpack.

"Why?"

"Because, from what once was, will be," Saphrael says.

"What?"

"It means demons generally inhabit the Quanta, so we put them back as part of the Draona, the ritual ceremony. It's communion, of sorts." Saphrael says.

"Communion… with demons?" Gabriel asks.

"I guess." Saphrael looks to Cadence.

"More like communion with demonic power," Cadence says.

"That doesn't make it sound any better." Gabriel adjusts the pack he offered to carry for Spud.

✦

The following cycles were spent breaking down the demon into parts, which included a lot of storing, sorting, and a pungent smell that reminded Gabriel of a pile of dead fish if they were left to rot in a batch of chlorine. All around them, various displays of demon corpses are posted in front of barracks, signifying that the time for battle approaches.

Cadence stretches some demon skin on a metal square to dry, as demon leather is valuable and can be used for repairs.

Gabriel, Cadence, and Saphrael are just outside the barracks, each busy with their own task.

"Cadence, what did you say when you killed the demon? The words didn't translate," Gabriel asks, keeping his mind off the tedious task of crushing bone fragments with a stone mortar and pestle.

Saphrael nods. "Sacred words don't translate from High Enochian when spoken in prayer."

"Prayer?"

"A blessing?" Saphrael answers.

"Maybe a curse?" Cadence suggests.

They both look at Cadence, who says "What? It can be. Anyway, I said grace in forgiveness, understanding in death."

"Oh." Gabriel falls silent, focusing on his mindless task. "Why don't you guys hunt demons more often? If you get items to trade from it?"

"We're only allowed to hunt at certain times, and we're also only allowed so many kills. It's a part of an agreement we have with the more intelligent demons," Cadence says.

"Agreement?"

"Yeah, basically they stay away from us, and we don't kill them or throw them in the pit." Cadence shrugs.

"What is the pit?"

"Yesod, an entire realm where everything and anything unwanted goes," Cadence explains.

"What are you talking about? What else is there?"

"Besides demons? Remnants, vampyres, faeries, daeva, dinosaurs, you know, anything we don't want around," Cadence says, his head down as he is finishing tying up the leather onto a square to dry.

"What? Wait those things are real? Remnants?" Gabriel asks.

"Yes, they are, Gabriel. Remnants, they are kind of like demons." Cadence says.

"Kind of like vampyres," Saphrael muses while continuing to crush dried plants.

"More like demons," Cadence says.

"No, they are the parts of the soul that were not cleaved. Demons are the severed pieces of the soul." Saphrael counters. "Most of them become vampyres."

"Or die," Cadence says.

"Right, or die," Saphrael agrees.

"What?" Gabriel looks back and forth.

"Don't worry about it," Cadence says. "They're in the pit."

Marce, using his black halberd accented with gold as a walking staff, makes his way to Saphrael and drops blood-red shards of some spiky flower-like crystal into his hands. Saphrael takes one and throws it in a bottle full of water mixed with plant material, and shakes the bottle. The little red crystals clink inside the glass before they dissolve, while the plant particles flow, dancing around like flecks in a snow globe. The color of the water turns a deep, dark red.

"What is that?"

"Sanguis. It's money," Marce says.

"Why are you dissolving it then?"

"It's also a drink," Marce explains.

"What?"

"It's made from a rare, dried berry. So, it can be re-liquefied."

"Rehydrated," Gabriel corrects him.

"Whatever, Earthling." Marce gives Saphrael more spiky red flower-like crystals, and Saphrael places them into a pouch on his belt. It isn't long before the others arrive. They head into the barracks after cleaning up in order to pack their things.

"Where are we going now?" Gabriel asks as they set off into Thale Forest.

"The Quanta," Saphrael says. "It's required that we go there to perform the Draona to make the lutum."

Near the middle of Thale Forest, they reach a deep ravine. Gabriel looks at a dilapidated, dark-gray wooden bridge, the steps of which are worn, some broken, and occasionally entirely missing. The ravine was carved by deep fjords that are now empty thanks to Gabriel.

Loth peers into the massive ravine, then glances at Gabriel. "I don't believe you burned the cursed water."

"It's 'I can't believe.'" Gabriel corrects him.

"No, literally, I don't believe that you did it."

"Believe what you want, Loth." Saphrael shakes his head.

Carefully but nimbly, they make their way across the questionably safe bridge. Loth and Cadence each wear a piece of the demon's rib, broken in half, displayed on necklaces. Gabriel was told it was a symbol of honor, to mark who scored the kill.

It is not long before they come to an open space. In the center of the small clearing is a lone moss-covered statue of an angel in a gambeson uniform. The discolored gray statue has its right hand open, two fingers pointing to the ground, palm facing up. Gabriel's anxiety spikes when he sees the expression on its face, the look of abject misery. He wonders what the artist was thinking when they carved it. Saphrael stomps on the ground. The rest, except Gabriel, follow suit, stomping and listening.

Saphrael nods to the others, who quickly move out of the way, except Cadence, who walks forward with his golden staff, closes his eyes, and lifts it into the air. He whispers a prayer that does not translate for Gabriel.

As Gabriel stands there, too lost in his own mind, Saphrael pulls him out

251

of the way just before Cadence uses a significant amount of force to drive the golden staff through the ground. Chunks of Basalt crash into the hole, along with Cadence.

Gabriel looks in but can only see darkness and a set of stairs.

"He's all right," Saphrael says, looking down before reaching into his pack and taking out a metal bowl and a light green crystal cluster. He places the crystal inside the bowl. The crystal formation looks like a pile of squares. Saphrael enters first, and as he descends, he pours a mix from a glass bottle onto the crystal. The square, light green crystal cluster glows with a dim light.

Not far down the stairs, the length of which cannot be seen in the darkness, Cadence waves and looks no worse for wear as they catch up to him. Feeling relieved, Gabriel switches his vision in an attempt to see just how far the stairs go. The gray stone stairs seem to go on forever. Then he gets hit with a flash of bright, shining light from the oversized crystals that seem to be growing everywhere.

"Agh!" Gabriel stops in his tracks, momentarily blinded. The light leaves bright white burn marks behind, even when he shuts his eyes.

"He looked, didn't he?" Loth says, sounding amused.

Marce sighs. "We told you not to use your magus vision in the Quanta."

"Yeah…. I know." Gabriel's eyes are finally adjusting to the dark again. "Shouldn't there be openings to this place somewhere closer to the barracks?"

"There are, but we have to go somewhere specific to perform the Draona. Besides, the ground heals itself after a while. This entrance is relatively well used, so the chances of us getting locked inside are much less," Saphrael explains.

"Good to know." Gabriel bumps into Spud. Saphrael turns around with the light so they can see where they are going. "There's… there's still water down here," Gabriel says, intently listening to the sound of rushing water.

"It's a vast cave system. I would be surprised if you reached all the cursed water," Cadence says, to which Loth scoffs.

As they descend further into the Quanta, the sound of rushing water becomes clear; he can tell it is a waterfall before he sees it in the dim light.

The waterfall pours from the edge of a higher level. Gabriel's fingers trace the smooth bumps of the brown rock wall laced with white to his right. Droplets of water sprinkle on him as they draw closer to the falls.

Saphrael veers off to the left onto a strip of land. There is not a whole lot of space, as it sits precariously close to the vast darkness of the abyss below. The waterfall ends in a pool near the vertical stone walls embedded with crystals. Everyone takes off their hiking packs except Gabriel, who doesn't own one. As he wanders forward in the dark, he bangs his knee into a large rock formation.

"Ahh!" Gabriel hit his knee at a particularly unfortunate angle.

"Be careful." Saphrael holds up the small bowl containing the glowing light green crystal. "And don't go off on your own. Sometimes, those who venture too far in the Quanta are never heard from again."

Saphrael sets down the metal bowl. Everyone sits in a circle around the rock formation Gabriel just ran into. There is a pop as Saphrael uncorks a bottle and throws it over the rock cluster. The formation starts to glow a deep red where droplets land before running down in small rivers along the stone. Streaks of glowing red appear, intensifying in color as it gradually lights up entirely, especially bright in places the water touched.

Everyone bows their heads and closes their eyes, except Gabriel, who is confused because no one told him how the Draona was to be performed.

Saphrael hangs his head down, exhausted, resting before he continues to arrange glass bottles and add various powders and liquids to them. His mouth moves as he works, but makes no sound, talking to himself about the measurements and order in which the ingredients are added. Then he places the prepared bottles on the glowing rock formation.

"So, what does lutum do again?" Gabriel asks.

"It depends on the type of demon you make it from," Marce answers as he stares at the center of the strange stone campfire. "This one was a fear demon. Lutum infuses you with their essence, at least for a short time, inspiring fear in others. It also enhances natural abilities like strength and prowess."

"...And you guys are usually successful at hunting demons?" Gabriel asks.

"Hunting demons isn't difficult, Gabriel." Marce tilts his head slightly, his brows furrow, and a curve at the corner of his lips indicates he is insulted.

"No, what I'm saying is maybe there's a detriment to using a power boost after it fades."

"You're suggesting that we don't use lutum in the fight?" Marce asks, disgusted. "You don't even know what you're talking about, and you think it's all right to give us instructions?"

Saphrael looks over, the weight of winning the next battle is upon his shoulders. The toll it is taking on his friend is noticeable.

"I'm just saying, if there are drawbacks and you guys always use it—"

"Because we always lose?" Marce finishes his sentence for him.

"It's just a suggestion."

"All opinions are valid," Saphrael says.

"Oh, where'd you get that from, Saph? You know for a fact that is not true."

"Okay, but if we don't factor in everything, what I'm saying is... maybe he has a point," Saphrael says.

"Utilize every possible advantage," Marce repeats what sounds like a mantra.

"In defense of oneself," Saphrael seems to finish the saying, before adding, "Preservation leads to opportunity."

"So, use it at the end?" Gabriel suggests.

"Not legal to use it after the battle has started but in a real fight, not a bad idea," Cadence says.

Loth is quiet. He's always mad. Gabriel assumes it's because he's mad at him, but he has no idea why. He hasn't ever done anything to Loth.

"Do we have enough for the free-for-all and right now?" Spud asks.

"Yes, but I think I'll take Gabriel's advice and not use it during the free-for-all," Saphrael says.

"You're going to listen to him?" Marce sharply turns to face Saphrael.

"Yeah, it's decent advice," Saphrael says.

"Terrible advice." Loth rolls his eyes.

"Remember, flexibility leads to longevity," Saphrael reasons.

"Flexibility leads to the loss of oneself," Marce says, head lifted proudly. "Never become what they want you to be because you'll lose yourself in the process."

"Or you'll become something new," Spud says.

"Something you're not," Marce counters.

"Be a brick on the road or be nature that reclaims all," Saphrael says.

"Just because you have a metaphor for everything doesn't make you any more correct than anyone else, Saph."

"Just because you're angry doesn't make you right," Saphrael says quietly.

"Say that to my face," Marce says, glaring at Saphrael.

"I said just because you're angry, doesn't make you right," Saphrael repeats louder.

"Good. You have a backbone, and you're not changing your opinion because you think you're right. Guess we're not so different after all."

There is a crackle from the bottles on the fire, and Saphrael removes them and sets them down in front of him.

"What's in that, anyway?" Gabriel asks.

"The bones you grounded earlier, plants from the forest, the unspilled blood from the hunt," Saphrael explains.

"Our... blood is in there?" Gabriel asks.

"You wasted your arrow," Loth points out.

"I wasted it driving the demon into yours. I'm the only reason you're wearing that trophy bone to begin with," Gabriel counters.

Loth rips his necklace off and throws it at Gabriel. It skids across the ground before being lost over the edge of the cliff.

Gabriel thinks of Semoel. He wants to tell his friends about him but was always warned not to. They wouldn't understand. They would call him crazy. *Dawn didn't find me crazy.*

"Gabriel, are you okay?" Cadence asks.

"What? Do I not look okay?"

"Yes." Cadence shrugs.

"I bet it's about Dawn. He always looks like that when he thinks about

Dawn," Spud says, looking thoughtfully at Gabriel.

"Maybe it's best to give up your obsession, Gabriel," Loth says. "When you give everything for something, you end up with nothing."

"I will fight for Dawn until the light has faded from my eyes and the world is nothing but darkness," Gabriel vows.

"What was she like, Gabriel?" Spud asks.

A half-smile forms on Gabriel's face, and he lets out a sigh. "She's intoxicating. Sure, she has problems but nothing that I didn't want to help with. She is intelligent… eyes you could get lost in." Gabriel is silent, thinking about her. Suddenly, her face morphs into Lucius's, and he thinks about how similar they look with their angelic narrow faces and high cheekbones.

"What did our princess do on Earth? Did she display any powers while she was there?" Loth asks, actually talking to Gabriel for once.

"Yes, I believe so. People died mysteriously after suffering an all-consuming obsession."

"Hmm… perhaps you're next, Gabriel." Loth smiles. "Her mother is more legend than fact. She could manipulate others as if they were an instrument, and they would dance to her tune. Any tune that she desired. I remember a story where she whispered into the ear of a town's magistrate and he killed himself, simply because she suggested it on a whim."

"Umm… I think it was a king?" Spud says.

"What's the difference?" Loth says. "Listen, Gabriel, archangel or not, the siren's call will drown us all."

Spud unwraps empty vials from his bag, one for each of them. He hands them to Cadence, who passes them to Saphrael.

"So, people died around her?" Loth says. "Interesting. You know, that's not a thing that just happens, Gabriel."

"I know—I don't know. I don't know why it happens. I'm only grateful that it does."

"You're happy that humans are dead?" Marce asks.

"No. I mean—they were trying to kill her."

"There aren't many beings that can just cause things to just die like that,"

Marce says.

"Maybe it's the Four," Spud says with a vaguely blank look on his face, as if he was telling a particularly scary part of a campfire story.

"The Four?" Gabriel glances over to Saphrael, who looked up when the Four were mentioned, pausing from mixing the vials.

Loth rolls his eyes and answers, "The Four are a myth, meant to scare us from not harming the humans."

"Legend has it there are four humans who not only have the power of angels but even that of the Archangel of Death himself," Marce says.

Spud shivers. "Azrael could kill us all if he felt like it."

"It's a good thing he never feels like it then," Marce says.

"Speaking of fears." Saphrael holds up a bottle of the mixed concoction. It is predominantly dark red with traces of other ingredients floating around. "You guys ready?"

"Ready for what?" Gabriel asks.

"Do you ever stop asking questions?" Loth says, reaching over, snatching a bottle from Saphrael before throwing his head back and drinking the entire serum at once.

"Slow down," Cadence cautions.

"Don't tell me what to do." Loth inspects the glass to see if any remains, then fills it with water to get the rest of the mix.

Once everyone has a bottle in front of them Saphrael raises his glass into the air and says, "Enjoy your time, while you can."

"You'll never be here again," Spud answers, raising his glass in the air.

"Was that a toast?" Gabriel asks.

"Yeah," Saphrael says, "it means that life is each passing moment, none the same as the next."

Gabriel uncorks the bottle and sniffs the pungent liquid. Closing his eyes, he drinks the bitter, warm, grainy liquid. Immediately, he feels like someone punched him on the side of his head, and the world starts to slow.

"What is your greatest fear?" Marce looks around the glow of the rock campfire. "No one? Mine is being alone. I know I push everyone away, but it's because I'm afraid of them leaving. At least this way, my fate is my own doing."

"I'm afraid of never making a difference, whether I live or die," Cadence says.

"I'm afraid of the archangels," Loth says. "Besides Emperor Lucius, of course."

Gabriel lifts his head, having trouble staying in the conversation. His vision doubles as he asks, "Why?"

"Don't ask him," Cadence says.

"You ever meet someone who's so sure of their 'morals' that they would kill for their beliefs just to prove to themselves that they were right? That is each and every one of them, besides our emperor. They have too much power. Things would be better off if they and the entire Crown didn't exist."

"I told you not to ask him," Cadence says.

"I miss home. I miss Hod. It's beautiful. I guess… what I really miss is being happy." Saphrael's shoulders slump as he leans forward. "Though I'm not quite sure I ever was. Although my greatest fear is that there may be nothing beyond the void."

Everyone is silent, contemplating the vast expanse.

"I'm afraid of the zombies from the lake," Spud says jokingly.

Everyone laughs. Gabriel feels lost in this moment with his friends, as if he has been there for countless ages. Conversation becomes background noise as he feels the drink warm his blood. His heart beats so hard he can feel it in his ears. Someone says his name, but he doesn't respond. Around him, those in their black with silver-accented uniforms morph into beasts with the heads of dead and rotting demons. Blood pours down their faces.

Gabriel stands aggressively, fire erupting from his palms. His body lifts into the air, hovering close to the ground. The dim surroundings turn a bright, blinding blue before he loses consciousness.

Chapter 22

A dam walks alongside Dawn through the narrow black stone halls of the citadel. The ever-present masked royal guards silently trail behind them on their way to Lucius's study. They just finished hand-to-hand combat training. Dawn is still in her military gambeson and her hair is tied back in a series of braids. As they walk, his mind wanders to a time not long ago when he instructed her in weapons training, or at least attempted to. When she dropped the sword, refusing to wield it, it felt like a failure on his part. Though it all, he can't help but admire her inner strength and kindness.

What a gentle soul, to be condemned to such a cruel and unforgiving place. They stop in front of the door to the study. Adam forces the thought from his mind as he opens the right half of the oversized black rune-engraved double doors.

In the dark parlor, Lucius stands to greet his daughter, gesturing to her seat. The princess cordially nods and takes a seat in her chair as Adam takes his place near the door. The emperor pays Adam no mind, as if he isn't even in the room as he talks to Dawn.

"I want to teach you how to properly use your powers. Although I am uncertain at this point what powers you have. I believe you have my gifts, as well as your mother's. As you know, I am the bearer of the purple psychic flame. I can see myriads of future paths. But I must warn you, even the most accurate psychic can only predict the most probable outcome. The

259

threads of fate are constantly in motion, sewn collectively by the actions and inactions of all. I do not have access to Azrael's Book of Life, Death, nor Fate. The Book of Fate contains that which has happened and that which is most likely to happen. From what I have gathered, you and Gabriel are, like the other archangels, an exception. You are simply not in the books. Tell me, has anything strange ever happened to you on Earth beyond your seduction aura?"

"Yes, well... I could control the rain, the clouds, the wind, even tornadoes. I could temporarily prevent it from raining or cause it to rain more."

"I see. I want to teach you how to use your powers to the best of your ability." Lucius pauses, and Adam senses a shift in his tone. "I need to see what you can do. That was quite a display you put on in the Axion."

She turns away.

"It's all right. What is done is done."

"It never should have happened." Dawn's voice cracks and she briefly looks in Adam's direction, pain evident in her eyes.

"Your reaction in the face of danger was impressive. Bear in mind, there were many around to protect you if you truly were in any danger. Which, I do not believe you were. I presume you can control demons. You just don't know how to yet."

"Who says that is something I want to do?"

"It may be useful someday, Dawn. Demons are simple-minded creatures. Your mother—" Lucius takes a moment to carefully find the right words. "She did things her own way, and now we are burdened with her... experiments."

"They are living creatures. Even kind of human in some way."

Lucius studies her for a long moment. "You are so much like her, and yet so different," he says more so to himself. "Stand up. We must begin. I need you to promise me to use your power in a way that is not self-serving."

Dawn nods and even though there is fear and uncertainty in her eyes, she holds her composure well.

Lucius stands from the middle of the couch and starts pacing. "If one strives solely to be in the light, they become zealous. Such a moral rigidity is unsustainable and invariably leads to the decay of oneself. Striving for an unattainable moral perfection and failing leads the broken self-righteous soul to seek control elsewhere and force moral purity upon others. This leads to hatred of perceived sins and a perverted sense of justice. Justice, in these cases, typically is just another word for death. You will say, but Lucius, I know where the line is. I know not to cross it. Passionate self-righteousness burns the line between love and hate, between saving a life or taking one. Therefore, do not act selfishly or self-righteously."

"I understand," Dawn says quietly.

"The purple flame in your room. Tell me about it." Lucius walks over to her.

Adam looks at the unlit candle sitting on the table in front of them.

"I don't know how to describe it. I'm drawn to it, like it is calling to me. When I touch it, it's cold." Dawn keeps her head down as she answers.

"That's natural. Power must always be tempered with caution. When you see the future, do not tell anyone but me. Most do not know how to properly handle such information." Lucius walks to the candle sitting on the table and ignites violet flame in his hand, which emits an unseen power signature that feels like the buzz of electricity. Lucius smiles and lights the candle. "Now, come and breathe in the flame."

The princess gets up and walks over to the purple-flamed candle. Lucius nods and she holds it in front of her face, closes her eyes, and breaths in the cold flame. Moments later, she opens her eyes, and her irises have turned deep violet.

Adam unconsciously holds his breath as he witnesses this moment.

Dawn stumbles, nearly falling. Adam runs across the room to her. He steadies her in his arms, and she weakly grabs hold of him, her fingers digging into the fabric of his sleeves as if she is holding on for dear life. Adam feels helpless as Dawn starts to convulse in his arms. He gently lays her on the ground. Dawn's body curls, stiff and strained. The muscles of her throat look as if she is screaming, yet no sound emerges.

"What have you done?" Adam struggles to maintain his emotions, torn between staying at her side or taking the punishment that comes with verbally disagreeing with Lucius. His body shakes, suppressing his visceral reaction, well aware of the abuse Lucius would inflict upon him if he were perceived to question him or step out of line.

Lucius impassively observes the situation before resting a hand on Adam's shoulder. "She will be all right. Have faith."

"She isn't breathing." Adam cradles Dawn's head, holding her limp body in his arms.

"She will. Back away," Lucius orders.

A familiar ozone scent fills the air, and Adam looks up in time to see flames ignite in Lucius's hands as if he were in the midst of battle. He barely gets out of the way in time before the fire envelops Dawn's body. The fire burns her hair ties, and her braids come undone. Her hair does not burn, nor does it singe the fireproof military gambeson she is wearing.

Adam rushes back to Dawn, kneeling at her side. "She still isn't breathing!" When he looks at Lucius, he is unable to hide his anguish or his anger.

"Take her to her room and lie her upon her bed, so that she may rest." Lucius says.

"Rest?" Adam shakes his head. "I won't pretend to understand your methods or what is going on, but I swear to you—"

Lucius cuts him off. "Do as you are instructed."

◆

"Dawn... Dawn." Gabriel murmurs as if will power alone could bring them back together.

Faintly, in the distance, he hears Cadence say, "Saphrael, you can't wait any longer. If you do, you'll miss your match. I'm sure Gabriel will be here when you return." The door creaks as it opens, and they begin to leave. "I hope the lutum-fueled nightmares won't scar him too much."

"The archangel? Yeah, I think he'll be fine," Marce scoffs before the door shuts.

Gabriel finds himself in a hall staring at a dark-brown wooden door in the distance. He is home, completely forgetting that it lay in ruins. And for the life of him, he can't remember what he did yesterday or even what he was doing now.

As he turns away from the strange door at the end of the hall, another door next to him swings open, and Dawn runs into him. He smiles. "Dawn," he says softly. Saying her name strikes within him a memory of pain, but he doesn't know why.

She kisses him, and he relaxes as he embraces her. They break from the kiss, he smiles, looking into her eyes, and feels that all is right with the world. The heavy watch sits in his pocket, and he remembers that this is the day, the day he is going to ask Dawn to marry him.

He brushes her soft hair from her face and smiles, resting his hand on her cheek.

"It's all right. You're safe with me. You will always be safe with me." Gabriel feels the weight of the pocket watch and says the words that he knows she longs to hear: "The pizza is almost done."

They walk outside, hand in hand. The fresh crisp fall air and the smell of pizza and wood crackling in the firebrick oven fill his lungs. He looks back at the old, weathered gray-brick cathedral-esque fortress that he calls home, feeling grounded. Dawn basks in the warmth from the rustic cement gray-brick oven, watching the pizza.

He walks to the round black mesh steel patio table beside the firebrick oven and picks up a glass candle Dawn made. As he lights it, he asks, "Do you need any more crafting supplies?"

"No, Gabriel. I told you, stop buying me things," Dawn says, still watching the pizza.

The scent of the candles, a combination of sandalwood, nag champa, and palo santo, blend with the aroma from the firebrick oven. He shrugs and explains, "It's an expression of love."

"Is it? To me, it feels like an expression of ownership." Dawn shivers even though she is in front of the firebrick oven.

"What? Dawn, no, I—" Gabriel fumbles his words.

"Like I can't do things on my own."

Gabriel shakes his head. "I don't mean it in any possessive or conde-scending way. I'm just trying to say I love you."

"Gabriel, if you want to say I love you, just say I love you." Dawn shakes her head and folds her arms, silently staring into the oven's fire.

"I love you. There isn't anything I wouldn't do for you. You know that right?" Gabriel says.

She looks back at him and smiles, and as she does, there is a loud crack followed by a bang, much like the day the branch broke when Dawn tried to hang herself.

"Did you hear that?" Gabriel asks, looking around, but Dawn doesn't seem to have heard anything.

Suddenly, they are back in the hallway near the door at the far end of the hall. There is a wooden jewelry box in his hands.

"Hear what?" Dawn asks.

"Nothing..." He stares at her, but she seems as if nothing is amiss. Nervously, he fidgets with a jewelry box before presenting it to her.

Dawn is silent, her expression bordering on suspicion as she opens the box. Inside, are three gold-accented, resin-preserved roses: one red, one white, and one black. "Gabriel..."

"They're real roses," Gabriel explains quickly, having just been repri-manded for buying her things too often. "Please... just listen. They are real roses, preserved in resin and gold. It wasn't expensive—I mean—I didn't want them to die."

Dawn picks up the black rose. Specks of silver shimmer as light dances across the surface of the night-colored rose. The frozen petals are artfully crafted, more so by nature than resin and gold. Beauty lies not in the profanity of excess but in the unique dips and bends of imperfection.

"Red, for love. White, for hope. Black and platinum for the stars above."

"Gabriel..." Her words fade as she is left speechless, holding the black rose. Gabriel removes a ring-shaped box from his pocket. Dawn's breath catches in her throat.

Inside is not a ring... but a small brass key that he places it into her hand and motions to the door at the end of the hall.

"Why don't you find out?" Gabriel says with a gentle smile.

She hands him the box, keeping hold of the black shimmering platinum rose and the key in her right hand.

She opens the door and walks into a newly constructed greenhouse. Sunlight streams through the stained-glass panels of the exceptionally warm room. Dawn is speechless as she walks through the rows and rows of flowers and herbs.

"I wanted to give you something living. Something you could care for. Something you might adore. I thought, hey, I could get her a bouquet of roses, but why not living ones?" he says from behind her, standing near the door.

"You know, from the way you've been acting, I half expected that you were going to propos—" Her words are cut short as she turns back to Gabriel, who is down on one knee, holding the beautifully engraved golden pocket watch. It is open in his hands, and inside sits a ring upon a small piece of fabric.

"Dawn, you are the only light I see in this world. Without you, there is only darkness. If you allow me to be by your side in marriage, I will dedicate my life to you. I already have but know that I do. Dawn, I love you. Will you marry me?" He smiles but his eyes cannot mask the fear that she might say no.

Dawn grips the black rose in her hand tightly, her eyes turn dark, and her hair changes into a more formal look. She has a detached demeanor as a cold wind from the hall blows into the greenhouse. Her clothes change, and she is wearing her black and gold military dress. The gem of the blood-colored pin sparkles on her chest.

"Marry, you?" She looks offended and amused, with a half-smirk on her face. The half-smirk is familiar—it mirrors one Lucius had the day he invaded their home, assaulted Gabriel, and abducted Dawn. Right before Lucius's expression changed and he threw him into the wall of his bedroom. That was the night everything in his life came crashing down.

Gabriel sits up suddenly and finds himself covered in sweat, his heart racing. He lets out a deep sigh and lies back on his cot inside the Wonder

Brigade's barracks. Closing his eyes, he thinks about the lutum that they drank in the underground caverns of the Quanta, but he doesn't remember much after drinking it and has no idea how he got back to the barracks. Gabriel wonders if he can see Dawn again if he goes back to sleep.

✦

Adam glances at Dawn, who lies still atop her blankets as if she were simply asleep. Her skin is pale, she is not breathing, and she has no pulse to speak of. Yet her body shows no sign of rigor mortis. Long ago, he was a doctor in Eridu, so he is well-versed in determining whether one is fully and irrevocably dead, even angels. Although angels move naturally toward ethereal regeneration and humans toward ethereal decay, with Dawn, he did not see progress one way or the other. It is as if she is trapped in a state of purgatory. Questions would not quiet in his mind as he turns back to the pages of the book he is reading, unable to focus on the words.

The doorknob twists. Adam stands, straightening his faded gray fatigues and sighing heavily, not from physical exhaustion, but from who was inevitably on the other side of the door.

Lucius strides in, passing by Adam without so much as a glance as he makes his way to Dawn's bedside. Inside, Adam can not quell feelings of unease and anger whenever Lucius stops by lately. So, whenever he comes to check on Dawn, Adam keeps to himself and waits for him to leave. Not that that wasn't expected of him to begin with.

Adam pushes aside feelings of repulsion as Lucius touches her soft red hair.

"Remarkable, she looks so much like she did the day I rescued her," Lucius says softly, his back to Adam.

Adam stands silent, saying nothing.

"Are you still upset?" Lucius asks, sounding amused.

Rather than responding brashly and saying something he would regret, Adam says nothing, so Lucius continues. "She isn't dead. I've assured you of that. No, my daughter is resilient. She will survive, have faith."

What if you are wrong, Adam wants to say but doesn't. Instead, he suggests aiding her potential angelic regeneration abilities in an area specifically designed to do so. "Have you considered taking her to Chesed?"

Lucius looks at Dawn and says, "The Silentes Fields are for soldiers, Adam."

"You've been training her as if she were one," Adam says, beginning to lose his grip on decorum.

"Control yourself, Adam, or be considered unfit," Lucius says, setting his gaze upon him.

✦

It is pitch black and cold, far colder than even in the citadel as Dawn walks toward a yellow-orange light in the distance. The light emanates heat that grows warmer the closer she draws to it. Soon, the crackling of fire becomes clear. All around her, the yard in front of Gabriel's home fades into existence. The smell of burning wood and food cooking mingles with her favorite scents: sandalwood, nag champa, and palo santo as she finds herself in front of a firebrick oven.

She holds her breath, and her heart seizes as Gabriel says, "Did you hear that?"

His voice comes from behind her, and for a moment she does not turn, as if he could not possibly be there. That she could not possibly be here. That, maybe, somehow, everything she has been through was all just another nightmare.

She turns around, and Gabriel is standing there waiting for her to respond to his question. Dumbstruck, she struggles to say something, anything. She wants to tell him the hardships she has endured. Most of all, she wants to tell him about the loneliness she has been suffering without him. Yet, *This has to be a dream*, she reasons, as she does not seem to be fully in control of her own body.

However, she is content simply to be an observer, even if it is just a dream. She finds herself in a rustic stained-glass greenhouse, staring at Gabriel, who is down on one knee, holding out her pocket watch with a ring sitting inside of it.

"Dawn, I love you. Will you marry me?"

She desperately tries to say *"Yes! Yes! Of course, I will marry you!"* But all that comes out is "Marry you?" The voice is hers but not her own. It has dropped an octave and sounds insulted. Inside, she screams at her body to do something other than sneer at Gabriel with disdain. He is still down on one knee, his once outstretched arm lowered to his side. His hand closes around the pocket watch that holds the engagement ring.

Impossibly, a cold wind blows, encircling them. Dawn finds herself in her military-style dress on the black diamond-shaped stage of the Laterem. The imposing figure in the silver mask grips his weapon, heading straight for her. Her heart races. She almost drops the blood-encrusted hook-sword as she stumbles back. Lucius steadies her. His hand grips hers painfully, forcing it to hold on to the hook-sword as he whispers a warning. "If you allow your weapon to fall, you are as good as dead."

The blade of the assailant's oversized weapon sings, slicing the air, heading in her direction. With nowhere left to turn, she desperately thrusts the hook-sword.

Yet when she opens her eyes, in her hand, she grips not the hook-sword, but Gabriel's throat. The sight of Gabriel's room at night blurs around her. Now, she is not in her body, but Lucius's, watching helplessly as Lucius hurls Gabriel against the wall. His body slumps to the floor as pieces of the house crash around him.

"Gabriel!" Dawn screams. There is no sound, except that of her own voice echoing back at her. Dawn reaches out in vain.

The last thing she witnesses before the world stops, becoming still and deafeningly silent, is hope fading from Gabriel's eyes. A dark-purple discoloration seeps from the corner of her eyes and spreads across this snapshot of reality. A stinging cold envelops her. She feels isolated and distant, internally begging for Gabriel not to leave her again. Color drains from the world, leaving only the still image, frozen in time, much like a pale black-and-white photograph eroded with age. But it too fades.

✦

Dawn's body sinks into the comfortable bed beneath her. She doesn't know where she is as she wakes from a deep sleep. For the first time since she had occupied her room, the thick, pitch-black curtains are drawn around her four-poster bed, blocking out all but the faintest light. She looks at the hauntingly beautiful torn rose carved on the headboard, confirming that she is, in fact, in her room in Lucius's citadel.

The curtain is drawn back, and Adam looks at her.

"I see you have finally decided to wake," Adam says evenly, but he can't mask his true emotions of surprise, and for some reason, relief.

"What happened?" Dawn asks, stretching her tight muscles, it feels as if she has been asleep for a very long time. Adam pulls the curtains back fully and secures them with the golden rope before offering his hand to help her out of bed.

"I can stand on my own, Adam," Dawn says as her feet, still in boots, hit the floor. She is wearing her training uniform instead of her typical nightgown. Then she remembers where she was last. "I was in the study. Lucius was showing me the purple flame and then—then I don't remember. What happened?"

Adam clears his throat and holds his head up, eyes briefly looking away from her. "I'm afraid, as usual, that is something you're going to have to ask your father."

"Really?"

"I am afraid so," Adam says reservedly as he straightens his fatigues.

Trying to get information from him is like trying to draw blood from a stone. She side-eyes him, annoyed as she walks over to her closet to look for a dress to wear.

"I'm afraid you are required to stay in your training uniform, Princess." Adam says, his head slightly bowed apologetically.

"Why is that, Adam?"

"Your father has requested that he be notified the moment you wake. You are to learn how to wield your father's flame. He has set up a training room down the hall." Adam opens the door and looks at a masked guard who walks away, leaving the other masked guard at his post, outside her door.

"If you would, Princess." Adam holds the door open for her. She sighs and shakes her head, grumbling about how no one ever tells her anything as she walks through the right half of the large wooden double doors.

They walk down the narrow hall dotted with faintly glowing blue crystal lights. Most doors in the citadel look the same, carved from black wood with what Dawn assumes is Lucius's symbol covering the top half of the door frame. Adam stops at a door that looks just like the others and opens it for her.

She walks into the spacious, high-ceilinged room. There are no adornments on the walls outside of the same lights that line her room. The only thing in the otherwise empty space are statues set at varying distances, they are ruin-like, in a dire state of disrepair. Most of the statues are of angels. Dawn quietly looks at one with its wings outstretched, depicted mid-battle, with a weapon in hand.

Another seems to be representative of despair, his arms outstretched, beseeching any who passes by. Not far from that statue is one of a pair, an angel guarding an injured human, his wings protectively wrapped around their forms. Dawn walks up to it and inhales sharply as she realizes that the companion statue is not human at all, as evidenced by broken bones jutting out of his back where wings once were.

Her hands run across the jagged broken bone. She looks into the statue's face. "Must be why he is in pain," Dawn says thoughtfully.

"Indeed," is all Adam says in response.

The door opens, and Lucius enters carrying a metal mask. Although she has seen the masks before, mostly as decorations around the citadel and being worn by many in the Axion, no one has bothered to explain what they are.

"Father." Dawn greets him with a nod and walks up to him. She hesitates, getting a clear view of the mask in his hands. It's shaped like a dragon... like the dragon she has seen so many times before.

She opens her mouth, but no words come out, caught between astonishment of seeing the dragon in a metal mask form and wanting to ask what the masks are for or what happened to her when her memory failed.

Unlike the other masks, which are silver, this one has a textured design of the metal itself, shading the silver a far darker gray.

"Your eyes—" Lucius says, before uncharacteristically not finishing his sentence.

"What about them?"

"Has Adam not informed you?"

"No?"

Lucius holds his dark silver helmet with the back facing her so she can see her reflection.

Her irises are a deep violet. She shakes her head in disbelief. "This doesn't make any sense."

"Pay it no mind. It is merely confirmation that you have incorporated the flame. Now, this is my Chokma mask," Lucius explains. "It is traditional, however, not required, for combat. The metals focus our magnus sight, which allows us to see far beyond the capacity of others. Each mask is symbolic, generally assigned to units of my army." He holds up the mask, examining it in the light. "With this, you will easily be able to see the beating heart of your enemy. Although once you are properly trained, you will not require the use of a Chokma mask to do so."

"What happened to me?" Dawn asks, interrupting him. "I remember inhaling the flame… then nothing—nothing but this strange dream."

"If you detail me with the account of your dream, of all of your dreams, including the one where I know Azrael contacted you, then I will fill you in on what happened."

"That isn't fair; dreams are personal."

"Dreams are far more valuable than most give them credit for, especially those of psychics. Do we have a deal?"

She nods, staring at the floor before looking up at him.

"All dreams from here on out, Dawn." Lucius judges her reaction.

"Only up until this point. As you said, dreams are valuable. If they are to

271

be used as a bartering tool, then I will keep hold of the value and determine for myself if I should share details. After all, Father, you wouldn't want me to devalue myself. For my own protection, of course," Dawn says, before she looks over to Adam, whose eyes speak of amusement.

Lucius is silent for a long moment before nodding. "Very well, you have a deal. But I require you to journal in detail the agreed-upon dreams and anything you can remember of your life, even if you think it is trivial. I will supply you with a Book of Literas, of which there are always at least two. The other I will have. When you write in one it shows up in the other. Typically, one writes back and forth, but in this situation, I will simply read what you have written." Lucius clears his throat. "Now, where would you like to start?"

"I require the knowledge of the beginning of everything to do with the archangel flame itself if I am to fully understand it. If you can, write back to me the history that I have been missing."

"The fire of the archangels is something that has always existed," Lucius says offhandedly. "Therefore, to start at the beginning is impossible."

"That is not entirely correct," Adam says, stepping forward from his place near the door. "There is a clear beginning of this current epoch."

"Before that was another beginning," Lucius says.

Dawn is even more confused.

"It is said that angels came from nothing, but what was beyond that first step has been theorized and subsequently—" Adam says.

"Thank you, Adam. That will be all," Lucius says, thinly masking his annoyance.

"Very well, sir." Adam walks back to his place near the door.

Lucius turns back to Dawn. "Now, what happened to you is quite simple. You incorporated the flame, and it takes time for one to adjust to the powers as it infuses into your essence. It burns away your old self and reconstructs you anew. I apologize for not informing you of this sooner. It happens even to archangels, at least theoretically. That period of adjustment knocked you unconscious. Now that you have recovered, we will train you in your abilities. Agreed?"

"Yes, Father," Dawn says softly, distracted once again by the statues littering the room.

"Dawn." Lucius calls her attention back to him. "Put the helmet on and we will proceed."

Carefully, she takes the helmet, thinking of the dragon that has stalked her for so long, but she knows Lucius is unlikely to divulge that information. Turning back to face the ruin-like statues, she puts the helmet on.

"I can't see anything," she says, voice echoing from inside the dragon Chokma mask.

"You must concentrate, Dawn. Release your understanding of how things should be and allow things to be as they are."

She strains to take in a deep breath, trying to concentrate. Still, she sees nothing. Then, all at once, telepathic disembodied voices assault her, and she loses her balance. Lucius has hold of her. The voices grow in number and volume. She screams, her voice echoing in the helmet.

Lucius rips the helmet off her. The black veil of nothing is replaced with the room around her. The voices go quiet as Lucius has a hand on her shoulder, his eyes closed.

Listen to me and only to me.

She opens her eyes wide at him. Not because he is speaking to her telepathically, but because she's heard those words before.

"It was you," Dawn says. "It was always you, wasn't it?"

Lucius looks at Adam, then says, "Yes, I have been watching over you since I came to be aware of your existence, Dawn."

"Those nightmares, the snakes, everything," she says, confused. Her body spikes with adrenaline, urging her to run.

"You can't always run," Lucius says, noticing her change in stance. "There is nowhere left to run. Do you understand that, Dawn? You are precisely where you are meant to be. Now, again."

"No, I can't see anything in that!" Dawn backs away.

"Dawn, this is the path that you must travel."

"I'm tired! I need to rest."

"You will find in battle that death does not care how tired you are. That you must persevere, if you wish to fight another day."

He forces the helmet back on her. This time, she feels as she did in the dream, when she had occupied Lucius's body. Except this time, he was possessing her. Her body moves on its own.

I am not your puppet, she says to him inside her head.

You will do as instructed, Dawn, Lucius replies telepathically.

He moves her hand, palm facing out in front of her, yet no flame is emitted—nothing.

"Perhaps the flame has not fully incorporated into you," Lucius says.

Then she smells a familiar ozone scent of fire. Desperately, she tries to get the helmet off as she is once again in control of her body. The ice-cold flame from Lucius chills the air nearby, growing colder.

"SIR! We almost lost her the last time. Is this a wise decision?" Adam says with urgency as Dawn gets the metal helmet off just in time to see the flame blast at her, enveloping her. She falls to the ground. The dragon Chokma mask lands beside her.

Adam places his hand on Lucius's shoulder. "SIR."

Through the haze of purple flames, Dawn sees Adam thrown like a rag doll into the statue of the angel with the broken wings and the other angel protecting it. Adam slams into the solid stone statue, which is far more resilient than it looks, not even moving as Adam hits the floor.

The icy flame vanishes. Lucius has a cold expression of disappointment. No, it's not disappointment she saw in her father's eyes, it is hollow indifference.

She isn't used to this and doesn't know exactly how to feel. Dawn closes her eyes and thinks, *Love always leads to disappointment.* Lucius turns and walks out of the room. Feelings of abandonment surface.

Adam, though bruised and beaten, offers her his hand. She looks up and accepts it. He helps her to her feet.

"I'm sure everything will sort itself out," he says reassuringly, then walks over to open the door for her. "You said you were tired, Princess. Let us find some peace in rest."

She walks to him and looks at him in silence before they head back to her room, and both masked guards follow. Dawn isn't talking right now, and Adam lets her be.

"Time in the warm bath may help," Adam suggests.

Dawn nods, still not talking as she walks alone into the adjoining room that looks like a small natural cave. Warmth hits her as she rests against the door. Refusing to give in to the depth of her sadness, she thinks about how much she will enjoy the relaxing waters of the hot spring-like pond. After removing her training uniform, Dawn sinks into the water, laying her head back on the warm stone ground behind her.

Chapter 23

In a small locker room on the ground level of the Axion, Saphrael sits alone. He pulls on the strap of his shoulder guard and buckles it in place. The sound of heavy footsteps calls his attention, as whoever it is stops at his door. Saphrael looks up, not expecting to see anyone before the free-for-all. The door opens to none other than Darius, his loyalty officer. For a long moment, Darius says nothing as he stands in the doorway, lifting his chin in the air and looking down at Saphrael, who is sitting on a bench at the far end of the room.

"Yes?" Saphrael asks.

"You're late." Darius does nothing to hide his disdain for Saphrael.

"Match hasn't started yet."

"I've never liked you, Saphrael. However, I do have an offer that may be of interest." Darius briefly inspects the cleanliness of the wall, gliding his finger across a line of dust.

"Can it wait until after the match?"

"I'm afraid… it cannot. This is a peace offering. Convince your friend, Gabriel, to surrender unconditionally to our emperor and our laws. If you are successful in your endeavor, I can guarantee you a spot in the championship rounds, no matter the results of today's match. Which means you and all of your friends will have the opportunity to escape your lowly position."

Saphrael freezes. That means he would get to go home to Hod. Closing his eyes, he physically turns his head away from the idea.

"Gabriel does not belong here; you know that as well as I do. There have been repercussions from Adam's reassignment. As the dust settles, we will be able to refocus our efforts on taking care of this... issue," Darius says.

Saphrael holds his tongue, trying to find the right words. When he finds none, all he says is, "I'll think about it." He avoids eye contact as he gets up and walks past Darius, Chokma mask in hand.

"I do hope everything works out for you and the rest of the Wonder Brigade," Darius says as he walks by. "Sheltering traitors makes one a traitor," Darius says to Saphrael's back. "I can only imagine the consequences."

Saphrael stops and shakes his head, fighting to keep uncertainty at bay. Gripping his Chokma mask, he continues down the gray stone hall, his Knights Templar sword, Solomon, at his side. He shakes his head and grits his teeth as he puts on his Chokma mask. Standing in the hall, he stares at the entrance to the Axion's floor.

◆

I could go home... to Hod. Come on, Saphrael, focus on the match, he says to himself as the procession of flag bearers marches past in perfect military formation. There are roughly fifty flags, each representing a champion from the lowest-ranking teams in their division. The line of flag bearers split and march out to opposite ends of the Axion.

Surveying the competitors, they look like battle-hardened warriors fueled by determination, as shown in their rigid stances. Saphrael knows better than to trust the outward facade, that what drove them to grip their weapons tighter, what aided their prowess, was in fact fear: fear of losing, fear of retribution, fear of pain.

Atop his standard Wonder Brigade gambeson uniform sits a small square chest plate on his upper left side, next to it is a similar metal shoulder guard. He also has on forearm guards and a single leg plate secured by demon leather.

He walks to the nearly empty weapon racks and takes the only thing left, a small dagger with notches carved into it, known as a sword-breaker. He grabs it quickly and turns back to the field. Saphrael hits the side of his Chokma helmet, forcing himself to focus. Surveying the field with magnus vision, points of light glow. Visible is not only their aura but the beating of their hearts, blood flowing throughout their forms down to the tiniest of branching veins, every muscle contraction, and if he strains their skeletal system.

The battle horn blares. Chaos erupts with the clang of metal on metal. Barbaric screams, laced with cries of pain, and cheers from the crowd all fade into silence in Saphrael's mind as he becomes intensely aware of what is immediately around him.

He allows his body to rest, muscle memory holding his sword at the ready. He takes a stance midpoint between offensive and defensive, one where he can switch his guard at a moment's notice. As usual, some competitors have teamed up—the skilled with the unskilled, which is commonplace in free-for-alls. The skilled are not worried about the unskilled, and the unskilled have little choice but to team with a more capable warrior. No one wanted to team with anyone from the Wonder Brigade.

Sword-breaker in one hand, Solomon in the other, Saphrael stands ready. The Tigris champion zeros in on him. *He thinks I'm an easy target. I'll show him.*

The Tigris team's champion swings his longsword at him. Saphrael dodges the first swing, blocks the next, and then parries, snaring the sword in the teeth of sword-breaker. Pulling the sword-breaker hard to the side, Saphrael forces the Tigris champion's sword from his grip. His opponent stumbles forward as he tries to keep hold of his weapon. Using momentum, Saphrael drives Solomon straight through his opponent's back, the front of his sword, skewering his adversary's chest. The Tigris champion falls.

Saphrael places a boot near the impact point and removes his sword from his opponent. Blood covers his blade, as well as his clothing. Briefly, he focuses on movement near him, as everyone else is heavily engaged in their own battles.

The Tigris champion slams his fists on the ground and gets up, letting out a scream as he runs at Saphrael. Saphrael runs at him as well, sword in hand. He fakes a swing. When his opponent blocks, Saphrael drops halfway and rams his shielded shoulder into his opponent's unguarded midsection. The Tigris champion loses his footing and stumbles backward. Saphrael briefly smiles beneath his Chokma mask, thinking about how mad he must be to be shown up by someone from the Wonder Brigade.

The Tigris team champion swings his sword wildly. Saphrael dodges the errant swings. He wants to tell him to just give up, that he would succumb to the wound he struck earlier. The opponent continues to swing his sword recklessly at Saphrael, who easily parries. After blocking another anger-fueled swing, Saphrael forces their crossed blades into the air. Through his magnus sight, he can see fluorescent blood growing and brightening a spot on his opponent's gambeson. Saphrael digs his boots into the ground, rooting his stance, then shoves the Tigris champion back.

The Tigris champion screams again and then runs at Saphrael, knocking him into a nearby wall. The already unstable and partially demolished wall starts to crumble on impact. Saphrael's vision gets knocked back to normal, and he sees nothing from inside the mask. In the darkness, he can hear the pieces of the wall falling. He runs, gripping his weapons and quickly switches his vision back to magnus sight. As he runs, Saphrael purposefully collides with anyone in his way. Most are too engaged in battle to realize the wall is falling. The structural collapse accelerates, taking out many opponents. Saphrael reaches the middle of the large arena, and only then does he look back to see that the majority of the remaining wall is now rubble. Plumes of dust obscure the battlefield like black flecks of static in his magus sight.

He wonders how many are buried beneath the rubble. Amid the chaos, he finds only himself and three others left standing. One wears an Anaconda Chokma mask holding a twisted dagger crafted to tear one open far more brutally than a traditional dagger could, and a small round metal shield, flanked by two champions. One has a Unicorn mask and wields a mace, and the other has a Behemoth mask and a glaive. They are working together, the unskilled leeching upon the skilled.

I made it this far, Saphrael thinks. *I can do this. I will do this, for Gabriel.*

Saphrael braces himself. The Anaconda champion tells the Unicorn to take out the Behemoth. The Behemoth stumbles back, unprepared for the betrayal. The Unicorn champion drops his mace and runs at the Behemoth, lowering his head and goring the Behemoth with the sharp spike of his Chokma mask, causing him to drop his weapon. The Unicorn lifts the Behemoth into the air with its body skewered on its helmet. The Unicorn champion dislodges the Behemoth using both hands and throws his body onto the ground. The Anaconda stands with his foot on the throat of the Behemoth's body. As the Unicorn champion turns back to the Anaconda, he is met with the Anaconda's spiral dagger into his side.

The Anaconda extracts the spiral knife, flips it upright, and jams it into the Unicorn champion's neck. Saphrael steadies himself, his bloodied sword in one hand and sword-breaker in the other.

The Anaconda's stance narrows in on Saphrael, his body stiff with anger. The Anaconda advances and blocks Saphrael's sword using his shield before Saphrael feels the cold bite of the twisted metal pierce his midsection.

The agonizing pain shocks his system, spiking adrenaline throughout his body. Saphrael kicks the Anaconda champion away and drops the sword-breaker, the spiral blade still stuck in his midsection. He fakes a swing from Solomon. When the Anaconda dodges, in one fluid motion, Saphrael grabs hold of the spiral dagger, rips it out of his midsection, turns it to face him and stabs the Anaconda champion in the throat. *For Gabriel,* he thinks, screaming as Solomon glides through his opponent's neck.

The Anaconda's body drops to the ground, his helmeted head landing beside it. The crowd erupts. After he sees no opponents left standing, he takes off his mask, and his vision switches back to normal. He screams a victory shout and thrusts his bloodied sword skyward, completely exhausted yet wired.

Healers wearing black with gold trim run to him. Saphrael is lightheaded from the blood loss but continues to hold himself upright, sword lifted in the air until the healers tell him they need to tend to him. Even in this moment with exhilaration surging throughout his body, the dark offer is inescapable in his mind.

Chapter 24

In the citadel's war room, Dawn's hands rest on a long, black metal, gilded table. She never took a good look at the beige parchments lining the walls when she was here before. The vaguely astronomic drawings fascinate her. She tilts her head and mutters, "It's like Leonardo da Vinci threw up on the wall."

A small smile pulls at the corner of Adam's lips as he sits at the far end of the table, turning a page in the book he is reading. Lucius stands behind a throne in the middle of the table, across from hers. The chairs in the room are a deep chestnut brown.

"Shall we begin?" Lucius says.

Dawn has on her amethyst-colored rose-petal inspired dress.

"Why do I have to learn how to argue?" She pushes aside feelings of inadequacy at failing to produce the purple psychic flame. "I don't even know why you're bothering anyway."

"Dawn, put your personal feelings aside, they do nothing for you. Now, critical thinking encompasses a far larger area than debate alone. It affords you the opportunity to think for yourself. Yes, I know, before you interrupt, you do think for yourself. At least everyone thinks they do. While most is not any actual deep thought, but a stream of consciousness. You must step aside from your thoughts and learn to observe them."

"Like in meditation?" Dawn asks.

"Yes, humans have the rather unfortunate disposition of being an animal of high intellect. Yet they allow their lives to be dictated by what they believe they think, without critical thought. Processing of thoughts are often mistaken for conclusion of thoughts. Man is a creature of habit, yet it is not properly exploited. Mankind must realize that most of their actions are dictated by base animalistic instincts that allowed them to survive the harsh terrains of a virgin Earth. Separate yourself from the false belief that every stereotype echoed back by basic processing are your own thoughts. Critical examination is imperative as well as identifying false information. Do you know about logical fallacies?"

Dawn shakes her head no and he continues.

"Most everyone will appeal to various things that have absolutely nothing to do with the argument itself. Since this is true, ergo, that must also be true—a failure in logic caused by faulty reasoning. I want you to study them. I want you to become intimately familiar with critical thinking."

"Why?"

Lucius sighs, resting his hands on the table, and leans forward. "Everyone should learn logical fallacies in order to identify them and make their arguments and line of thinking more sound. I simply want you to take your place someday."

"That place is full of arguments?" Dawn asks. "I'm not a lawyer."

"Your place is one that requires sound reasoning."

"What is it you want me to become?"

"I need to teach you how things work in the cosmoverse."

Dawn looks confused at the word cosmoverse. Lucius notices and explains.

"The cosmoverse is a name for the universe you know, plus the outer realms, neutral space, the edge, and the various Ethereal Realms. Now, back to why you need to learn logical fallacies. There are tribunals and councils, governing bodies that debate and decide how to interpret the law. Some of our laws are based on treaties. There are separate laws that govern our system and the Crown Realms. You always ask about what is fair in the cosmoverse, about how to change things. Beyond clear action, the rule of law and the interpretation of it can bring your change to fruition. That is why fallacies are important."

Dawn nods. "Okay." She sighs, looking at the stack of papers in front of her. "I'll study."

Lucius leaves the room, and several hours pass.

The door opens, and Lucius returns.

"Do you understand fallacies better now?" Lucius inquires.

"I believe I do."

"Good, remember that reality itself is concrete, obscured by liquid, malleable opinion. The court of public opinion is therefore flawed. It reacts to surface rumors, is easily swayed, and in the end is mob mentality. Be true to truth, always. Growth and prosperity happen when one admits their perception is faulty and then makes a conscious effort to change it. Do not poison perception with falsehoods. In a debate, keep your composure. In restraint, there is power because there is choice. Unless, of course, reaction works in your favor." He pauses a moment. "Words hold power. Do not defend simply your point of view, but the concrete truth. Tell me something you have been wrong about."

"Nearly everything in my life," Dawn says.

"Admitting when one is wrong is the first step toward correcting your course of action. Name a specific thing you have been wrong about."

"How the world works, I guess? Everything I knew was wrong."

"Tell me a truth that you have known."

"Well, I guess I don't know the truth. I trust the memories of the blood flower."

"It is still a hallucination of the past and not concrete."

"Then nothing is concrete?" Dawn asks.

"Some things are concrete. Find those truths, hold them close, and guard them. There is one more thing I must address. You, regardless of whether you want it or not, are a symbol. Everything you do reverberates. You must act with the utmost care in all that you do. There will be some who love you for who you are. There will be some who want you dead for who you are. You are beholden to them as they have you in their hearts and in their minds."

"Why am I not free to live as I choose?"

"You must act responsibly with caution and foresight. A symbol is not an individual. You can be a powerful force that changes the path of the future for the positive or negative. That is the power that comes with being a symbol, but you lose freedom. It is the chains in which we are bound."

"Are you beholden to the population?" Dawn asks.

"Of course," Lucius says. "Everything I do, I do for for them. That will be all for the day. If you need me, I will be in my study."

Adam shuts his book after Lucius leaves and says, "Well, that was interesting."

She walks over to the door as Adam holds it open.

"Take the papers with you," Adam says.

"But I've already read them."

"You might want to read them again."

Dawn sighs, trudges over to the papers, and picks them up.

✦

Dawn wakes from a dreamless sleep and looks over to the door at Adam, who is sitting where he normally does, reading his book. He looks over and notices she is awake, then gets up and walks over.

"Ah, you are awake. Did you sleep well?" Adam stands properly next to her bed.

"I'm fine. No dreams or nightmares to speak of."

Adam nods. "Good to hear, by the way… while you were asleep, this came for you." Adam motions toward her silver table. Sitting upon it, next to her candelabrum, is a long black wooden box with a silver latch etched with patterns.

"What is it?" Dawn asks. The box vaguely reminds her of a coffin.

"Why don't you find out?" Adam suggests, walking up to her, looking at the box. "You will find that today's combat training will differ from what you are used to."

"I hope so." Dawn unhooks the silver latch and opens the box. Inside she finds an elegant medieval-esque black sword with purple accents, a gem in the pommel in the shape of a rose, and a heart-shaped crystal in the center of the emperor's crest in the handle.

"I know you've been depressed. Your father is hoping that this token of affection will help guide you toward forgiveness and understanding. The metal is recycled from hook-swords. Of course, the one you used is in the blade."

As she runs her fingers along the bumps of the handle, she can't believe that something so crude could transform into something so magnificent. The blade is sharp and has angelic sigils etched in purple along its fuller. The sigils arrange themselves to translate to the word Beloved. The tapered cross guard resembles black wings. Light reflects on the grooves of the embossed handle.

"This emblem is another gift from your father. It is to be known as your sign." Adam points at the emperor's crest at the center of the cross guard. It always reminded her of two moons over a Celtic cross. This emperor's crest is adorned with a heart-shaped purple gem.

"I don't want to fight."

"Dawn, this is to protect you. Perhaps you should give it a name."

"A name? Why would I give a sword a name?"

"Because, Dawn, it goes where you go from now on."

"Maybe I should call it Adam," she says with a smile.

"If you wish."

"What about Cain?"

Adam moves his head slowly and looks at her. "What about Cain?"

"For the name of the sword… you know, world's first murderer."

"World's first *recorded* murderer," Adam corrects her.

"Wasn't he—" Dawn doesn't finish her sentence. She doesn't feel as if it is her place.

"Yes." Adam pauses for a moment. "And do you plan on wielding it in that fashion?"

"Of course not." Dawn admires the beauty of the elegant blade. "It is divine."

"Why don't you just call it that, then?"

"Divine?"

Adam nods.

"I guess that works."

Behind the sword box is a black-and-purple sheath. Adam picks it up and hands it to her, along with a belt.

Dawn touches the embossed metal of the handle, then runs her hand along the clear coating protecting the rose gem in the pommel. Finally, her eyes rest upon her emblem, a heart in the center of the emperor's crest. It seems appropriate and noble. She is honored and feels like this gives her life meaning, rather than just death and suffering. The only other time she has ever felt this way was when she was in Gabriel's arms.

✦

Inside the citadel's indoor Blackstone arena, Dawn flows gracefully as if she were dancing. With her sword in hand, Divine sings as it slices through the air. Her movements are strictly controlled in a well-practiced manner. Her deep red spiral curls are down, and she has on a standard gambeson uniform. Lucius and Adam watch as she practices her forms.

Lucius turns to Adam. "The personalized sword and emblem were an excellent idea."

"It was a passing thought."

The emperor walks up to her. She turns to him, Divine in hand.

"How is it?" Lucius asks.

"It's hard not to have a fascination with it. I loved it from the moment I saw it. Thank you." Dawn smiles as she looks at her long black medieval sword accented with purple before sliding it into her sheath.

"It looks well on you," Lucius says, walking over to the weapons rack on the wall and removing a sword. "I want you to get to know other weapons, of course, but become intimately familiar with the one you are wielding."

Adam watches as Lucius turns to her, sword in hand. Dawn actually smiles. Her hand grips the crystal rose pommel and then glides down to the hilt and grabs hold of her sword, removing it from its sheath.

"I designed it as a one-handed sword so you can wield flame in the other. Rest your hand on the pommel and the guard, but rest more so on the pommel. Try to navigate your sword swings that way," he says, moving her hand to the proper position. "If you can throw your opponent off psychologically, he will be fighting two battles, one of which he is sure to lose."

Dawn practices with the hand placement that Lucius has shown her and finds it much easier to control the sword, giving her greater accuracy. Lucius steps back, placing his sword in front of him.

"Keep your defense. Wait for opportunity. Do not allow an opening in your guard. Know your stances. Practice sword training with Adam every morning from now on. You can practice attempting to wield your flame in the evening. Otherwise, I want you to study."

Dropping her guard, Dawn takes a deep breath and nods. A sword comes flying at her, she blocks just in time. The swords reverberate with the clash of metal on metal.

"Never drop your guard," Lucius warns her.

"Yes, Father," Dawn says softly. He turns to put the weapon away, and Dawn thrusts her sword at him. Lucius half turns, using centrifugal force to knock her sword out of her hands. It skids across the black stone floor.

Adam walks forward and picks up Divine.

"You can allow the princess to do some things herself, Adam. How else is she ever going to learn?"

Adam looks like he wants to say something, but instead he nods. "Of course."

✦

Dawn sighs at the large stack of books and papers sitting on her table. Most of the books are brown with beige paper sticking out. Read, train, read, train is all she ever does anymore. She brushes her long, deep red hair off her shoulders, sweeping it to the back.

"What should I read today?" Dawn says to herself out loud. Adam briefly looks over, then goes back to reading his book. She finds learning most everything interesting. It isn't that she has to read, it is the strict schedule she dislikes. But no one has ever had expectations of her before. Already feeling like a failure as she is unable to produce her father's flame, she needs to prove that she is capable and worthy.

Pushing away a pang of sadness, she browses her stack of books, one catches her eye. It is a relatively small navy-blue book in the middle of the stack. There are no markings on the cover. Dawn picks it up and sinks into a chair near her barred, flower-shaped window.

Her mouth moves as she reads a chapter headline. "Discere Centers?"

She glances over at Adam. Who is sitting in his chair near the door, engrossed in reading as well. So, she goes back to the small navy-blue book.

Hours pass as she absorbs information, reading as fast as she can because it's clear she is not supposed to have access to this book. Briefly, she wonders, *What if it's not real? What if it is exaggerated?* Turning the pages, she keeps her composure and reads about the systematic cruelty that governs the Sine System from the damnation of Lucius from the Crown Realms to the torture of those who seriously under-perform and the shadow networks of loyalty officers. Briefly, she thinks about the attendant who worked with Ketis, the one who specialized in tradition. Only a small portion of the book remains unread. She turns the page to a new chapter titled Applied Sociological Programming.

"What is it you are reading?" Lucius asks.

Dawn unconsciously takes in a sharp breath as she looks up at her father. She hadn't even realized that he was in the room.

"Oh, just something from the latest delivery of books." She closes the book and holds onto it.

Lucius rips the book from her grasp and opens it. Adam walks up, standing beside him.

"Adam, were you aware of what she was reading?" Lucius asks, turning to him and shoving the book in his face.

"No, sir. I'm afraid not."

Lucius swings the book inches from hitting Adam, slamming it onto the table, causing everything on top of it to tremble.

"My sincerest apologies to you both," Adam says with a bow.

"Who delivered this set of books?" Lucius demands, his eyes fixed on Adam.

"I confess I haven't been paying enough attention to matters at hand today. It was one of the standard sets of guards. Nothing was out of the ordinary."

Dawn looks back and forth at their exchange.

Lucius turns to her. "My dear, you must disregard anything written here. It is twisted poison written through the eyes of traitors."

"What about it is lies?" Dawn demands, her eyebrows raised, tears forming in her eyes.

"This is exactly—" His tone changes. "Dawn, these angels are dangerous. They believe in their own rhetoric. They bend the truth to fit their own malformed agenda." Lucius turns to Adam. "I suggest you discover the source of this misinformation before I have no other choice than to find it to be a lapse in your judgment."

"Yes, sir, my lord. Permission to leave Dawn's side to conduct an investigation."

"No, your absence is what they may be waiting for. I will conduct my own investigation."

"Sir, I am well suited for this task," Adam insists.

"You have your duty. Ensure this does not happen again."

"Father?" Dawn stands up. "What in the book is a lie?"

"This is nothing more than propaganda. They are a terrorist organization whose sole purpose is the destruction of our way of life." His eyes lock with hers. "They haven't contacted you before, have they?"

She remembers the dream, eyes widening in realization.

Adept at reading her reactions, Lucius asks, "When?"

"A while ago," Dawn says quietly.

"Where?"

She looks away.

"Dawn, these dissidents are a threat. Where did they contact you?" Lucius demands.

"In a dream." Her voice wavers as she confesses. Tears fall down her face.

"Why haven't you said anything before now?" Lucius's gaze is fixed on her.

Lifting her head, she looks straight at him. "You told me to be the judge of everything for myself. The one who contacted me is not a threat."

"Dawn, no one on the opposing side is to be trusted. Do I make myself clear?" Lucius says.

In her mind, she is back in the dream, feeling the breeze of the guillotine blade as it slices the air in front of her face.

"Is this one of the dreams you didn't want to log yet?" Adam asks.

Dawn looks back and forth between them. She shakes her head and lets out a deep sigh, deciding it's best to just not say anything.

"Get the name," Lucius orders Adam. He turns and leaves without another word.

"Do you know who it was?" Adam asks. "Who contacted you?"

Dawn holds his gaze and does not look away. "Yes, but I will not turn him in."

Adam raises an eyebrow. "Lucius will place blame on everyone if you don't tell me who it was."

"How can I be sure? It was a dream, after all."

"Don't play games with me, Dawn. This could mean my head as well."

"Surely, Lucius knows you have nothing to do with this."

"One can never be too cautious."

"Apparently, one can," Dawn says in defiance.

"Dawn, this group wants nothing less than the destruction of your father and everything he stands for. You do understand that?"

"It was just a dream," Dawn says, staring off into the distance.

"Tell me everything," Adam pleads.

"First, tell me if what is written in that book is true," Dawn says.

"What parts, Dawn?" Adam asks with a sigh of resignation.

"All of it."

Adam picks up the book and flips through the pages, stopping on a section on how to tolerate torture. Snapping the book shut, he shakes his head.

"This is something I am not going to address," Adam says.

"Why?" Dawn glares at him. "Because you know what is written in there is true."

"It is not my place to tell you about what is written in that book."

Adams looks at the pile of books sitting on the table. As he picks up the stack, loose papers fall out. Dawn's eyes widen as she sees Gabriel's name written at the top of the paper.

Dawn grips the papers, reading as fast as she can. "Gabriel? Treatment Plans?"

She scans the papers that have a list of problems and solutions for both of them.

"Increase dependency? Desensitization? Validation? Weaknesses?" She is dazed and disconnected. Briefly, she gets a glance at Gabriel's page. "Anxiety exploit? A list of traits?" As she turns the page over, Adam rips the papers from her. Dawn fights to keep hold, causing the treatment plans to tear. She is left only with the crumpled edge of the papers that list their names, but even that is torn.

"Adam… what's going on?"

He ignores her, confiscating the rest of the books, leaving her with the evidence in her hands.

"Adam?" Dawn demands, tears falling.

He doesn't answer. Instead, he flips through the pages, checking for anything out of the ordinary.

"Adam, tell me what's going on."

"Your father only wants what is best for you. Trust in his judgment."

He flips through a copy of the *Treaty of Ordo*, finding a part underscored in red, an addendum.

"What is it?" Dawn asks.

Adam closes the book with the treaty in it. "It seems that they want you to know what you may already be aware of."

"Oh, and what is it I am already aware of?"

Adam sighs. "That the legal successors of the primary signers of the *Treaty of Ordo* are also bound by the same restrictions as the respective leaders."

"If they wanted me to have this information, why would you tell me?"

"One, I assume Lucius has already gone over the fine print with you. Secondly, it is something you should know going in."

"I see. That means if I become successor, I am bound here?"

"Is that unacceptable?"

"I suppose not, but it isn't fair."

"It is so successors cannot be used as a loophole," Adam says. "Converse with them again and we may all pay a heavy price, Princess."

"I promise nothing, other than that I will abide by the law."

Adam raises an eyebrow. "You are aware, your father's word is law? You don't have to be named successor. That is something you must accept yourself, Princess."

There is a loud crash outside the doors, down the hall. Adam gets up, opens the right half of the double doors, then firmly shuts it.

"It's your father. Seems as if he's found the traitor."

Dawn gets up to see what is going on. Adam places a hand on her shoulder, stopping her.

"Allow this to happen. It will anyway. Best not make it worse," Adam says quietly.

She shakes her head, bats away his hand from her shoulder, and goes to the door. Adam stops her, getting in front of the doors.

"I cannot allow you to leave this room, Princess."

"How did Lucius find him so quickly?" Dawn asks.

"Dawn, first of all, you are already aware of who it was. If you know, he knows. Secondly, when you pass along something as sensitive in nature as this book, someone must pay the price. My guess is he was ready to turn himself in for the sake of protecting others."

"If there are others."

"There are always others, Dawn."

Chapter 25

Dawn, having just woken up, has yet to change from her silk black nightgown embroidered with purple roses as she listlessly turns a page in the book she is studying. It is a compendium of the last thousand orbiums of tournament champions. To Dawn, it only highlights the brutality of the system. It makes her sick to see it held in such high esteem. A scream echoes inside of her head causing Dawn to grip the table, closing her eyes, before she sharply turns to her flower-shaped window. Rushing over, she stops and peers through the bars, seeing the same muted landscape that is always present.

"Dawn," Adam says in a warning tone as he walks over.

As she is about to give up, she spots a small gathering partially obscured by the mists that hang low in the air. Adam looks over her shoulder and ushers her away from the window.

"I'm just looking," Dawn protests.

"Best not to spy on others," Adam says.

A psychic cry, louder than before, causes her to inhale sharply. She turns back to the window.

"You can hear that? Right, Adam? You can hear that?" Dawn asks, desperately straining to see what is going on.

"Princess, you need to focus upon your studies, not what is going on down there." Adam puts a hand on her shoulder to move her away from the window.

Before he can, Lucius's voice comes from the doorway. "You needn't shield her from this. Dawn, put your overcoat on."

Dawn sighs and throws on her long black overcoat with purple highlights running from the lapels to the long ends, which reach the floor. It takes her a minute to button up fully.

"Don't forget your belt," Adam reminds her.

Dawn grabs her belt and ties it around her waist. She takes a moment to adjust her solid metal emblem that sits just off center to the right. Divine rests on her left side next to her pouch of tarot cards.

"Come now." Lucius gestures for her to follow. "I'm sure Adam has properly informed you of the traitors known as the resistance?"

Dawn stays silent as Adam hasn't said much about them.

"They are a pitiful group of madmen and so-called idealists," Lucius says without looking at her as they walk. "They move blindly, without knowing who is on their side. Most everyone you meet is a part of a shadow network colloquially known as the unseen hand. They keep everything and everyone in place. This includes the visible, such as loyalty officers, down to the nearly imperceptible. Everything has a place, and everything stays in that place, lest the balance is upset. The last thing anyone needs is chaos. Some do not understand. They fail to comprehend the security that order provides. This must be corrected quickly and punitively, lest a chain reaction causes society itself to collapse. Where would we be without order and society, Dawn?"

Dawn remains silent as they walk.

"On Earth, where would you be without society?" Lucius prompts her again.

"A lawless wasteland?" Dawn says as they come to a set of spiraling stairs.

"It would be no different from the cruel and unforgiving mercy of nature. Without order, there is only chaos," Lucius says, the front doors of the citadel come into view.

Lucius opens the doors to a few high-ranking military officers, including Zunael, congregated on the landing of the grand stairs. They quiet as soon as the door opens. Dawn looks at them, but they are looking at Lucius.

Adam puts his hand on her shoulder as if he is trying to tell her something, preventing her from going forward. A dark-red droplet falls directly in front of her. Feeling disconnected, she stares at the splotch of blood on the ground. She looks up into the air, and her eyes widen. Adam keeps his hand steady on her shoulder. A series of ropes are tied together, suspending a beaten and bloodied body still in his royal guard's uniform, but without his faceless metal mask. Blood continues to drip in front of her. Her heart wrenches as she recognizes him as the guard from her dream.

"He will be corrected once he repents," Lucius says.

The youthful-looking guard's mouth is sewn shut. There is a symbol burned through his uniform's upper right chest, almost too far away to see clearly, but Dawn is certain it is Lucius's symbol. It glows orange as if he were currently being branded. The officers chat, paying no mind to what is, to them, more decorative than alive.

The tortured angel's eyes meet Dawn's. The world quiets; the officers' conversations fade into silence. Every breath the guard takes seems to inflict pain. The rope wrapped around his body also binds his arms behind his back as he is suspended in the air. Dawn fights to hold back tears, thinking, *All this over me?* She tries to remember the conversation from her dream but can't remember it as clearly as she would have liked. *It wasn't worth it. What was his goal? What is Lucius's goal?* Dawn feels sick as her mind races.

"I called you here to announce that Princess Dawn will officially be crowned my successor. This orbium's Circle Gala will double as a coronation. I trust you all will have enough time to get everything in order by then?"

There are murmurs and nods.

"Why wasn't there a successor named before now?" an officer asks.

"Adam quietly filled that role until a rightful successor could be found."

Before more questions could be raised, Lucius sharply says, "That will be all."

Without so much as a glance upward, Lucius turns and heads inside.

"It's time for us to go back inside as well, Dawn," Adam says.

Dawn is still looking up at the bound and tortured royal guard. Adam ushers her inside, she keeps her eyes on the guard until the door closes behind her.

She says nothing on the way back to her room, and Adam lets her be. Dawn sits down on her bed, trying not to look at the barred, flower-shaped window. And for once, Adam doesn't try to get her to do her daily tasks.

"How long will he be punished?" Dawn asks, finally saying something.

"As long as is necessary," Adam replies, looking up from his book.

She knows he won't give her answers about the guard or the methods of so-called rehabilitation, so instead she asks, "The word orbium? What does that mean?"

"Orbital cycle, Dawn. It means year but aligned to Tiphareth's orbital cycle."

Dawn nods, then looks to the window. Her gaze is soft and disconnected.

✦

Eventually, Dawn returned to her studying. Her hair is down in large waves of curls that cascade down her back. Although she grows tired of the elaborate dress, makeup, and jewelry every single day, she never complains because she knows what it was like to be without. Her dress features a heart-shaped purple bodice and a black skirt covered in layers of lace textured with patterns of roses and leaves cut from the lace, paired with matching gloves that extend just past her elbow.

There is a knock on the door. Adam answers it and talks quietly with someone on the other side before he motions for her to come over. One-half of the large wooden double doors opens fully, revealing the visitor to be the tortured guard. Lines on his skin where he had been whipped shine red. He is still in his royal guard uniform, although it is tattered and torn in several places. The beaten guard reluctantly looks up at Dawn. His eyes are light hazel with flecks of gray. His expression is tired as he falters, having difficulty holding himself upright.

"I—I wanted to tell you how sorry I am, Princess. How wrong I was to violate my contract and speak to you," he says while averting eye contact.

Beyond him, the other guards are at their posts beside the doors, one holding it open. She half expected Lucius to be standing behind the disgraced guard.

"I wanted to see you. I was wrong. There is—there is no threat." The disheveled guard steps forward, his hands shaking as he holds out a black wooden box in front of her. "Don't do this. Please consider the consequences."

Adam strikes him with a backhand across the face.

"Once a traitor..." Adam says, taking the box. "If you care so much about Raziel here, your father has made a request."

Raziel closes his eyes, his head down.

Adam opens the box. Inside is a purple heart-shaped gem attached to a silver chain. Accompanying the necklace is an elegant, matte-black crown. The centerpiece of the crown is Dawn's emblem, a purple heart gem with the emperor's crest behind it. The tips of the crown are topped with small cerulean jewels.

"The crown is for when you are legally designated successor. For now, it is merely a reminder," Adam says as he pulls out the necklace. The purple gem turns in the air as he holds the chain in his right hand. "You will voluntarily wear this at all times. In exchange, Raziel will be placed on a more merciful probation."

"Why?" Dawn asks, watching the light reflect in the series of triangles cut into the edges of the gem.

"This crystal transmits psychic resonances—thoughts that are too loud, telepathic transmissions," Adams explains.

"So, everything will be recorded?"

"In essence, yes, even dreams. To keep you safe from stalkers and would-be assassins."

"Doesn't Lucius already have this ability?"

"Some things are given of free will. Show him you trust him. You faltered by not telling him of your encounter with Raziel—now known conspirator against the crown."

"Dawn, don't—" Raziel's words are cut short as Adam punches him in the mouth.

"It also enhances psychic abilities. It is your choice, but you do not have eternity to decide. Guards." Adam nods toward the door. The guards escort Raziel away.

Dawn watches as he leaves, wishing she could do more. The door shuts behind them. Adam places the necklace in her palm. She closes her hand around it, feeling the gem pulse with raw power. There is even more energy radiating from it than she has felt from her tarot deck.

"Will this allow me to talk to Gabriel?" Dawn asks.

"I'm afraid that would be entirely up to Lucius."

"I'll wear it."

"This is not to be taken lightly. You have not been given any stipulation as to how long you will be required to—"

"I said I'll wear it. I have nothing to hide."

"Famous last words." Adam picks up the necklace, places it on her, and clasps it shut.

It weighs heavier on her chest than she thought it would.

"Your father wants to see you," Adam says.

"I don't want to talk to him right now."

"Don't act like a child." Adam holds the door open. "Come along."

Dawn sighs and follows Adam to Lucius's study. Lucius sits silently on the couch, head tilted back and eyes closed. Dawn looks at Adam, who nods to her chair. She walks over to her seat. After waiting for quite some time, she looks over to Adam, about to say something. He shakes his head and motions for her to be patient. Finally, Lucius opens his eyes and lifts his head into an upright position. He looks at Dawn, fully aware they are there.

"I know you are upset with me. I admire that you are." Lucius focuses his attention on Dawn, who reluctantly looks at him.

He picks up a chalice of Xerotes and breathes in its sweet aroma before offering Dawn a glass. She accepts it and takes a drink. The liquid warms her.

"You have such conviction. Albeit misplaced ethics," Lucius says.

"I have misplaced ethics?" she repeats, pointing at herself with one hand and carelessly whipping the chalice with the other, spilling some Xerotes onto the floor.

"Yes." Lucius lounges back, holding his glass. "Dawn, consider the consequences of careless inaction as it pertains to societal law, for just a moment. The higher the place of power, the heavier the burden. I shoulder the responsibility for everything that happens here. I was going to show you how things worked, but you were not ready."

"There is balance." Dawn lifts her head defiantly. "Between freedom and law."

"Dawn, consider the failings of the balance of freedom and law as to where you are from. Do you believe that simply because one says they are moral through words and not action, that they are moral? Or what about those who cast off the chains of responsibility, are they ethically superior?"

"What do you mean?"

"When the law fails and someone dies, it is regarded as no one's failure because of the illusion of freedom. You come from a place so morally deficient that they often intentionally err on the side of negligence. This leads to much pain, suffering, and death. Something to think about."

Lucius motions for Adam to retrieve her. Adam approaches her chair. Dawn finishes her drink quickly; her hand briefly rests on the necklace she is blackmailed into wearing, although she does not mention it. Dawn looks at Lucius carefully as she sets the chalice on the table and turns to Adam. She can feel his eyes upon her as she leaves the study.

◆

Dawn warms up to spar against Adam, flowing in her forms as her sword sings, slicing through the air. She wears her black gambeson uniform, and her hair is tied in large chunky braids pinned together near her ears and rests on her shoulders. Adam watches, occasionally instructing her on form. As she holds Divine mid-thrust, she flashes back to when she was in the hallway, under attack by the masked royal guards. Her breathing becomes heavier, and her eyes widen. She feels as if her sword is the hook-sword skewering her assailant. Dawn nearly drops Divine.

"Dawn," Adam's stern voice jolts her back to the citadel's indoor Blackstone arena.

He walks up to her. "Are you all right?"

She nods, not answering, hoping he won't press her about it but knowing that he will.

"Dawn," Adam repeats.

For a moment, she tightens her grip, causing her hand to shake, before she places Divine into its sheath.

"Dawn..." Adam repeats in a softer tone.

"I don't want to talk about it." Dawn keeps her head down.

The door at the far end of the room opens, and a pair of masked royal guards enter. Unconsciously, she puts her hand back on the hilt of her sword. The guard on the left has a chain in his hand that leads to the wrists of a masked figure clad in a plain black uniform. Another set of guards follows close behind.

"For this session, you will have a sparring partner besides myself," Adam says, watching as they drag the sacrificial lamb to the center of the room. The prisoner's silver Chokma mask is forged to resemble an owl.

"I won't fight." Dawn looks at Adam. He has a sword for their sparring match in hand.

"I'm afraid this will be a morally painful lesson for you today, Dawn. If you do not engage with him, I have orders to kill him."

Adam walks to the prisoner and rips the Chokma mask off revealing familiar short blond hair.

Dawn's heart seizes, *Raziel*. Somehow, he looks even worse than the last time she had seen him, which was only earlier this cycle. His skin is pocketed with bruises, dried blood, and wounds. He leans forward, having an issue keeping himself upright. Nonetheless, he offers her a weak smile. The guards remove the chains from his wrists.

"How am I supposed to have an even match with him if he can barely stand? Let him recover first."

"My, you do have your father's tongue, do you not? I'm afraid you cannot talk your way out of this one, Dawn."

Adam tosses a sword unceremoniously in the direction of Raziel.

"It's all right, Dawn," Raziel says softly. "Do what you have to."

Dawn shakes her head. The royal guards take out their weapons and point them at Raziel. His eyes plead with hers as much as they did when he was strung up in front of the citadel.

"Pick up your sword," Adam orders Raziel.

Raziel slowly picks up the sword. "It's okay."

"Stop talking," Adam demands.

"How do I know when the fight has been satisfactory?" Dawn grips the cold handle of her weapon.

"When you win, Dawn," Adam says.

She sighs and draws her sword before looking into Raziel's eyes. The understanding she thought was there is broken as Raziel charges in her direction, sword aimed at her midsection. She dodges and half turns, swinging at him, but Raziel continues running forward before turning to face her.

Their swords clash. Dawn wants to close her eyes but forces herself to stay in the fight. She boots him in the midsection, causing him to stumble backward. Raziel answers by swinging his blade skillfully, slicing her lower left forearm through her gambeson. She looks at him in shock. Blood runs down her fingertips, dripping onto the hilt of her sword. She dances with the blade, muscle memory coupling with intensity quickly puts Raziel on defense. He stumbles back, losing his balance. Dawn increases her onslaught, the clash of metal on metal rings as Raziel manages to block right before falling to the ground.

Dawn holds her sword to his throat, ready to deliver the killing blow. Her hand starts to shake, and she takes in a long, deep breath before dropping Divine. Her sword clangs against the black stone floor.

She turns away from Raziel. Her heart strains inside her chest. Adam walks over and picks Divine up. He has a hollow expression in his eyes as he advances toward Raziel. Suddenly, he stops, turns sharply, and gives Dawn her sword. Gripping her hand forcefully around the hilt, Adam points the sword at Raziel. "Fight him or I will have failed, and there will be more than one death haunting your memories this day."

"What?" Dawn backs away, tearing her arm away from him, and faces Adam. "You want me to fight?" She grips Divine tightly. "I'll fight you."

"Dawn, that is not the lesson we are here to learn today."

"Perhaps it should be." Lucius walks into the Blackstone arena. "I see the experiment was only partially successful. Perhaps positive reinforcement can only do so much. That is enough for today."

"But, sir," Adam protests.

"I said that is enough." Lucius is visibly irritated that Adam has the audacity to question him. "We will try again tomorrow and the following cycles, until we are successful." Lucius addresses the royal guards without looking at them. "String him back up where he belongs until it is time to try again."

Tears fill Dawn's eyes as they force the metal cuffs back on Raziel's wrists.

"I'm sorry, Dawn," Raziel says, right before royal guards force the owl Chokma mask over his head.

"Dawn," Lucius says, putting his hands on her shoulders. He turns her away from Raziel. "I know this is a difficult lesson, but it is one that you must learn."

"What lesson is that?" Dawn feels as if she is choking as she talks.

"Sometimes life gives you no choice other than the path ahead of you. You cannot choose the circumstances, like when you must fight to survive. Raziel is being made an example of, and that, too, is valuable."

"Valuable to what?"

"To keeping the peace. So that things like the assassination attempt are quelled before they get to that point. Trust me, this is for the best."

Chapter 26

Gabriel sits alone in the barracks, passing the time by studying his worn book on combat techniques. No matter how hard he tries to concentrate, he can't shake the sight of Dawn staring at him with those emotionless eyes when he asked her to marry him in that strange dream. He shivers, not from the cold, but from the possibility that she may already be gone.

He gets pulled away from his nightmarish daydream as the door opens. Gabriel sets the book down and stands. Saphrael, covered in blood and dust wearily looks at him before clunking his Chokma mask on top of his cabinet and dropping onto his cot.

"Are you okay?" Gabriel asks.

"I'm okay. Are you okay?"

"I'm all right now. What happened? Did you go to your fight?"

"I did. I won." Saphrael sits up, his face is solemn. "After I carried you back from the Quanta."

"Where is everyone?" Gabriel asks, looking at the door, expecting the others to walk through.

Saphrael shakes his head, taking a moment to collect himself before he looks down. "I didn't want to tell you."

"Tell me what?"

"I—" Saphrael struggles to find the right words. "Before the match, I was approached by the authorities. They want me to convince you to turn yourself in. They threatened to mark me a traitor if I refuse."

"I'm surprised they didn't do something sooner."

"It might be the power structure change. It could be something else. I don't know," Saphrael says.

"What did you tell them?"

"Not much. I said I would think about it," Saphrael says, starting to remove his gear. "I'm not going to turn you in, Gabriel."

"Aren't you afraid they'll send you back to discere?"

"Let them," Saphrael says. "I would much rather die for something than to live for nothing."

"I thought you couldn't die."

"Metaphorically speaking. Also, there are ways to permanently kill angels. It's just very difficult."

"So… how?" Gabriel asks, sitting down on his cot.

"What do you mean how?" Saphrael looks up from undoing his leg plate.

"How do you kill an angel?"

"Well, the easiest way I know is with the sword Eternus. You need the fire of the Archangel of Death and the sword. It was forged to hold the flame. It's how we lost two archangels in the time of the Promethean Angels."

"Okay? Is this something I should be worried about?"

"Unless Lucius can get both the sword and the Archangel of Death to empower it, I wouldn't be too concerned."

"So, where is the sword now?"

Saphrael shrugs. "Some say Lucius has it. Others swear it is well protected in the Crown." Saphrael's half-laugh ends in a scoff. "Wishful thinking. I'm hoping Azrael has it because he'll never use it… and if it is truly lost, I hope that it remains so."

The door swings open, screaming on its hinges before it halts, unable to be opened farther. Marce storms in. "Why is he here? Do you have any idea what they're going to do to you? To all of us?"

"…No?" Gabriel answers.

"Of course you don't, outsider."

Gabriel raises an eyebrow at the stark response. Saphrael stops removing his gear and walks up to Marceriel, half his shoulder guard hangs down undone.

"What do you want?" Saphrael asks. He stops, his face inches from Marceriel's.

Marce glares at Gabriel then meets Saphrael's challenge. "I'm here to ensure the messages are delivered."

"What messages?" Gabriel asks.

Saphrael adjusts his foot to one side and rests his arms in a defensive stance.

"Have you made your decision or has Gabriel made it for you? He's not supposed to be here. They made that perfectly clear. We will all be labeled traitors if you continue to plead ignorance," Marce says, looking directly at Saphrael.

"I will fight on Gabriel's side for as long as I am needed," Saphrael says.

"Why?" Marce grits his teeth.

"Fighting is useless there is something to fight for. Unlike some," Saphrael pauses to make his point clear, "I don't turn my back on my friends."

"Fine. Traitor." Marce aggressively tilts his head up while looking at Saphrael.

Saphrael punches Marceriel in the jaw, which is countered by Marceriel's boot to Saphrael's shin, then Marce uppercuts Saphrael with the underside of a Chokma mask. Gabriel's eyes widen as he watches Saphrael's blood run down the side of the metal of a Tigris mask.

"And you call him a traitor?" Gabriel rushes over to intervene.

"Stay out of it," Marce orders Gabriel, shoving him back. While Marce is distracted, Saphrael tackles him. The back of Marceriel's head ricochets off the black metal wall. Marce shoves Saphrael away.

"Turn yourself in," Marce says, pointing at Gabriel.

"What happens if I do?"

"How am I supposed to know? I'm just the messenger." Marce shrugs, keeping a wary eye on Saphrael.

"Do I have time to think about it?" Gabriel asks.

"You have until Saphrael's next scheduled Axion fight." Marce looks briefly at Saphrael. "Same goes for you, traitor."

"So that's it," Saphrael says, "A minor inconvenience and you switch sides?"

"Minor? A minor inconvenience? You've lost your mind, Saph." Marce's eyes narrow. "Don't forget whose military you serve."

"As if I have a choice!" Saphrael's voice breaks.

"None of us do. It isn't about choice, Saphrael. It's about duty, it's about honor, it's about—"

"Loyalty?" Saphrael steps forward, challenging him, to which Marce rips the Wonder Brigade's banner off the black metal wall, wraps it around his hand and punches Saphrael in the right temple. Saphrael doubles over but recovers quickly, grabbing hold of the banner, momentarily throwing Marce off balance. The fabric of their flag stretches and threads begin to pop before Saphrael pulls back sharply, ripping it apart.

"Oh, nice job, Captain!" Marce throws his hands up, letting the torn piece fall to the ground.

Saphrael looks at the piece of the flag he has and closes his hand around it. "Just tell me why you left..."

"You're the one who left, Captain. You left us, all of us. You left us with no choice but to follow orders."

While they continue to argue, Gabriel picks up the torn piece of the banner Marce had dropped. He stares at it for a while as their shouting fades into the background. Gabriel clears his throat to get their attention.

"Guys..." Gabriel says, but they are too busy arguing. "Guys!" Still, they ignore him. There is a subtle shift in Marce's stance as he leans ever so slightly forward, readying to attack. Having enough of it, Gabriel slams his fist, denting the metal wall. That gets their attention. "Grace in forgiveness. Understanding in death."

Both Saphrael and Marceriel are thrown off enough by hearing the Wonder Brigade's creed to stop fighting. Saphrael lets his shoulders drop and Marce relaxes as well.

"We have until my next fight? Why don't you stay while we figure this out?" Saphrael suggests.

"Why? What is there to figure out?" Marce asks, spreading his arms to the side.

"Hey," Saphrael places a hand on his shoulder briefly. "You'll always be a loser. That's what we are, right? The Wonder Brigade."

"We were losers. At least we were losers together," Marce says looking at the floor. "I'll stay, but not for long."

"Understood." Saphrael smiles wearily.

"Are you familiar with the parable of Job? God and Satan had a bet," Gabriel says. "Who would Job turn to? So Satan took away everything. His family, his material possessions, his health. Yet, Job didn't turn to Satan. Instead, he turned to God."

"Um, okay?" Saphrael says. "Inaccurate but go on."

"Satan made a mistake by taking everything away from Job. Once everything but God was taken away, you have nowhere else to turn. If you want a man to turn away from God, instead, give him everything."

"So, what, you're faithfully righteous now?" Marce asks.

"Only to Dawn. No, my point is when everything is taken away, you value what is left. My former life is gone..." Gabriel says as he holds the torn piece of the banner. "Can I keep this?"

"Uh, sure, Gabriel. No one cares if you keep that," Marce says.

Gabriel walks to the door.

"Where are you going?" Saphrael calls out after him.

"I need to think. I'm going for a walk."

The door to the barracks shuts behind him.

✦

Why does it still call to me? Gabriel sighs, slouching as he stands on what once was the shore of the Black Lake. The voices of those lost to the obsidian waters whisper to him, *You're not good enough.* Gabriel closes his eyes. *Maybe they're right... maybe I'm not good enough,* he thinks mournfully, looking into the crater. He decides to search for the Lost and flies into the air propelled by his blue flame.

After searching the area for some time and finding nothing, he gives up and rests in the treetops. The uppermost branches of the oversized, twisted gray tree bounce slightly as he settles comfortably against it. Taking in a deep breath of fresh air, Gabriel feels the wind against his face. Then he looks out across the familiar forest. It isn't long before he drifts off to sleep, lost in thought.

In his mind's eye, his spirit flies through hoops of blue neon circles. A vision comes into focus: the cursed lake's foreboding, coal-black waters as they once were, then a blinding flash of light leaves a discolored photographic impression behind. After his sight acclimates, he looks out upon the lake. The curse is not only lifted but the water itself is luminous. A light source emanates from the center of the purified waters. In his vision, he watches several Lost go into the water and then emerge, their scars seared shut. Their movements no longer disjointed, their healing accelerated.

Gabriel sways in the branches, waking from his vision.

"How can I do that? Semoel? Are you there?" There is no response. Gabriel sighs. "Maybe I should talk to Saphrael."

Gabriel jumps off the branches and flies to the crater of the lake, landing beside it.

"How am I supposed to do this? Was it just a dream? Would they even want to be purified?" he mumbles to himself.

Gabriel lifts off the ground and flies dodging around the twisting treetops, leaving a streak of blue flame. He lands close to the edge of the forest and opts to walk the rest of the way.

When he gets back to the barracks he finds Marce, hunched over, sitting on his cot.

"Well, look who's back," Marceriel says. "You've got some nerve."

"What did I do?" Gabriel asks, pointing to himself.

"We have little time left and you spend it alone. You don't even tell us what you want to do."

"I had to think."

"What is there to think about?" Marce asks.

"I want to talk about something else. Where is Saphrael?"

"He'll be back soon."

"I had a vision. You know, I never really thought too much about visions, but this one seemed... real."

"You're going to have to leave the doubt on Earth, Gabriel. Visions are real. Tell me what you saw."

"The Lost—the lake was filled with purified water. After they went in, they stopped rotting and were freed from the curse."

"You know that won't change why they went into the lake to begin with."

"I know."

"By the way, it's called a baptism," Marce says sarcastically.

"Right... so, how do I do it?"

"A baptism?" Marce laughs. "You want my help to perform a mass baptism on creatures that aren't even angels anymore? Going to throw a couple of demons in there as well?"

Gabriel wonders what would happen if a demon was forced into purified water. He puts his head down and closes his eyes as he talks, "I hear it... the lake, calling me. Holding me down. This cursed residue it tells me things... like I'm not good enough, like I can't do it, that everything is pointless."

"You sure that's not just depression, Gabriel?"

"No, I mean it is, but this is different."

Their eyes meet each other's evenly.

"All right, I'll help you," Marceriel says with a shrug, standing up.

"Really?"

"Yeah, you want to baptize the Lost. Sounds like fun. Should we wait for Saphrael?"

"Maybe I shouldn't be here," Gabriel says, doubts forming in his mind.

Marce scoffs. "Is that what you really want to do?"

"What?"

"Run away and hide when bad things happen?"

"No?"

"Then stand your ground. Look defeat in the eyes and tell it to screw off. The only other option is to run away and hide. You turn from predator to prey when you run away and hide."

"Okay, okay. I get it. Don't run."

"No matter what, Gabriel. You think this is bad? That losing everything is bad? That's life. You think the Wonder Brigade wanted to be torn apart? We were a team. You can't have anything good here. Not unless you're a part of a team that wins. And even then—" Marceriel lets his words die without finishing his thought. "That is why I am on the winning side. That is why I am on Emperor Lucius's side. Do not forget that."

"After you keep getting sent to discere? After they severed your wings? And you call me weak. You're acting like a victim staying with their abuser because it's safer. It's not safer, Marce. You need to make a choice. That choice is yours, but it's one that you're going to have to live with. I understand if you believe there is safety in numbers."

Marceriel tightens his fist as he walks up to Gabriel.

Saphrael opens the door, breaking the tension. "What is going on?"

Marce briefly rests his hand on Saphrael's shoulder. "I'll explain on the way."

"The way to what?" Saphrael asks.

"We're throwing a baptism!" Marce hurls his hands into the air as he walks by.

Saphrael tilts his head and gives Gabriel a questioning look.

✦

Saphrael, Gabriel, and Marce stand at the edge of the deep crater, staring at the black crystalline spikes that jut up from the ground.

"Where do you suppose all the water went?" Saphrael asks.

"What?" Gabriel turns to him.

"The water has to go somewhere, Gabriel," Marce says.

Saphrael points to the sky. "It has been a lot cloudier since the lake got burned."

"Okay, archangel, let's see what you're made of," Marce rubs his hands together and then points at the crater. "Flood it."

"What?" Gabriel shrugs with his hands open.

"You said in your vision you saw a pool of holy water," Marce says.

"Well, it was purified water."

"What is the difference?" Marce rolls his eyes. "Fill it with water."

"How am I supposed to fill it with water?" Gabriel asks.

"Your girlfriend could," Marce says. "Remember the arena? There has never been weather like that since fire consumed Geburah. If anyone could refill this lake, it's Dawn or archangel Azrael."

"Could the real Archangel Gabriel fill it with water?" Gabriel wonders.

"Guys, those aren't suggestions that are going to help right now," Saphrael says.

"I can do it. I mean, maybe," Gabriel says. "Okay, besides Dawn, give me an example."

Saphrael and Marceriel silently exchange a look.

Marce shrugs and says, "The flood, Gabriel."

Gabriel nods. "Noah and—?"

"There are a variety of legends of the flood. The flood of Mesopotamia was an act of angels." Marce looks out into the distance as he talks.

"Why?" Gabriel asks.

Saphrael and Marceriel exchange another look. Neither of them answer him this time.

"Guys," Gabriel says, "what?"

"A long time ago, in Sumer, some of us went to Earth. We wanted to help guide humanity to prosperity. Writing, pottery, medicine, society itself was nurtured," Marce explains.

"We saw potential in them," Saphrael says. "The archangels were there… things… happened."

"Tell him," Marce says.

"We were supposed to be guiding them. Lucius—he—I can't say it."

"I can. Lucius, known then as Lucifer, fell in love with a human. A high priestess named Lilith. He trained her. His philosophy is that all information should be free, so he gave her access to forbidden knowledge. I guess he thought that only those who have free will are able to choose their own path."

"Lilith was lost to dark magick. Maybe it just brought out her true nature," Saphrael says.

"Does it matter? Look, the point is we gave humans civilization. Lucius gave Lilith access to dark magick. Two archangels died. In the chaos, the Divine Council's initial solution was to simply eradicate the humans. Erase the mistake. They feared the destruction that humanity's selfishness could lead to. Lucius objected. Even though he was the leader and Gabriel his right hand, Uriel disagreed. In the end, after all the debating, it didn't matter. What mattered was what Uriel decided. Being the Archangel of Death at the time, she had the power to see to their end herself. War and death followed. The Battle of Eridu ended with the destruction being washed away by the flood. She lost her place as the Archangel of Death for what she did," Marce says.

"The Divine Council removed magick from the world. There is residue, but not the free-flowing magick that once was," Saphrael says.

"How does this help me?" Gabriel asks.

"You might be able to control floods." Saphrael shrugs.

"I don't think so," Marce says. "He isn't the Archangel of Death."

"Well, what am I supposed to do?" Gabriel sighs.

"How do you use your flame?" Saphrael asks.

"I meditate. I just do." He opens his gloved right hand and a blue flame erupts, hovering above his palm. He closes his hand, and it dissipates.

"Then meditate," Marce says, sounding annoyed.

Gabriel sits on the ground and inhales deeply, closing his eyes. Time slows down. He remembers Dawn's words when she guided him through meditations. *Feel the grass outside, the trees, the droplets of water hanging onto the grass. The air between it all.* He concentrates on a single dewdrop on a blade of discolored grass. Then he connects to the water in the air and the electricity in the atmosphere. Without warning, a lightning bolt strikes the ground close to Marce. He nearly trips backward while moving away. "Watch it!"

"Don't interrupt him. Keep doing what you're doing, Gabriel," Saphrael says.

Dawn, Gabriel says in his mind, *aid me.* He is only vaguely aware that flames have ignited in his hands, which are resting on his knees, palms facing up. A grumble of thunder crackles in the distance. The gentle breeze speeds to a howling gale-force as it starts to rain. In moments, it becomes a downpour.

"Direct it to the crater," Marce yells over the storm.

Gabriel lifts his hands in the air, then sharply pulls them down. His blue flame erupts into blinding pillars that light up the gray storm clouds. Thunder and wind increase, centering upon the former lake as water alters its natural course, racing into the crater.

Saphrael and Marce look at each other, both drenched with water.

The blue flame vanishes, and the storm stops as quickly as it had started. Gabriel opens his eyes and looks out upon the new lake.

"Now you have to purify it." Saphrael looks at the oddly calm, clear waters.

"Isn't it already purified? How do I even do that?" Gabriel asks.

"Meditate?" Saphrael shrugs.

Gabriel sighs and breathes in deeply, allowing his thoughts to disappear as he looks inward. Time passes in his meditation. Marce and Saphrael sit quietly on the shore.

Gabriel turns to Saphrael. "What about those relics where we first met? We could throw one of those statues in it. Would that do it?"

"Couldn't hurt." Saphrael shrugs.

✦

"What caused this, anyway?" Gabriel asks, observing the broken tablets and worn statues that litter the Ruins of Daath.

"War, Gabriel," is all Saphrael says.

"The Battle of Eridu you were talking about earlier?" Gabriel pauses to look at a large, fractured mural, the one he had seen when he had first arrived: Angels fighting above humans working in fields.

"Something like that..." Saphrael says quietly. "It used to be a library... well... it's whats left of the once great library and pieces of Daath itself, of course."

"Why hasn't Emperor Lucius ever collected all of this?" Marce wonders aloud.

"Maybe they remind him of something that he doesn't want to remember." Saphrael shrugs.

Marce raises an eyebrow.

"Now, to find something that works." Saphrael looks around.

"Maybe we should fan out," Gabriel suggests.

"I'll search that section." Saphrael points east. "Gabriel, take the middle. Marce, the other end."

Gabriel trudges along in the cold, dark ruins, wondering just what the punishment is for trespassing. *Couldn't be any worse than what they are already planning to do to me,* he reasons. A pristine-looking statue catches the corner of his eye—not because of its condition but because of who it is. His breath becomes shallow. He scarcely believes what is standing before him as he turns to face it fully. There is no doubt in his mind that it is a statue of Raphael, the man who claimed to be his father on Earth.

He stares at it silently, as if it were only a trick of the mind and the statue would reform into one not so familiar. "Guys! I have a question!"

"What? Did you find a statue of yourself?" Marce calls back.

"No!" Gabriel yells, unaware that Marce is already at his side.

Marce nods, crossing his arms as he examines the statue. "That will do."

"No—but—I mean, who is it?" Gabriel asks.

Marce sighs, but before he can answer, Saphrael comes up beside him. "Raphael," Saphrael says, "perfect."

"Why... is it perfect?" Gabriel says with strained vocal cords. His body shakes as he tries to contain his anger and confusion. "Guys?"

"Raphael is the Archangel of Healing." Saphrael points to the medical staff the statue holds. "Why?"

Part of Gabriel wants to reach out to the statue, the other part wants to destroy it. "He was my father... at least he said he was... on Earth."

Marce and Saphrael give each other a silent look. Anger flares inside, his hands ball into fists, and blue flame ignites around his gloved hands.

"Gabriel, if you destroy that statue, we're going to have to find something else to help purify the lake," Marce says.

He strains to hold himself back. Where there once was trust, now remains only questions and a hollow yet familiar feeling of abandonment. As he starts to spiral emotionally, he turns away and closes his eyes, attempting to hold on to what he does have: Dawn, his friends. Nonetheless, he can feel the stone eyes of Raphael boring into the back of his skull. Gabriel unclenches his fists and the fire dissipates.

"I trusted him," Gabriel turns back to the statue and kicks the dirt in front of it. Dark-gray dust flies into the air in a small cloud that falls like ashes. "He lied to me."

"Maybe he lied to protect you?" Saphrael shrugs.

Gabriel screams in frustration and drops to his knees, head tilted down. Dirt around him flies up on impact.

"We can find something else," Saphrael says quietly.

"We won't find anything better than this," Marce says, pointing at the statue. He forcefully stands Gabriel upright and faces him directly in front of it. "Look at it."

Gabriel closes his eyes, turning away.

"Look at it," Marce repeats, pointing at the statue. "Just because he lied to you doesn't mean that you can sit here and let your feelings get in the way of what you want to accomplish. There are few roads that lead to success. There are many roads that lead to failure. Pick a road."

Gabriel screams again, the echo of which resonates throughout the ruins. Saphrael wearily looks behind them, past the ruins, toward the empty expanse.

A horde of Lost appear, heading in their direction. Most do not cross the boundary of the sacred ruins. A single decayed Lost takes a step closer and then stops. The trio takes a defensive stance. No one moves. After a few moments, Gabriel drops his guard.

"I see you're taking the road most traveled," Marce says, keeping his eyes on the Lost. "Make him carry it." Marce shoves Gabriel closer to the statue. "Carry it back. What? You don't want to help those poor lost souls anymore?"

"Shut up already," Gabriel says and awkwardly picks up the heavy statue with one hand. The statue hangs down as Gabriel jets back to the lake, leaving a blue streak of fire behind him.

✦

Gabriel sets the solid statue on the shore of the lake and lands beside it. For some time, he stares up at the statue as it towers over him, his heart filled with grief over everything he has lost.

Blurs of black and silver speed toward him, stopping just behind him as Marce and Saphrael appear.

"Where's your halberd?" Saphrael asks Marce.

"Somewhere safe, I didn't think I'd be gone for this long," Marce says quietly as he observes Gabriel, who is still staring at the statue of Raphael. "You want to heal others? Start with healing the wound inside of yourself."

"Marce, I don't think that is good advice," Saphrael says.

"No, it is." Gabriel shrugs. "It's just that... I have nothing to say to him."

"Yes, you do," Marce says.

Gabriel sighs. "How is a statue supposed to help, anyway?"

"It's from a sacred spot in the Crown Realms before it fractured. Not only is it ancient, but stone absorbs, stores, and transmits energies," Saphrael explains.

Gabriel takes a deep breath, choosing restraint over anger, he reaches up and places his hand on the face of the statue. "Dad... I need your help. Maybe if you were here, things would be different. I wouldn't even need the statue."

Dirt covering the statue sheds, and it straightens itself upright. Rain begins to fall.

"Is that you?" Marce asks, looking up at the sky.

"No." Gabriel picks up the statue and dives into the water.

In his mind, he can see white light emanating from the center of the waters, as shown to him in his vision. As he descends, he thinks about how odd it feels to be in the lake but not suffer from overpowering depression. He places the statue in the dead center of the new sanctuary, at its lowest point between the jagged crystalline spikes.

Lightning strikes. The bolt travels through Gabriel on its way to the statue, as if it were made of metal and not stone, before it redirects back out of the statue, electrifying the entire lake. Gabriel is not in pain; instead, he feels energized as the heavy feeling he has been unable to fully shake since he was trapped in the lake is gone. He swims up and breaches the water, feeling renewed. Even the pain from the poison infecting him hurts a little less. Gabriel pulls himself out, stands up, and looks at the water. It shines with an unearthly luminosity. The soft glow reminds him of a full moon on a warm summer's night.

Marce and Saphrael walk up beside Gabriel. Saphrael asks, "How do you feel?"

"I'm still angry, but I feel better."

"How do we do this? Hunt them down and throw them in?" Marce asks.

"No," Gabriel says. "I assume most went in willingly. They must be given a choice."

"Gabriel, they're mindless creatures." Saphrael shakes his head. "As much as I want to believe that those we lost are still in there somewhere—"

"They are," Gabriel says. "Trust me. I was connected to them before, maybe I still am."

Gabriel lowers his head as if in prayer, connecting to the hive mind of the Lost. Whispers of their voices, laments of despair, harmonizing in a disjointed fashion, flood his mind. The feeling that he would succumb to the suffocating embrace of depression and be among the lost forever creeps into the back of his mind.

With his eyes still closed, he speaks the words as they come to him. "I know it feels like there is no reason to continue and nothing left to fight for. I know what it feels like to not belong anywhere. To be alone. I seek to offer understanding, but I beg you, offer yourself forgiveness. I don't

319

know if it will help, but I'm hoping that it will. You are welcome in this sanctuary."

After a few moments of silence, Marce says, "Death comes in many forms, few of which are permanent."

Something deeply unsettles Gabriel as he gazes across the pristine hallowed ground. The transformation doesn't erase what once was... but maybe, just maybe, there is hope for a better future, no matter how bleak the past.

"Do you think that will work?" Gabriel asks.

"Don't know, Gabriel." Marce shrugs.

"You've done all you can. I think you handled it well. Let's head back," Saphrael rests his hand on Gabriel's shoulder.

They begin their trek through Thale Forest. The three friends talk and laugh while walking to their empty barracks, as if nothing at all were wrong.

"Just think of it, Emperor Gabriel... if he marries Dawn..." Marce shoves Gabriel playfully.

Gabriel regains his balance, "At least I have someone."

Marce laughs, "You think being alone bothers me?"

"Yes."

"Yeah, I'm wrong... We all know where you'll end up," Marce says.

"Marce..." Saphrael looks at him warningly.

"Oh yeah, Marce, where's that?" Gabriel asks.

"With your head on a pike," Marce says with no trace of humor.

Gabriel slows down for a moment before shaking his head and then catches up with them.

Chapter 27

Saphrael walks into his temporary locker room in the Axion. After setting down his equipment, he thinks about his last fight, when Darius, the loyalty officer, had shown up and offered him everything he had ever wanted, the ability to go home to Hod. It would be selfish to abandon Gabriel. *An unforgiveable sin*, he thinks to himself. *But I've abandoned the rest of them because of it.* Saphrael hangs his head down, grief-stricken over the loss of his team, the loss of his friends.

It had been a lonely couple of cycles. The barracks were practically empty, besides Gabriel, who was constantly gone, walking around in the forest trying to sort himself out. Marce disappeared back to his new team, and that left Saphrael insufferably alone. Closing his eyes briefly, he thinks about his last victory and how he should be overflowing with joy... but instead he feels empty. By winning his way up the ranks, Saphrael should feel an undeniable glimmer of hope, except for everything looming: the threat of discere of being branded a traitor.

Before heading to the match, Gabriel told him he didn't have a plan and that he is considering turning himself in for the good of the Wonder Brigade. Saphrael reminded him that the Wonder Brigade was already gone. *"Do what is best for yourself, not for us. Okay? The Wonder Brigade, we—we're already gone,"* he had told him.

Saphrael presses his forehead against his Chokma mask, which is tilted toward him. "Offer me strength to see this through," he mumbles to himself.

"How does that human prayer go? Yea, though I walk through the valley of the shadow of death, I shall fear no evil."

The locker room door creaks open, breaking Saphrael's meditation. He stands defensively, gripping his Chokma mask as his former teammates walk in. Marce is in the lead with a grim expression.

"By all means, continue your prayer. You're going to need it," Loth says in his trademark low-toned, mocking demeanor. He stands to the left of Marce. Spud is on the other side and Cadence is further back.

"What do you want?" Saphrael's eyes narrow, heart racing.

"I'm sorry!" Spud blurts out.

"Don't apologize." Marce orders as he extends an arm, blocking Spud from walking forward. "He understands the price of treason. If anything, he owes us an apology. Gabriel has always been dangerous, destined to bring ruin to any who aid him." Marce points at Saphrael. "He sacrificed you for him. He sacrificed all of us, for what?"

"For honor," Saphrael responds.

Marceriel punches Saphrael in the jaw. Saphrael breaths in slow, controlled breaths as he calculates his next move, but he knows he has little chance.

"We have our orders, Captain," Loth says, but instead of addressing Saphrael, he looks at the door as the Tigris champion walks in wearing a full set of combat gear and Chokma mask.

Saphrael realizes that no one has a weapon. His sword, Solomon, sits on a bench just out of reach. He looks into the eyes of his friends, his former unit, searching for a hint of remorse. Millennia of this empire, dedicated to order and severely punishing those who step out of line, have sharpened their cunning, ruthless, and bloodthirsty nature. But he knows that this, this is as much a punishment for them as it is for him.

Daring to appeal to empathy, Saphrael places his Chokma mask on the bench he was sitting on and holds his hands open at his side.

"Do what you have to. But we've been through so much. We can fight back, together." Saphrael's final desperate plea falls upon deaf ears.

Loth scoffs, "I told you he was a part of the resistance."

For Saphrael, it feels as if time itself stopped, that is until his heart painfully constricts in his chest. Saphrael lunges for his weapon. Marce grabs hold of his shoulder and pulls, forcing Saphrael off balance. The Tigris champion lounges near the door as Loth grabs hold of Saphrael's hair and drives his face into his knee. Numbing pain radiates across his cheekbone, dazing Saphrael.

A flurry of fists, boots, elbows, and knees assaults him. A kick forces a boot into his calf, knocking him down. His face swells, and he can taste blood as he gets beaten. Try as he might to think of something else, anything else, he can't. The pain of hit after hit does not allow him to escape.

For some reason, they back away in a semicircle around him. Loth boots him once more in the midsection. Saphrael screams internally, *Get up!* Then, his eyes widen as he hears the familiar sound of Solomon being unsheathed. His arm wavers as he pushes himself up off the ground. The Tigris captain headbutts Saphrael with his Chokma mask, knocking him back down. The imposing figure has Saphrael's sword in hand. He turns to Marce and hands him Saphrael's sword.

Marce looks at the masked champion with a blank expression before his fist tightens around the blade's hilt.

"They said no weapons!" Cadence screams at them, rushing to stop Marce, but he gets blocked by the Tigris champion.

"A little payback for the free-for-all never hurt anyone... except, of course, maybe him." The Tigris champion punches Cadence for insubordination.

Marce locks eyes with Saphrael before letting out a scream and dropping down to one knee, driving Solomon through Saphrael's upper right chest. Then Marce stumbles back.

Loth holds Cadence's arms behind his back, locking him in place as the Tigris captain slowly extracts the sword from Saphrael. Then, without warning, he turns and drives Solomon through Cadence's leg, just above his kneecap, using a hammer fist to nail the sword in as far as it will go.

Cadence's screams fade into silence as Saphrael's hearing fails and the world blurs. As Saphrael loses consciousness, the last thing he sees is a piece of paper placed on the ground beside him. His blood stains the paper like watercolor, spreading across a logo: the mark of the resistance.

✦

No matter how hard she strains, she sees nothing. Dawn wonders if she has gone blind. Howling wind deafens all other sounds as pellets of ice-cold rain sting her skin. *I am outside. Why am I outside? This is a dream... it has to be,* she reassures herself.

The wind ceases as well as the rain, allowing her to see. Wind-whipped beads of pitch-black raindrops hang suspended midair all around. The temperature plunges, crystallizing the obsidian raindrops. A loud sound blares, and what was first a horn becomes a siren. Dawn drops to her knees, which get cut and torn, by what, she does not know. Desperately covering her ears does not stop the piercing noise from growing louder and louder until it morphs into static laced with screams and whispers she cannot discern. Then, worst of all, the sound stops. Why Dawn found the dead silence far more disturbing than the worst sound she has ever heard, she does not know.

Taking in carefully controlled breaths, she watches the vapor in the air as she exhales. Beneath the field of crystallized black raindrops are plants, as far as the eye can see. On closer inspection, she realizes that they are unopened dark-purple roses. The jagged stems and haggard leaves made it difficult to discern. Dawn jumps when the pellets of crystallized raindrops fall all at once as if someone had just turned on gravity.

Above all, Dawn feels... alone. She lets out a sigh, closing her eyes and begging the pit of despair in the center of her chest to quiet.

"Gabriel?" Dawn scans the field of unopened roses, hoping that maybe she will see him in this dream as well.

There is a creaking sound of something growing rapidly. Instinct urges her to get away from the roses as fast as she can. Dawn starts to run, breaking crooked stems and crushing petals, foliage as well as crystallized raindrops that pop beneath her bare feet. The hem of her nightgown and skin get sliced by thorns as she runs, but she runs nonetheless. She thinks about just giving up, about lying down in the field of strange roses and falling asleep. Shaking her head, tears start to flow as she thinks, *I can't do that to Gabriel.*

Looking up at the dark sky, she screams, "Gabriel! Where are you? God dammit! I need you!"

Her breathing comes in faster and harder as she tries to get… somewhere, anywhere, to find him. Dawn stops running, because the sound of fire and scent of ozone fills the air. She looks around and sees nothing, except the roses.

The roses bloom, peeling back leaf by leaf. All at once, everywhere, blossoming. The ground is aglow with countless dark-purple roses alight with violet flame. The neon glow of fire comes from the very center of the rose and crawls out, moving up the petals. Dawn draws her hands in near her chest protectively, yet she watches the roses out of curiosity.

Anxiety provokes her heart to beat faster. Looking up, Dawn thinks that the sky looks just the same as the one in the Ethereal Realm. In the sky, veins of black expand, crawling across whatever space is up there. Dawn ducks as tendrils shoot down, piercing the ground.

The glow of the purple roses intensifies until it starts to burn the petals, which turn quickly into ash. A cold wind blows, throwing the dust into the air. It falls like snow, yet unlike snow at all. The light flakes of dust rock back and forth as they fall to the ground.

Dawn cannot help but inhale the flower dust. Her throat starts to close, and she coughs violently.

Then, she is met with darkness, finding herself in her own bed. Light pours in as Adam draws back her bed curtains and looks at her, alert for danger.

"Dawn, what is the matter?"

"I'm fine…" Dawn looks at him and she knows he doesn't believe her. "I thought my nightmares were going to… get better…" Dawn hangs her head down.

Adam sighs. "When it comes to these things there is no easy fix, Dawn. I'm sorry your nightmares are growing worse."

"Do you think it has anything to do with—"

"With what, Dawn?"

"With Lucius," she says, touching the purple crystal heart pendant resting against her chest.

Adam straightens up and nods. "What do you mean, exactly?"

"I smelled fire... the purple roses, a field of them... as far as the eye could see. The black raindrops froze, hanging in the air. They fell before the roses opened all at once."

"The roses... opened... all at once?" Adam repeats.

"Yes. Before they turned to ash. The wind blew, and that's why I was coughing. Adam, do you know what any of this means?"

Adam is uncharacteristically silent for a long moment before he says, "I've never been adept at dream interpretation, Dawn."

"But this felt real."

"Sometimes dreams do," Adam says softly. There is a sadness in his eyes that inspires a hollow feeling inside of Dawn. "Was a single rose spared?"

"What?"

"Was a single rose spared?" Adam repeats.

"No, wait. Yes, one."

"One?"

"Yes. Why?" Dawn searches Adam's expression for answers. She finds none.

Adam takes a deep breath before saying, "And sometimes dreams... are just... dreams."

✦

Saphrael shivers from the cold. He finds himself shirtless and stripped of his plate armor. Weakly, he lifts his head, trying to ascertain where he is. Slick black stone walls of the cramped holding cell are not the pristine white walls of the discere centers he expected to see. As he moves, chains rattle. Each arm is forced down, pinning him to the cold, black stone floor. Closing his eyes, tears fall as the attack replays in his mind. The cold, detached look Marceriel had disturbed him far more than the pain of his own weapon being driven through his back, exiting at a slight angle in his upper right chest. Depression weighs heavy inside, tightening his throat and making it difficult to breathe.

"It's not their fault. It's not their fault," Saphrael repeats, mumbling to himself like a madman.

Taking in a deep breath, he closes his eyes and focuses on the familiar ice-cold feeling of the metal chains clasped around his wrists. The door creaks open, shiny black boots clank against the ground as a figure approaches. Saphrael keeps his head down, as is custom. A deceptively gentle hand wraps around his chin and forces him to look up. His eyes widen as he locks eyes with Emperor Lucius. Saphrael stays still to not show fear, even as he spots a flagrum in the emperor's hand. The device, designed for torture, has a black metal handle, the ends of which are a series of demon leather strips held in place by a loop in the middle, which keeps the weighted ends of the flagrum from getting tangled when used.

"Tell me, Saphrael," Emperor Lucius says in a sickly soothing yet dominant tone. As he talks, he takes out jagged pieces of silver metal from a small tin and begins attaching the broken metal to the ends of the flagrum. "When did you get involved in the resistance?"

"The what? No. I haven't—ever."

Lucius removes the bloodstained evidence from his pocket and unfolds the piece of paper with the mark of the resistance and shows it to Saphrael before crushing it in his fist and dropping the crumpled paper to the ground.

"You were found with resistance propaganda. I don't suppose you have an explanation for that?" Lucius continues nonchalantly screwing on the forged but sharp metal pieces to the ends of the flagrum.

"I was attacked by my teammates—it was planted—" Saphrael begins to plead, but he is met with a smirk of satisfaction, followed by a loud crack as the emperor whips him with precise accuracy across the side of his face. The open wounds burn with a sharp sting that grows into as searing numbness as metal digs in and rakes stripes of flesh from his face. Blood and bits of flesh spray on Lucius's clothing, the walls, and the flagrum, as well as Saphrael.

Unable to hold back, Saphrael screams, which echoes within the holding cell before he reacts instinctively trying to stand to fight. Chains clink as metal strains, holding him to the ground.

"Now, Saphrael, confess. Intelligence reports state you were found with treasonous propaganda. That is why you were subdued and taken into custody. Now, you are blaming the loyal soldiers who apprehended you red-handed? With your track record?" Lucius pauses before adding, "Pray you do not permanently get branded a traitor."

"What do you want?" Saphrael's voice wavers as he keeps his head facing the black stone floor.

"What I want is a civilized solution."

Saphrael can't help but laugh. This is quickly reprimanded. The flagrum nails him across the bare skin of his back, tearing the already deep wounds of where his sword, Solomon, had impaled him. Holding back immediate reactions, he shakes in pain before the flagrum cracks harder causing him to arch back. Despite it all, he refuses to give Lucius the satisfaction of screaming again.

"Once, you were one of Hod's finest champions, were you not? There was a time that you were, without a doubt, the most promising soldier of them all. Hod's great champion with records that remain, to this day, unbroken." Lucius turns his far-off gaze back to Saphrael, his lip twists with sadistic pleasure. "Fallen so far, so fast. Your championship-winning Chokma masks once hung in the halls of my citadel. Now... well... it is amazing what Chokma metal can do. The longer one wears it the more ethereal resonance gets exchanged between the mask and its user."

Emperor Lucius cracks the whip across his back again. Saphrael hangs forward, chains holding him in place.

"I had one of your championship masks destroyed... It is broken... just like you. Are you not, Saphrael? You have been for so very long."

As Saphrael looks up, hair matted to his forehead mixes with blood, sweat and pieces of flesh, Saphrael's eyes widen with the realization that the formations on some of the larger end pieces of the flagrum fit together like a puzzle. It's his mask, one of his former championship masks, now used to flay the skin from his body.

The emperor reaches into the tin once more and takes out a small vial and looks at it, "Demon's blood with some modifications. Our alchemists have been working quite hard on this, and I have been waiting for the perfect subject. Supposedly, it inhibits regeneration, enough demon's blood and you may never be able to regenerate completely. But, of course, this is all theory."

"You didn't answer me," Saphrael dares to say, turning his head, bracing to be hit again.

"What I want is beyond your concern. What I need is your cooperation."

Saphrael inhales sharply, begging himself to hold it together, trying not to show how much pain it is to even breathe.

"You, apparently, fail to understand hierarchy. Perhaps, you still understand consequence. Conspire with traitors, stay branded, lose everything. Honor your duty as a soldier of my army and perhaps I may find a place for you outside of the lowly station you currently occupy. There is a power vacuum due to Adam's reassignment. I could find a way for you to take over Azazel's position as Lord of Hod. It is also entirely possible that you could run the tournaments as overseer. All I ask is what you have already pledged, your loyalty."

"...Tell me what you want," Saphrael says weakly, lifting his head to look at the emperor.

"You will guide Gabriel to me. I hear he has only grown in power..." Lucius pauses, lost in thought. "But he is no match in a confrontation. He is untrained at best. His mission is doomed. Surely, you can see that. I cannot—I will not part with Dawn. I have the upper hand in this rigged game. If he insists on playing, he will lose. You are a puppet. Play your part, be rewarded. Continue to act as a loyal friend to Gabriel yet know where your true allegiance lies. Gabriel has possession of a cosmoversal crystal. Bring it to me or otherwise destroy it. Fail to do so and I will personally oversee the repercussions."

"How do you know about what Gabriel has?" Saphrael locks eyes with Emperor Lucius, who looks coldly down upon him.

"There is little that happens in this system that I do not know."

"When do you want it done?"

"Soon, everything aligns, including when the crystal will be active. I am utilizing the equity of trust you have built in order to give you this opportunity to prove your loyalty. The tournament has been canceled due to the absence of an overseer; however, there is still cause for celebration. The Circle Gala will hold a coronation for my daughter. She will legally be named my successor. Dare I say, Chancellor Gabriel yearns for the same opportunity for his son in the Crown?"

"Why are you telling me this?"

"So you can tell Gabriel. When she is legally named successor, Dawn will be bound to the Sine System. If Gabriel takes his father's offer, he will will be confined to the Crown Realms. That is the only reason he has possession of the cosmoversal crystal. It is only fair to give an opponent the chance to forfeit."

Saphrael stays silent with an unreadable expression in his eyes. Breathing in deeply the stuffy air of his cell, he closes his eyes and allows his head to lower, either a sign of respect or resignation.

"See that it is done or say goodbye to everyone and everything for eternity."

Lucius pounds his fist upon the cell door three times. A royal guard with a faceless mask and hook-swords walks in and hands him a glowing branding iron. Saphrael shakes his head and recoils. "No!"

The emperor smiles as he looks upon the ever-burning brand, the mark of the traitor, which is the resistance sign, typically branded upside down with three strikes through it. Taking the brand, he nods to the door and the royal guard who brought it leaves. Saphrael closes his eyes and tells himself, *This isn't happening... This isn't happening...* He breathes in painfully and looks at Emperor Lucius.

"Please don't do this," Saphrael pleads, and instead of uselessly thrashing against the chains, he looks at the glowing orange end and puts his head down. "Please, I beg you."

Emperor Lucius ignores his pleas and takes methodical steps in his direction before shoving the brand right upon his chest, pressing the burning metal against the spot where his sword impaled him. Lowering his head, Saphrael starts to shake and grits his teeth as the brand sears his open wound shut.

"Disobey orders and you will discover what true pain really is." With a sadistic smile, he holds the brand on Saphrael much longer than necessary.

Finally, he releases him and drops the branding iron on the ground, which glows tipped upon its side. Saphrael breathes in sharply, body racked with pain. Beaten and tortured, he watches as Lucius turns on his heel and leaves. The door to the holding cell closes behind him.

Continuing to shake from the pain, he closes his eyes and thinks, *What did I do? I didn't do anything.* Tears start to form in his eyes. *I did what is right... and I'd do it again.*

Chapter 28

Gabriel sits alone in the crowd of the Axion, awaiting Saphrael's match. Although the deadline had come, no one had approached him about his choice. No legions of soldiers lined up to seal his fate. Not even a guard approached. It was as if nothing were wrong... except everything was.

A loud horn blares, and the crowd turns restless. Gabriel has no idea what is going on as the fighter waiting for Saphrael seems to be declared the winner, with Saphrael nowhere to be found.

Murmurs travel through the crowd, most speaking disparagingly. "Wonder why they bothered to show up," he hears someone in the crowd remark.

"Heard he threw himself in the Black Lake," says another.

"Coward," the first responds.

Gabriel ignores this as he pushes through the crowd, searching for Saphrael. *He has to be here; we came together,* Gabriel thinks, breaking away from the spectators to the sparsely used locker rooms that line the wide halls of the Axion.

Most of the back halls are empty. Rubble blocks the end of this hallway. The gray stone walls darken near where it suffered structural collapse. There have been no flags for a some time, and Gabriel thinks about turning back. It is then he spots the Wonder Brigade's flag posted outside a lonely door ajar at the far end of the hall.

"Saph—" he begins to call out, but the word dies on his lips.

Strewn about are bloodied pieces of Saphrael's gear, including his Chokma mask and Solomon's sheath. After taking what gear he can, carrying it by putting it on, he buckles the sheath around his waist.

What happened? is all he can think. Blood and signs of a struggle are all he has to go on. *It had to have just happened,* he reasons again, panic coursing through his veins. Gabriel grabs Saphrael's bloodied Chokma mask and puts it on.

Just then, a noise comes from behind. The door creaks open.

"I'm sure it's still here," says a voice. Two dressed in standard gambeson uniforms and Tigris masks enter the locker room, talking loudly, not expecting anyone to be there.

They freeze and look at each other. One looks to the sheath at Gabriel's side, clearly what they had come to retrieve.

"Take it from him," the average-sized one says to his taller companion. He responds by shaking his head but cracking his knuckles while approaching Gabriel.

Fire lights up the locker room with a burst of blue. A punch lands on Gabriel's midsection, and another follows on his left temple, nearly knocking him off his feet. Half-stabilized, Gabriel leans in and rams his head into the attacker, knocking him back. The taller of the two runs into a bench while trying to find his footing, falling to the ground. The average-sized assailant has already fled.

Gabriel pulls in his flame and picks up the assailant by his throat, mimicking Lucius the night he held him by his neck. After squeezing his fist tight around his throat, Gabriel throws him into the wall.

"You'd better be breathing," Gabriel says, walking up, blue fire alight in his eyes.

✦

Striding with purpose out of the locker room, Gabriel leaves the door open behind him. A fresh coat of blood covers the walls. The unfortunate attacker is sprawled out, beaten but alive, as evidenced by the rising and falling of his chest as Gabriel walks away. He carries the attacker's Tigris mask in hand while donning Saphrael's blood-marred mask.

"Captain forgot the sheath. Our match was about to start," the poor soul begging for mercy had said. Gabriel didn't like it, but he wasn't sorry about it.

Shoving those in his way aside, he goes to an inner gate and peers through the metal bars. The crowd roars, but all he sees are stands and figures atop them. The metal latch screeches as the gate opens.

Bursting forth with the blue flame behind him, no longer caring about trying to hide, Gabriel flies into the Axion's main floor and into the air. Below him, in the opposite end, are five elevated stands. Perched on each stand are members of the Tigris team, they have crossbows in hand and swords at their side. The air is punctuated by the screeches of raptors, held in by a temporary makeshift wall.

He spots Saphrael's sword Solomon in the hands of the Tigris team's captain. Then he hurls the Tigris mask with all his strength at the captain, who blocks it and finally looks up. The bloodied Tigris mask falls to the ground far below the tops of the stands, landing on its side in the dirt.

Diving down, he speeds directly at the champion, leaving a bright blue streak in the air behind him. A ball of flame erupts around Gabriel, encasing him in fire. The Tigris team's captain barely has time to register what is about to happen before Gabriel rams him with his shoulder, knocking him off the stand. While he is falling, Gabriel maneuvers, shifting direction, and catches Solomon midair. Then he grips the Tigris captain by his chest plate. Gabriel is emotionless as he turns and increases speed, headed straight at the only remaining inner stone wall. He holds the Tigris captain to the unforgiving brick as they crash across it. The raptors below scream, attempting to flee, especially when Gabriel draws near.

Flames swirl around Gabriel as he glares at the Tigris team, all of whom aim their arrows at him. He holds up the Tigris captain as a shield. The Tigris team skewers their captain with arrows, one of which gets lodged in Gabriel's gambeson. Gabriel lets go of the Tigris captain and briefly watches him fall to the ground.

His eyes narrow, and he sheaths Solomon before flying directly at one on a stand, leaving a blue streak of flame behind him. Gabriel collides with the opponent, knocking him to the ground. Gabriel dives after him, driving the arrow he has straight through his arm, pinning him to the floor. The crowd a loud disjointed symphony of rabble. A rain of arrows targets Gabriel but they have no effect.

"Where is Saphrael?" he screams.

The opponent shakes his head, refusing to say anything. Gabriel holds Solomon to his throat before he decides he can't properly interrogate someone in the middle of a fight. Leaving him pinned to the ground, Gabriel flies into the air again. The ozone smell of the fire is familiar and comforting.

He points Solomon at one struggling to reload his crossbow, his hands shaking in fear. As the opponent fumbles, Gabriel impales him with Solomon and flies straight up into the air, propelling the skewered opponent with him. Gabriel pivots and dives back down, crashing through the ground.

Pieces of the Axion's floor fly into the air. Beneath the surface, Gabriel and the unfortunate opponent find themselves in a cage filled with dinosaurs. The dinosaurs are terrified of Gabriel, and they desperately claw at the walls, trying to escape. The fireball encasing Gabriel dies down as he removes Saphrael's Chokma mask.

"Where is Saphrael?" Gabriel demands, his voice booming, his ice-blue eyes glowing, highlighted by the darkness of the Axion's lower levels.

"I don't know! I don't know!" The opponent backs away.

"Tell me what happened." Gabriel walks toward him slowly.

"We got paid to attack him. That's all I know."

"Who?"

"Darius."

In one swift move, Gabriel roughly pulls Solomon out of his opponent before gritting his teeth and tightening his grip on the hilt. Instead of driving the sword through him again, he tears off the Tigris Chokma mask and right-hooks him in the jaw. There is a bone-splitting crack and the opponent's jaw hangs unnaturally to one side. After pushing him further into the dinosaur holding cell, Gabriel puts on Saphrael's Chokma mask and flies up through the opening, leaving him to their mercy.

Picking up speed, Gabriel flies at anyone reckless enough to continue to attack. He hurls the nearest opponent straight into another's sword, impaling him.

The crowd tramples one another as they scramble to reach the exits.

Gabriel grabs the opponent whose sword impaled his teammate, rips off his mask, and starts punching him relentlessly. The Tigris team member falls, his head bouncing off the ground. Gabriel continues to throw punch after punch. Stopping only when the angel loses consciousness, just like the one in the locker room.

Flying up into the air, Gabriel surveys the area, leaving a blue streak of fire. He hovers above the Axion, flame in his left hand, the bloodied sword resting in his right.

◆

Gabriel paces within the cramped confines of the Wonder Brigade's barracks. *What do I do? Where is everyone? Is Saphrael all right?* Day turns to night, at least according to the light fading in his time crystal, yet Gabriel continues to pace and stare at his map. His mind reels as it searches for solutions. Inside, he feels hollow, confused, and above all, lost. The familiarity of loneliness no longer comforts him as it once had.

The few times he ventured out, instead of the typical gawking, he was outright ignored with a distinct undercurrent of fear. He couldn't blame them after the way he retaliated against the Tigris team.

The door creaks open. Gabriel stops and puts the map back in his cloak pocket.

Saphrael stumbles in, as if drunk, face covered in festering wounds coated with a dark green substance. Rushing over to help, Gabriel picks up Saphrael's arm and places it over his shoulder, offering support. He gets immediately shoved back.

I forgot the way things are here, Gabriel reasons, helplessly watching Saphrael stagger over to his cot and collapse upon it.

In exhaustion, Saphrael allows his head to drop to the side. There is something in his eyes that speaks of loss, of pain rooted so deep that it cannot be hidden nor ignored. Gabriel wonders why his wounds are coated in a dark green substance, then the memory of the scent hits him: demon's blood. Then he remembers Loth complaining about demon's blood dripping on him on the way back from the hunt. He said something about the degradation of natural healing abilities, but Gabriel wasn't paying close attention. While studying the discolored bruises, swelling, and lacerations littering Saphrael's face, Gabriel takes in slow, controlled breaths to quell the anger inside.

"Saphrael... what happened?" Gabriel asks too calmly.

Saphrael shakes his head, presses his lips firmly together before taking in a deep breath. "It's not their fault."

"It's not whose fault?" Gabriel asks.

Saphrael shifts uncomfortably and opens his mouth, but when he does, no words come out. When he adjusts, Gabriel spots a strange bright orange glow beneath a poorly patched hole in his gambeson on his upper right chest near his shoulder.

"Saphrael... What aren't you telling me?" Gabriel looks to the door. "Do you think the others will return? Do you think maybe Marce—"

"No," Saphrael says, averting his eyes. "They're gone." His statement is made with such finality that Gabriel doesn't press, at least for now.

Saphrael shakes his head, then spots his sword and gear sitting on top of an empty cot and sighs in relief. Then he lies back in a more strained than relaxing way.

"They want me to bring you to Emperor Lucius."

"Good."

"What do you mean *good*?" Saphrael half sits up before lying back down.

Gabriel shrugs. "That's where I'm going once I have a plan."

"Gabriel, you have no plan. You will never have a plan. Not only do they have the home-court advantage, they have everything. Everything. You have one move besides forfeiture."

"That is?"

"Walk into the trap. Use it as a springboard to get what you came for and leave." Saphrael sits up looking at Gabriel. "Lucius says he can't let Dawn go, so you are in for a fight."

"You… talked to Emperor Lucius?" Gabriel says in a hushed tone.

Saphrael nods. "I was assaulted and framed. Then, I woke up in a holding cell. The emperor was waiting for me."

"The Tigris team already paid for attacking you. I made sure of it," Gabriel says in a monotone voice, looking off at nothing.

"What do you mean?"

"I mean… I took care of it." A bright blue flame burns briefly in his hand.

Saphrael half-smiles with a distinct look of sadness in his eyes. "It wasn't them… well, not most of them, anyway. It was… everyone else."

"What do you mean everyone else?" Gabriel looks around the otherwise empty barracks.

"You know what I'm saying."

Gabriel shakes his head and restrains himself from punching the wall. "You can't be serious."

"I am and I have no reason not to be," Saphrael says distantly. "Forget about them. Have you thought about where you will go?"

"Back to Earth, I suppose." Gabriel shrugs.

"You better do it before she gets crowned successor."

"What are you talking about?"

"At the Circle Gala, Princess Dawn will be crowned and legally designated heir. When that happens, she can't go back to Earth. She can't go to the Crown Realms either, according to the laws."

"That's not fair."

"I know, Gabriel. Nothing's fair. Lucius said that your father is Chancellor Gabriel and that he wants to name you as his successor to the Crown Realms."

"What?"

Saphrael nods. "So, what's your plan?"

"Plan? I have no plan!"

"I know, Gabriel, but given the information you have, maybe you should start thinking about one?"

"Save Dawn and… then… go home."

"You have no home."

"I know that! Don't you think I know that? Take her to the Ethereal Realm or the Crown Realms?" Gabriel says, his hands open at his side.

"Are you asking me?"

"Get Dawn. Go to the Ethereal Realm. Figure it out from there."

"I wouldn't stay in the Ethereal Realm for long. Demons and others can access it from here," Saphrael explains.

"What?"

"Yeah…"

"Take her back to Earth."

"And then what, Gabriel?"

"I don't know! Ask Raphael for help?"

"That's the most reasonable thing I've ever heard you say."

"Really?"

"Yes, if you can get over your… issues with him, he would make a fine ally."

"Why… why isn't he here?" Gabriel wonders.

"Why doesn't the Crown just take over the whole Sine System? First, Gabriel, to them, this is enemy territory, sovereign territory. Secondly, are you even aware of the *Treaty of Ordo*? Raphael isn't allowed here. Besides Emperor Lucius, the only other archangel allowed in this system is Azrael. It all has to do with the great war. Azrael is innocent."

"Raphael isn't?" Gabriel asks.

"Well… you try telling the Archangel of Death what to do."

"Ah," Gabriel says.

"Healer or not, Raphael did fight in the great war. Let's just say he wasn't on Lucius's side."

"Tell me about my father."

"What is there to say? He looks like you, exactly."

"Then what am I? A clone?"

"Considering angels can't have kids, maybe." Saphrael shrugs.

"How do I exist?"

"I don't know, Gabriel."

"Are there other clones?"

Saphrael shakes his head no.

"Wait. How does Dawn exist?" Gabriel asks.

"I. do. not. know."

"Is she a clone?"

"Does she look like a clone?" Saphrael says, exasperated.

"I don't know!"

"Dawn's mother, Lilith, was something else in the end: not human, not angel, nor demon. None of these things yet at the same time all these things, or so the legend goes. I find it entirely possible that Lilith really was her mother."

"You said *was*. Is she no longer with us?"

Saphrael shrugs. "No one knows for sure. Rumors are that Lucius has been waiting for her spirit to arrive in the Ethereal. It never did."

III

Part Three

Chapter 29

Alone in the chapel, Adam stands at the altar, pushing aside uneasy feelings of not being at Dawn's side. Lucius requested he take a short absence to test the loyalty of the remaining royal guards. He assured Adam he would keep a close watch on her through the gem in her necklace. It gave him a rare reprieve, and Adam did not want to waste his time.

Removing a square metal tin from his jacket, he opens it, revealing crushed blood flower petals, which he adds to a clay vial already filled with powdered blood. Briefly, he runs his fingers along a name imprinted on the side of the vial, written in Sumerian cuneiform: Eve.

Adam has never mixed Eve's blood with the flower before. He is hoping to see her or at least regain some memory from that era. After opening a flask, he pours water into the clay vial and swirls it around. The elixir is dark red, thinner than paste but thicker than water. Adam tilts his head back, drinking the grainy blend in one shot.

"Talk to me," Adam says, closing his eyes and sitting on a pew in the front row. The metallic taste of blood lingers on his tongue.

"Why can't I remember?" Adam allows his head to rest.

Should I ask Lucius for help? No.

He is unsettled by what this experiment might bring as he leans against the hard wooden pew, giving the blood flower time to work its way into his system.

"I love you, Adam." Eve's gentle voice surfaces in his memories.

The world around him shifts. Adam is in the past, embracing Eve. Her body sinks comfortably into his, her head resting on his shoulder. He loses himself in the feeling, if only for a moment. Closing his eyes, he tightens his grip around her, breathing in the scent of juniper incense that always seems to cling to her skin. He breaks to look at her delicate features. Her warm brown eyes meet his, and a smile forms on her lips.

Her smile. How could I ever forget her smile? he thinks, as he brushes part of her long, dark-brown hair from her face. Her smile contorts into an expression of pain. "Eve?" he says, as Adam of the past screams, "Eve!"

Eve fades from his arms. Her body now on the floor with the high priestess's ceremonial knife marked by its dark-blue lapis lazuli handle plunged in her chest. Blood soaks into her light-blue dress, staining it a dark red. To his left is Lilith, breathing heavily, her long cardinal-red hair disheveled. Fresh splotches of blood rest on her skin, and several drops race down her arm. Her hand is formed into a fist as if she were still holding the knife.

Then, Adam hears a noise that haunted his memories for as long as he had them... a sound he had long forgotten. It is a desperate gasping for air punctuated by a strained gurgle as Eve coughs up blood. In the blood flower memory, he is hit by a rush of adrenaline. Modern Adam's heart strains as he does his best to distance himself. No matter how much he tells his brain that this is the past, he knows that no amount of time will lessen this pain. If anything, time rotted his wounds without the benefit of decay.

The world narrows in his daze. Adam screams and attacks Lilith. She picks up a solid wooden chair and swings it at him as he lunges at her. The chair nails his rib cage. There is a loud crack and sharp pain in his lower right side. He hits the ground hard, landing next to Eve. Adam gets up and runs at Lilith, blood from his rib puncturing his side, soaking into his shirt. Lilith grabs hold of him and guides his momentum into the white mud-brick wall.

With all his strength, he keeps hold of her wrist as he strikes the wall.

His body goes numb as he crashes to the ground. Lilith slams hard against the wall and falls with him, landing on top of him. They look at each other. She slides her hand down his arm. Adam pulls away. Lilith leans in and kisses him. He turns his head, screaming at himself internally to stop. His body doesn't listen as he places his hand behind Lilith's head and pulls her in close and forcefully kisses her.

Eve lay dying, but all Adam can see, all he can feel, is Lilith. Adam lies Lilith beneath him and mounts her. He fights with every ounce of strength to turn to Eve, but Lilith keeps him facing her, and he is certain he isn't entirely in control of his own body. Adam of Eridu's vision is obscured by a dark halo blotting out the world around him, everything except Lilith.

Just before the light fades from her eyes, modern Adam observes that it is clear from her expression that Eve witnessed the betrayal. Modern Adam turns away from his old self, who is engrossed with Lilith. He didn't realize it at the time, but this Adam knows what Lucius's influence feels like.

Adam, former hierophant of the Sine System, knows he was possessed and that angels can inflame emotion and even remove them. That isn't even factoring in Lilith's seduction aura. Watching it—the worst mistake of his life—happen brings a tear to his eyes as he sits on the pew.

Spirit separated from old Adam's body, standing to the side of the couple, modern Adam looks at Eve's corpse, shaking his head in the real world. *What have I done?*

Adam strains to suppress his anger, his hands form into fists. He knows he cannot retaliate against Lucius for this revelation. Opening his eyes, he is conscious again in the mostly forgotten chapel. Adam leans back against the hard pew and takes deep breaths as he tries to shake the feeling of Lucifer occupying his body.

Adam stands but a head rush forces him to sit back down, his mind once again lost to the blood flower's effect. This time, he finds himself a distance from Eridu, in the wilds. Lilith reaches out to him from the ground.

"Please!" Lilith manages to choke out, blood pouring from a cut on her throat. She holds her neck, trying in vain to prevent blood loss. She looks different now, emaciated and dying—but very clearly pregnant.

Her brown eyes plead with Adam's. She clutches his shirt sleeve, leaving a bloody handprint when she lets go.

With great effort, she writes cuneiform in the dirt: save child, Lucifer, free. Drawing a line through the name Lucifer, she shakes her head. She lies back weakly, her hand resting on her stomach, and her crimson-red blood-matted hair rests in a halo around her.

Adam of Eridu nods, knowing what she is trying to say. She wants her child to be free from Lucifer's influence. He roots around in his medical satchel and pulls out a knife. Carefully, he takes time to clean the knife with water from a canteen and the skin of her abdomen. Impatiently, Lilith grabs the knife and cuts into herself. Gently, he puts his hand on hers.

"I will do this," Adam assures her.

Carefully, he slices into her abdomen, layer by layer. The overcast skies darken as day turns into night. Dogs bark in the distance. *She is being hunted,* Adam thinks, working faster. Finally, he grabs hold of the infant and pulls it out. The child has the same deep cardinal-red hair as her mother.

"It's a girl." He turns the infant over as there is a blue light emanating from her back. "The child has wings?" Looking over to Lilith, temporarily forgetting the current circumstances, his expression fades as he realizes Lilith is dead. Cradling the newborn, he checks her breathing—she is, but just barely. The baby is not crying.

A figure approaches Adam.

"Father," a man with a deep voice says. "We cannot stay here."

"Not now, Able," Adam says, cleaning the infant with water and his own shirt. "I will take the child. Burn Lilith's corpse. And son," Adam says, giving him a sincere look. "Thank you."

Adam starts to take his shirt off. Able stops him and gives him his shirt instead. The blue light dims as he swaddles the child in Able's shirt.

"Go, I will take care of this," Able says, picking up Lilith's body.

A terrible boom cracks throughout the sky—not thunder, but an instrument. A warning sound that reverberates and increases in volume, causing goosebumps and hair on his skin to stand on end. Adam holds the child close. The earth grumbles with quakes as the noise begins to fade. The sky turns white, bright, and strange, lighting up the wilds around him, so much so he can see Eridu in the distance as if it were midday.

In the chapel, modern Adam wonders about the truth hidden in the old legends of Eden, wondering if everything, from the name Eridu, the forbidden fruits of sex, the knowledge of dark magick, and the snake, were all metaphors, secrets and warnings passed down throughout the years.

In an instant, his mind snaps back to Eridu. Adam rushes through town covered in dirt and blood. Even in his state of panic, he draws little attention as the streets are nearly deserted. Those who have not fled are looking up.

Adam kicks in the door to a small, unassuming domicile.

"Raphael!" Adam shouts.

Modern Adam takes in this revelation. Adam of Eridu was seeking help from his mentor, whom he knew was archangel Raphael.

His mentor is nowhere to be seen. Frustrated, Adam turns and leaves, searching for help. Briefly, he looks at the newborn, who is still not crying.

While not privy to all his former memories, Modern Adam can hear the thoughts of old Adam. *Where should I go? The government center. The rest of the angels are there.*

He makes his way to the government building. Opening the door, he shouts, "I need help! I know you are not what you appear to be!" His voice echoes throughout the empty room as he cradles the infant.

A single person appears from a back room. They have short black hair and green eyes speckled with brown. "What do you need?"

"This child. She is one of you. Born of High Priestess Lilith. She requires protection and to be hidden from Lucifer." Adam reveals the wings on the infant's back.

"I can see to that," the man says. He is wearing robes with tribunal markings. "Give me the child. I will be sure she is taken care of."

Adam looks at him wondering, *Can I trust him? Do I have a choice?* He has nowhere else to turn, so he forces himself to let her go.

"Take care of her," Adam says.

The kind soul who accepted the child nods.

His mind wanders back to his cardinal sin of forsaking Eve and having sex with Lilith. *Could I have saved her? No, the knife cut straight through her heart and lungs. What have I done? How could I do this? No, it happened and there is nothing I can do to change it.* He doesn't know how to deal with this flood of emotion, guilt, and shame. Breathing in slowly in an attempt to calm himself from being completely overwhelmed, he is grateful that at least now he knows. It was an unforgivable act. This is undeniable to him.

Adam's hands shake as he stands and then drinks water from his flask. His eyes are dead set upon the altar. Slowly, he walks up to it and opens the dark-cherry wooden box and takes out Eve's heart encased in a clear material that has preserved it, the right half of her heart is torn open. There was no way she would have lived, even if he had applied medical treatment. He places the relic back in the wooden box and closes the lid.

He rests on a chair near the altar. His heart is heavy and feels like Eve's— ripped and bleeding on the inside. He tries to remind himself that he is now Adam, former hierophant, not Adam doctor from Eridu. He knows he can handle this, at least that is the lie he tells himself.

Adam, however, is not oblivious to the fact that he had sex with Lilith, and then she had a child. *Could Dawn be my own? Did they do something to her? Is it possible that Lucius, Lilith, and I all had a child together? How would Dawn react? What would she say if she knew? What if I am wrong? I love her, but I might love her like a father. I don't know. I need to find out.*

✦

Adam heads straight to Lucius's study. He stands before the towering wooden double doors, closing his eyes and straightening out his faded-black fatigues before he knocks on the left side of the doors.

"Come in," Lucius says.

Keeping his form proper, Adam walks into the room and stops a fair distance from Emperor Lucius, hands resting behind his back.

"Sir, I have important matters to discuss."

"Is that so?"

"Yes. I used the blood flower mixed with Eve's blood."

"Oh?" Lucius leans forward in his large ornate chair. "I'm listening."

"Yes, I—I believe that long ago, in Sumer—that we—" Adam pauses clearing his throat. "That I cut the infant, Dawn, from Lilith's womb. I was following her request. The last I saw of Dawn was with a tribunal member in Eridu. Lilith had begged that Dawn be free from your influence."

"I see." Lucius pauses, his reaction is subtle, too subtle for Adam's liking. "It is a conclusion I have already drawn." Lucius waves his hand dismissively.

"If I had known, I would have told you long ago."

"Of course," Lucius says, curling his fingers one by one until they form a fist. "Tell me, Adam, do you believe that you made the correct choice?"

"I—I don't know, my lord. Obviously, I made a mistake. I had nowhere else to turn. I was following Lilith's dying wish. Dawn has suffered hardships on Earth. Perhaps, her mother's judgment was incorrect."

"I see," Lucius says, his tone far too even, masking anger. "Well, Adam, I don't blame you for what you have done. You are loyal now. Are you loyal to me or are you loyal to Lilith?"

"I don't quite understand the question." Adam keeps his position steady.

"It is a simple question, Adam. Who are you loyal to?"

"You, of course," Adam says, a little too quickly.

"Are you certain?"

"Yes, my lord."

"How is my daughter doing?"

"Same, as always."

Lucius nods. "Get back to her."

"Yes, sir."

As he places his hand on the door handle, Lucius says, "Oh... and Adam... I know that you know." Lucius stands to his full height. "That I am her father. She had wings after all."

Adam grips the cold metal of the door handle.

Lucius walks up behind him. "Logic dictates—"

"Do not think me a fool," Adam pleads, his voice wavering.

Adam opens the door. Lucius firmly shuts it. "Perhaps, you are better suited for tasks other than guarding the princess."

Adam turns to Lucius. Their eyes meet evenly. For once, Adam is showing emotion. He works to steady his hand from shaking.

"Come now, Adam, things do not need to be this way. After all, you can still spend time with Dawn… if I allow it."

His jaw clenches, eyes locked with Lucius's, but he knows better than to say anything rash.

"She is not yours. She belongs to me," Lucius says to him, uncomfortably close.

"You know, Lucifer, I know when you're lying."

"Wouldn't you rather her not be your child, anyway, Adam? You could take what I know you want. If I allow it. Dawn, rights to the throne."

Adam physically turns his head away from the idea. His mind involuntarily flashes back to Eridu and the feeling of being possessed.

"Are you certain that she is not of my flesh?" Adam asks, desperate for answers.

"Keep your position, for now, and Adam—"

"Yes, my lord?" Adam falls back into his familiar role.

"It's best not to confuse her with—"

"The truth?" Adam asserts firmly.

"Facts that we may not be entirely certain of. Tell her of what you suspect, and I will ensure you never see her again."

"I have done everything you asked. My only payment is that you honor your word." Adam takes a step closer. "You agreed to my position as her personal guard if I threw her into the Axion. Which I did. I took the blame. I was your shield. With her wings, your sword. Just let me go back to my rightful place."

Adam's mind drifts back to the dark day Dawn arrived in the citadel, remembering the ice-cold dark-blue shard he used to sever the bones that connected her wings to her shoulder blades. Dawn was sedated and strapped to a chair specifically designed for this grim task. The immense amount of pain had woken her. Fortunately, she was blindfolded. Dawn thought it was just another nightmare. She had told him as much.

"You only speak to Dawn because I allow it." Lucius's threatening tone snaps Adam back into reality.

"No. You made a deal. Why was this not a factor for you, anyway? Either you are manipulating me, or your head is so far into the future that you forgot about the past."

"I stand by my word," Lucius says.

"I know you will." Adam turns back to the door.

"Oh, and Adam. You are to protect her, at the cost of your life, if necessary."

"I know my oaths," Adam says with his back to Lucius.

Chapter 30

Inside the citadel's indoor Blackstone arena, Dawn practices sword fighting with Adam. Exhausted, she sighs, placing her sword into its sheath. The top of her hair is pulled into braids, with loose hair hanging down her back and shoulders. She has on her gambeson uniform.

"Dawn, I know you're tired, but you must continue." Adam holds his sword at the ready.

Dawn nods and unsheathes Divine. She moves, dancing with the blade, flowing in formations she has been taught, allowing muscle memory to direct her movements. The blade sings as it blocks Adam's maneuvers.

"That's enough, Dawn," Adam says. "You must understand the purpose of this training."

"I know. I know. War is apathetic to suffering, to death." Dawn slides Divine back into its sheath. She rests her hand on the pommel, feeling the metal of the hilt down to her emblem. The tips of her fingers rest on the purple heart gem in the center.

"Dawn, I apologize in advance for this next phase." Adam bows his head respectfully.

"Am I not done?"

"No, I'm sorry. I don't set the training schedule. If I did, I wouldn't—"

"Wouldn't what?"

"Never mind." Adam closes his eyes for a moment. "Bring him in."

Masked royal guards enter. Limping behind them, led in by chains is their prisoner, Raziel. There are fresh red lacerations on his skin. Dawn's heart wrenches. Raziel looks far worse than the last time she saw him.

He looks at her. In his eyes, she sees compassion and poorly masked agony. Raziel briefly nods to her.

Adam watches them closely.

"Kill him," Adam says, pointing his sword at Raziel.

"What?" Dawn turns sharply to Adam.

"I said kill him," he repeats. "It is simple. Cut his head off."

"No." Dawn backs away, gripping her sword's handle. "I won't."

"Dawn, angels don't die, not really."

"What?"

"I've been meaning to tell you this for quite some time. I had to run the details by your father before I could relay the information in full."

"Okay." Dawn crosses her arms. "Then explain."

"There is a massive cemetery, if you will, on Chesed known as the Silentes Fields. Blocks of solid stone where we place the dead. Given time, they return and, of course, need to be re-educated through discere."

"I will not harm an innocent. Hasn't he suffered enough?" Dawn's jaw strains in anger. "I'm wearing the necklace. I thought Raziel would be given a more lenient sentence."

"He has, Dawn. Death is merciful. Follow orders."

"No. I won't!"

Adam sighs. "There are worse punishments than this."

"What alternative punishment do you suggest?" Dawn says.

"I don't know. It isn't my choice. Talk to your father," Adam says as he places his sword on the weapons rack mounted on the wall.

"Why not allow him to continue to be a guard?" Dawn takes a step closer to Adam.

"Why would we ever allow such a thing?"

"Because, that way you can keep an eye on him. Turn him into counterintelligence."

"This is something you have to talk to your father about, not me. First form," Adam says, ordering Dawn to take a specific fighting stance.

"No. Take me and Raziel to see my father. I want to see if there is another way."

"Come along, then, Dawn." Adam faces the royal guards and nods to the door.

As they walk down the hall, Dawn's mind reels, trying to sort her way through this mess. She looks over at Adam, who is walking beside her, and asks, "What would you do?"

"You wouldn't want to know what I would do."

"You know, just because you made a mistake doesn't mean that you have to keep making it—knowing the destruction at the end of the path and the rebirth of the same cycle. I will take no part in it."

If she didn't know any better, she would have sworn that Adam gave her a sympathetic look. They arrive at Lucius's study. Adam knocks on the door.

"Come in," Lucius says.

Adam opens the door and holds it for Dawn as she walks in. The masked royal guards lead Raziel in by chains.

"What is this about?" Lucius asks, setting down the papers he was reading.

"Your daughter has something she wishes to discuss," Adam says.

"Do you now?" Lucius's eyes move from Adam to Dawn. "What is it, darling?"

"I'm wearing the necklace. I want Raziel to be free. Allow him to return to his post."

"No." Lucius picks his papers back up, but Dawn continues pleading.

"You could make him work for you, be counterintelligence. Watch him at all times but allow him to go back to his sworn duty."

Lucius sighs and sets his papers face down on the table. "I don't know why you care so much about this specific angel." Lucius nods to the royal guards and points to his wrist. The guards unchain Raziel. The disgraced guard stumbles, nearly falling. No one besides Dawn seems concerned. She goes over and helps him walk to a chair.

"May he sit, Father?" Dawn asks.

Lucius inclines his head. Raziel sits in a chair and keeps his head down.

Dawn takes a chair between Lucius and Raziel. Adam stands behind Dawn.

"Raziel, is it?" Lucius says, studying him. Then he looks toward the door and says something that does not translate, but the meaning is clear as the masked guards leave the room.

"Tell me, Dawn, why do you care so much for this particular angel?" Lucius asks, leaning forward and searching her reaction.

Dawn takes a deep breath, then looks into his eyes.

"Because I have to. My morality doesn't allow me to turn away," Dawn says.

"Oh? And what would happen if you did?" Lucius sits back and waits for her answer.

"My insides would scream at me until things were made right."

"Quite the moral compass you have, my dear. Perhaps you would feel better by alleviating yourself of it," Lucius says.

"I don't even know how I would do that," Dawn says, feeling bile rise inside.

"There are ways, proven methods to desensitize you," Lucius says, waiting for her reaction.

"N—No." Dawn, for once, feels frightened by him.

"Dawn, you must understand hierarchy, structure, and order. Things are done the way that they are for good reason."

"I disagree."

"Dawn, you have a decision to make. I leave this as your choice."

Dawn draws back; she wasn't expecting that. "Why?"

"You are my daughter, and because of that, you need to learn how to manipulate the world around you to achieve what needs to be done. Not just for you, not just for Raziel, but for the good of the Sine System as a whole. You ask how to bring about change, and I am showing you. Send Raziel to discere until he learns his place."

"I will do no such thing." Dawn's eyes lock with his as anger rises inside.

"Why not, Dawn? Even if he orchestrated the previous attacks on you?"

"Have you proof of this?"

"No, but it isn't out of the question. Is it? He is a member of the resistance.

The very organization who assaulted you."

Dawn feels a seed of doubt forming in her mind. She shakes her head. "I will never send someone to discere."

"Dawn, you must learn that these things maintain order, stability, and peace."

"Peace? Peace through pain?"

"Peace is always achieved through pain."

"Why not allow him to return to his place as a royal guard?"

"Dawn, please listen. Raziel is dangerous. He is not to be trusted. He violated his oath when he talked to you and sent you false information."

"What about the information was false?"

"It is propaganda designed to turn one into an extremist. You must disregard false information when you know it is incorrect."

"It seemed to be accurate to me."

"Dawn, it is extremist propaganda. Has it turned you against me?"

Dawn's heart beats faster. She closes her eyes, head down, not answering.

"Give me an answer, Dawn. Has he turned you against me?"

"Of course not! Father, Raziel is not a threat. If anything, he is an ally. Considering turning him into your spy." Dawn looks at Raziel, who has his head down, pretending as if he isn't there.

"If I may," Adam says, "it's not a bad idea. However, there does need to be some form of punishment."

Lucius leans back on the couch.

"What say you, Raziel?" Lucius asks the broken angel.

"I will never spy for you," Raziel says, lifting his head and looking directly at Emperor Lucius.

"Very well, Dawn. He said no. Now what?"

"Hasn't he suffered enough?" Dawn pleads.

"String him up another seven cycles to prove our point and then allow him to take his place. I disagree with making him a royal guard again, but it is not my choice," Adam suggests.

"Perhaps I could find the benevolence to allow this," Lucius says, looking at the purple heart gem necklace resting on Dawn's chest.

"Does it have to be this way?" Dawn looks sorrowfully at Raziel's bruised and torn skin.

"Dawn, what I am allowing is an act of mercy," Lucius says.

"This isn't mercy. Mercy is kind no matter the circumstance."

"Mercy gets you killed. I once believed in mercy, but then everything and everyone turned their back on me. I was lost. Until I founded this empire. That is something that cannot be achieved through mercy but the power of persuasion accompanied by violence."

"Why take away freedom? What happens in the discere centers?"

"Many things, Dawn. Maestros analyze the individual's specific psychology to help guide them in the proper direction."

"What is a maestro?" Dawn asks.

"Maestros are specialized individuals who psychologically profile the subject. Then, do what needs to be done in order to achieve the best possible version of that angel."

"You know that's wrong," Dawn says.

"Tell me, Dawn, beyond physical torture, what exactly is wrong about discere?"

"I don't know."

"I will get a maestro to watch over him. In exchange, I grant you your version of justice."

"Will you still hang him for seven cycles?"

"Yes."

Dawn sighs.

"This is the best deal you're going to get." Lucius looks to the door, says something that's lost in translation, and the guards reenter the room. "Take him to his place."

Dawn looks away as if this isn't happening.

"It will be over soon." Lucius leans back casually, studying Dawn's reaction.

Raziel's head is down as they escort him out of the room.

"Why not make him my personal guard? For when Adam is gone."

"Dawn, that angel is dangerous. He is not to be trusted and you want to spend time with him?"

"I trust him," Dawn says.

"Trust is a beautiful, fragile thing. It can shatter in an instant." Lucius seems to be far off inside of his mind. "No, you should trust no one. Especially anyone in that zealous cult whose only goal is to destroy me and anything that they can, including you."

"I want him to rotate with Adam. Honestly, I don't—I can't after what happened—trust the guards."

"Dawn, you are supposed to fear them. If you're afraid, then an assailant will be afraid. Trust is a valuable resource, but so is common sense. He is in the resistance. He cannot talk to you."

"Why?" Dawn asks.

"If I may, they have built a rapport with one another. They have an understanding," Adams says.

"The traitor is not allowed to speak with you." Lucius picks up his papers. "I will place him back on duty at my side, where I can watch him."

Dawn sighs, resigned.

"My dear, you really must begin to understand how things work."

"Dawn, it's time to study," Adam says, offering her his hand.

Dawn sighs and takes it. She turns to her father and nods to him. Lucius closes his eyes and nods in return.

◆

Inside the Wonder Brigade's barracks, Gabriel and Saphrael sit in the middle of their respective cots, leaning forward and talking to one another. The room looks nearly the same as it had before the others left, except that their signature weapons are gone. Everything else was abandoned, as if it didn't matter what they left behind.

"Go over your strategy again," Saphrael says.

"Get in. Avoid Lucius. Get out."

"Okay, sounds reasonable enough." Saphrael pauses and takes in a deep breath. "There is something I need you to understand. Whatever happens…

don't worry about me, okay? I am ready to sacrifice myself for your cause."

Gabriel looks at his best friend, searching for words but finding none.

"Emperor Lucius offered me a deal," Saphrael confesses.

"You already told me this."

"I know. But I didn't tell you everything. He told me if I brought him your cosmoversal crystal, that I would be promoted to a tremendously higher position. Don't worry, I am not going to do that even if it would save me. Living here teaches you things, like there really is such a thing as evil. That it isn't confined to just one side or another. Sometimes, things are so dark you can't see the good in anything. If I never see you again after you rescue Dawn... I have come to terms with it. If I get reprimanded for my part in this, I am prepared to face the consequences."

"Why?"

Saphrael shrugs. "Like I said before, if you die for something, you don't live for nothing. Figure of speech, of course—there are much darker paths that are not as favorable nor as kind as death."

"Being able to exist will always be better than death, Saphrael."

Saphrael shakes his head. "You've never been to discere. They break you in order to reshape you. Your mind... your spirit... everything. Have you decided where you are going to go?"

"I'm still planning to ask Azrael or Raphael for help."

"Even though Raphael lied to you your entire life?"

"I'm not even sure if that was real," Gabriel says, looking off to the side.

"What do you mean?"

"Memories of my life... they are different from the memories I have now. I think I've only had real memories for a few years before I met Dawn."

"I wish I had answers," Saphrael says.

Gabriel lifts his gambeson and looks at the poison marks on his skin. They are a shade lighter than they were before he went into the purified water.

"How are your injuries?" Saphrael asks.

"Painful, still advancing... just not as rapidly as before."

"It's going to take everything we have if you're going to stand a chance against Emperor Lucius," Saphrael says. He gets up and walks over.

Standing before Gabriel, Saphrael reaches for his Knights Templar sword, Solomon. The sound of it being quickly unsheathed causes Gabriel's pulse to quicken, the memory of being skewered by it during training clear in his mind.

When Gabriel looks at his friend, he finds the blade aimed horizontally rather than facing him, resting in Saphrael's hands as he holds it out to him.

"I want you to have this."

"I couldn't take Solomon from you, Saphrael."

"I'm serious. Take it."

"I can't. That sword is important to you." Gabriel looks at the ancient blade with Latin engraved in the fuller and the red cross on a shield in the rounded pommel. "I couldn't."

"Dammit, Gabriel, I'm serious. You need this more than I do. It's yours now."

"But Saphrael, this is all you had left from Hod."

Saphrael shrugs. "Other than the team's symbol."

"The Tiamat came from Hod?"

"Yeah, captains get to keep their symbol if they change teams. Besides, after it represented me and my incredible losing streak, everyone thought it was nothing but bad luck."

Carefully, Gabriel lifts the sword and nods to his friend. "Thank you, Saphrael. You know, I don't think I could do this without you."

"Yeah, I know." Saphrael punctuates his sarcastic response with a cheeky half-smile. "You should know the legends that follow that sword. The most common one is that it once belonged to one of the last Knights Templar, who was wrongfully accused and sentenced to death. The knight, tied to a stake, said those who are guilty would pay. Those responsible for his execution died shortly after he did. Some say it is cursed but cursed with righteousness. That it compels the bearer to act justly. I'm not sure if it works on archangels, but it seems to work on everyone else." Saphrael looks at the floor. "I won that when I was champion. I was brutal. I was bloodthirsty. I was good. Then, I started doubting myself. Was I doing the right thing? I think it was the beginning of my decline."

"Why are you giving this to me?"

"Because you need it. It will do great things in your hands, I'm sure."

Gabriel's hand tightens around the hilt of the sword, feeling unworthy of the blade, of everything.

✦

Cycle after cycle, Adam vigilantly keeps watch over the princess. Compared to what his life was for so long, guarding her has been a much-needed reprieve—one he hopes will last. Truths recently uncovered constantly claw at his mind, never quite allowing him peace.

He glances over to Dawn who is sitting on her bed reading a book. Quietly, he allows himself to indulge in a moment of appreciation and love he cannot deny.

I forgot to review the books that arrived, Adam thinks as his attention is drawn to the recently delivered stack of books sitting on her table. One book in particular captures his attention. It is a small, dark-red leather book. Written along the spine, in cuneiform, are the words the *Songs of Lilith.*

Adam walks to the table. Trying to calm his racing heart, he grabs the faded leather-bound journal.

"Where did this come from?" Adam looks at Dawn.

"It's been here for days, Adam," Dawn says. "It's poetry and mythology, I think. I'm really not sure."

Has Lucius left it here to haunt me? Have the contents been altered to poison my thoughts? he wonders as he returns to his seat near the door. Dawn sits on the edge of her bed, watching him.

Opening the book, he reads. *Rotten fruit decays, all crops failed. So many seeds lost that will never bloom*

Adam breathes in, taking a moment to fully absorb the text.

"How much of this have you read?" Adam asks.

"A lot, but none of it makes sense. I think maybe something is lost in translation. Do you understand it?" Dawn intently waits for his reply.

All she wants to know is about the past, everything I cannot say. So, instead, he stays silent. All he wants to do is tell her. Tell her everything that he knows, but he can't, not without risking losing her forever.

"Yes, Dawn, but until I know exactly what it means I—I cannot tell you what I think."

"Why?" Dawn looks injured at his statement.

Adam considers her long, spiral, cardinal-red hair. Her features pang his memory of Lilith. His mind wanders. *She looks like her mother. She looks like Lucius. If she is in fact my own, why does she not look like me?*

"Because... I may be wrong," Adam says, Lucius's threat to take her away fresh in his mind. He decides that, without direct evidence, it is best not to tell Dawn of what may be.

Adam goes back to reading the text.

My first love helped plant a tree. Roots of the earth. Red rain from the sky nourishes the sapling. Spring has arrived.

I died in Eridu. Everything that I was. Dead skin shed like a serpent. I am no longer free. I belong to him.

A lifetime ago, the first man on Earth to ask me to stay. Now, despite our tree, despite the growing fruit. I cannot return. Pride burned to ash.

Adam sits back and contemplates the passage, *Red rain from the sky nourishes the sapling. A reference to archangel Lucifer and blood magick.* Dawn watches him, waiting for his insight.

Adam carefully says, "In the early days, things were often passed down in verse. This seems to be a fragmented transcription. Probably inaccurate at best. I would pay it no mind." It pained Adam to blatantly lie to Dawn, but he could not tell her.

"Oh." She fails to force a smile.

There is a knock on the door.

Adam stands and greets the visitors. Ketis, the tailor, walks in with a gown resting in his arms. He is followed by a few assistants carrying boxes.

"How nice to see you again, Princess." Ketis nods.

"Hello." Dawn returns a nod of acknowledgment.

"Traditions unable to dictate formality, as we haven't had any for this type of occasion before," Ketis says.

"What about my mother?" Dawn asks.

Adam looks from Dawn to Ketis.

"She was never—it's not my place to—something to ask your father," Ketis mumbles before attempting to change the subject by showing Dawn the gown he designed. It's a beautiful midnight-blue ball gown, with gems in various places that glitter like stars. The middle of the skirt and bodice are darker than the rest of the dress and embroidered with vines and roses.

She smiles. "Thank you; it's lovely."

Ketis bows respectfully. As soon as they are finished setting down the items, the tailor and his assistants leave.

Dawn turns to Adam. "Tell me about Eridu," she says, looking at the book in his hands. It wasn't even a question, it was a demand.

"Dawn, there are certain subjects I cannot talk to you about. I do not have all of my memories; therefore, I cannot give you accurate facts. As for the legends, there are so many variations, only some of which contain truth."

"Why don't you just tell me what you know—even the legends? How do you not know everything? You were my father's right hand."

"Of course, having been your father's right hand granted me access to knowledge of a great many things. It does not, however, grant me knowledge of everything that your father knows, much less all knowledge in the omniverse."

"Wait—I thought it was a cosmoverse?"

"The cosmoverse is the sum of the universes as we know it: the Ethereal Realms, Earth's universe, the Crown Realms, the Sine System, and neutral space. The omniverse is our cosmoverse—the void, and any other potential cosmoverses that may or may not exist," Adam explains.

"So, there is more out there?"

"Our perspective only allows us to see so far, Dawn."

"Even the perspectives of archangels?"

"Presumably."

Dawn is silent as she slowly walks over to see what Ketis has brought her. The boxes are filled jewelry and accessories, as well as coordinated makeup. Out of the largest box, she pulls out a silvery light-blue metal circlet. She picks up a slip of paper from the box and reads it.

"It's a halo. Like a tiara? Worn as a signifier of what is to come. I guess it's like a promise ring for your head."

"I imagine Ketis is taking the opportunity to impart new traditions," Adam says.

Dawn puts it on. It fits, resting like a crown upon her head. Her hair will have to be wrapped around it for the Circle Gala and coronation. She stands in front of her full-length dressing mirror and holds the night-sky-inspired ball gown in front of her.

Chapter 31

D awn glances over at Adam, who is seated in his chair near the door. His clothes remind her of the first time she met him so long ago. He is fully decked out in a ceremonial dress uniform with absolutely everything in place.

Suddenly, the door to her room swings open without anyone knocking or announcing themselves. Dawn quickly places the tarot card she is holding back onto the deck as Adam jumps up, tightening his fists while adjusting his stance. His shoulders relax once he sees it is Lucius.

Without a word, Lucius stares at Adam and makes a curt nod in the direction of the door. Adam closes his eyes, his body language stiff. Nonetheless, Adam leaves the room without comment.

Lucius walks up to her, his boots clacking on the stone floor in a rhythmic pattern she has grown familiar with. Like Adam, he too is dressed far more formally than even he typically does in his tailored floor-length Victorian-style overcoat and black pants, completed with a vest embroidered with silver vines.

Dawn sits in a chair in front of her vanity. She nods cordially to her father before turning back to the mirror to continue applying makeup. From the corner of her eye, she notices the top card of her deck is askew. Hesitating briefly, she hopes he won't notice.

Outwardly, her appearance is pristine. She is dressed for the gala in her stunning midnight-blue dress that sparkles with cerulean gems reminiscent of the night sky. The dress's skirt is embroidered with small roses and twisting vines. A pile of thick, loose braids rests in a bunch on the top of her head, some of which are wrapped around her light silvery-cerulean halo. The rest of her soft, vibrant hair rests in large spirals down her back.

There is silence between them as he stops behind her. Looking at him through the mirror, Lucius has the usual unreadable expression on his face. If she isn't mistaken, his expression softens before the hollow coldness that typically marks his demeanor returns.

"Father," Dawn says.

Lucius inclines his head.

"Why did you send Adam away?"

"I simply want to spend time with you alone before the festivities." Lucius's eyes lock with hers in the mirror. "You look so much like your mother."

Dawn tries not to roll her eyes and nods at his reflection.

Lucius strokes her hair and rests his hands on her shoulders.

"She would be proud," Lucius says.

"I haven't done anything."

Lucius has a half-smile as he squeezes her shoulder. "Your mother cannot be here, yet if you permit me, I would like to talk about her. The final memory I have of your mother is from the day she left me. She was pregnant. We had been trying and failing for so long. Then, when everything seemed to be headed in the right direction… it went so very wrong. Her anger, her defiance, led directly to her grim fate. She was my singular purpose… and now, nothing remains of her but you. My greatest fear is that I have truly lost her forever. My second greatest fear is that I will lose you as well. Dawn, my dear, grant me your assurance that you will not leave. Swear to me that you will, under no circumstance, leave the Sine System."

Dawn pauses, the weight of what he is asking heavy upon her. "Never see Earth again? Never see…." She can't finish her sentence as grief wells, traveling up her throat. Her eyes dart to the tarot deck, then quickly look away.

Lucius studies her reflection in the mirror. His cold, unnaturally bright copper-colored eyes lock with hers. Without hesitation, his hand moves to her deck and picks up the card sitting askew. Closing her eyes, she expects anger.

"The Knight of Cups." When she doesn't answer, he continues. "You may speak of him." Lucius squeezes her right shoulder.

Dawn's voice breaks as she says. "Gabriel… Will I ever see him again?"

Lucius tilts his head up and removes his hand from her shoulder as he bows his head slightly. "I have a confession."

Her eyes flicker to him as he places the card back into her deck.

"I have not been entirely forthcoming. You must understand, it is my duty to protect you, my darling. Gabriel is here in the Sine System." Lucius slides a book from the pocket of his overcoat and places it before her on the desk of her vanity. "Consider this an apology. For both failing to inform you of Gabriel's presence and the lack of information in the book on the Promethean Angels. I am hoping this makes it up to you."

Dawn picks up the journal and flips through it. The entire sleek, black, leather-bound book is filled with entries in Lucius's handwriting. Dawn stops at a page and pulls out papers that are folded within the journal. They are the treatment plans that she has seen before, sent to her by the resistance.

"I hope that this more than makes up for keeping you in the dark for so long. Trust that everything I have done, I have done for your protection."

Overwhelmed, Dawn's hand shakes as she holds the book. *Gabriel is here. Really here? He hasn't come to see me?*

"You have all the time in the world to read later. Dawn," Lucius says in a low, calming tone. "I need you to swear to me, as soon-to-be-crowned princess, that you will not, under any circumstance, leave."

Dawn is silent, breathing in harder. Shaking her head, she grips the book.

"Dawn," he says again, brushing her hair softly before taking the book and setting it upon her vanity. "I can't bear to lose you, not like I lost your mother. Promise me that no matter what happens, you will stay within the Sine System."

"I won't leave you!"

"Swear to me."

"I swear. I will stay here, with you, no matter what."

Hot tears stream down Dawn's cheeks as Lucius firmly embraces her, holding her against his chest.

"I pledge to you my guidance and love as your father. I will never abandon you, regardless of the letter of the law, regardless of your inadequacies in wielding the flame. I have the utmost faith in you. I will not leave you, not like Gabriel."

"What do you mean?" Dawn pulls away from his embrace.

"Gabriel's movements within the Sine System have been thoroughly traced. He has, thus far, made no attempt to contact you. All of the information is in the journal. You deserve the truth. Trust is one of our most valuable assets. Do not squander it on those who do not deserve it."

"Has he been looking for me?"

"My sources informed me he has known your location for quite some time."

Dawn quiets into silence as tears stream down her face.

Lucius kisses her forehead. "I will see you at the gala." He squeezes her upper right arm before he turns to leave.

Lucius heads out the door. Adam comes back inside, holding Lilith's book. As he passes by, Lucius rips the small red leather book from his hands and, without comment, leaves.

"Meaningful chat?" Adam asks casually, then his expression changes when he notices she is crying. "What did he say to you?"

◆

"I miss her, Saphrael. I miss her more than anything," Gabriel confesses as they walk through the nearly empty streets of Arali. They are not far from the arena where they often train—close enough to see it, but far enough away that the large structure is out of focus.

"I know, Gabriel," Saphrael says, stopping at an open space just outside of the engraved symbols that marks the teleportation leyline.

Gabriel has on his father's breastplate, which has a light-blue centerpiece that looks like a compass star in the center. It is mostly hidden by Azrael's cloak. Besides the matching armguard, the rest of his plate armor is filled out with a patchwork of pieces, most of which would have been thrown out long ago by anyone else. Beneath the plate armor is his grayed Wonder Brigade uniform. Solomon rests in its sheath at his side. Saphrael wears his standard black and silver-accented Wonder Brigade uniform. The dagger, sword-breaker, rests on his left side.

"What if I don't—" Gabriel begins to say.

"Don't what?"

"What if I don't succeed?"

"You'll be fine, Gabriel."

Gabriel looks at Saphrael, expecting to see unease for his own future, but instead finds compassion and determination.

"How can you be so sure?"

"Because you are strong, Gabriel. You have a mission. You have to succeed."

"Wait!" a familiar voice shouts from behind.

Gabriel turns to see Marce running up to them in full combat gear and cape, halberd in hand. Beside him, Saphrael clenches his fists as the corner of his lip twists in irritation before he fully turns to face Marceriel, body language stiff.

As soon as he reaches them, Marce opens his mouth, which gets promptly shut by a right hook as Saphrael's fist connects with his jaw. Marce blinks, halfway moving his hand to his face before training takes over and he shifts into a defensive stance.

"What? Not finished with me yet?" Saphrael shouts, sharply planting his feet into the ground.

Marce stumbles back, blocking hit after hit. The rage-fueled punches rock him, yet he manages to continue blocking with his forearms. With a scream of frustration, Saphrael grabs hold of Marce's halberd. Marce looks at his weapon before shouting, "Would you listen to me?!"

Saphrael, however, is in no mood to listen to anything he has to say.

While keeping hold of Marce's weapon, Saphrael stomp-kicks Marce, his unforgiving boot driven into his kneecap. Gabriel watches in silence as Marce buckles, crumpling to the ground. As he falls, Saphrael twists the weapon from his grip and reorients his stance. The air sings with the sound of the black and gold halberd's blade as Saphrael swings the weapon around, aiming it at his former friend's throat.

"I'm here to help!" Marce pleads from the ground.

"Help? Help?! Is that what you call it?" Saphrael grits his teeth, his stance is solid and without tremor. Marce swallows hard as Saphrael repositions the halberd's pointed end directly at his eye.

"I deserve it... I do," Marce says with a grief-stricken, glossy look before resting his head on the ground, accepting his fate. "I know I do. I submit myself to your judgment, Captain."

Time slows to a standstill as Saphrael tightens his grip on the halberd. Screaming in anger, Saphrael hurls the weapon like a javelin. The weapon's pointed tip lodges into the ground, inches from Marce's face. Saphrael shakes in anger, breathing hard as he drops to the ground and lands on his knees, back hunched forward.

"I'm sorry. I'm sorry," Marce pleads, his voice breaking. "There is no reason to forgive me. I wouldn't forgive me. I don't deserve your forgiveness. I never will. But you always said that isn't what forgiveness is about."

"He's right," Gabriel says, walking up beside Saphrael. "As wrong as it feels, he's right. And he's here. No one else showed up."

Saphrael picks himself up. Unable to look at Marce, he turns away from him. Gabriel offers Marceriel his hand.

"Thanks, Gabriel," Marce says, grabbing hold of Gabriel's wrist as he helps him to his feet.

Marceriel dislodges his halberd from the dirt and wearily leans upon it.

Gabriel punches him in the jaw and warns him, "Don't mistake mercy for weakness."

Marce smiles, amused despite it all. "You'll make one of us yet, Earthling."

"I can't—I can't forgive him," Saphrael says, talking to Gabriel or perhaps himself.

"You don't need to. But how 'bout you not be stupid and take help that you both clearly need," Marce says with his usual undertone of anger.

"I don't need you," Saphrael continues, looking away from Marceriel.

"Oh, you clearly do, Captain," Marce says.

"Stop calling me that!"

"Why? Because the team is broken? You can't get rid of me that easily." Marce lifts his head proudly.

"It's suicide," Saphrael says blatantly. "Do yourself a favor, stay out of this one."

"No." Marce walks in front of Saphrael, who finally looks at him. "I can't let you two go alone. You are prepared but so are they. That no outside weapons allowed in the citadel rule? Well, this year it's weapons welcome."

Saphrael nods. "I see."

"I'm sorry that it took me too long to realize that… this, this is where I belong." Marce pounds on the upper right-hand side of his breastplate. "I will fight by your side."

Gabriel nods. "Good to have you back, Marce. Anyone else coming?"

"I'm afraid that's unlikely, but I don't know. I've spent the last several cycles alone in the woods." Marce falls silent for a few moments, keeping his head down. "I realized that you're the only true friends that I have. I don't want to lose that. I've lost everything. We all have. Don't make me lose what little I have left."

"It's fine," Saphrael says. "Do you believe him?"

"We need any help we can get," Gabriel says before turning to Marce. "I thought you were loyal."

Marce looks up with an injured expression. "I am."

"To your emperor. Isn't that what you said?" Gabriel presses.

"Guys, I really am on your side."

"We'll see," Saphrael says.

Marce notices that Gabriel has Solomon on his belt and tilts his head. "You gave him your sword?"

"Yeah, I did. He needs it. Like he needs us."

"So, what's the plan?" Marce asks.

"We don't really have one." Gabriel shrugs.

"You don't have a plan?" Marce opens his free hand questioningly.

"Still in?" Saphrael asks.

"Uh, yeah, of course. What's the point in committing only light treason?" Marce says.

Saphrael rolls his eyes.

"What? You are."

"Whatever, Marceriel." Saphrael looks away.

"No, Saph, get it through your head. You are committing treason," Marce says.

Saphrael uncomfortably shifts his weight from one side to another.

"What, you can't handle being labeled a traitor?" Marce says.

Saphrael unclasps his shirt hinges and unfolds the corner near the edge of his shirt collar, exposing the ever-burning traitor's mark branded into his skin. For the first time, Gabriel sees it clearly—it is a reversed emperor's crest with three distinct strikes through it.

"Reserved for the most treasonous. I was branded after you assaulted me and handed me to Emperor Lucius."

"Saphrael," Gabriel says, staring at the mark, still haunted from the day Saphrael stumbled into the barracks after his abduction and torture. "I don't want you to get hurt because of me."

"I'm going to get hurt no matter what, Gabriel. It might as well be for something worthwhile."

"We're going to lose," Marce interjects. "You know that, right? Look at what we are up against. Emperor Lucius, his army, everyone. We are monumentally screwed."

"It'll be fine," Gabriel says.

"Fine?! How is it going to be fine?" Marce asks.

Gabriel walks away from him and onto the teleportation sigil. He looks at the spot in the sky he knows is Tiphareth, the forbidden realm.

"So... plan?" Marce asks.

"Avoid Lucius. Get Dawn. Get out," Gabriel explains.

"How do you propose to leave?" Marce asks, leaning on his halberd.

"I have a cosmoversal crystal."

"You have a what?" Marce says. "For how long?"

Gabriel shrugs. "Since before I came here."

"What's the plan for us? Saphrael and I can't just leave."

"I told you, there is no plan. If you're not okay with that, then leave," Gabriel says.

"No, I want to help. It's just—" Marce says.

"Suicide?" Saphrael reiterates.

"Okay, I get it." Marce looks at the ground.

"You are a warrior, Marceriel. Fight for something," Saphrael says. His hand briefly rests on Marce's shoulder.

"I'm no warrior. You're the warrior, Saphrael. And you, you're an archangel; of course you can fight."

"We are all warriors as long as we fight. Don't be prey, right?" Gabriel says with a smirk.

"Yeah," Marce answers with his own smirk. "Don't be prey."

"Remember, they don't know that either one of you is a threat. So, use that to your advantage," Gabriel says.

They step into the large symbol burned into the ground and fade into an electromagnetic field of light.

◆

The silence of the empty streets morphs into a crowd of voices. Gabriel's eyes widen as he looks up at the imposing coal-black structure with jagged spires. His perspective only allows him to see a part of the citadel. Swallowing hard, he struggles to keep his anxiety at bay. Instead, he focuses on the crowd around him and flips up the hood of his tattered cloak. There are so many milling around that no one takes notice of him.

"Use your wings. There shouldn't be anyone around back," Saphrael says and then nods to Marce. "We can blend in. Do some scouting."

Gabriel slips through the crowd and finds himself alone in the back of the citadel. Taking a moment to look up again, he feels overwhelmingly cold and intimidated by the structure whose pitch-black stone spires twist organically into the sky. Gabriel launches into the air, using his fire to boost his ascent. He lands on a ledge of an oversized window. Willing his flame into a concentrated jet, Gabriel begins to cut the glass.

Breaking the window takes more effort than he anticipated. Once it starts to crack, he easily directs the flow of damage. The window shatters, pieces fall noiselessly to the ground.

His worn regulation boots set down upon a floor made of the same black stone as the outside of the citadel. The room he finds himself in is filled with nothing but statues and artifacts. *It must be a storage room*, he thinks, but to him it feels like an abandoned mausoleum.

He stops, listening for sound. When he hears nothing, he cautiously walks toward the door. Soon he finds himself wandering a myriad of narrow halls, some of which contain paintings, Chokma masks, and, occasionally, lines of statues.

The seemingly endless halls of the citadel have high ceilings, yet are dimly lit and oppressive. Surprisingly, he hasn't run into a single guard or worker as he wanders through the empty halls of the upper levels. *I bet they think that no one is this stupid...* Gabriel thinks.

Slowing his pace, he comes across a large set of dark mahogany-colored double doors. His breath hitches in his throat as he sees a carving of Dawn. Gently, he rests his hand upon the image of the falling woman carved in the door. *It looks just like her. This has to be Dawn's room.* He takes a step back to view it more fully. The mural on the other door is Emperor Lucius chained and reaching out for the falling woman... *It must be Lilith*, Gabriel reasons.

His eyes narrow, focusing on a metal bolt lock running across the center of her doors. It's the only lock he has seen on any of the doors he has passed. A flash of anger mixed with sadness and regret is quickly replaced by a feeling of inadequacy.

Metal screeches against metal. The sound travels down the hall as he unbolts the door. Gabriel looks down the dark, narrow hallway. It is as still as it was before. Without thinking twice, Gabriel grasps the metal door lock and tears it off its hinges. It clangs as it hits the ground. Gabriel enters the room.

Briefly, his eyes are drawn to the far wall and the flower-shaped window lined with bars. Next to the window is a silver metal table with a black metal candelabrum that holds four yellow-orange flamed candles and a center one topped with purple flame. He talks to himself as he absentmindedly walks toward the candelabrum.

"Dawn," he says softly, "I don't know what you have been through. I only wish I was here to help shoulder the burdens you must carry." Without thinking, he reaches out and touches the purple flame.

"Ow!" His hand jolts back from the searing pain.

A book sits open on the ornate silver-colored metal table next to the candelabrum and other stacks of books. *She must have just been reading this,* Gabriel thinks. Briefly, he admires the elegant, slanted script written with black ink upon the strangely textured light gray pages. As he reads it, he realizes that it must be Lucius's handwriting. He reads: *I know you care deeply for Gabriel. And for that, I apologize. I have always acted in your best interests. Please, my dear, forgive my transgressions.*

"What a load of bullshit." Gabriel tosses the journal back onto the table, and it lands askew.

To the right of the table is her vanity. It has been recently used, judging by the pieces of vintage-styled but new-looking cosmetics lying about.

Turning to the other side of the room, a trifold mirror sitting in the corner near her bed captures his attention as the frame is glowing. Gabriel takes off Azrael's cloak, exposing his midnight-blue semi-translucent archangel wings as he walks up to the mirror.

Unrelenting self-doubt plagues him like a sickness that never quite heals as Gabriel stares at his reflection, not recognizing the man staring back at him. Still not used to his white-blond hair and ice-blue eyes, he looks down at his grayed gambeson, black gloves, and scuffed Wonder Brigade pieces of armor. The brilliance of the Crown Realm's armor shines with soft ethereal light.

"Is this who I am? Who I have always been? If it is, then why do I feel more lost than ever? I know hell and that is life without you," Gabriel says quietly. "The only time life ever made sense was when you were in my arms."

There is a crack in the upper right corner of the center mirror panel; one that travels down and branches into smaller veins. Lightly, he rests his fingers on the crack in the mirror thinking, *I wish I knew what happened.* Then he looks at the top of the mirror. His heart sharply constricts with pain at the sight of the mirror's centerpiece, a faintly glowing, large purple stone rose. It reminds him of the rose on Dawn's dress that she wore the day he failed to reach her in the Axion.

Allowing his vision to shift into magnus sight, Gabriel looks in the mirror and sees damage from the soul poison infecting cells emanating from his bloodstream. Every cell is highlighted by his blue flame, burning especially bright in his irises. The only areas he cannot see through are the pieces of his father's armor. He watches as his blood circulates, muddied by the poison, that darks the fuchsia color that is typically seen in this vision. The darkest hues are near his chest, just outside of the edges of the armor, where he had been stabbed by the soul poison blade, twice. He has grown used to the pain. There is nothing he can do about it, and there are more important matters at hand this day.

He speaks softly, as if in prayer. "Dawn, my love. Have you missed me as I have missed you? Are your days filled with misery as they were on Earth? Would you even want to return?" Gabriel allows himself to breathe out heavily, his vision returning to normal. "Maybe things can never go back to the way they were. But I know that as long as you are by my side, everything will be all right. It has to be." Resting his hand on the mirror, he bows his head.

"I'm trying to hold on. Sometimes it doesn't feel like there is any hope left to hold on to... but—I have to... I have to. I refuse to live without you. Do you remember the day you came into my life? I can't forget the look of despair in your eyes. I swear, I will do everything in my power to ensure that you will never know what that feels like again."

CHAPTER 31

Moments later, he lifts his head and looks at his reflection, determination in his eyes. He throws the Archangel of Death's cloak back across his shoulders, takes in a deep breath, and steadies himself for what is to come.

Chapter 32

The sounds of music and chatter in the distance spike anxiety in Gabriel as he peers down a narrow hall lined with Chokma masks hanging above rows of deteriorating statues. The rows of statues are set in front of twin stone water pathways, all leading to an imposing set of black doors looming in the distance. A strange sense of calmness washes over him as he swallows hard, wondering what lies beyond the elegantly embossed wooden double doors. Inside, there is only one answer: Dawn. Something warns him to turn back while he still can.

I have to, he tells himself. *There is only one path for me, and that path leads through those doors. Dawn, I'm sorry if I neglected to appreciate you enough when you were by my side. I took for granted our peaceful life on Earth. I'm sorry I wasn't strong enough to prevent this from happening, and I pray you don't hate me for it. But I'm here now.*

The harmonic symphony of stringed instruments becomes crisp and clear as the right half of the doors swings open. A white-haired angel surrounded by a small entourage walks past Gabriel without so much as a glance in his direction. He waits for them to pass and then walks into the ballroom.

The first thing he does is look up, as the entirety of the ceiling glows with a gray light. In the center of the gray crystal ceiling is a large black emperor's crest, so large it casts a shadow upon the floor. Etched in circles around it are countless names and what appear to be dates. *Maybe it is a commemorative gravestone of some sort?* Gabriel wonders until he sees Saphrael's name written for rings, then he realizes it isn't a gravestone, it's a list of champions.

Get it together, Gabriel. Remember why you're here... Suddenly, he feels hollow. His mind wanders back to the dream, where he asked her to marry him, and she rejected him. Forcing the disturbing image from his mind of Dawn in military attire the last time he saw her, he tells himself to focus and surveys the massive crowd in the expansive ballroom. Glinting in spots here and there are assortments of bladed weaponry—most everyone seems to be armed. The majority of the crowd is dressed in the black gambeson uniforms with different accents of color and insignia; some have armor on as well. There are a healthy number of officers in dress uniforms, milling about. Most are naturally conversing with their units or socially dictated groups based on rank.

Standing out among the crowd is a lone couple dancing to the soothing melody of violins, violas, and cellos.

Dawn... Gabriel thinks, watching silently as Adam, in full officer's uniform and cap, puts one hand behind Dawn's shoulder. His heart swells as he watches her move gracefully. The skirt of her midnight-blue ball gown ruffles while keeping its form as she dances. Scant candlelight shimmers off her dark ball gown, points of cerulean light twinkle here and there, reminding Gabriel of nights spent stargazing with Dawn.

A pile of large loose braids sits in a bunch at the top of her head, some of which is wrapped around her faded silvery-blue halo. The rest of her hair hangs down her back in large, soft curls.

Adam pulls Dawn closer and dips her to the side. As he does, Dawn's large, soft spiral curls sway, and what he sees makes Gabriel's blood run cold. He stares at two large, distinct scars on her back. The same scars he has seen on his friends.

Bright blue fire erupts around him, encasing Gabriel. "You cut off her wings?"

Without thinking, Gabriel speeds toward Dawn, plowing through anyone unfortunate enough to be in his path. He stops a short distance from her, afraid that he might accidentally hit her.

Dawn turns, breaking from Adam. When her violet eyes lock with Gabriel's. It feels as if time has stopped. *She looks so different. Does she even want me here?*

Desperately, he tries to read the look on her face. Her initial shock sinks from confusion into despair as her eyes brim with tears.

"Gabriel?" Her soft voice wavers, choked with emotion. "Gabriel... where—"

Adam grabs her arm and says something to her Gabriel cannot hear. Ever the hardened soldier, Adam is difficult to read, but not Dawn. There is a well of emotion in her eyes, confusion, and above all, pain.

It's still her, he tells himself. "Dawn, please don't listen to them." Then, as much as he doesn't want to, Gabriel turns to Emperor Lucius and yells, "You cut off her wings?"

"What?" Dawn is clearly unaware of what he is talking about.

Adam steps in front of her, standing between her and Gabriel.

"You don't know?" Gabriel looks at Dawn before turning to Lucius.

The corner of the emperor's lip is twisted in amusement while he lounges in a large black throne on a raised stage. Lucius straightens his silver-buttoned, Victorian-esque overcoat that nearly reaches the ground. Beneath the overcoat is a satin black vest embroidered with silver vines and formal black pants. Emperor Lucius leans forward on his throne, elbows resting on his legs, hands together as if in prayer. Gabriel's ice-blue eyes are met by Lucius's unnaturally bright copper-colored eyes.

"You cut off her wings?!" Gabriel repeats, demanding an answer as blue fire encases him once more.

"Adam... removed her wings," Lucius says.

Adam's reaction speaks louder than words as he shifts his weight uncomfortably from one foot to another,

"Why?!" Gabriel twists Azrael's cloak to the side, revealing his large midnight-blue ethereal archangel wings. In his anger, his wings extend to their full length. The fire around him grows ever brighter.

"The same reason everyone here has no wings. It is cultural. It's tradition.

It is how things are done," Lucius explains.

Gabriel looks at the crowd and spots Saphrael not far away. His posture is held upright, in pride, yet in Saphrael's eyes is a detached, far-off look of grief. Gabriel realizes that wings represent what they used to have and everything they used to be. As Gabriel scans the unspoken reactions throughout the room, he realizes that everyone here has suffered greatly.

Turning back to Emperor Lucius, Gabriel eyes narrow, "Why? Your own people! Your own daughter?!"

Lucius relaxes in his chair before leaning forward. "Come now, Gabriel. Respect our culture."

"You mutilated her!" Gabriel screams.

"Grace in understanding... forgiveness in death," Lucius says in a flat tone.

Thrown off by hearing the Wonder Brigade's mantra, or at least Lucius's mangled interpretation of it, Gabriel tells himself to *stay focused. I'm here for Dawn.*

From a distance, Dawn locks eyes with his, but Adam has a grip on her arm and is still lecturing her. The only words Gabriel can make out are the words honor and duty.

Adam releases Dawn's arm, and she takes a step forward, her voice unsteady as she cries, "What took you so long? Do you even care?"

"Gabriel will abandon you again, my dear. That much is certain," Lucius says from his throne.

"Dawn..." Gabriel ignores Lucius, and the blue fire around him fades. His heart tells him he has failed her. "I swear that everything I do, I do for you and you alone. I would do anything for you."

She turns away and looks at Lucius, tears welling in her eyes. He has no idea what is going on between them. Confusion sparks anger inside.

Lucius casually waves his hand from his elaborately carved black throne and says, "Wonder Brigade, the opportunity to demonstrate your loyalty has arrived. Come forth and prove your loyalty."

After Gabriel exchanges a solemn look with Saphrael, he searches for the others in the crowd. Marce is nowhere to be found, but Loth is pushing his way roughly through bystanders.

Placing his hand on Solomon, Gabriel prepares to fight. His sword is halfway drawn when Saphrael walks up and puts an arm out to stop him.

"An archer who shoots to win loses focus on his target, making his goal two impossible targets when he only has a single arrow. Besides, this is our fight," Saphrael says, eyes narrowing at Loth.

The open wounds on Saphrael's face from his encounter with Emperor Lucius haven't healed. If anything, they look worse than when he stumbled into the barracks. Despite this, he shifts naturally into a fighting stance, determination burning in his emerald-green eyes as he grips the sword-breaker.

From the far end of the room, Spud, in a Tigris uniform with his large broadsword at his side, makes his way to aid Loth. Marce cuts him off before he reaches them, emerging from the horde, his black halberd with gold accents in his left hand. He drops his cloak on the ground. Spud stops, and they stare at each other, waiting to see who will make the first move.

Meanwhile, Loth tosses his restrictive dress jacket to the side, revealing an array of sharpened knives hanging from his trademark bandolier. Then he quick releases several knives and hurls them at Saphrael.

Saphrael dodges five of the six knives, but the sixth skewers him in his left shoulder. With no time to waste, Saphrael allows the knife to stay lodged in his shoulder. Carefully watching as Loth runs at him armed with a pair of circular metal wind and fire wheels

Loth swings the dangerous-looking weapons, aiming for Saphrael's throat. "Stupid. Treasonous. Captain!" Loth yells, swiping aggressively with every word. Saphrael easily backs away, dodging the low range of the wind and fire wheels. Altering his stance, Saphrael runs directly at Loth, sword-breaker in hand. Loth aggressively swings at Saphrael, becoming more erratic in his movements. Loth yells in frustration and boots Saphrael in the chest, hitting just below his wound and ever-burning traitor's mark. For a moment, Saphrael loses his balance and stumbles backward.

Metal tings against metal as the sword-breaker catches one of Loth's metal wheels, just before it hit him. Loth pulls hard on his weapon, but it is caught firmly in the metal teeth of the sword-breaker. Saphrael's arm is held upright, and he sharply twists the blade from Loth's grasp. The wind and fire wheel falls to the ground. Loth nails Saphrael with the other wind and fire wheel. It's blade drags across the side of his face and sprays blood.

For reasons Gabriel doesn't understand, Loth opts to retrieve the wind and fire wheel that was pried from his grip. Saphrael shakes his head, grabs Loth's hair, and drives his head into his knee. Stumbling back, Loth looks astonished. Saphrael picks up the wind and fire wheel that Loth had failed to retrieve and uppercuts him with his own weapon. The spokes of the wind and fire wheel get lodged into Loth's upper throat just below his chin.

Instead of letting go, Saphrael yells and uses his strength to pull the wind and fire wheel down, slicing Loth's throat open. The former teammate looks at Saphrael, trying but unable to speak before losing consciousness and dropping to the ground.

Saphrael grabs a knife from Loth's array and cuts every major artery in his body. A massive amount of blood covers Saphrael as he catches his breath. When he stands, Loth's blood pools around his boots in dark-red puddles. Breathing heavily, Saphrael finally pulls out the knife stuck in his shoulder and throws it away from him.

Marce, who has been blocking Spud from aiding Loth, tightens his grip on his halberd. Spud was preoccupied with watching the brutal match between Saphrael and Loth anyway. Now that the fight is over, Spud turns his attention to Marceriel, standing defensively with his broadsword in hand.

"You're nothing but a traitor, Marce," Spud says, words laced with self-righteous indignation.

"You think blindly following orders like a good little soldier somehow makes you right? Absolves you from all sins? You are damned... we all are. You are what you've always been, Padrael; a coward too afraid to think for yourself, to make your own choices. You want to be a puppet? That's your choice. I choose to defend my friends."

"Like you defended Saphrael?"

His eyes filled with regret, Marce makes the mistake of looking back at

Saphrael, who is drenched in blood and making his way to them. Spud charges at Marce, who turns, swinging his halberd in a controlled and decisive manner. Spud is no match for the long range of the halberd, and the axe-like bladed edge of his weapon cracks Spud's skull open. Padrael falls to the ground. Marce puts his foot on Spud's chest, holding down his body as he extracts his weapon and sets it upright. Streams of blood race down his weapon, while more viscous internal material clings to his blade.

"Padrael forced your hand," Saphrael says, placing a hand on Marce's shoulder.

"By the way, Marceriel, I never did properly thank you for this trinket," Lucius says from his throne, dangling something gold and shiny from his right hand. A chill runs through Gabriel. He feels disconnected as he stares at Dawn's pocket watch.

"It's not what you think," Marce says, shoving Saphrael's hand to the side and backing away. "Guys, I—I'm on your side."

"You'd better be." Gabriel turns his attention back to Dawn, who is blocked by Adam. The former hierophant-turned-personal guard is flanked by an entire line of masked royal guards on both sides. Adam stands with the poise of a battle-hardened soldier. In his hands are a set of black hook-swords, each surrendered from two different guards.

"Dawn…" Gabriel says calmly, talking to her through the wall of guards. Their sleek, faceless, silver-white masks make him feel as if he is facing a line of stylized robots clad in black martial arts uniforms.

Before he can do anything else, one of the royal guards spikes his mask on the ground and raises a black hook-sword to the sky, screaming, "We are not your dogs! Cerberus, rise!"

Adam shouts, "Raziel!" and turns to him as battle erupts. He pushes Dawn toward Lucius, who grabs hold of her arm and pulls her to him, saying something that Gabriel cannot hear over the sounds of battle. His heart wrenches when her eyes connect with his; her gaze is glossed over with detached sadness.

The storm of the chaotic brawl is deafening, punctuated by the clang of metal on metal. There are more resistance fighters and sympathizers than

Gabriel expected.

Adam advances on Raziel. The renegade angel swings first, and Adam blocks, forming his hook-swords into an X. Adam shoves Raziel back, gliding his hook-sword to the end of Raziel's weapon, locking the ends of their weapons together. Adam pulls forcefully, knocking Raziel off balance. Nearly lacerated by the crescent hook guard at the end of his own weapon, the renegade angel stumbles but quickly regains his footing.

The emperor sits Dawn on his throne before walking slowly toward Gabriel, tilting his head from one side to the other, cracking his neck. Inside, Gabriel is cold and fighting the instinctual urge to back away as Lucius's unnaturally bright copper-colored eyes stare unblinking in his direction before he shoots into the air. Purple fireballs erupt, shooting at Gabriel in succession.

Gabriel's blue flame ignites, encasing him. Without thinking, he flies directly at Emperor Lucius. The line of fireballs are neutralized by his blue flame. Throwing a punch at his face, Gabriel screams, "What have you done to her?"

"She has the free will to choose her own path. You don't have any idea what it would be like for her anywhere else, Gabriel. She is safe here," Lucius says, easily dodging him. If Gabriel didn't know any better, he would swear Lucius had teleported ten feet away.

Gabriel shakes his head. "I'm taking her home. I'm taking her to the Crown Realms."

"Charming. Mark my words, if other archangels take possession of Dawn, her very existence would be in danger. You have no idea what they are capable of."

"What did you do to her? Why is she acting like this?"

"Gabriel, Gabriel, Gabriel. You pitifully inadequate, lonely child. There is much you do not understand."

The words strike Gabriel to his core. He feels as if he were trapped in the Black Lake, with overpowering hopelessness paralyzing him.

Focus, Gabriel tells himself as he looks up at Emperor Lucius. "Have you brainwashed her against me?"

"I have only told her that which is true," Lucius says.

Down in the brawl far below, a single royal guard stands out, pacing back and forth, eyes fixated on Dawn. His fists tighten around his hook-swords as he shouts, "Evil must be eradicated!" The royal guard charges, running at Dawn.

Adam and Raziel immediately disengage and run to her defense. Instinctively, the flame protecting Gabriel dissipates as he dives, speeding to her. Lucius flies faster, catching Gabriel by the back of his breastplate and redirecting him into the floor. The impact launches stone fragments into the air. Lucius lands, stomping on the center of Gabriel's back. Through the disorienting haze, Gabriel keeps his attention focused on Dawn.

"Come now, Gabriel. Dawn can stand on her own. After all, I have trained her well." Lucius leans more weight onto the back of his breastplate. "Have you no faith in her?"

Gabriel strains as he watches the fight between Raziel and the assailant. The entirety of the attacker's focus is foolishly set upon his target. Raziel hooks the offender's ankle and pulls. The attacker falls hard, face-first onto the black stone floor.

"Hurting the innocent will never be the right thing to do, Zaphaiel," Raziel says, aiming the sharp end of the hook-sword at his target.

"Innocent? You know as well as I do that there is no such thing, Raziel. They are but a plague," Zaphaiel says, picking himself up in an aggressive stance, ignoring Raziel's blade.

"Yes, Zaphaiel, there is such a thing," Raziel says.

"All who stand against me, stand against justice!" Zaphaiel says.

Adam comes up from behind and holds the crescent blade of the hook-sword to his throat. He starts to cut into Zaphaiel's neck when a jet of purple flame encompasses them. Adam dodges, but the flame is directed at Zaphaiel's face. Adam looks confused as he realizes that the source of the flame is not Lucius, but Dawn.

She has a strong, resolute stance as she directs highly concentrated flame at the assailant. The flame burns brightly, melting the royal guard's mask, fusing it to his skin. She holds her ornate black sword with dark-purple accents in her other hand. Lucius has a half-smirk on his face, watching her. Utilizing the distraction, Gabriel yells and throws Lucius off him.

Adam puts his hand on Dawn's shoulder and says, "That's enough, Dawn."

She glares at Adam, her irises a bright, rich purple. Faithful royal guards line up, standing to each side of her. Lucius hovers in the air as Gabriel flies, racing to Dawn. Lucius reaches Gabriel and redirects his momentum by grabbing the same upper edge of his chest armor and throwing him with intense strength through a wall.

Lucius speeds through the opening after Gabriel. Moments later, Gabriel emerges, Lucius directly behind him. Cursing silently to himself, Gabriel tries to increase his speed but falters as he was never properly trained.

"You have power but lack experience. Abandon this pointless crusade," Lucius demands.

"Fuck you." Gabriel unsheathes his sword midair and swings the blade, aiming for the emperor's head. Lucius moves so fast an imprint of where he was is left in the air.

Desperately applying more force, Gabriel swings harder, as if that could make up for his lack of technique. Lucius grabs hold of his shoulders, pulls him forward, and headbutts him. The ballroom blurs. Lucius takes hold of Solomon as Gabriel's head whiplashes back. Gabriel screams as the cold steel of his own sword impales his midsection directly under his breastplate, near where Adam had hit him with the secondary dose of the soul poison.

Pulling the bloodied sword out of Gabriel, Lucius watches him spiral to the ground, then speeds down and drives the sword into Gabriel's upper shoulder, where there is no armor, pinning him to the ground.

Gabriel screams. No matter how many times he has been stabbed, it never hurts any less.

"Gabriel!" Dawn runs to him but is stopped by Adam, who places his hand on her shoulder. Purple fire crackles threatening to ignite around her, but in that moment, Dawn and Adam share a wordless exchange, and he lets her go.

She sheaths her sword and runs to Gabriel. Lucius stands to the side, allowing them to reunite. Planting her feet on the ground, Dawn grabs the sword, Solomon, and pulls, painfully extracting the blade from his shoulder. Sword in hand, Dawn turns to face Lucius, pointing the bloodied sword directly at him.

"That's enough, Dawn," Adam orders.

Gabriel picks himself up. A half-smile forms on Lucius's face as Gabriel grabs the handle from behind Dawn and places his hand over hers. He shoves the sword forward, driving the blade through Lucius's midsection.

"Very amusing," Lucius says, allowing the blade to rest in him before pulling it out, showing no change in expression as he does. The wound seals itself immediately.

No amount of time could prepare me to face such a threat. I need to get Dawn out of here, now, Gabriel thinks as he leans to one side from his injuries. The room is silent. Fighting has ceased.

In quick succession, Dawn hurls violet fireballs at Lucius, unsheathing her sword at the same time.

Lucius does not even feign blocking and absorbs the flame. "My dear, the purple flame is one we share. It can't possibly harm me."

Out of nowhere, Dawn violently jolts back, her arms spread to each side as if she were punched in the chest by an object traveling at high speed. The momentum causes her head to whiplash. Gabriel catches her as her sword clangs, crashing upon the ground.

"Dawn?" Gabriel begs, holding her close before looking at her, trying to figure out what is going on. She stares back at him, and her richly colored violet irises darken to mahogany before the light fades from them completely. Her eyes shut, and her body goes limp.

Holding his breath, panic rising inside, he frantically thinks, *This is it, I'm never going to see her again...* "Dawn! Dawn! God, Dawn! What's wrong!" He bows his head and presses her still-warm body as close to him as he can. "Don't leave me! You can't leave me! Not after all this. God, please!" Tears begin to flow, but his despair quickly hardens into anger.

Lifting his head, he glares at Emperor Lucius, ready to charge at him regardless of his skill in power or battle experience. Breathing in slowly,

Gabriel becomes confused because it doesn't even look like Emperor Lucius is paying attention. Even though the sword, Solomon, is still pointed directly him, Lucius's eyes are closed as if in meditation.

"Switch your vision!" Saphrael yells from a distance.

In the blink of an eye, Gabriel activates magnus sight. The ballroom dims to a near pitch black with the exception of brilliant auras that fluoresce off every living thing. Even inanimate objects, like those made of stone, shine with a dull glow. Yet it is difficult to see anything in the air above—it is as if the vacuum of space dropped closer to the surface and lay far too close for comfort.

Both Dawn and Lucius's cells are backed by a violet glow. A stream that starts out as purple smoke forms and twists in the air, directed by the wind. Entrails of smoke lightly steam around the crystal heart necklace sitting upon Dawn's chest, making it appear as if it were burning. The smoke in the air coalesces into a stream of purple light whose intensity in hue only darkens as it becomes concentrated.

A second light source, a nearly colorless, faded gray stream of light, entwines with the violet in a helix formation. It travels from Dawn into the center of Lucius's chest, and vice versa. The light exiting the center of Lucius's chest is the faded gray stream.

Everyone is silent, watching as the helix light streams, connecting Lucius and Dawn, twist together in the center between them, forming what can only be described as a swirling spiral arm galaxy.

The galaxy, composed of light, explodes outward with an intense blast of bitter cold. The shooting stars, or rather specks of light, all race to Emperor Lucius, who holds his free hand open, eyes closed. As the dots of light disappear into him, the color backing his cells darkens to an even richer, more concentrated violet.

The light streams vanish. Gabriel shields Dawn, holding her close before examining her in magnus vision. Tears threaten to fall as he stares at Dawn's completely motionless heart and lungs. Even the blood running through her veins has stopped.

A groan, like that of an ancient ship being torn asunder by the merciless tempest sea, fills the air. Gabriel looks up. His heart races as the black dragon encircles above, highlighted by his own black flame. Chains of purple light shoot out from Lucius's palm and wrap around the black dragon. The dragon, like the shards of light, gets pulled into Lucius.

The ballroom is disturbingly quiet as Gabriel switches his vision back to normal. It sharply focuses on Dawn and then on the blade pointed at his throat. Adam forcefully removes Azrael's cloak, confiscating anything Gabriel has in his pockets. The sword, Solomon, crashes to the ground after Lucius tosses it beside him.

"The time for games has passed." Lucius extends his hand, then forms a tight fist, sharply twisting it in the air.

As Lucius pulls down his fist, the pain of the soul poison's infection running throughout his body intensifies. His throat tightens, making it difficult to breathe. Shaking, Gabriel fights to keep his balance, holding onto Dawn with all the strength he has. It feels as if Gabriel is being burned from the inside out. Unable to hold back a cry of distress, the thought passes that *Now I understand what Saphrael meant when he said there are fates worse than death.*

On his skin, he feels veins of soul poison splinter open. Internally, His blue flame warms as it fights against it. The black veins glow with a hint of blue, creating illuminated shades of gray. The veins of living wounds advance throughout his body, snaking out like cracks of glass. Holding Dawn tighter, his vision blurs as he notices that the glowing cerulean gem in his breastplate seeps with blood-red corruption.

His fingers curl, stiffly shaking. He screams in pain, still holding onto Dawn's body. Even though he feels as if he is losing his grip on consciousness, he manages to yell, "Lucius!"

Lucius levitates, landing nearby as Gabriel shakes, nearly paralyzed, but still standing. Gabriel strains to look up at him. The shining metal of his father's armor tarnishes with rust-like splotches of onyx rapidly overtake the silver-colored metal.

Emperor Lucius has a small smile. "Resilient, aren't you?" he says, slowly walking up to him.

The resistance is losing. In the distance, Gabriel can see Saphrael and Marceriel surrounded not only by the Tigris team but a slew of high-ranking officers.

I don't think I can hold on much longer. I'm sorry, Dawn. Losing control, he falls, shielding Dawn with his own body as he hits the ground.

A flying, decayed angel swoops in past Gabriel. The Lost come pouring en masse through the large black double doors held open by masked royal guards. Leading the charge is Cadence, limping heavily, leaning on his golden staff. The Lost swarm the battlefield. Cadence nods and smiles to Gabriel before heading into the fray. Voices of the hive mind of the Lost flood his mind.

Do not give up, Gabriel.

We are here.

We are here for you.

Battle reignites. The majority of the Lost surround Gabriel, some flying in circles above before landing beside him. Many of the decayed former angels lean to one side, as their anatomical structure can no longer support an upright stance.

Lucius raises his hand but Gabriel's pain doesn't intensify. Instead, Dawn's unconscious body is ripped from his arms and hovers in the air. Every weapon is forced from the grips of their owners and levitates, all pointing at Dawn. Her own black ornate sword with purple accents is beneath her body, ready to impale her.

"Stop!" Gabriel begs. "Please! Stop! I'll do anything!" Gabriel stares up at Dawn.

"Call off your side, and I will call off mine. We should have a civilized discussion. Come, listen to what I have to say," Lucius says, gesturing to the thrones.

The Lost respectfully move aside for Gabriel to pass. Broken, Gabriel nods to them and then limps onto the raised platform. He sits on a throne next to Lucius—a throne he is sure is reserved for Dawn. Adam walks up to Emperor Lucius and gives him the items that were in Gabriel's possession. Lucius hands Adam the ragged cloak and keeps the other items.

Lucius amplifies his voice, shouting an order that does not translate. Many stop fighting immediately. Gabriel raises a fist in the air, hoping those fighting on his side will stop as well. In turn, Raziel shouts something untranslated, telling the resistance to hold. The weapons fall crashing onto the ground except Dawn's sword, which is rotates directly beneath her unmoving body.

"Well, that was fun, for a moment. It makes me nostalgic for times long past," Lucius says, taking a seat on his throne.

"Dawn... is she all right?" Gabriel asks, unable to keep from staring at her unconscious body suspended in the air.

"That is entirely up to you. Tell me, Gabriel, what is it that you want?"

"Dawn."

"Is that all?"

"Yes. I mean, I want my life back."

"I'm afraid your life as it was is no longer possible. Tell me, Gabriel, if I offered you a safe haven and for Dawn to make up her own mind—I do know how deeply she has missed you—would you consider staying here? Stay here, marry Dawn, if you truly wish to be with her. The Crown Realms will not accept her. It would be dangerously foolish to take her there. Earth is not safe. This is your only option."

"What if I say no?"

Gabriel strains to keep his face a steady mask, as he does not want to show how much pain he is actually in. The living wounds have utterly altered his appearance. At least the pain in his shoulder and midsection isn't as noticeable because of it. Gabriel looks up at Lucius, his eyes veined with soul poison.

"I can lessen the pain, yet I will not remove the poison. Most would not survive, not with the amount of soul poison in you."

"What do you want?" Gabriel asks.

"Our goals are not entirely misaligned, Gabriel. I do not have to be your enemy." Lucius closes his fist, forcing the soul poison to crack his skin more. "Swear an oath to me and I will guide you. Stand."

Reluctantly, he gets up, stands before Lucius, and stares straight into his unnaturally bright copper-colored eyes, clenching his fists.

Gabriel takes a deep breath and allows himself to relax. "For Dawn," he says with his head down, one arm pressed against his chest, massive wings folded behind him.

"Will you abandon your pointless crusade?"

Keeping his head down, Gabriel replies, "Yes," followed by a heavy sigh. Emperor Lucius unclenches his fist, and the intensity of the pain eases a little. Scanning the crowd, Lucius addresses them in a booming voice. "Let it be known that Gabriel will not save any one of you this day."

Looking across the crowd to Saphrael and Marceriel, Gabriel says, "I want my friends and anyone who fought for me to not face retaliation."

"Gabriel, there is a method to order. Show me the cracks in the foundation so I may fix them. Besides, you are in no position to make demands. However, tell me what it is you want."

Gabriel looks up at Dawn, as he has been for nearly the entire conversation. "Besides Dawn?"

Lucius nods.

"I want my friends to be okay."

"Very well. I have a position that requires someone trustworthy and powerful—hierophant. I will send all the traitors you requested to the empty land of Geburah. You and Dawn shall make your citadel there, now that it is no longer covered in fire."

Gabriel nods, not believing that he would concede control of the fate of traitorous angels.

"Dawn... my successor, my heir, my child. She needs to learn how to rule, properly. As do you. Submit to my training, and I will ensure a place for you. Take the entirety of your Wonder Brigade and do with each of them what you will."

Saphrael and Marceriel are on their knees, surrounded by officers. They, like everyone else in the ballroom, are silent and listening.

"I will take you in... as a son," Lucius says.

"Why?"

"I want what is best for my daughter. You are willing to sacrifice everything for her." Lucius pauses, then says, "I have one more thing to tell you, Gabriel."

Emperor Lucius pulls something out of an inner pocket of his overcoat. Gabriel's heart rate spikes as he looks upon the river stone that Raphael threw into the stream so long ago.

"How did you get that?"

"None of your concern," Lucius says, tossing the stone into the air. He looks at Gabriel, straight into his gray-veined ice-blue eyes, searching for his reaction.

"That means—" Gabriel begins to say.

Inside his head, a familiar voice answers, *Yes, Gabriel.*

Lucius says the last part out loud. "I am Semoel."

Breathing in sharp, soft breaths, Gabriel's eyes widen as he processes this revelation. Lucius tosses him the stone. Gabriel looks at it in disbelief. It is the same stone. He would know it anywhere.

"Thanks?" he mumbles.

"Gabriel, I want you to know that I was there. I was the only friend you had. For a long while, your life was synthetic," Lucius explains.

"What?"

"You were in stasis. When I was made aware of your existence, I tried to aid you through it."

"Okay? Was any of my life real?"

"The last few years, yes. Most of the other archangels conspired to write your fate, always believing they know best. They implanted memories of a simulated life. Near the end, stasis could no longer hold you. Then, they left you with Raphael."

"Do you know my father? Archangel Gabriel?" he asks, still staring at Dawn.

"Yes, at one time, he was the greatest friend you could ask for."

"How do I exist?"

"There are questions I do not yet know the answer to. When I do find out, I will pass on the knowledge to you. Do not forget that I was your friend. I helped you through a great many things."

"Like night terrors?"

Lucius has a small smile on his face and shrugs. "Psychological warfare. Use every weapon at your disposal."

"What? How can you call me a friend when you induced night terrors that haunt me? Not to mention, you brought those night terrors to life one night."

"True. I see the paths of most futures, Gabriel. I molded you, to temper you to the correct path, to me."

"Why?"

"Perhaps in time you will understand."

"I have one last request. I want to be named as your successor, legally. So Dawn doesn't have to carry that burden. You say you take me in as a son. As my friend, give me the legal title. Crown Dawn princess, but do not bind her here."

"I'm afraid she is already honor-bound. She has vowed to stay within the Sine System."

"Why?"

"Gabriel, nowhere else is safe for her. This is her home. She is meant to be here. On Earth, she was miserable and homeless. The Crown Realms will think her an abomination. Who knows what they would do."

"Please, name me successor. You think I am strong enough to become your hierophant? To rule a new town? But not to carry the burden of being legally bound? Please, put that hardship on my shoulders and not Dawn's. She doesn't deserve to be trapped here."

"Gabriel, she is protected here," Lucius says.

"I am begging you, make me your successor," Gabriel says, lowering his head again.

"Very well, I will legally name you my successor in the responsibilities and burdens tied to the *Treaty of Ordo*. However, if I am incapacitated or somehow killed, Dawn will become empress and inherit everything. There are no laws that state your legally named successor also gets your titles and position. You are bound to these restrictions immediately if you agree."

"Agreed." Gabriel nods.

Saphrael has a knee-jerk reaction, bolting to his feet, but is quickly forced back down.

"There has to be another way," Saphrael shouts.

Gabriel looks over in time to hear Marceriel say, "Shut up."

"Gabriel, don't do this!" Saphrael pleads.

Marce, with his hands tied behind his back, headbutts Saphrael in the chin. Those surrounding them take out their weapons and aim them at Saphrael, who looks down, defeated.

The room is silent. Gabriel's heart beats heavily in his chest, painfully constricting as the poison circulates through it.

"Tell me, Gabriel, to what extent of suffering would you endure for Dawn. What would you sacrifice in her name?"

"Everything—absolutely everything. I can't believe you even have to ask. But if you require clarification, know that there are no lengths I would not go, no hell I would not cross, no sacrifice I would not make for her."

"Love..." Lucius says thoughtfully with a quiet indiscernible expression on his face. His gaze is firmly set on Dawn's unconscious body as it rotates slowly midair. Gabriel shivers as the temperature plunges, although he isn't sure it actually has or if it just feels that way. Lucius's eyes shift into an eerie, markedly hollow demeanor that Gabriel will not soon forget. The tone of Lucius's voice, laced with undercurrents of malice, drops but is altogether unsettlingly even. As he speaks, his eyes never leave Dawn's body. "Love is an affliction, a disease of the mind. Chains of love not only bind, they suffocate, they strangle. This disease will rot you from the core until nothing but ash remains."

"You're wrong." Gabriel stares at him with fixed determination, unable to hide the anger rising within. As Emperor Lucius turns his attention fully back to Gabriel, something inside urges him to strike at Lucius, but he knows he is outclassed, at least for now. "Love is sacrifice. Love is a promise—"

"Love is weakness."

"If love is weakness, then it is one that I accept wholly and without condition."

"Very well, may it be the chains in which you are bound. But remember, one can only know the true extent of suffering in the darkest of days only if the brightest ones came before it. Now kneel and repeat these vows."

Gabriel looks at Dawn's unconscious body before closing his eyes, taking in a deep breath, and dropping to one knee, his head bowed.

"On my honor, I, Gabriel, do hereby pledge loyalty and submit myself in servitude to Emperor Lucius."

Gabriel repeats his vows, keeping his head down.

"I vow to protect Dawn with my very life, if required."

"I will always protect Dawn, no matter the cost." Still kneeling upon one knee, Gabriel raises his head, and his eyes meet with Emperor Lucius's.

Lucius waits for him to complete his vows correctly.

"I vow to protect Dawn with my very life, if required."

Lucius reaches into his pocket and takes out Dawn's engagement ring. Gabriel keeps his composure, masking a torrent of emotions as he stands and accepts the ring from Lucius.

"One more thing you should be made aware of. Adam is a package deal with Dawn. He has been my trusted adviser for a very long time."

"You know he threw me in the cursed lake," Gabriel says.

Lucius shrugs. "C'est la vie. Dawn's coronation will be delayed in order for you to be crowned prince. Preparations will have to be made for this change in events. I will guide you, if you allow me to do so. You may take Dawn to her room," Lucius says.

Lucius pulls out a small, elongated diamond-shaped vial hanging from a silver chain. The water shining within is a luminescent light-blue. "Take this healing water from the realm of Zera. Its properties will speed healing time. Dawn will wake on her own, of that I am certain. However, anoint her with this, specifically her head and heart." Lucius motions to his forehead and then heart before tossing the vial to Gabriel.

Placing the silver chain around his neck, Gabriel looks at Dawn's body in the air. Adam clears his throat, calling Gabriel's attention, and hands him Azrael's cloak. Gabriel puts it on and then places the ring into the inner pocket of his cloak. Dawn's unconscious body lowers into Gabriel's arms.

Her sword floats down to rest on the ground. Raziel places her sword back into its sheath, which is hanging at her side.

"Thank you," Raziel says from beside Adam. Raziel hands Gabriel his sword. Gabriel sheaths Solomon after putting his cloak back on.

Turning to Adam, Gabriel asks, "Are you coming?"

"I will fulfill my oath and protect the princess with my life. I am not going anywhere, Gabriel."

Gabriel nods, jealousy gnawing inside. "Let's go then."

Together they walk, making their way back to Dawn's room.

"Why did you cut her wings off?" Gabriel asks as they walk down the long hall.

"I was ordered to," Adam says.

Chapter 33

Gabriel carries Dawn to her bed and lays her gently on top of her black blanket that's laced with golden vines before sitting on the bed beside her. Ever present, Adam stands near a black wooden pillar of her canopy bed and looks at her unconscious body with a reserved stature, yet he is unable to hide the depths of concern in his eyes.

"So, what exactly is it that you do?" Gabriel asks.

"I guard the princess. She has been made my sole concern," Adam explains as he walks over to his seat near the door before taking a small book from the pocket of his jacket.

"Why?" Jealousy flares in Gabriel's voice.

Adam shakes his head. "Everything is so violent here, everything exudes darkness. I simply want the best possible life for Dawn. If I get to take care of her as well, that's a bonus."

"Would you leave if I asked?"

"Possibly. In the end, it would be up to Emperor Lucius."

"Why do you care about her so much?"

Adam looks at Dawn with an unreadable expression. Then he turns to Gabriel. "That I cannot tell you."

"Why?"

Adam shakes his head.

"Did you sleep with her?"

"No, of course not. I'm afraid you have the wrong impression of our relationship. This is a responsibility I have undertaken, and I will not have it compromised because of you."

"You gave up your highly successful position just to guard her? Do you love her?" Gabriel asks defensively.

"Yes, deeply. Nothing has ever happened between us. Think of me as an overprotective father figure. The princess needs protection, and I am the most qualified. I specifically requested this assignment."

"Really? What was your job, anyway?"

"I had many responsibilities: hierophant, Lord of Geburah, tournament overseer to name a few. If you're asking about the distant past, I was a doctor in Eridu."

Gabriel winces as the soul poison running through his veins is especially painful for a few moments. His mind wanders to the battle he had just lost. "I didn't think I was going to lose."

"Why? You had an impossible mission. Did you really believe that your untrained, newly found powers were enough to defeat Lucius?"

Gabriel sighs. "I just wanted to save Dawn."

"Lucius was right when he said anywhere else would be too dangerous for her. With her seduction aura, Earth is not safe, especially combined with her personality. It may be bleak, but this is her only option. Do what you want, Gabriel. But know this, if harm crosses her path because of you, you will answer to me."

Gabriel gets up and walks calmly over to Adam, albeit too calmly. "I don't trust you. I think you care about her too much. It's inappropriate."

Adam stands, closes his book, and holds it in his right hand. They are nearly even in stature.

"Gabriel, not only is this my job, it is my choice. You may not understand now, the lack of freedom, the lack of choice we are given in this military order, but you will soon learn."

"Really?" Gabriel takes a step closer.

"Some lessons can only be learned through experience, and in that you have none," Adam says with no trace of humor.

"I went through hell to get here!" Gabriel starts to lose his patience and balls his hand into a fist.

"And I have suffered this existence, trapped within this way of life, for thousands of years."

Gabriel doesn't know how to respond to that. His eyes travel to the book in Adam's hands. "There isn't a label on that book. What are you reading?"

"None of your concern."

"I'm sorry, I thought I was hierophant of this military, and as such, I outrank you. Hand it over."

"I will not. But if you'd like to run and cry to your new master, the door is right here." Adam opens the door for Gabriel, who snatches the book from his grip.

Gabriel flips through the book and holds his other palm out facing Adam, blue fire crackling from the center of his hand. Adam instinctively blocks with his forearm, as if it could shield him from the flame. Yet it is not directed at him. Instead it forms a wall of blue fire, filling the air with an ozone-like smell. The wall encircles Adam.

Opening the book, Gabriel's brow furrows as he recognizes the handwriting. "You and Lucius writing love letters to each other?"

"Gabriel, that is not yours to read," Adam says from within the ring of fire.

Gabriel continues to feed the wall of fire with his free hand as he reads. *I do believe that the typically subtle shifting in the shade of Dawn's eye color is connected with her abilities. Why do they lack the full brightness they should naturally have? I fear the unwanted but necessary impurities are to blame.*

The handwriting changes in the following paragraph. *It is my possibly flawed opinion that Dawn's abilities may be strongly tied to her emotional state, as volatile as that can be. The subtle shift in the intensity of her eye color is ever present if you pay close attention. I find it prudent to take an observational wait-and-see approach in this matter.*

"Gabriel, I beg of you. I will offer you information on this or any other matter you seek if you do not tell Dawn what is in that book."

"No."

"What do you mean, no?"

"Why is this so important to you?"

"This is part of my duty of protecting the princess," Adam begins to explain.

"You're spying on her." Gabriel speaks his mind without thinking. "You need her to trust you so that you can manipulate her with Lucius. How are you any different then him?"

"It is not my choice."

"Earlier, you said it was."

"That isn't what I meant. The complexi—"

The blue wall of fire fades as Gabriel unsheathes Solomon and shoves the blade at him, stopping only inches from Adam's throat. "You are nothing but an unworthy yes man, a mindless drone… victimizer… an abusive murderer whose hands will never be clean of the blood you have spilled. But deep down, we both know what you really are."

Adam takes a step forward. "And what is that, Gabriel?"

"A coward. A coward who believes he is worthy of absolution, for all of his sins to be forgiven. For what? Why? Because you were directed to commit them by someone else? Is that your defense? Take responsibility for your actions, or I will ensure that you do."

"You believe I fear your sword? As if I have never known the bite of a blade? There are more important matters at hand than bravado." Adam looks to Dawn, who lies unconscious upon her bed. Slowly, Gabriel lowers his sword and resheathes it before turning back to her.

A mix of emotions flood his mind as he walks to Dawn's side: worry, regret, victory. Sighing, he sits down beside her, head bowed, while resting his hand upon hers. *She looks like she is sleeping. If only,* Gabriel thinks. His gloved fingers grip hers a touch tighter. After placing the book inside his cloak, he lifts the elongated diamond-shaped corked vial at the end of the silver necklace and stares silently at the luminescent light-blue water.

After a long moment, he closes his eyes, struggling against the temptation of using it on himself. The painful soul poison burns like acid in his veins. Without leaving Dawn's side, he looks at his reflection in the trifold mirror beside her bed, seeing for the first time his mutilated appearance. Even though he knows the lightning strike-like scars run throughout his entire body, he sets down the vial and removes his gloves to look at the marks on his skin.

"You bargained yourself for her," Adam says from across the room. "I would have done the same."

Would it work? Could the water heal the infection? He doubts it, but part of him says... *maybe.*

"I can't," Gabriel says out loud.

"You cannot what, Gabriel?" Adam asks.

"I can't risk it," he says, turning to face Dawn. "Lucius said she'll wake up anyway..." Gabriel picks up the vial with his scarred hand and looks at the water. "Even if this cured the poison entirely... I can't."

"It is for you to decide. Tell me, Gabriel, would it be worth it? If everything went according to plan, could you silence that voice inside that urges you to take the proper course? The voice that offers you no peace when you know you have done wrong? Could you live with yourself knowing what you have done to her?"

"No. Of course not. Who could?"

"Many would ensure their own selfish needs then be left to bargain continually with reality in order to convince themselves that it was out of their hands. When what they consider to be the truth and reality cannot be rectified, they suffer."

"Then they suffer justly," Gabriel replies.

Adam simply looks at him, saying nothing in response.

Removing the silver chain that holds the vial of healing water, Gabriel uncorks it and pours half of it on Dawn's forehead and the other half over her heart, which soaks through the bodice of her dress.

Time ticks by, and nothing happens. Gabriel closes his eyes, praying she will wake and maybe, just maybe, everything will be all right. Slouching, Gabriel's heart pounds heavily in his chest. A deep inhalation catches his attention, and he looks back in time to see Dawn's eyes flicker open. She sits up, looking dazed.

"Gabriel?" Dawn asks, confused, brushing away some of her mussed hair from her face before rubbing her eyes. "What is going on?"

"Dawn." Gabriel places his hand on hers. "I love you."

"I love you, too, Gabriel," she says, her eyes tracing the veins of soul poison running across his skin. She reaches out and lightly touches a strand of his white-blond hair before resting her hand against the breastplate covered by Azrael's cloak. The breath in Gabriel's throat catches as her caress sparks electricity in its wake. She lightly traces the poison veins along the skin of the back of his hand. Her violet eyes lock with his damaged ice-blue eyes. "What happened? You look like you got hit by lightning."

"I would do anything for you. You know that, right?" Gabriel squeezes her hand. "I'll explain everything to you later, I promise. Dawn, I have something important to tell you. Soon, you will be crowned princess. I will also be crowned. I am to be named successor, legally only. Everything else goes to you." Gabriel can't help but kiss Dawn. "I wanted the line of succession in order to ensure your safety. I don't want you to be trapped here."

"But I will be here, nonetheless," Dawn says softly, her eyes downcast.

"Don't you want to leave? Go home or somewhere that isn't here?"

"Gabriel, I'm happy here."

"You like it here?"

"Yes."

"You are okay with me being named successor, legally?"

"It's fine, Gabriel." Dawn looks into the distance before saying, "You can control fire, too."

"Yes, Dawn. I absorbed the flame under the Axion and cleared Geburah. Lucius says we will be living there soon."

"Is this true?" Dawn looks at Adam.

"Yes, Dawn, that is what your father said," Adam replies.

"But... I am at home here," Dawn says.

"In this prison?"

"I'm safe here."

"Lucius said he will have a citadel built for us," Gabriel reaches for Dawn, but she turns to address Adam instead.

"Adam, are you still going to be my guard?"

"Yes, Princess. I will not leave your side."

Gabriel kisses Dawn before she can say anything else to him. As he embraces her, he wishes to be lost within this moment forever. He stands and gathers his courage, giving her a small, nervous smile before kneeling down on one knee, taking her hand in his.

"Dawn, you are the only light I see in this world. Without you, there is only darkness. If you allow me to be by your side in marriage, I will dedicate my life to you. I already have, but know that I do. Dawn, I love you. Will you marry me?" He fumbles around the inside of the cloak for the engagement ring. Telling himself to *calm down* as he presents the ring to her. Dawn is speechless as she stares at the slender platinum band with two diamonds surrounding a light-blue translucent teardrop that glitters with pieces of sand, gold, and silver and is held in place by a Celtic heart knot.

"You... asked me before... but it was in a dream," Dawn says to Gabriel's surprise. "You bought me a greenhouse with stained-glass windows. It was nice..."

Gabriel stays silent, remembering the dream he had after he drank lutum in the Quanta. He doesn't know how they shared the same dream—maybe it was the lutum, maybe it was something else. He starts to panic when he notices that she is glaring at him. Suddenly, his mind flashes back to the end of the dream that turned into a nightmare when she rejected him. His heart strains, afraid that it will happen again. *Has she changed too much? Does she no longer love me?*

Moments tick by as a flood of confusion renders him speechless. Nonetheless he holds his composure, trying not to give way that his throat is closing up. "Dawn..." His voice cracks as he chokes up. As his eyes plead for an answer, her face softens before she turns away, shoulders hunched.

"What took you so long to find me?" she says, her voice broken and barely audible.

It sinks in that she feels abandoned, again, as she has her entire life.

"Dawn..." Gabriel sighs, looking up, his shoulders relax, and he briefly averts eye contact. "I don't know. I didn't have passage until the resistance sent me one. I had to wait until I could slip in and find you. I thought the crowds would give me cover. Everything I have done, I swear I have done for you. I need only you, no matter the cost. I would die a thousand deaths if it meant I had but a chance to be by your side."

At first, she doesn't answer him. The pounding of his heart increases his heightened anxiety.

Dawn looks at him for a long moment, not saying anything before she breaks out in a smile. "Yes, Gabriel. Of course I will marry you."

While still on knee, Gabriel vows, "I pledge to you my honor, loyalty, fidelity, and love."

He takes her hand and slides the ring onto her finger. Standing up, he lifts her into his arms, squeezing her tightly. After moving strands of hair from her face, he tilts his head and kisses her.

Dawn laughs as he gently and playfully drops her onto her bed, keeping hold of her as he falls along with her, landing on top of her before settling onto his side and staring at her as he had so many nights so long ago. Everything he has wanted—everything he has fought for—was right here in front of him.

She wraps her arms around him, nuzzling against his neck. Breathing in softly, she looks up at him and smiles. Her expression changes as she presses her hand against the corrupted blood-red gem in the center of his breastplate.

"Are you okay?" Gabriel asks.

"Why?"

"Because you were knocked unconscious and had your power drained." Gabriel stares at the purple heart necklace resting on her chest.

Dawn shakes her head. "I got lightheaded… the world faded. I saw the black dragon."

"I've seen him a few times, Dawn. Nearly every time you were in danger, the black dragon appeared. I'm not sure anyone else can see it. No one's ever mentioned it."

"What happened when I was unconscious?"

"Lucius siphoned your power, adding it to his own. He used you like a battery and then threatened you with your own sword," Gabriel says.

"No."

"Yes, I saw it with my own eyes."

"When you came into the ballroom, you were screaming. I had wings?"

"Yes, Dawn."

"Is there anything else either of you need to tell me?" Dawn asks, looking back and forth from Adam to Gabriel.

Adam shakes his head.

"I don't know where to start," Gabriel says.

"How did you get those scars?" Dawn asks.

"It's a poison."

"What happened?"

"I got stabbed, twice." From the corner of his eye, he looks at Adam to see if he has any reaction. Adam makes no response, seemingly minding his own business.

He turns back to Dawn and says, "I love you. I could have sought help for my wounds, but then I might never have been able to find you. Dawn, I once told you love is a promise that, in the absence of reason, I will be there for you. Well, here I am."

"Gabriel." Dawn smiles and kisses him. "You're an idiot."

"I am not," Gabriel says, laughing.

He rests his arms around her, never wanting to let go. They lay side by side, spending hours talking about everything they've been through.

As if she reads his mind, she says, "You're worried about them, aren't you? Your friends."

"Of course I am."

"Why don't you go see how they are?" Adam suggests.

Kissing Dawn, Gabriel pulls her body close to his and says, "Why don't you come with me?"

"I'm afraid that isn't possible," Adam says. "We have had breaches, as you may be aware, and Dawn cannot just wander about. For her safety, of course."

Ignoring Adam, Gabriel looks into Dawn's violet eyes. "I won't go if you tell me not to."

"Go. I can see how worried you are. I'll be fine. Adam's here."

Gabriel's jealousy flares inside once more. He tries and fails to not let it surface.

"I'm sorry, Dawn. I just—I can't help but feel jealous," Gabriel admits.

"It's okay. It is not like that at all. Is it, Adam?"

"Of course, Princess," Adam says and then looks at Gabriel. "There has never been anything between us."

Part of Gabriel doesn't believe him. For a split second, Gabriel reaches for the book inside his cloak, pausing as he fights against giving in to anger. Instead, he lets go of the book and caresses the side of Dawn's face. She closes her eyes and leans into his touch before he kisses her again.

After they break from the kiss, Dawn locks eyes with him. "Is everything all right?"

"It's nothing..." Gabriel says with a smile, yet there is a look of concern in his eyes. Inside, Gabriel knows that she trusts Adam, but should she? Against his better judgment, Gabriel decides not to expose Adam's betrayal, at least not yet.

"If you are going, can you check on someone for me?" Dawn asks.

"That Cerberus guy, Raziel?" Gabriel guesses.

"Yes. Make sure he's okay, would you?"

"Of course."

"Come back as soon as you can."

"I will." Gabriel squeezes her hand before he leans in, allowing himself to indulge, losing himself in the moment. All of his worries, his fears, his anxieties melt away, replaced instead by the feeling of her lips pressed against his own.

His expression changes as he stares at Adam on his way to the door.

"Adam," Gabriel offers him a curt nod. Adam acknowledges him, nodding in return. "Take care of Dawn in my absence, or I cannot guarantee favorable consequences." Gabriel punctuates his threat by placing a friendly hand on Adam's shoulder, gripping it with a fair amount of force. Gabriel gives him a cocky smile, taps the fabric of the cloak where the book is and leans forward to whisper, "Your secret is safe with me... for now." Then he turns and exits the room.

After the door closes, despite his living wounds, despite the pain, despite the loss, he smiles. He got what he wanted. Dawn was his.

✦

"Are you ready?" Gabriel squeezes Dawn's hand softly, eyes fixed on the massive front doors of the citadel before turning to her. He can't help but pull her in close, resting his hand against the small of her back, allowing himself to indulge, he kisses her, becoming lost in the moment. As he holds her, he revels in the way her body fits comfortably against his own. His large archangel wings are exposed, casting a soft blue aura across her complexion. Azrael's cloak rests, bunched up, draped over his left side.

"Anywhere is heaven as long as you are around. Pain, misery, suffering, none of that means anything when you're in my arms," he says.

Dawn's eyes meet his, and she shyly turns her head before saying, "Gabriel... I—I never thought I would see you again. You're far more than I deserve."

Shaking his head, he smiles and says, "There is not a single soul in the omniverse worthy of your love. Guess you'll just have to settle for me."

Dawn laughs and playfully pushes against the bright, dark-red tetragram center of his matte-black corrupted chest plate. Inscribed in a circle encompassing the tetragram piece are red words written in High Enochian; it says *loyalty, honor,* and *dedication.* Light from the red glow of the tetragram and the blue of his wings meet, casting a gradient mix of purple light on the back of Dawn's hand. The rest of his plate armor, beyond the pieces of his father's tetragram armor, has been filled out with matching matte-black plate pieces resting above his worn grayed Wonder Brigade uniform.

Silently, he locks eyes with her, hoping she can see the genuine love that he has for her before pulling her in for a kiss, careful not to flatten the giant crystalline fabric amethyst rose on the bodice of her newly restored dress.

The ribbons in her hair, as well as her large, soft spiral curls, rest against his hand. She is adorned with a flower crown of dark-purple metal roses, each rose secured to her faded silver-cerulean halo. A braid hangs from each rose.

"My princess," Gabriel whispers to her, playing with one of her braids.

Dawn tilts her head and looks at him. "Don't call me that."

"It's what everyone calls you…" Gabriel's voice trails off. "Sorry… my love."

"I'm sorry. It's just—"

"It's a lot. I know. You don't *have* to call me a prince, but you can if you want to." Gabriel grins at her.

"Well, it fits. I always thought you were a spoiled—"

Adam clears his throat, gesturing to the door he stands beside. "Your guests await."

Masking his annoyance, Gabriel looks at Adam and nods. Stepping forward, he intends to open Dawn's side of the doors, but Adam already has. Turning to Dawn, Gabriel waits for her to adjust the sword resting at her side, which hangs beside a pouch containing her tarot cards, and interlocks his fingers with hers. The doors are held fully open by royal guards posted outside.

Hand in hand, they step out onto the landing at the top of the long staircase. The black stairs are lined with rows of elegantly crafted black wooden arches. At the apex of each arch is a modified version of Dawn's emblem. The heart in the center of the sign, which sits atop the traditional emperor's crest, glows a brilliant mix of purple and blue. The series of lights that shine from the emblems, as well as the purple and blue fire, fueled by stones smoldering in evenly spaced pillars under each arch, remind Gabriel of a misty airplane runway on a cold winters night. Beyond the rows of arches is the courtyard, lit with points of light here and there, glowing from crystal hearts atop scroll banners featuring their engagement celebration emblem. Like on the black wooden arches, the moons are gone from the crest, leaving the circle above the cross more prominent. The centerpiece heart-gems, like those on the arches, glow a bright pale blue and purple.

They approach the first arch and stop as they have been instructed. After a few heartbeats, a horn blares, quieting the crowd who all look up the grand set of stairs. Music starts—a string quartet Gabriel is sure is from the Circle Gala, or at least they don the same stylized uniforms.

As they walk, he notices how reserved and poised Dawn is. Knowing her, something about it doesn't sit right with him. Ever the loyal guard, wearing a dress uniform, Adam walks a few paces behind Dawn, keeping far to the left. He is proper and reserved, as usual. Gabriel is more than aware of Emperor Lucius's abusive Machiavellian philosophies. In the back of his mind, he starts putting together the cause and effect of why Adam acts the way that he does, and the fact that he's doing the same to Dawn. Gabriel pushes the thought out of his mind, at least for tonight.

Emperor Lucius waits to greet them in the courtyard at the bottom of the stairs, dressed in the same clothing he had worn the night Gabriel's nightmares manifested into reality. The night Lucius ripped Dawn from his arms in his own bed. He wonders if he chose this outfit on purpose just to screw with him. It's possible that he wasn't even aware of what he was wearing that night. The luminescent gold buttons of Lucius's overcoat shine, emitting their own source of light. *I can't think this way,* Gabriel tells himself. *To underestimate him would be a grave mistake. This is no coincidence.*

"Thank you all for coming to celebrate the engagement of Gabriel and my daughter, Dawn." Lucius addresses the crowd before lowering his voice. "Gabriel, a word."

"Dawn, come along. Let's greet your guests." Adam walks forward and motions for her to follow.

"But—" Dawn stammers.

"I require a word with your fiancé alone. It won't take long." Lucius turns to face Gabriel.

"Dawn," Adam says, but Dawn doesn't move.

"It's okay." Gabriel grabs her hand and kisses it. He closes his eyes and feels the warmth of her skin against his cheek. "I'll just be a minute." He smiles at her, and she can't help but smile in return.

411

"Dawn," Adam calls again.

Reluctantly, she pulls her hand away from Gabriel's, and he watches her leave.

"Gabriel, I do hope you are pleased with our arrangement." Emperor Lucius regards him with a look of reserved disdain. "Something you must understand is that no matter what you do, Dawn belongs to me, and I will utilize her and her abilities as I see fit."

Anger rising, Gabriel bites down hard in a bid to hold his mouth shut as Emperor Lucius continues.

"She is mine just as you are now as well. You would be wise to remember your sworn oaths." Lucius lifts his chin and looks off into the distance.

"I won't ever forget." Nearly imperceptibly, Gabriel relaxes his hands to keep them from forming into fists. "But I thought that the deal was that she belongs to me and I answer to you."

"The deal was that I allow you to stay within this realm, enjoying the luxury power provides and granting you the opportunity to ask for her hand in marriage." Lucius takes a sip from an elegant metal chalice. "You would be wise to respect hierarchy and order." Lucius's eyes drift across the soiree to Dawn, silent in contemplation before he says, "Enjoy your time together."

"Whatever." Gabriel rolls his eyes, winging his right hand carelessly to the side.

Lucius's tone sharpens. "Watch yourself, Gabriel. Do not forget, my word is law, and I will not suffer a treasonous soldier, much less a treasonous hierophant. Perhaps, you require specialized training on Chesed before I grant you more time with your fiancée."

Controlling himself, Gabriel breathes in slowly. "If you take her from me..." His voice wavers with anger.

"Oh, I believe I already have. I see your pathetic associates made the guest list. Poor choice, in my opinion. One can often be defined by whom he surrounds himself with. Do not allow that to rub off on my daughter, would you? Now, come, there is something I would like to show you."

Lucius starts walking in the opposite direction that Gabriel wants to go, which is to be at Dawn's side. The soothing music from the string quartet and celebratory atmosphere are almost enough to make him forget the underlying dark nature that envelopes everything in the Sine System.

Interrupting his thoughts, Lucius abruptly stops in front of a glass case that containing a single pitch-black twisted plant that seems to consist only of a stem and a closed dark-purple bud.

"Is it dying?" Gabriel looks at it through the glass.

"No, Gabriel, in fact, it has not yet lived. This is a mori rose." Lucius produces a dagger with a gold handle.

Gabriel stands his ground and waits for him to continue.

Lucius cuts his own hand and allows his blood to drip onto the soil of the mori rose, then looks at it closely and says, "It has the chance to bloom for a single day, but not until a thousand years after germination—if it is lucky enough to get the chance. A mori rose is innately connected with death. When one blooms, that day is marked by prophecy."

"What does it mean when a mori rose opens?"

"That a great death has or will occur, large in stature or in number. Something that affects the course of fate." Lucius gestures to the jagged stem of the mori rose. "We use them as canaries. They let us know when to be on guard."

"I see." Gabriel looks over his shoulder across the gathering to Dawn, who is reservedly conversing with some high-ranking officer. Adam, of course, stands at her side.

"You know, Gabriel, Dawn's existence is rarer than a mori rose blooming. What little time humans tend to have. I will do everything in my power to ensure that fate does not befall her, if it even can. She has only begun to blossom. It is up to you to cultivate her love and create a proper environment for her to thrive. Should you fail and instead salt the earth, you would send her back to me."

Lucius turns and walks away, leaving Gabriel alone. Feeling helpless, he begins to realize the true cost of the deal he has made.

✦

On his way to Dawn, Gabriel stops and stares at the life-sized statue Emperor Lucius commissioned of him and Dawn. The copper or bronze statue of himself has one arm around Dawn while she nuzzles the crook of his neck. The metallurgists captured their likenesses with a quiet brilliance.

"Gabriel?" Saphrael's voice startles him, as he was not expecting to hear his name.

Turning to his closest friend, he smiles. "Saphrael. Where is everyone else?"

"I'm right here, Archangel," Marce says from behind Saphrael with his usual tone of sarcasm.

"Cadence is around here somewhere." Saphrael walks past him, heading to a gallery display. "Come on, I want to show you something."

Held up on black metal stands are various relics and artifacts, mostly weapons surely broken in combat. Saphrael stops in the middle of an intimidating row of Chokma masks set at varying heights. Quietly, he looks up to the mask in the center, raised slightly above the others. Marce is uncharacteristically quiet.

Carefully, Saphrael removes the Chokma mask, holding it in his hands, he says, "This was my old mask... When I was champion of Hod." His fingers stiffen, gripping the silver metal helmet.

"I could ask if Lucius would return it to you," is all Gabriel can think of to say.

His expression is solemn. "No." Saphrael shakes his head. "That's not who I am anymore. Not sure it ever really was."

Leaning in to take a closer look, Gabriel studies the design of the silver metal mask. "Is that a serpent?"

"No. It's a dragon," Saphrael says, in a barely audible whisper. "Few have ever been granted the right to use the sign of the dragon... It's a high honor... reserved... for the most... terrible."

"Saphrael, whatever happened in the past—"

"Effects the future, without fail," Saphrael argues in return.

Sadness fills Gabriel as he looks at his friend, wishing there was more he could do. Placing a hand on his shoulder, Gabriel says, "After everything you've done, you stood by my side when no one else dared. Let me talk to Emperor Lucius. Maybe—maybe I can find a way for you to go home, where you've always wanted to be, Hod."

Saphrael pulls away and then puts the mask back onto its stand. "No, first of all, Gabriel, that's insulting."

"What?"

"I wouldn't have earned it. I might take whoever's rightful place it is to be there. Besides, I'd rather stay with you and everyone else on Geburah. There's a lot of work to do."

Marce nods in agreement.

"I understand," Gabriel says quietly before he undoes Solomon's sheath and holds Saphrael's sword out in front of him.

Saphrael looks at the sword for a long moment then shakes his head. "You've done more than enough. Keep Solomon. I have a feeling you're going to need it. And, Gabriel, thanks for getting the traitor's mark removed."

Gabriel is at a loss for words, so all he says is, "Thanks, Saphrael, for everything."

Saphrael nods and turns to the side. The imprints on his face from being torn open by a flagrum are visible but healing. The friends head over to a table, and Gabriel is handed a metal chalice, embossed with vines. Picking up one of the many carafes, he pours something that looks like brandy or wine. The pungent smell overwhelms him as he raises the cold metal to his lips, tasting the strange liquid.

"It's been a long time since I've had Xerotes," Marce says as he fills his chalice with the red liquor. "I can't wait to meet your fiancée."

"What?"

"Relax, archangel." Marce rolls his eyes.

Turning away from Marce, Gabriel goes to find Dawn. He spots her walking with Adam in between entertaining guests. Gabriel hurries over before they get caught talking to someone else. Kissing her on the cheek, he offers the second chalice he got for her.

Dawn smiles, closes her eyes, leans her head forward in a sign of appreciation, before accepting the drink. *God, she is adorable*, he thinks. Gabriel kisses her and takes her hand, gently tracing her fingers. Bringing her hand to his lips, he sees her engagement ring sparkling like starlight even in the scant light. Marce stares at Dawn's engagement ring, once held within the pocket watch. They have never talked about what happened.

"I'm sorry," Marce mumbles. "When I took your watch, I thought I was doing the right thing. I thought—"

Gabriel puts a hand on Marceriel's shoulder. "It's all right."

They share an uneasy moment of silence, before Saphrael gracefully changes the subject, nodding to Dawn and giving her a charming smile.

"It is a pleasure to meet you," Saphrael says, lowering his head in a sign of respect.

"You were insane in the Axion," Marce says.

"Marce." Saphrael turns to him.

"What? She was! An insane show of strength."

"Forgive him, he lacks decorum," Saphrael says.

Dawn laughs, and Gabriel kisses her cheek and smiles at her before nodding toward his friends, pointing as he introduces them. "Marceriel, Saphrael, and Cadence is around here somewhere. The Wonder Brigade, at least what's left of it."

"I'm here," Cadence says, walking up from behind Gabriel.

Gabriel nods to his friend. He hadn't seen him since the Circle Gala, even though he has seen Saphrael and Marce several times. From what Saphrael told him, Cadence was avoiding them as well.

"I've been meaning to ask, Cadence, how did you end up with the Lost?" Gabriel asks.

Cadence looks down and then swallows the remainder of his Xerotes in one gulp.

"I was there... the—the assault on Saphrael," Cadence says, his voice fading.

"It's okay, Cadence. You didn't do anything wrong." Saphrael says.

Tears form in Cadence's eyes. "I almost—I almost had to. I couldn't— After I tried to stop them, they threw me into the Black Lake. Which helped my wound more than anything. With nowhere else to go, I stayed there, trying to reason with the Lost that the waters were beneficial. I helped as many as I could. The resistance heard about the healing powers of what they're now calling Sacra Hallow. I'm worried about Spud and Loth. Although, given time, they will be made whole."

"What about their minds?" Gabriel asks.

"That's something else entirely," Cadence says.

"What are you going to do about them anyway?" Marce takes a sip of Xerotes.

"Emperor Lucius suggests I learn a lesson: how discere is beneficial," Gabriel says. Everyone quiets. "...Of course I'm not going to do that, but I don't know if I can just welcome them back with open arms."

"It's not welcoming them back to allow them to live their lives, Gabriel. It wasn't their choice," Cadence says.

"You have a point," Gabriel says.

"Dawn," Adam calls from behind. "Your father requires your attendance."

Dawn kisses Gabriel, squeezes his hand, and then looks at his friends. "Nice to meet you all. I'm sorry, I have to go."

Gabriel lets out a sigh, watching Dawn following Adam.

The Wonder Brigade share a toast of the rare burgundy liquid, clinking their glasses together.

"By the way," Marce says, pointing all around Gabriel's body. "How much did it hurt?"

Gabriel rolls his eyes. "A lot."

"Was it worth it?" Marce asks.

Gabriel's attention shifts across the gathering to Dawn. "Yeah."

Raziel walks up to the group. "Gabriel, a word?" Raziel stands near him, waiting. Gabriel nods, and Raziel walks into the circle. "I wanted to thank you again for putting yourself on the line for us."

"I really didn't do anything, Raziel."

"You did and you didn't have to. You may not think so... but you saved us. It was a selfless request, Gabriel. I hope you know that."

"How did you guys manage to get the Lost to Tiphareth anyway?"

Saphrael asks.

"It wasn't easy. We could only manage the ones who had been purified. They've been relocated to Geburah for now. By the way, guys, applications are open." Raziel winks.

They all laugh, and Raziel wanders away. Gabriel made sure that Raziel was among those protected who will be sheltered under their own subset of laws on Geburah. So he walks free, wearing a standard uniform instead of the confines of a royal guardsman.

When Gabriel turns back to the group, Cadence is distracted, looking off into the far distance up the grand stairs. "I thought there wasn't a champion this year. Why do they have the sword pole?"

Gabriel doesn't know what Cadence is talking about and looks up the stairs at a procession of banners. Lines of soldiers in dress uniform carrying banners flanked by rows of those playing drums and odd sets of ornate triple trumpets, march in perfect formation down the stairs. The music gets louder the further they descend. Then, Gabriel sees what Cadence is talking about. Among the banners is one that looks like the hilt of a giant sword, carrying the torn Wonder Brigade banner just to the right of a large pole that displays three flags. Of the triple banners the highest rectangular-shaped banner in the middle bears the mark of the emperor's crest, the right is adorned with Dawn's emblem, and the flag to the left carries the symbol of Gabriel, which matches the tetragram sigil on his chest plate.

Marce squints, "Is that? No. It can't be."

"What?" Cadence says.

"It's... It's the Wonder Brigade flag..." Saphrael says in disbelief.

Everyone turns to Gabriel, who shrugs and gives them a half-smile. "There wasn't a tournament champion this year, so... Lucius left the decision up to me."

Saphrael shakes his head and laughs to himself before taking a sip from his chalice. "...And you picked your own team?"

The thought had never occurred to him that he could choose another team. Gabriel winces and says, "Yes?"

Saphrael nods. "If it was a test on pride, I'd say you failed."

"Maybe his next test is to get stabbed again. You're pretty good at that," Marce says.

"Oh, and you're not?" Gabriel replies.

"Touché, archangel, touché."

They all laugh until Lucius's booming voice projects loudly across the gathering. Gabriel looks over to Lucius, who has his chalice held up as everyone goes silent. "We have a surprise for you this evening. One that will surely be a symbol of our new era. Progression is built upon tradition. While we move forward, we must move carefully, with wisdom and purpose. One thing we can all agree on is that the realms of this system are far too cold."

Standing just to the right of Lucius is Dawn, whose guard, Adam, is nearby, facing the crowd. Lucius motions for Gabriel to join them. Gabriel hands his chalice to Saphrael, who looks thoroughly confused. He nods to his friends before walking up to Lucius and Dawn, his eyes on his fiancée the entire time.

She stands on a sigil burned into the ground. Not far away is a matching sigil. Briefly, Gabriel looks at the violet heart gem necklace Dawn always wears before turning his attention to Lucius.

"The blue flame is that of spirit. For several millennia, it has fueled the fortitude of fighters in the Axion. Now we attempt to bring that strength to the entire Sine System." Lucius nods, signaling the royal guards.

The royal guards walk up in a line, then split formation and stand flanking Dawn and Gabriel. Ceremoniously, the newly engaged couple ignite their flames and offer them to each lead royal guardsman's lighting torch.

In turn, they pass the flame down the line of guards. When complete, they march off and stand beside giant scroll banners setting them alight. Yet, the banners do not burn; instead, writing in flame appears. Depending on the flame, the text glows cerulean or a deep purple. The scroll banners have two variations that say, *Bind the night into the day. Forever we shall stay this way.* And the other says, *Bind the day into the night, for I will set all things right.*

The lit banners are their cue. Gabriel kisses Dawn before they turn in unison. They lock eyes and smile before facing Sine and shoot rivers of fire into space. Gabriel's jet stream is purposefully larger than Dawn's and aims at the core of the star, while Dawn threads concentrated dark-purple flame with finesse and precision along the outside.

Closing his eyes, Gabriel feels the powerful energy of the flame as it flows. There is a grumble in the distance that escalates into terrible crackling from space, followed by a deafening boom.

Reborn, Sine's brilliant glow shines a bright blue with solar flares and spots of purple. Light soon begins to fall upon the realm, illuminating what it touches, yet defining the darkness in places of shadow. Everyone talks loudly, marveling at the star. Lucius places his hand on each of their shoulders, signaling for them to stop.

Gabriel embraces Dawn, kissing her, placing his arm around her as they look at the newly rejuvenated star. Closing his eyes, he breathes in her scent and interlocks his fingers with hers, indulging in this moment—this moment of happiness. He has everything he needs, but at what cost?

Chapter 34

The Lux Dominus, seat of power in the Crown Realms, is a massive, stunningly luminous architectural masterpiece, composed primarily of towering decagonal crystal rods that fan out at an angle in an art deco fashion. The entire structure smolders with a soft golden glow that, in conjunction with the pale, barely yellow clouds, acts as the main light source for the system.

Chancellor Gabriel paces, his midnight-blue archangel wings folded behind him. His boots with soft inner lining click and clack in a rhythmic pattern against the glass-like crystal surface. The air is crisp and still. Encompassing a vast area is a sigil etched into the illuminated floor of the gardens that sit atop the Lux Dominus. Fruit trees and hanging floral vines are artfully placed, with symbols etched in the crystal flooring around the trunks. The tree's roots penetrate the ground, veining through the crystal surface like a disjointed spider's web.

The sigil is inscribed with the original names of all the archangels. Quietly, he stares at Lucius's former name, Semoel, written beneath the name Lucifer.

"What happened to you? Why do you always let your ego dictate your actions? Don't you understand the harm you cause? Do you care? Are you capable of caring?"

"Am I interrupting something?" an old friend's voice calls from behind him. Chancellor Gabriel turns around and nods. Raphael has his arms folded in front of him, wearing beige robes similar to Gabriel's light-blue ones. His own archangel wings rest behind him.

"Raphael. No, I was in contemplation—trivial matters, pay it no mind."

Raphael's brunette hair hangs down his back. He inclines his head and silently looks at the Lucifer engraving in the crystal flooring.

"I need to talk to you," Raphael insists.

"Of course, old friend. I always have time for you. What is it?"

Raphael gathers his thoughts and says, "It's about Gabriel."

"What about Gabriel?"

Before Raphael can answer, a terrible boom thunders from space. They both look up in awe as a blue star laced with violet accents explodes into existence, causing the realms to shift. This induces motion sickness, but only temporarily.

"This is impossible," Chancellor Gabriel says. "We may be in far more danger than anyone realizes. There are reports of my son causing a weather shift, directing floodwaters. He may even be responsible for the earthquake that destroyed his home."

"Yes, but, Gabriel, I implore you, he is not your son."

"Don't you think I know that? Tell me again what you saw."

"While he was in stasis?"

"Yes."

"I thought they were nightmares. I paid them no mind. Now, I am not so sure. I believe when Uriel opened the time portal, it was not a time portal, but a space-time portal."

"So, the other Gabriel is from an alternate point in space-time?"

"I think he may be from a different cosmoverse entirely," Raphael says.

Chancellor Gabriel looks up at the newly birthed blue star and shudders at the sight of an omen of such magnitude. He considers the implication of the purple lacing throughout.

Gabriel muses, "When nightmares become reality, reality becomes indistinguishable from fiction."

Acknowledgments

I would like to thank my beta readers, friends, and supporters; my editor, Crystal Durnan; and cover illustrator Breno Girafa. Finally, my husband and co-creator, Jason.

A mori rose sits in its glass case in the center of the war room table. Its twisted stem has grown larger, but the bud remains closed. Lucius raises an embossed metal chalice to his lips and takes a long sip of Xerotes.

"I believe Chancellor Gabriel is concerned over the power imbalance that the two represent," Zunael says before adding, "You will certainly not allow them to leave the Sine System."

"Of course not." Lucius waves his hand dismissively. "It will be as it should."

"I beg of you, walk with caution. We do not know what we are dealing with. There is so much we do not know. If we could only—" Zunael quiets, refraining from finishing his sentence. The scars of discere are visible on his face and hands.

"If we could—what, Zunael?" Lucius lifts his chin up and looks down at him, daring him to finish his thought that he wants to experiment on Dawn.

"Nothing, honorable Emperor." Zunael makes no change in the rigid way he sits in the chair—carefully, properly, and methodically organizing his notes. There is a touch of fear in his normally cold eyes as he purposefully turns his gaze away from the mori rose.

Lucius smirks as he takes a sip from his chalice. "I believe there is something you are not telling me," he says before carefully setting his glass upon the black metal table.

Zunael looks at the chalice and then up at Lucius. "No, there isn't anything."

"No further indication about the vision Dawn had?"

"The field of mori roses?"

426

"Yes."

"No. It's as if it were just a dream, an unfortunate side effect of the disposition of her creation. Of her being part human."

"She is not part human," Lucius sneers, quieting Zunael.

The head architecta lowers his head and nodding. "That is why you felt the need to break protocol, in that statues may be only constructed for the dead."

"Or an archangel," Lucius states.

"Yes—yes, of course my lord," Zunael says, his voice shaky. "Of course the council will not—"

"This is natural law, Zunael, not a constructed one."

"But—"

"That will be all."

With that, Zunael picks up his papers and leaves Lucius sitting on his throne-like chair near the center of the war room's table. Lucius's eyes fall to the mori rose. He watches it intently.

Not long after, Dawn comes in, alone as she has been instructed. Adam waits near the door.

"Gabriel's been so busy lately," Dawn complains as she sits down.

"That happens when you decide to accept the marriage proposal of someone in such an important position," Lucius says, waving his hand in the direction of the mori rose. "Tell me, Dawn, what is it that you see?"

"What do you mean?"

"Here in front of you, what do you see?"

"The empty glass case?"

"Empty?"

"Yes, empty. Why?" Dawn looks understandably confused.

"You may return to your room, Dawn."

She gets up and her mouth hangs open before she says, "Did... did I fail some test?"

"No, never you mind," Lucius says before bringing his chalice to his lips once more to taste the pungent, bitter liquor.

Each prophetic flora is connected to a soul. Only those to whom the

427

mori rose belongs cannot see it. After the door closes behind her, Lucius looks back at the twisted black-stemmed mori rose. A name is inscribed on the top of its glass case. The name: Adam.

Welcome to the Mori Rose Saga